The Godmother's Secret

ELIZABETH ST.JOHN

Published by Falcon Historical Press 2017, republished 2025

Books by Elizabeth St.John

The Lydiard Chronicles | 1603 – 1664
The Lady of the Tower
By Love Divided
Written in their Stars

The Princes in the Tower Mysteries
The Godmother's Secret
The King's Intelligencer

Counterpoint Novelettes
Theo, Earl of Suffolk
Barbara, Lady Villiers
Henry, the King's Cavalier

"Her world and characters are so real I wanted to remain there. The Lydiard Chronicles are now on my list of all-time favorite historical novels.
A fantastic read."
Editor's Choice, Historical Novel Society Book Review

"The authenticity and historical research displayed within this story is immense and exquisite. Ms. St. John is sure to be a newfound favorite for all historical fiction fans who adore rich, immersive prose.
Historical Fiction Company 2022 Book of the Year

"One of the best books I've read in ages."
Richard III Society

"Probably the best novel of history and mystery that I have read, with barely a pause for breath, in a long while. Ms. St.John must rank as one of our top independent writers.
A hard act to follow."
Helen Hollick, USA Today Best-Selling Author

Acknowledgements

The joy of writing this novel came from not only the research and archival discoveries, the numerous books and papers I read, but also the conversations I enjoyed with so many people during the past three years. It turns out everyone has an opinion on what happened to the Princes in the Tower, and every one of those opinions is different.

That one question was a conversation starter everywhere I went, and my sincere thanks to all the enthusiastic staff, volunteers and visitors at libraries, council offices, churches, cathedrals and archives, festivals, concerts and pubs across England who stopped to chat. Special thanks to members, staff and volunteers of numerous societies and locations, including the Richard III Society, the Bosworth Battlefield Heritage Centre, the King Richard III Visitor Centre, The National Archives, The Tower of London, Bolton Castle, and Middleham Castle, as well as The Friends of Lydiard Park. And a special thank you to those who kindly invited me into their private homes and libraries, sharing their own family histories.

So many people who threw their time and energy into reading various drafts, ad nauseum. This was not an easy novel to write, and a huge thank you to my brilliant writer friends, Cryssa Bazos and Amy Maroney, who absolutely walked this journey with me and saved me from giving up on several occasions. Also thanks to the entertaining and ever-truthful Thursday night writing group at San Diego Writers, Ink., and my wonderful beta readers of Lynda, Judith, Karen, Deborah, and Sandy, for their generosity in sharing their own unique expertise, questioning motives and providing positive feedback. Incredibly special gratitude to my extraordinary editor Jenny Quinlan, who rescued me from plotholes and stayed the course when I had no clue where I was going. Finally, my heartfelt love to my family and friends who have traveled with me, checking in and cheering me on. Emma, my darling girl, thanks for always being on the road with me.

www.ElizabethJStJohn.com

The Lydiard Archives are a unique digital collection of objects, records, reports and ephemera documenting the thousand-year history of Lydiard House and Park. Created by volunteers with a passion for preservation and accessibility, The Lydiard Archives are managed by The Friends of Lydiard Park, an independent charity formed to protect, conserve and educate people about this beautiful historic estate with its Palladian house, ancient church, walled garden, and rolling parkland.

www.TheLydiardArchives.org.uk
www.FriendsofLydiardPark.org.uk

Main Characters

St. John

Elysabeth St. John, wife to John "Jack" Scrope, 5th Baron Scrope of Bolton
Oliver St. John, Elysabeth's brother, married to Isabel Scrope, Jack's sister

Beaufort

Margaret Beaufort, Elysabeth and Oliver's half sister, married to Lord Thomas Stanley

Welles

John Welles, Margaret and Elysabeth and Oliver's half brother

Tudor

Henry Tudor, Margaret Beaufort's son by her first husband, Edmund Tudor

Stafford

Harry Stafford, Duke of Buckingham, Margaret Beaufort's nephew by her second marriage to Henry Stafford

Zouche

Meg Zouche, Elysabeth's stepdaughter from her first marriage to William Zouche, Fifth Baron Zouche, and wife to William "Will" Catesby

Scrope

John "Jack" Scrope, 5th Baron Scrope of Bolton (Elysabeth St. John's husband)
Isabel Scrope, Jack's sister and Oliver St. John's wife
Agnes Scrope, Jack's sister and Richard Ratclyffe's wife
Ralph Scrope, Jack's cousin and husband of Cecily of York

The Plantagenets

Edward IV, King of England
Edward V, "Ned," Prince and King of England
Richard, "Dickon," Duke of York
Richard, Duke of Gloucester and subsequently Richard III of England (Edward IV's younger brother and uncle to Ned and Dickon)

The Woodvilles

Elizabeth Woodville, wife and queen consort to Edward IV, King of England
Anthony Woodville, Lord Rivers, her brother
Bess Woodville, Elizabeth's daughter, wife to Henry Tudor
Cecily Woodville, Elizabeth's daughter, wife to Ralph Scrope

Richard III's Councillors
William "Will" Catesby (Meg's husband)
Francis, Lord Lovell
Richard Ratclyffe, member of King Richard's inner council
Thomas Stanley (Margaret Beaufort's husband)

England, 1470

The Wars of the Roses have been raging for twenty-five years, decimating families, ruining the land and exhausting commoners and lords alike. Now, the future of England balances on a sword blade. Two anointed monarchs battle for the throne. Mad Henry VI's faction is presently in power, supported by the House of Lancaster. Exiled in Flanders, Yorkist King Edward IV is amassing an army to reclaim England, while his pregnant wife, Elizabeth Woodville, has fled to the safety of sanctuary in Westminster Abbey with her young daughters.

King Henry's healthy son is the Lancastrian hope to rule England. Will the House of York greet a new prince to secure its own dynasty? Or does the claim from a young Welsh Tudor challenge England's embattled monarchy?

Never before has so much been at stake for peace in England.

1

Autumn 1470 | Westminster Sanctuary

A secret has been conceived . . .

"Entry, in the name of God and King Henry!" My guard clouts the iron-clad door of Cheyneygates, challenging the sanctuary of Westminster Abbey. "The Lady Elysabeth Scrope demands entry!"

A murther of crows startles from the gables, cawing and whirling around my head and circling up into the clouded heavens. I join three fingers in the holy trinity and cross myself; head, chest, sinister and dexter. These ancient purveyors of death do not disturb me, for I have not survived this war to be hindered by a superstition. If there were a crow for every dead soldier, England would be a huge raucous rookery. But it never hurts to invoke God's protection. The crows swoop and squabble and alight singly among the gargoyles on the parapets of the soot-stained Abbey. Like the granite tors of my Yorkshire home, these walls are impenetrable and inaccessible. And just as hostile. God offers protection to all who claim sanctuary. And men erect walls to keep them safe.

No stirring from within. I sigh. Not unexpected. "Knock again," I command the guard. "Let them know their visitors will not leave."

The waning October afternoon trickles shadows into the well of the courtyard. I pull my cloak closer, thankful I had chosen my finest weave to keep the warmth in and the damp out. The sun had shone golden when we rode out from London, but upon reaching Westminster we collided with the rain clouds streaming in from the west.

Fallen mulberry leaves clog the stone steps rising before me, rotting unswept in the hollows. Someone isn't taking care of the abbot's house. It is clear that no one has left nor entered for a while. The

2

guard's hammering is unanswered, and yet to the right of the door a candle flame glimmers through a browed window and a shadow flits elusively.

I push back my hood, and a spatter of rain needles my face. *Here, gatekeeper. Here's reassurance I bear your fugitive no threat.* I am of middling age, graceful, fair of face, my countenance pleasing, I've heard say. Hardly a threat.

The rain unfurls in sheets. I raise my voice. "I am not asking the queen to break sanctuary." God knows the wretched woman would make it easier on all of us if she did. I motion the guard aside and edge up the slippery steps to the door. "I am here to join her." My voice competes with a dripping gutter and gets lost under the pitter-patter.

At the foot of the stairs, my stepdaughter, Meg Zouche, hums with a redhead's restless energy; her curly hair springs wildly from her hood, laced with jeweled droplets of Thames mist. "The queen thinks to defy fate with a barred door." Meg scowls at the blank and blackened oak.

"She will admit us. Eventually. Even one such as she cannot birth her child alone," I reply. "I may not be her choice for an attendant, but a captive has no say in their guard." Temper's blood warms my cheeks. I stand resolute at the door, ignoring the invisible eyes taking my measure. If this time in sanctuary is to be the battle of wills I anticipate, then I must win the first foray. I plant my feet in the composting leaves, ignore the damp seeping from the stone into the soles of my boots, and wait.

Bolts grate top and bottom, and the door creaks open. I swallow a last breath of rain-washed air, hoarding the fresh scent for the stifling weeks to come, for the queen's confinement shapes my own prison sentence. Reaching for Meg's warm hand, I cross the threshold into the abbot's house. The splashing steps of our guard fades, his duty done, mine just beginning. And if I fail and the child dies, I will be shown no mercy from Henry, the king that rules, nor Edward, the king in exile.

We are herded like moorland sheep into the cramped entry corridor, and the steward squints down his drip-tipped nose and sniffs. Meg glares back at him until he drops his gaze. She may be only nineteen, but she has been mine since she was two years of age, and I have trained her to run a great household. She will brook no truck with an insolent servant. Let Meg practice her learnings on the poor man; he is, after all, the enemy.

3

"Escort my mother to the queen," Meg commands, "and then show me our lodgings."

He grudgingly dips his head. "Wait here, Dame Zouche."

So the household expects our arrival. They just don't choose to welcome us. Of course, there is little that will escape the queen, for certainly she has her spies and informers even as she invokes sanctuary to protect her unborn child.

"This way, Lady Scrope."

I kiss Meg's warm cheek. "Make friends with him, Meg," I whisper. "We're going to need all the help we can muster. I'll return shortly."

She grins and winks. "*Bon chance,* Belle-maman."

The steward sets off at a brisk trot through a passage that runs alongside the entry courtyard. He does not look back to see if I keep up nor to extend me the courtesy of a deferential bow nor even a head tilt that my rank demands. So. This is how we will engage.

He leaves me at the open door to a dim chamber, and I pause to let my eyes adjust to the shadows and to reclaim my dignity. I am aware that whoever is in the room sees me before I see them.

The lofty wood panelling is underlit by half-burned candles struggling in the damp air. At the end of the chamber is a diamond-paned window, beyond which the Abbey lurks, blocking the waning light. Resting in a high-backed chair before the hearth, her pure profile dark against the blue flames of a meagre fire, is Queen Elizabeth—I still think of her as Elizabeth Woodville—her belly swollen under a beaver-fur mantle. Three little girls huddle on red velvet prayer cushions at her feet, the youngest child perhaps eighteen months.

So this is the commoner queen and her brace of healthy children. Yet still no male heir to claim the throne. What are the odds this next child is a boy? High, I reckon. Especially given the wellspring of prayers God must be receiving daily from the queen and her followers.

The girls are sweethearts, little honey-and-pink roses, quietly curled together like dormice in a pillow. My heartstring is tugged by my own two-year-old daughter at home in Yorkshire. It was so hard to leave my girl; she is the precious only child of my second marriage and later years, when hope had bled dry. Worse still is the melancholy of my newly dead son, for after his perilous birth there can be no more. I shoo away the picture of his tiny coffin, dig my fingernails into my palms, and firmly close the lid on my grief.

4

"Your Grace." My greeting competes with the hissing logs struggling to heat a room with a ceiling so high midnight drapes the vaults. I drop a court curtsey and raise my voice. "I am Lady Elysabeth Scrope. Wife to Baron John Scrope of Bolton Castle. I am to attend you in your confinement."

The truth of my appointment yawns like a gorge between us; the men may fight across hill and dale, but the women draw their own York and Lancaster battle lines across planked and herb-strewn chamber floors.

The queen scowls at my rain-drenched hem. "I did not invite you here." She lifts her face and darts her head forward, spite widening her silvery cat eyes.

"I did not ask to come." I secret a fist in my skirts, sign to ward off evil. This queen's mother was tried for witchcraft; her daughter is tainted with the sorcery. I have no proof, but the rumours of how she bewitched the king are enough to convince me it is so.

"And so we are both here against our will." The queen shifts and grimaces, grips the lion-head chair arms. "Come closer so I may know the face of my enemy, Lady Scrope. Your husband's family are true to York's cause. You, I hear, are not."

So already I enter a skirmish. After all these years of war, there is no truce. Two monarchs claim England's throne, but a kingdom can only bear one ruler. Jack's loyalty shines clear; my husband's ancestors are generations of Yorkshire barons. Mine is as murky as a moorland fog, for I am still in my heart bound by my blood family's Lancastrian allegiance.

I stare at the queen's stomach. "I'm sent by King Henry to attend you, bear witness to your child's birthing." *And not a day too soon. She looks ready to whelp at any time.*

"Not so. That lunatic directs you to spy on me," the queen retorts.

"No, madam, he does not," I reply. *In his madness, he commanded me to far worse than spying.*

"King Henry is but three weeks in seizing the throne, and already his French wife is back in the saddle, riding him to war. And you," she rakes me with scornful eyes. "You are Margaret Beaufort's sister, are you not? She whispers in Henry's other ear."

"Half sister." My correction is trite with use. Margaret has been the celebrated heiress in our family since she was born. "We share a mother. Her father was the Duke of Somerset. Mine was Lord St.John."

"When she is not advancing her Tudor son, she's negotiating favours for her family." The queen continues as if I had not spoken. "And in arranging your marriage, I hear Margaret married you, her widowed sister, to a York ally."

This is exasperating. I am being interviewed by a woman who has no authority to appoint. I am her gossip and her gaoler. Take my help or leave it be.

The queen is owed no explanation of a marriage contract that blossomed from convenience to love. "I think not. As a widow, I made my own match," I say shortly. When Lord Zouche knew he was dying, Jack promised to advise me on my wealth, protect my lands. I did not plan on falling in love with my advisor.

"And so you have. A nice widow's portion. I am sure Margaret saw that Jack Scrope was aware of your holdings." The queen glances at a scrap of crumpled embroidery held up by her eldest daughter, presses a fleeting caress on the princess's cheek. "So, Lady Scrope, where lies your loyalty? Where is your truth? With your Lancastrian sister or your Yorkist husband? You have a tangled family, to be sure."

Her witch eyes see conflict too clearly. Margaret and King Henry callously move me across England's battle board, castle me with their enemy to watch over her birthing. My marriage to Jack may have been my choice, but this confinement was at the bidding of my king. I could not refuse. And even Jack appreciates the ten pounds that accompanies my appointment. A tangled web, to be sure.

I untie my cloak, shake a shower of raindrops to the rushes laid upon the floorboards. At least these are freshly changed, the leaves still green and pungent from the reed beds. One advantage of this gloomy lodging situated so close to the river. "You left the Tower of London to come here to Westminster?"

"You haven't answered my question," the queen demands.

"I am here. And why did you leave the Tower? It is both a palace and a prison. You should have felt secure there."

The queen shrugs. "My husband, King Edward, thought me secure in his stronghold. But I know better. Whoever holds London holds the Tower. And London favours Lancaster. I am safer under God's watch than the crown's."

She is right. "You'll be protected. And untouchable."

Claiming sanctuary is as old as time itself. God only knows how long this woman will hide within the Abbey confines. Now I am lashed alongside the Woodville queen on her Fortune's wheel, a passenger on a journey not of my choosing, and that is the only truth that matters.

"A measured response," the queen replies. "Do you always see both sides of the coin, Lady Scrope?"

"Perhaps both colours of the chessboard, Your Grace," I say carefully. "Our lives resemble the conflict of black square and white. Perchance while the kings fight, the queens hold the power."

Queen Elizabeth shifts in her chair, peers down at the girls. They are quiet, too quiet in my opinion. I do not think this mother thought much of her daughters' well-being when she fled to Cheyneygates. I wonder who last sung them a lullaby, cuddled them to a peaceful sleep.

"I think the conflict is of our rose emblems of red and white," the queen says, interrupting my thoughts and returning our talk to the politics that have ruled my world for most of my life. "Do not be too assured, Lady Scrope. My husband amasses an army to reclaim our throne. You may consider yourself under the simpleton's protection. But for how long? Choose your colour wisely. You are merely a pawn in this game of kings."

I ignore her goading, try to bring our conversation back to neutral territory, for I must impart more news. *Don't falter now.* "There is another matter, Your Grace. A command from the king."

The queen places her hand protectively over her belly. "What design now from Margaret Beaufort and the simpleton, Lady Scrope?"

I hold out the letter, worn with my folding and unfolding. "You know I am to witness your child's birth. Here is the command that the king also appointed me the baby's godmother."

On Margaret's advice. This is not my choice.

The queen snatches the paper and tears it into pieces, the shreds floating and dissolving into the rushes. "Godmother? A godmother is a relative of the blood. Is there no end to my humiliation?" Elizabeth Woodville gestures to the door, hands fluttering like moths through the dusk. "I will not accept a parasite in my family. You have no right to be here. Get out."

"My duty, Your Grace, is to ensure you are safely delivered and your child well cared for." Enough of this war of words. I am equally at risk in this place, and I will not let her arrogance rule my destiny. I curtsey

7

to the queen's turned head. "May I suggest you rest now. I will see you in the morning."

I have a responsibility, whether this commoner likes it or not. Time to find Meg, discover what is available in this barren house of men to carry out my duty of witnessing this birth, bringing this child safely into the world. And that is all I can think about. Despite all of Margaret's manipulations, I still don't know if I can truly stand before God and swear the godmother's oath to join the House of York.

I cross the endless chamber floor, and my damp skirts chafe at my calves, bind dismally around my ankles. I will not let the queen see my weariness.

Don't falter, don't fall. Don't falter, don't fall.

A clashing of bells fractures the stale air, so close above my head they could have flown from the belfry and buried me. Vespers. And so will my days now be measured, in God's time, until salvation comes. Whatever that might be.

"And be warned!" the queen shrieks, a previously hidden country accent now coarsening her voice. "Be warned, Lady Scrope and all those who commanded you to this sanctuary. Your godmothering is worthless if I bear a daughter. But if I birth a boy . . . if I birth a prince in this prison, his life lies in your hands."

2
Autumn 1470 | Westminster Sanctuary

In our small square room tainted by kitchen odours and an open drain under the high, horned window, Meg and I make scant suppers of hard cheese and rye bread. The steward takes pleasure in delivering us to the cold-tiled pantries and damp larders and points to the dented pewter service on the ceiling-high dresser. No doubt Abbot Millyng dines nightly on silver, mopping his venison gravy with fine white manchets, but no invitation comes to join his table. He obviously does not consider us worthy of notice, and so fend for ourselves we do.

After restless nights, I arise my chilled bones to go about the business of preparing for the birth. Each morning I break the ice in the water bowl and splash my face, gathering strength for the day ahead. Thank heaven for Meg's presence, for together we can overcome most things. I have loved my stepdaughter as my own since the motherless little girl was two years old. My arranged marriage to Lord Zouche bore no fruit, and I learned early that love does not ripen in an old man's body. Meg was the last of his offspring, and I am eternally grateful for her in my life.

Despite its painted panels and floor-to-ceiling tapestries, the Jerusalem Chamber affords no comfort for the queen's confinement. This is a room designed for men's deliberations, powerful and intimidating. I walk slowly around the perimeter. How ironic that the Arras tapestries portray the Adoration of the Magi. These priceless cloths would all be removed in a few weeks for Advent and draped within the Abbey, leaving the wood panels naked. They would adorn the altar for the Christ child, but not rebuff the cold for a king's baby.

The room is dominated by a polished oak table as big as my fishpond at Bolton Castle, hefty armed chairs rooted to the floor; there is no tolerance for women in this male enclave, even if they herald a royal birth. The men may have named the chamber to say they had died shriven in Jerusalem, but it is no salvation for a woman facing childbirth's dangers.

Where else could the queen deliver her child? After several frustrating interviews with the abbot that go nowhere despite my attempts, I seek out for myself the kitchens, stillroom, and chapel—food, medicinals, and a place to pray for all but the direst emergencies. I direct the abbot's carpenter to immediately fashion a birthing stool from a library chair. Meg orders a wooden trestle bed and kindling dragged into the boteler's pantry. The room is small but warm, hard by the kitchen flue. There is no cradle and no money to purchase one. I empty the trunk in my room and stuff it with a soft wool blanket from my bed. This baby will be warmly, if not royally, welcomed.

The queen ignores me still and takes no interest in the running of her household, albeit one locked down under God's protection. I wonder who cared for the little girls before I arrived but have no time to find out. Finally, I manage to extort coin from Abbot Millyng to order fresh marrowbones and beef from the butcher. Meg sends the spit boy to gather armfuls of nettles from the Abbey fields and to pick up the wormy windfall apples from the orchards beyond the walls. Now, at least, we can make broths and tisanes to sustain the queen; they will not come amiss for us either. My hurried appointment under the duress of war and threat of invasion gave scant notice to prepare for this role, and the queen's delivery is upon us. The responsibility of her well-being weighs on my shoulders, drives my furious preparations. Should the birthing go awry, I will be accused of negligence by either Lancastrian or Yorkist. This must go well.

Worse, the queen refuses to take to the birthing room, and the woman insists on remaining fully dressed in the Jerusalem Chamber. Certes, this is the commoner in her. Or the fugitive.

At the end of our long days, Meg joins me in the kitchen as I finally sit down on a hard bench by the blackened fireplace. Pottage bubbles in a pan hanging over the flames, but in truth I am usually too exhausted to eat. The abbey bells have tolled for Compline, and I think that I too am buried and waiting for the Final Judgment, like the death of Christ this service honours.

"I think we are prepared, Belle-Maman," Meg says with the optimism and faith of the young. "The queen has given me the name of Marjorie Cobbe, her midwife. She insists that we call upon the woman when her time comes."

10

"The queen spoke to you? She still refuses to accept I am here." I ease my shoes off, stretch my stockinged feet towards the fire, and wiggle my toes to ease the ache. Meg chafes my hands, rubs my aching shoulders. Sweet girl.

"She will come around," Meg replies. "The queen knows what is best for herself and the health of her baby. And being angry is not good for either of them."

"Maybe so, or not," I say. "She had better summon the magic of her ancestors, for I cannot do more for her in this prison. And if I fail and the child dies, I am in God's hands. I cannot falter these last few steps."

The following morning is the Day of the Dead, and the queen attends Mass. I kneel at her side before the simple altar in the icy Cheyneygates chapel, the spirits congregating around us. The wax-white face of my own infant hovers like a vision under my eyelids, suppressing every prayer, bringing forth hot tears of guilt on my frozen cheeks.

Meg takes my hand, her familiar touch comforting. "I am praying to the Virgin for your lost child," she whispers. My stepdaughter understands the nightmare I inhabit, my son's empty cradle, Jack's empty eyes.

"God grant him protection on his first All Souls Day," I reply. "Blessed Virgin Mary, care for my beautiful boy."

"Aargh!" The queen crosses herself and attempts to rise; she sways, clutches the base of her spine. She grips her gown between her legs. A dampness spreads from her pelvis, darkening the green velvet to black, puddling on the floor before her.

I meet her eyes. "Your baby comes. We must go to your birthing room."

The queen stands proud. "I will go to the chamber. My child will be born in Jerusalem."

I stand taller. "If you go into labour in that miserable hall, your child will be born dead." And I wait.

The queen rocks on her feet and then gasps as a birth pain clenches her in its fist. She lifts her crucifix to her lips, murmurs an "Ave Maria."

I lock eyes with her. *Get on, woman. My life depends on your child's survival.* "Come, Your Grace, it is best for you. Your husband would want you to care for his heir."

"It is not your place to tell me when to leave."

The queen has already delivered three children. In my experience, this birth could go quickly.

"It is not safe for you to stay." I turn to Meg. "Please send for the midwife; tell her to come quickly."

The queen gasps as another birth pain doubles her over. "I must remain to hear mass."

"Enough, Your Grace. We must go now."

Three more birth pains of increasing frequency and the queen shuffles forward. As if she has a choice and all the time in the world, she lets herself be walked haltingly from the chapel to the womb-like room and lays down.

"It is a bad omen, deserting God," the queen moans. "Where is Goodwife Cobbe? She is the midwife, not you."

I ignore her words, build up the fire, and heat a tisane of chamomile.

As a toll marks the end of mass, Meg returns, and the midwife arrives in a swirl of fog and wood smoke with her bag of scissors and linens and vials of mugwort and pennyroyal electuaries, a rabbit's foot, and St. Margaret's birthing girdle to ensure an easy labour. The crone smells strongly of her workroom spirits, but her hands appear steady.

The relentless abbey bells mark the longest hours. The room is so dark night loiters within. The scent of purifying lavender oil mingles with stinking melting tallow and smoke from the damp logs. The hours pass with no sign of the child, and then creeps over us a sharp odour of fear-sour sweat, drenching the queen's moans.

"This is not like the others," she pants, her stomach mounded over her long slender legs. "There is something wrong."

The midwife leans over her, casting a humpbacked shadow on the wall. "Hush, my lady," she says. "Your child is just slow to arrive. Bite down on this kerchief, and do not push further, for just a moment."

The queen cries, her body rigid. Meg bathes her forehead with a damp cloth. I beckon the midwife to the fireside. The crone's lined face gleams with perspiration, and the smell of fear is strongest from her.

"What is happening?" I demand. "The queen employed you because she trusts you. This birth is going on for too long."

The midwife wipes her mouth with the back of her hand. "The queen is narrow," she says. "And the baby is large. That is all." She turns away from me, hunches over her bag, and rummages for another curative. This time she places a dried toad upon the queen's stomach, arranging it this way and that with deliberate care, chanting an unintelligible rhyme as she does so.

I turn my back on the woman, shaking my head. I do not put much store in these witching tokens, but if the queen does, then it is her decision.

"Belle-Maman!" Meg hisses. "Look!"

The midwife is tipping a stone bottle into her mouth and drinking the contents. She sees me looking at her and quickly drops it back into the bag.

"What are you doing?" I cry. "Are you drunk, woman?"

The midwife laughs and pulls the bottle forth. "Want some? Prepare yourself, Lady Scrope."

"Get away from me." I smack her hand.

The crone sneers. "And you think you can do more? From what I've felt, the cord is wrapped around the child. If it is not freed, the queen will kill it. And likely herself too."

"Dear God, leave the queen's side." I push her to the fireplace, force her to sit on the bench.

She hunches over, swaying and mumbling. "Their deaths are on your head."

I grip the crucifix at my breast until Christ Jesus is imprinted on my palm.

Not again. My precious son. Holy Mother Mary, do not lay another child's death on my conscience.

Meg catches my thoughts from beside the sweat-drenched bed, where the queen lies prone and whimpering. "Do not revisit your own ordeal, Belle-maman. We will guide this child safely into the world."

I stand at the queen's side, my hand crushed in her pincer grip, wipe her face, smooth lavender oil on her temples. I swat away the dead toad and place the frayed linen birthing girdle across her stomach.

Sweet Saint Margaret, have mercy on this child and sustain this woman with the hope of motherhood. Grant me, oh Lord, thy grace and thy love. Hear my prayer. Hear my prayer . . .

The girdle failed my own son.

Hear my prayer.

"Save my baby . . ." The queen's voice breaks, its rich notes pain-racked. She turns her head, those brilliant eyes fierce in the dimness. Her blond hair clings to her temples, sweat-lankened. And still she is beautiful. "Goodwife Cobbe, I am in your hands. Let me die so my child may live."

"You both will live." I hold her gaze, move to block her view of the drunken crone slumped on the bench. "I promise you."

This child will not die as mine did.

Hear my prayer.

Enough of these prayers and tokens and girdles.

Enough of this dark magic.

"Get her up, into the birthing chair," I command Meg. "Hurry. I must try to unloop the cord."

Between us, we get the queen into the chair, Meg standing behind her with her arms supporting her. I kneel on the floor before the queen, with room now to reach inside her. I have never done anything like this in my life, but there is no time to think, only time to try to save a life. The queen screams and strains, and I shout at her to stop. The baby's head is showing now, and I hold my fingers between its neck and the cord, hoping that if the weight of the baby and the downward shift of the chair work together, the birth will happen quickly and I can pull the child free.

When the bells toll for Lauds, the queen's head lolls to one side.

The midwife shrieks and mutters, and I shout over my shoulder to shut her up.

"Meg, make the queen push when I tell you." We have one chance, I think to myself, before they both die.

The fire surrenders, and grey light slips beneath the window covers, the winding cloth of a chill dawn. The crone snores in her drunken sleep.

Now.

"Push, Your Grace, push to bring your child into the world." I fill the stifling room with my order. "Push to give your husband the York heir he so desires." No men's battle lines now. This war is between mother and child.

The queen screams and shudders and pushes, and the child almost somersaults from the womb, and I spread the cord and pull the child free.

14

Mary, Mother of God. A boy. A boy born to the triumphant cries of women, who together conquered darkness and delivered light into the world.

The child sucks air, shudders. He is one breath from living, one breath from dying. The future of the House of York squirms in my hands. Holding the newborn to my breast, I embrace life, a mother's instinct over men's conflict.

"A boy! A lively boy, Your Grace." I am in tears, and so is Meg. The queen lifts her head, fixes her eyes on me with a look of surprise, and then closes them again as we help her back to the bed.

My first duty is done. If that is what King Henry and Margaret Beaufort intended. God's witness to the birth of their enemy's heir. Would Margaret have fought so hard to save his life? Will the king recall his insane command to me? I quickly push the disturbing thoughts to the very back of my mind.

Queen Elizabeth's son, King Edward's successor to the throne. I bow my head. And now the conflict begins.

I am to be godmother to a York prince.

God protect him.

God help me.

3

Winter 1470 | Westminster Sanctuary

I linger in the heavy-ceilinged corridor wending from the queen's birthing room to Abbot Millyng's study, my kidskin slippers sticking to the icy flagstones. The wall torches do little to light my path, their meagre flames shriveled by the cold. Has the news of a newborn prince ever been greeted with more trepidation? Not that I can imagine. I cannot yet think of his reaction when King Henry discovers that King Edward now has his own son to continue his dynasty. Or what will be demanded of me when my oath will join me with the Yorks.

How had I known how to save the child's life? I can't say. Was it Saint Margaret? Or the hand of God? Or is the instinct deep in a woman's heart, some visceral survival sense? I can't say. But my whole body vibrates with the awareness that if I had not cast out the wretched midwife and her dark arts, if I had not countered the queen's direction, if I had not banished decorum, then the child would be dead and likely his mother too.

My hand grips the iron latch, praying to freeze forever this moment. When the news is heralded, the world will tremble on the battleground of kings again. But it is not my secret to hold. I must tell and survive the consequences. For it is not two kings, but now two dynasties that ravage England's throne.

The abbot is hunched over his desk, and he looks up sharply from his writing as the door hinges groan. This time he is forced to acknowledge me, for he knows I bring the news he is waiting for. Deliberately placing his quill in the inkpot, he meets my eyes, makes the sign of the cross.

"A boy," I say with no cushioning. I want the words to shake him out of his smugness.

He steeples his fingers, resting his fat chin on the ink-stained tips. "King Edward's heir to England's throne."

"England already has an heir," I remind him of King Henry's own healthy son, a child born after one of his brief periods of lucidity when carnality did not chafe him like a hair shirt.

"And now we have two. I'll send word to court." He grates the words from tight lips and eyes me sharply under brows that cling like beetles to his domed forehead. "The queen? How fares she?"

I shrug. "Well." She is already sitting, suckling her newborn like any farmer's daughter. And still does not speak to me.

Abbot Millyng pushes himself away from his desk, lifts a parchment to read by a great branching stand of candles. Beeswax at that. "King Henry's orders appoint you the child's godmother." He squints at me in the glare. "Are you prepared to swear the solemn oath that this role brings? Stand at the font and pledge your loyalty and life to the York heir?"

I bow my head. As my Lancastrian king commands. As my York husband demands. God knows my heart is entwined with both. But where lies my own loyalty? I cannot say yes, and yet the ceremony approaches.

The abbot takes my gesture for agreement. He is used, no doubt, to women who have no voice.

"Indeed. Prepare to stand before God with true loyalty in your heart. He sees everything. Including the promises of false witnesses." He looks beyond me to the door. "Go and tell the queen we shall baptise her child within the abbey. I shall stand as godfather." The abbot picks up his quill again, returns to his scratching. "Go. On your way."

I have no intention of leaving. This may have been the longest conversation I have had with this so-called man of God since I arrived, but I am not done.

The bells ring the passing hour.

Dear Lord, when will I get used to this relentless tolling?

"Abbot Millyng." I count until the clashing ends, force his gaze up me. "This honour was bestowed upon me by King Henry himself a week ago at the Palace of Westminster." I have his attention now, for his fat cheeks redden, puffing like a toad under a heron's threat. "I would thank you to pay me the courtesy my rank demands." I may struggle with my inner conviction, but I will leverage my new position.

He examines a speck on his gravy-stained gown. "Your rank is tied to Lancaster's fortune. For as long as it lasts."

I ignore his jibe. "At that same audience, King Henry recognised his namesake, my nephew Henry Tudor, as his heir. I would say my fortune rides on both the Lancaster and York wheels of destiny. I am aunt to one heir. And as godmother, I am considered a blood relative to the newborn prince and King Edward. Your role is official. Mine is personal."

And just like that I am elevated above him, now a member of the royal family and a woman he must defer to.

Satisfied, I leave the odious man squatted among his earthly luxuries, contemplating his own Fortune's wheel that has rolled over his perquisites. Whether he is for Lancaster or York, he is most uncivil, so confused is he for his own vacillating loyalties. But this is where the wars have brought us all—looking first for division before reconciliation.

Outside his study, in the dark corridor, I slump against the wall, the uneven stone blocks cutting into my back. The bracing cold air is now welcome, the dampness of the old foundations reminding me we are just a mere hundred paces from the soaring splendour of Westminster's banqueting hall.

Just a week ago and a lifetime away, Margaret brought me before King Henry in that same building, where noble Lancastrians assembled to welcome the return of the victorious king and his French wife. My sister and my nephew were given a family's place of honour.

The king's watery gaze rested on me as I looked for signs of his madness, for in truth it was his brain fevers that had left our country in such shambles. No frothing at the mouth, no rolling of eyes. He seemed perfectly normal.

"She will suit the position." His voice was soft, mild-toned. "An excellent suggestion, Margaret." He waved his hand vaguely in the air as a matter closed and abruptly leaned forward towards Henry Tudor, standing tall between us. "You are a fair young man, named in my honour, and I foresee a noble future in your face. The Tudor and Lancastrian blood in you runs boldly."

The hall fell quiet, his words silencing the chatter. Henry Tudor humbly knelt, and a whispering rustled around the courtiers as the king reached forward and raised him. "After my beloved son, you are my closest male relative, my child. If God chooses to take him on the battlefield, you will be my heir."

There was a gasp throughout the court, and the queen scowled and crossed herself against the wanderings of her husband's feeble mind and the black omen he had just uttered.

Well, that should make Margaret happy. That is as good as calling Henry the heir to the throne if anything comes of the king's son. I turned to my sister. "What position will I suit? What does the king refer to Margaret? What have you done this time?"

"A great honour, Sister," she replied, keeping her eyes on her son. "You are to serve Elizabeth Woodville in her forthcoming childbirth. And be the child's godmother."

I can still feel the shock that punched me in my stomach. "Join the York queen in sanctuary? What were you thinking?"

Margaret gave me one of her enigmatic looks. This one was as if the cat had stolen the cream. "Just placing a cuckoo in the York nest, Sister. Hedging risk, Elysabeth. Hedging risk."

The king was watching us, a bemused smile splitting his hollowed cheeks. "She will follow my instructions, Margaret? Ensure there is no heir to York's throne?" He rocked back and forth and fell into mumbling prayers and invocations to God and the apostles.

"What in God's name does he mean?" I hissed at my sister. "Ensure no heir?"

"Shh," she whispered. "It is his lunacy talking. Forget you heard those words."

I remember biting back a flash of anger. The king leaned forward, pulled on the arm of Henry Tudor, and then kissed his cheek, stroked his head as one would a favourite dog. My nephew looked startled, slipped a glance at his mother, and then bowed obediently under her nod. He turned to the king, knelt again, and kissed his hands and the Bible they clasped on his lap. Truly, Henry was very astute for one so young.

"War demands much sacrifice," my sister continued, a triumphant smile playing around her tight lips. "We must be prepared to give everything for our beliefs. You included."

And now, in that dank abbey passageway with the exiled king's newborn under my care, and the godmother's holy oath looming before me, I start as the clash of the abbey bells shake me from Margaret's words. I must return to the queen's bedside. And pray to God for forgiveness if I am to swear an oath with my lips and not my heart.

19

The command from King Henry comes within hours and in no uncertain terms tells me my duty. As the appointed godmother, I must get the child baptised immediately. Folding the message in half, I let the candle flame catch a corner and devour it to ash.

"I have to follow my destiny," I tell Meg. "No matter if this places me in the centre of the House of York."

Meg drapes a shawl across my shoulders, hugging me as she does so. "You will find a way to steer between both paths, Belle-maman. Your sister may have the cunning, but your integrity will light your way."

I return her embrace. As usual, Meg's optimism comforts me. "And so it shall be," I say. "Please go and tell Abbot Millyng that the ceremony shall be held in the abbey tomorrow. I have had enough of him for one day."

The queen has returned to Jerusalem, taking back the chamber and insisting that it is the only place within Cheyneygates fit for her son. I order the meeting table to be shoved against a wall; the palatial chairs are now stacked like empty tenements in a corner. Carved benches and soft plump cushions ring the fireplace, a woman's gossip circle replacing the men's war room. It is a small victory, but significant when the abbot did as I bade. The tapestries are back from their duty in the abbey and have been rehung in this lofted room to keep some of the drafts away. Wooden screens ornate with angels are dragged in from storage and placed in a cordon large enough to hold the queen's bed around the fireplace. I insist the floor cushions remain, for now she has deprived the rest of the room from the fire's heat, I do not intend Meg and the little princesses to freeze under the decorative but useless Arras tapestries. It is a struggle, but the queen concedes.

As I slip around the screen, the queen looks up from nursing the babe, her breast full, her nipple rosy under the child's pursed lips. A sharp pain pierces my own bosom, where just a few weeks ago I had brimmed with milk.

"It is time for the prince to be baptised, Your Grace." I come straight to the point. I have no interest in flowery court language.

"And I suppose you are still appointed his godmother." The queen caresses the child's cheek as he suckles. "It is a tragedy that I have no choice in my own son's godparents."

I will not show her my own struggle against my role. I have no choice either. "The king wishes him to be baptised immediately." I push away the terrible thought of King Henry's fatal wish for the boy-child that I had refused to obey.

The queen's face lightens for a moment before she realises I mean King Henry. "It is of no business of his when my son is baptised." She is brazen in her dismissal.

"The king most certainly takes a deep interest in the son of his enemy," I continue. "He commands me to proceed immediately. I have already told Abbot Millyng to make arrangements."

I reach out my arms, but the queen does not lift the child from her breast. Instead, she holds the baby closer, half turning aside. "You have no loyalty to me or my husband. Why should I think you would devote yourself to my son?"

I ignore protocol and sit on the bed next to her.

"Because if it was not for Meg and me, your son would not be alive today."

The queen whips her head up. "Marjory Cobbe is my trusted midwife for life. She knew what to do."

I stare at her. "Marjory Cobbe was drunk and resorting to magic."

"She would have delivered my child safely."

"She would have killed you both."

The baby stirs against her breast, turns his face towards me. For the first time, I see his perfect features and pink cheeks. Something shifts inside me in answer, a deep tremor within my own womb.

My godson. My son from God.

"God has granted me a son to love as my own lost boy." I let my words fall around her and softly stroke the baby's tuft of golden hair with my fingertips. The first touch of him sends a warmth through my body, soothing the ache in my linen-bound breasts.

The queen does not move him from my touch as she kisses his forehead.

I gather strength. Perhaps this is Saint Margaret's final gift to me. "Entrust me your child, Your Grace. I will swear to you that which I swear before God. I will protect him from evil, show him the light, and prevent those who would hurt him from ever doing so."

The queen hesitates, and I let her come to her decision. She has little choice, after all, but best she think it is hers to make. She lifts the child and places him in my arms, his sweet rosebud mouth still mewling for his mother's milk. The queen meets my eyes, and I know we are both thinking of the night he was born, the decision I made that saved their lives.

I sniff his hair, taking a deep, warm breath of God's miracle. This child has survived because of me. We are forever linked on our shared wheel of life.

"You will be safe and beloved, my prince," I whisper. "Safe and beloved."

Abbot Millyng meets us at the door to the abbey, and although I am relieved to be away from Cheyneygates, we are as meagre a procession for a prince's christening as ever could be imagined. Meg has fashioned the queen's ermine-lined cloak into a robe to keep the baby warm, for the day is bitter from a freezing east wind, and our breath wreaths like spirits in the brittle air. Before he allows us to enter the abbey, the abbot makes me open the prince's mouth so he can place grains of salt on his tiny tongue to keep the devil away. He has already tested me in the prayers I must recite, the Ave Maria to prove my worthiness as God's mother on earth to the prince.

The little princesses accompany their brother as part of the baptismal procession; four-year-old Bess of York solemnly carries the chrism. Such a humble ceremony in such a grand setting. No doubt the queen chose to give birth within the sanctuary of Westminster Abbey intentionally, knowing that her child would be baptised among kings and that the shrine of the Confessor would be the backdrop for her own Edward's anointing. Nothing surprises me about the Woodvilles, for they are masters of manipulation and will approve of this staging. No choir nor audience, no nobles nor clergy. Just me, a Lancastrian appointee, and the abbot and prior, all paid by the king to surround the York heir with those loyal to Henry's rule.

And yet, as I stand within those hallowed walls and lift the lighted taper to signify God's grace, perchance this child represents hope, not conflict. A feeling of peace warms me as I hold him and swear the sacred godmother's oath to protect him from all those who wish him harm. Perhaps, I implore in my own silent prayer, perhaps he will be the healing of our nation, not the tearing apart.

Perchance there will no longer be warring factions, no need to claim loyalty to York or Lancaster. Perchance, just as Jack's and my child would have joined our houses, this child is the future peace of England. And maybe war will cease before it reaches these sons of kings and, somehow, this generation will end the conflict of their forefathers. For is it not always the mother's prayer to hope for peace for her children?

Little Bess holds the chrism aloft, her sweet beauty shining in the dim light of the great abbey, her gaze fixed on the baby.

"My brother, Edward. Prince Edward of England," the princess whispers; her innocence and joy brings an unexpected warmth to this solemn ceremony. "My little Ned." Whether her mother has told her to say this or it is her own childish thought, I know not. But her simple words hang in this burial ground of kings, this holy pilgrimage site, and drift into the very fabric of the royal banners that adorn the stones.

God's grace commands undying loyalty to the young prince, and in this moment there is no House of Lancaster or York, but simply a child pledged to God and my holy vow.

Jack would say this young family might be the healing of their nation.

I pray to God he is right.

For now I am confirmed as the prince's godmother, they are my family too.

4

Spring 1471 | Westminster Sanctuary

This winter, this bitter winter, where the child wails from the gripe each night, his pained, pitched screams jarring the very bell tolls. My feet tread a pilgrimage back and forth across the Jerusalem Chamber as I rock Ned and murmur lullabies onto his soft hair until he calms. I doze and arise red-eyed to snow cornered in the windowpanes and a furry frost coat to scrape with my fingernail and admit the grey morn. Each day seeps into the next, our captivity enforced by the bands of soldiers standing guard at the abbey gates and doors. There are twenty-eight of them in total, each in their place, for I count them morning, noon, and night.

Lately, it has been impossible to send a letter to Jack; the abbot ignores my requests and informs me that his intelligences to and from the king are more important than domestic tittle-tattle. News from home is sparse, for the remoteness of our Yorkshire stronghold discourages messengers from struggling through the snow-filled dales. Perhaps Jack is not even at Bolton Castle, for Meg hears from the cook that armies are moving swiftly across England's exhausted counties again.

When letters from Margaret cease, my isolation is complete.

In the early hours before Cheyneygates stirs and the children awake, and my day begins all over again, Jack's presence is closest; I can lose myself in uninterrupted thoughts of him before the worries cloud in. The memories of our dawn lovemaking flood my mind, his ardour that awakened my frozen heart, created our beautiful daughter.

As my morning catechism, I pull Jack's notes from my bodice. He is not one to write often, and the two letters that made their way into sanctuary are faded and worn with reading, their stale dates kept fresh by hope. *Stay safe*, he assures me, *for I am of good heart, and our cause is not lost. I am looking after you, I promise.*

Those were his first words to me after my first husband's death.

"I'll look after you now," he said abruptly, calling at my home with his condolences while the dirt was still fresh on William's grave.

What was his promise?

"I pledged to Lord Zouche I would marry you."

What neither of us had admitted was the strength of our attraction to each other, the not daring to believe that perhaps there could be a future, that time and Fortune's wheel had aligned. My loyalty to my arranged marriage had kept my eyes lowered and my thoughts hidden. When Lord Zouche had departed this earth, I could look at Jack fully and take pleasure in the lust rush in my limbs, imagining his strong body next to mine, his soft beard on my breast as he kissed me to oblivion. We married as soon as my mourning was respectably behind me.

The queen may have taken to sanctuary to bide time, but for me it is a slow bleeding of lost days that can never be regained. Jack's absence gnaws like a canker in my heart. As if mocking Lent itself, I have given up on all contact with my family and my penance truly begins.

It is Good Friday, the holy day of mourning, and I watch from the window to see who will be creeping to the cross in the abbey.

I greet the guards as old friends, the twenty-eight men who keep me safe and keep me a prisoner.

Good morrow, Redbeard, Hawknose, Scarcheek.

Do they look up and hail me too, this solitary woman with a babe in her arms, peering down upon them from the abbot's prison?

Greetings, Ravenhair. But . . . where stand Broadshoulder and Flatfeet? I crane my neck to see if they are on the other side of the wall, but I cannot find them.

What changed their routine? I have heard no news. Something has happened. I count again. Only sixteen remain. I must ask Meg if she has noticed them elsewhere on the abbey grounds.

"You are restless, Lady Scrope." The queen shifts Prince Edward and helps him latch on to her left breast. After nearly three months, she still feeds him herself, no wet nurse being allowed into sanctuary. I suspect King Henry's French wife probably rejoices in treating the queen as the commoner she is. What she doesn't see is the vibrant beauty motherhood bestows upon this most captivating of women.

I walk to her side and tuck Ned's tiny foot under the robe. "I awoke this morning in a dole humour," I admit. "In this isolation, there is no controlling the moods that encroach upon us. The uncertainty of each day is hard to overcome."

The queen agrees. Our conversations have become civil, if not intimate. She respects my experience. I admire her tenacity. And deeply hidden is our unspoken shared memory of the dark magic on the night of Ned's birth. The queen may deny it happened, but she watches me differently now.

"The waiting is difficult when the end is unknown," she replies. "And yet have faith, Lady Scrope, that this will also pass and that better times lie ahead." The queen smooths her son's cheek and leans over him. I can barely catch her words. "Soon, Ned, you will greet your father, and he will be so joyful, so happy to meet his young prince and heir to the throne."

Had I heard correctly? "Have you news, Your Grace?" It wouldn't surprise me if messages are still being smuggled into sanctuary. The queen turns to see if any of the abbot's retainers are close by. The chamber is empty. No need to eavesdrop on women's fireside chats.

"I have heard from your sister."

"From Margaret? How? When?"

"Just yesterday. Does this surprise you?"

In truth, no. Margaret wouldn't waste ink on domestic pleasantries with me when there are matters of state to discuss. More curious is that she corresponds directly with the Yorkists.

"What does she say?"

"Her husband, Henry Stafford, has been commanded to muster for King Edward."

"Another battle?" Fear for Jack shrouds my heart like a widow's cowl.

The queen gazes over the sleeping head of her baby. "My husband sails to reclaim England with an army. Those who have the courage ride to welcome him back to his rightful kingdom. Margaret made a wise decision." Standing, she hands the prince to me, shakes out her skirts. "Your sister is always one who plans for the highs and lows of Fortune's wheel. Think carefully where you will be when the wheel turns for you, Lady Scrope."

26

On Easter's Sunday, as with every morning before and every morning ahead that I can predict, I walk through the Jerusalem Chamber to the tall mullioned window looking down upon the precincts of the abbey. I pull a face at the griffin gargoyle that flies from the adjoining roof. He has become my own spiritual protector as well as the cathedral's, his constancy my silent companion in prayer.

These wars. These wars that men fight and women endure, waiting for news, for their men to return home—or not. This new prince, born into conflict, swaddled by dispute, and nursed with vengeance. This wheel of destiny as old as mankind. No one questions if it can be halted. At least no man does. And the women walk behind God's chariot of war as they always have and salvage the wreckage.

"We've come to hear the singing," Meg's voice interrupts my musings. She walks across the chamber, holding Bess and Cecily by their hands. "Have they begun yet?"

I blink away tears. "Not that I have heard. But I was far away." I beckon the girls to the great west window. I try to make the most of each day for the sake of the princesses. Bess is a precocious child and one whom her mother already relies upon greatly; but it is little Cecily who steals my heart. She is near the same age as my own daughter, and although no substitute, I take comfort in playing with her and hope that at home Jack's sister Isabel is caring for my girl.

The fog has settled around the abbey precincts, creeping between the grey stone buildings and drifting in curling silver ribbons on an invisible river breeze. We hear the singers before we see them, and I open the window to let the joyful songs of praise and resurrection fill the chamber.

This Lenten season has been the longest I can remember, and our fasting, combined with the bleak routine of prayers and confession, worship and devotional reading, has drained light and joy from all of us. I usually appreciate this reflective time of year, but time imprisoned within sanctuary, far from those I love, weighs heavy.

"Change is coming soon," Meg whispers as we lean from the sill, our hands pressed against the cold stone.

"What have you heard?"

Meg shakes her head and looks around. The boy is cleaning out the fireplace, and another is bringing the logs. She knows something; her friendships with the abbot's servants have given her information.

"We cannot be expected to stay here forever," Meg says. Then she leans in closer and whispers even softer, "I'll tell you later, when we are by ourselves."

I fill my lungs with the morning air, welcoming the fingers of damp mist caressing my skin. The singers walk under the window towards the west door of the abbey, their sweet music gradually fading until the morning enfolds them and silence rolls in. A glimmering in the east promises a hidden sunrise struggling to break through, and as the glow strengthens, I rub my eyes to clear my eyelashes of the misty drops. *Surely not . . .*

"Meg. Meg, look. Now!" Surely I am dreaming; the mist disorients my perspective. "King Henry's guards—"

"Dear Mother of God," exclaims Meg. "The guards are no more. It is true!"

We both lean from the window and peer through the thinning fog. A crack of blue sky breaks beyond the abbey roof, melting the mist before us, revealing an empty yard. The only evidence of guards are the churned footprints of dozens imprinted in the mud, all leading away from the abbey.

"What could have happened?" I stretch even farther, searching the grounds past the Abbey towers towards the river. No army. No soldiers. Just a clutch of singers threading their way past the primrose banks, their chatter and laughter floating up through the open window. "There is no one guarding us, no one standing sentry. It is as if they never existed." Fear and hope clashed in my heart. This is a sign that a war has been lost. Or won.

"We must tell the queen." Meg jumps from the windowsill, straightens her gown. "King Henry's guard no longer protects London. We may be in great danger."

"Or . . ."

"Or we may be free," Meg finishes.

We turn as the queen sweeps into the chamber, radiant as the April sun that now streams through the coloured glass panes, casting a jewelled net of reds, blues, and greens across the dark floor. She clutches Ned in her arms.

"King Edward has won a great battle at Barnet," she says, her voice hoarse with emotion. "Henry is captured."

"King Henry no longer rules? He is deposed?" I swallow a sudden sourness burning my throat. "And his son is . . . ?"

"The Prince of Wales has yet to show his face. It will not be long before my husband kills him." She grips Ned so tightly he wails. "My son is the rightful heir to England's throne."

Dear God. The omen King Henry forecast just a few months ago when embracing Henry Tudor has come about. They will all be gone. Except my sister's son.

I hold out my arms to take Ned from her, for she holds him awkwardly, and I am afraid she will drop him in her ecstasy of victory. "Your Grace, let me hold Ned for you."

The queen hesitates and then shoves him at me. "King Henry is under lock and key," she repeats triumphantly. "For good, for he has fallen into madness, and my husband has imprisoned him in the Tower. York reigns again." The queen's golden hair and golden gown catch the morning light, illuminating the Jerusalem Chamber with her incandescence. She resembles a holy painting, for surely that is a halo shimmering from her golden crown. "Your sister Margaret made her choice to join us just in time. The Lancastrian dynasty is finished. And my son has a kingdom to inherit."

I rock Ned gently, and his crying stops. He falls asleep in my arms, as he has every day since he was born. A shiver runs through me, and I hold him close to my breast, cherishing his warmth and sweet, peaceful breathing. "And what now, Your Grace?"

"My children and I are to be escorted to the Tower of London to join the court. You will remain here until I summon you. My wait is over. Peace has come to England."

But has it come to me?

My mind recalls Margaret's triumphant smile as King Henry blessed her son, pronounced Henry Tudor his heir. The last Lancastrian king may be on his knees in a Tower cell praying for God's mercy before insanity overwhelms him. There is no doubt in my mind that in her own private chapel, my sister, the last female Lancastrian, is on her knees praying too.

I hope she will spare a thought and say a rosary for me. I have never had more need of God's help.

5

Spring 1471 | The Tower of London

I stare dry-eyed and parch-mouthed across the slate-grey waters of the Thames. Gripping the leather strap nailed to the barge to steady against the chop, I am being rowed along the fast-flowing river to the Tower of London, as ordered by the king. He has finally taken London, after weeks of skirmishes and a terrible final battle at Tewkesbury. Will he honour me now as his blood relative, as the church decrees? Or will he imprison me as his enemy, as politics dictate?

The queen's words roll over and over in my mind, keeping time with the dipping oars pulling me closer to my destiny.

Peace, she said. But whose peace?

Henry VI, the last true king of the Lancastrian dynasty, is insensible under lock and key in the Tower, his queen fled in exile, his heir slaughtered by his own countrymen.

Peace? At what cost?

Destruction. Carnage. Annihilation. This is war's legacy.

I shudder away from a vision of my husband bleeding into the tender grass of spring on Tewkesbury's fields. I have yet to hear of Jack's fate, and I cannot think of my own destiny without agonising about his. I am a soldier's wife, and with that comes the deep and constant fear that gnaws every time he leads his army for the king.

"What will happen today, Belle-maman?" Meg's voice is fractured by the shrieks of gulls squabbling over rubbish on the riverbank. Her green eyes reflect my concern, and I wish I could give her more than cold comfort.

"I stand before the king as his child's godmother. And as his Lancastrian enemy."

"But surely he knows you had no choice."

"In my oath? Or in saving his son's life?" And there lies the heart of the matter. If King Edward refutes my appointment, labels me King Henry's spy, I do have a choice.

"You would not tell of the witchcraft of that night?"

"To save you and me from being imprisoned as Yorkest traitors?" I pull my cloak closer, brace myself against a gust that cuts like jagged glass against my throat. "I will know when I stand before the king. And my God."

On the north bank, just an arrow's flight away, York Palace slides by, immutable and blank-faced. As we turn the great bend that slings the river east to the cold German Sea, the spiteful headwind whips whitecaps across its broad stretch and the oarsmen strain against the tide. Fickle April has hidden its sunshine behind a shroud of clouds, and the cold creeps into my marrow and settles in my bones.

We travel by barge, for the streets are impassable with the crowds pouring from every home and merchant's shop to celebrate the return of King Edward. London turns its back on King Henry and all those who follow him. This is a hostile world, and my time in sanctuary seems safe and sacred, for what does life hold for me now? Uncertainty churns my thoughts sour, and I find no comfort in freedom's wide horizons.

The Lancastrian royal line is no more.

Except for Margaret. And her Tudor son.

I clutch the strap until it chafes my palm red. God's wounds, Margaret carries the last of the royal Lancastrian blood in her veins. But as a mere woman, she cannot muster men to support her claim to the throne. England will not tolerate a warrior queen.

But Henry Tudor as a warrior prince? She would think so.

"We are here, Belle-maman." Meg's soft voice carries over the slopping of water against the side of the barge. "We are at the Tower."

I alight at the water gate under St. Thomas's Tower, and the king's guard walks me up the slight hill by the Garden Tower to an imposing iron gate. Instead of entering the whitewashed stone keep, I am escorted into the Inmost Ward through a complex of stone and wooden buildings. I have arrived at the Royal Palace.

Palace and prison. For this is no ordinary royal residence. The Tower of London is the most secure gaol for the most important prisoners in the land. No merchant robber or cattle thief is kept here. No, these are cells for bishops and dukes, statesman and rebels. For those who have challenged the king. Or simply been put in the wrong place at the wrong time.

Before me crowd timber-framed structures that house the royal apartments, the great hall, musician's galleries, all surrounding the cultivated gardens. At least I think they are here. I am still struggling to make plans now that my king is no longer in power and I cannot see anything beyond my immediate fate.

I could retire to Bolton Castle. *Dear God, where is Jack? Is my daughter safe?* I could hide with Meg in the St.John home at Bletsoe. *Where is Margaret?* And would I even be allowed to leave the Tower? I rush from one future worry to another and then realise that I must deal with the present first.

"Are you ready?" Meg breaks my thoughts, brushes my dusty skirts. On the other side of the doors is the royal court, King Edward, Queen Elizabeth, the victors assembled to celebrate the return of the House of York.

"As I will ever be," I reply. "When we enter, stand back while I approach the king. If I am to be painted with the same brush as King Henry, I do not want you to be brought down with me."

Had Jack been on the battlefield with King Edward? His last words beat in my heart.

"I will always look after you."

I draw back my shoulders and lift my head. If I am to be publicly castigated as King Henry's pawn, I will not let anyone see my fear.

The great hall is so full of people I cannot make out one face from another, and the talk crashes over me like a great wave, throwing my balance and halting my steps. After months of sanctuary silence, the sounds of the world are louder now than I ever remember. Nobody notices when I first enter the hall, but as I am escorted towards the dais, voices drop and a hush descends.

King Edward and Queen Elizabeth sit under a canopy of state, their clothes stiff with gold thread and ornate with jewels. The backdrop of richly embroidered banners and walls painted in hues of crimson and gold, vermillion and azure is simply dazzling. Just as I had become used to silence, so had I only seen gloom and muted shades.

Don't falter, don't fall.

I finish what feels like the longest walk in my life before arriving before the king and sinking into a deep curtsey.

"Lady Scrope." The king's voice is rich and deep, as befits his great height, filling the now-silent room. "You have been treated with respect within sanctuary, I hope?"

I stare down at my feet. My shoes are scuffed at the toes. All that pacing with Ned, those sleepless nights, those cold, barren dawns. I inch the hem of my dress to cover the worn leather.

Not treated at all well by Abbot Millyng. Nor your queen. "Yes, Your Grace."

"Come forward, please."

The king wears a crown resting lightly on his golden hair. He is as handsome as they say, fair of face and a physicality that has every woman in the room looking at him with longing. My own pulse sounds in my ears, but not due to lust. What is my fate?

"My wife tells me you kept her company during her sojourn at the abbot's house." The king reaches for the queen's hand. "And that you came appointed by our enemy King Henry to spy upon her."

I have a choice

I prepare to do battle. And I had thought perhaps the queen and I had reached a truce in our mutual love for Ned. "I—I was appointed by King Henry to care for the queen in her confinement."

There are words I can say that will stop this dead.

The queen leans over and whispers. I see the love light in his face for her as he hearkens to her.

He continues, his sentences rolling over my head, pronouncing my fate. "And I understand that you, a declared Lancastrian, also assumed the role of godmother to Prince Edward."

"I was given the appointment, Your Grace, and carried it out to the best of my ability." There lay the truth between us. I cannot honey-coat nor tell it any other way. "My birthright is Lancastrian."

The king beckons me closer. "So you are as a cuckoo in my family, placed by my enemies, aligned with those who would wish my queen and heir dead."

I feel the same way, but I cannot admit to his truth. "My husband, Lord Scrope, is for York. Perhaps within a woman's world, our priority is not that of sides, but of life. If I did not choose correctly, then so be

33

it." If I am to be guilty, let me die knowing I saved a life, not snuffed it out.

God knows I had the choice.

Behind and around me, the courtiers edge closer. I feel their breath, and I am the quarry. The king gestures at a woman standing on the dais holding a child, and the queen takes my godson from her. She hands him to the king, who receives him as carefully as if he would break. Such a contrast, this tiny newborn swaddled on his board and the conquering warrior.

I ache to take Ned myself, but I am not invited.

The king strokes the baby's cheek and looks at me over the child. "I hear Ned may not have survived. My son, God's precious gift, my most desired treasure, almost taken from me." His expression is stern, his complexion white where he is clenching his jaw.

Here is my moment. "I had to make a choice that night . . ."

"And the queen may have died." The king pauses, as if weighing a decision. I press my hands to my sides to quiet their trembling.

In the silence lies my fate. I dread and yet crave his next words.

"Lady Elysabeth Scrope, I hereby grant you a full pardon for your Lancastrian beliefs . . ."

My knees buckle, so great is my relief.

". . . and welcome you to our family as an honoured godmother. The queen tells me you were brave and decisive and your actions helped her beloved midwife deliver them safely."

I glance at the queen, who stares steadily at me, her cat eyes unblinking.

The king continues. "May I remind you that you will always serve my son under the oath you swore in Westminster, guide him, give him wise counsel, and protect him from those who would wish him harm."

"I will, Your Grace," I reply.

I am pardoned. I am safe.

I address the queen, paraphrasing my godmother's oath. "Until the day I die, I will always protect him."

"And if that means shielding him from those closest to you?" The king drops his voice. "Your Beaufort sister has yet to declare her allegiance, although her husband, Stafford, fought gallantly."

"My first duty is to my godson and my sacred oath."

"I expect no less of you." The king glances over my shoulder, as if impatient now to move on from the world of women and children "And are you wondering about your husband, Lady Scrope?"

My throat constricts, the elation of the king's pardon crumpling under an appalling anxiety. "Yes, Your Grace."

"Lord Scrope served me well—"

"—and led us to victory on the right flank of the battlefield," a pleasant voice interrupts us. Who would dare?

"Richard." The king laughs. "You were there with Jack, Brother. Tell Lady Scrope of her husband's feats."

Grinning at the king, the Duke of Gloucester steps forward, inclines his head to me. He is small-boned and sallow-complected, no likeness to the dazzling king. "Lady Scrope, Jack fought like the true Yorkshireman he is. Fearless in battle, loved by his men, and eager to put down his life for his king and country."

Oh God. I sway then, my traitorous legs betraying me at my husband's fate rather than mine.

"Nay, Jack is alive, and simply . . . tidying up the field of combat," Gloucester reassures, "and will be here with us shortly. He is my trusted friend; I have commanded his return to Bolton Castle to sit on our northern council. As a fellow Knight of the Garter, I will rely on his loyalty as we rebuild our country."

Such relief surges through my limbs; blood rushes to my cheeks.

Jack is safe. And we return to Bolton Castle.

The queen is still looking at me. Our bond has grown tighter in these moments, the tangled web she identified in sanctuary threads between us. "It seems you and your husband will be important to the future of our rule as we rebuild our alliances across the Houses of York and Lancaster," she remarks. "I am pleased you chose the right path, Lady Scrope. Now for you to persuade your sister to do the same."

"Margaret Beaufort stays close to her son's family," the king continues tersely. "Jasper Tudor was absent from the field of battle, and I have yet to see him pledge his allegiance to us. Your sister is slow to recognise our victory. Heed my words, Lady Scrope, and be aware that not all in your family are in my favour."

I incline my head and curtsey, for I have no ready answer, nor would I dare put voice to Margaret's ambitions. Silence is the best response.

After a weighted pause, the king waves me away.

As I walk back through the crowded hall, I now can recognise courtiers from the blur of faces. Some smile; others bow their heads. Apparently, I am now welcome as one of this court.

How suddenly this wheel has turned.

When the news comes the next morning from the Duke of Gloucester that Henry VI tragically died in his sleep that night and that the war truly is over, I pause and wonder how Henry Tudor feels on the news of his uncle's death. Just a few months past, the king's demise would have elevated my nephew to the throne and made my sister the king's mother. Now Margaret is an exile in her own country and the House of Lancaster is no more except a diluted bloodline in my sister's veins.

My choice has been made for me. I must relinquish the house of my birth and return to Bolton Castle.

My future lies with the House of York.

6

Spring 1483 | Bolton Castle

The falcons have hatchlings, and I walk down the hill from the castle to the mews to see them, through the fragrant lavender beds, the well-stocked apothecary garden, and around the maze. As I approach, the birdcalls become loud, and I see that three have been taken from their cages and are now on perches under the oak trees. Standing before them, their hands on their hips like adults, their heads bright in the April sunshine, Ned and his brother, Dickon, converse with Jack and the falconer with all the seriousness of seasoned hunters, nodding and listening to their replies. These are the moments I want to hold in my mind's eye, the forever blue skies, the boys' golden hair, my husband's tall figure, the freedom that gilds this day.

Instead of joining them, I pause by the meadow kissing gate to watch the boys. Young men, I should say, for at twelve and ten Ned and Dickon are growing fast. Each year they stay with us at Bolton, they dash to the charcoal lines on the whitewashed wall of their room to see how much they've grown. This April, Ned is at my chin and Dickon reaches my shoulder. Growing too fast, I say.

I look back at the castle, for I love the view from this meadow, and catch my breath at the pennants flying high from the tower in Ned's honour. It was April twelve years ago that the Scrope banners were swooping over the castle towers like the hawks, the azure background blending with the soaring skies, leaving the gold bar to flash like lightning in the breeze. Proudly flying the king's sunne in splendour and Gloucester's white boar emblems, Bolton Castle had welcomed me back as a member of the royal household. I had left home as a Lancastrian and returned as a Yorkist.

Now, after a decade of peace, my family prospers and Jack has flourished in his position as Gloucester's favourite. His rewards have been many. Land, patronage, revenues, enrich our life and raise us to the highest positions of power among the influential northern barons. Even Margaret is impressed with our affluence, and that says a lot for someone as particular as she is. I mentally check that I have prepared her room the way she likes it when she stays with us, including arranging the small prie-dieu and candles in the window alcove for her devotions. I sigh and wonder what bargain with God she's negotiating in her prayers this time.

A footfall behind me and I turn at the familiar sound.

"All is well, my love?" Jack links his arms around me. His kiss is warm on my neck as he holds me close. "You seem preoccupied."

"Just anticipating Margaret's arrival this afternoon, her usual way of getting under my skin."

"Don't let her bother you."

"She's going to want me to plead her cause with the king. I know she's not coming here just because she misses us."

"And you will handle her request the same way you have managed her in the past. Don't fret." He squeezes me closer to his broad chest. It feels so reassuring.

I smile up at him. "You look most fine, Husband. The boys' maturity reminds me that years are passing, and yet you are as handsome to me as when we first met."

"And you are not a day older than when I first saw you, all flushed and radiant in your garden, your hands full of flowers." Jack caresses my cheek, cups my chin to kiss my lips. "That is a sight I will never forget. For it was that moment that I knew I could never love as I love you."

I smile. "Even if I was another's wife?"

"It was just a matter of waiting my time. And being first in line of all the suitors that would hurry to your door."

I laugh and lay a finger upon his beautiful mouth. "No other suitors. That day will always be with me too."

Jack kisses my finger and then lifts me from my feet, making me cry out as he whirls me in a circle. The boys look up and run across the field, laughing and calling out to me. They are back to being children again as they bump and race each other to get to me first.

"Make the most of this glorious day, and tonight we have the Hocktide feast to enjoy," Jack says as he puts me down, breathless. "Even Margaret can't spoil the fun we have planned."

Laughter and bursts of song echo from walls and rafters as pages thread through the trestles carrying aloft great smoking platters of roasted meat. I catch sight of Jack at one of the lower tables, sitting with his tenants as if one of them, a charming host with a word for everyone. The candlelight picks out the silver around his temples, and there are threads of grey in his beard. But still one look from him and I know exactly what he is thinking. And how it will feel later, in the privacy of our chamber. He catches my eye and makes his way to my side.

A storm of drumming resounds from the stone walls, and our family and friends hush their talk as the musicians beat an insistent rhythm and other instruments join. Night has stolen across the dales as we feasted, and now branching stands of our finest beeswax candles light the great hall, illuminating the rich reds and blues in the wall hangings and casting a warm glow on the faces of those I love.

We are all gathered to celebrate Hocktide, the traditional time to feast and dance after the deprivation of the Lenten season and the solemnity of Easter. It is one of the most important weeks in our tenants' year, where we enjoy sports and games and settle up on rents and dues. We love to reward them all by throwing open Bolton's great hall and inviting everyone to attend.

A glint of gold catches my eye, and I laugh at Ned's bobbing head as he skips a dance to the drone of the hurdy-gurdy. It is an old song that encourages the young men of the village to capture a coy maiden, and although Meg pretends to ignore her young admirers, I catch my stepdaughter winking at the young prince and his corresponding crimson cheeks. With a husband and three fine boys of her own now, Meg knows how to turn a man's head and teach a boy manners.

"Ned loves to be here with us," I say to Jack. "We are fortunate that Lord Rivers thinks us worthy of his precious charge."

My husband pulls a rueful expression. "I'm not sure we can live up to Lord Rivers's standards of chivalry and learning. But Prince Edward will learn the ways of the knights who will be his most loyal followers when he becomes king."

"Not for a long time," I reply. *Don't let my boy grow up too quickly.* "He is but twelve."

"It's never too early to learn who your friends and enemies are," says Jack. "And I am afraid in the protected air of Ludlow, Ned gets little chance to judge for himself who is of good character and who is not to be trusted."

I agree. "True indeed. And important skills when he becomes king in the distant future. It sounds as though you and my brother Oliver are teaching Ned more than horsemanship and telling tales of your exploits in battles." I enjoy the prospect of Ned smiling from ear to ear now, not hiding his delight as the dance of the young men increases pace and each steps forward to perform a solo jig. I am so happy to see him drop his formality and behave as any other lad. And thank God that Jack has taken in the young prince as if he were his own son. My own sad prediction at Ned's birth had been correct. God did not bless us with more children of our own.

"Oliver's experience of fighting in France and my wars with the Scots give him real stories, real battles, not the make believe of Lord Rivers's Arthurian legends." Jack's voice says it all, his contempt for the world of stories and chivalry loud and clear. "Anthony Woodville is more concerned with honing his likeness to a knight of the Round Table than dealing with life in the real world."

"There is nothing wrong with admiring the stories of King Arthur—"

"I love the knight's tales." Ned arrives at my side, red-faced and puffed. He sneaks a look at Jack, who silently pushes his tankard towards my godson, whistling and looking the other way as if it were moving itself by magic. "Shall we tell stories when the dancing is over? You know, the ones we admire, like Sir Lancelot and King Arthur."

"From what I remember, Lancelot was not such a good friend to King Arthur," replies Jack. "If you are going to learn anything from these tales, Your Grace, learn how even the best of friends can turn into mortal enemies."

"Jack," I scold, both for his words and his plying of drink to Ned. "Let us enjoy our stories without putting your own views on them." I smooth Ned's hair from his perspiring brow. Because he has grown several inches this last year, he is as tender as a young shoot—and as vulnerable. "Come, sweetheart, rest for a moment, otherwise you will overheat and catch another fever." Ned's health is always frail when he first arrives at Bolton Castle, no doubt from the long days Lord Rivers favours at his studies, with his only exercise dominated by instruction, not play. "I was just playing a memory game with Lord Scrope, thinking of the happiest occasions in my life that I mark time with. What are your special memories, Ned?"

The boy thinks for a moment, and then his face brightens. "Do you remember the joust at Westminster, when my brother was betrothed? When my Uncle Rivers challenged my Uncle Buckingham, who got angry because he was beaten by Lord Rivers in the joust and Lord Rivers had the most beautiful horses, and he arrived as the figure of Saint Anthony, and then Buckingham swore to avenge his loss, even though he and Lord Rivers had once been friends because Buckingham is married to his sister."

I smile at him and want to hug him in all his breathless, innocent excitement. I remember the joust differently, with Buckingham in his usual boastful way arriving with an excessive number of horse and retainers, all dressed in gold and purple. Lord Rivers, the queen's brother, had been dressed as the saint in his hermitage, in pure white and with white horses and retainers in white. He had beaten Buckingham in quick measure.

"I do remember." Ned's father has set the fashion for chivalry and the worship of King Arthur, and Ned has taken it to heart. I point across the room. "The Duke of Buckingham has not joined us, but his aunt, my sister Margaret, is sitting at the head table. She came a long way to celebrate with us today."

We both look in silence. Margaret cuts a stern figure, sitting by herself, her face white under her nun-like wimple, her back rigid.

"I hope she's enjoying herself more than she appears," whispers Ned, choking back a giggle. "The music looks like it's giving her a megrim."

Meg flings herself down on the bench next to us, fanning herself with her hand, her auburn hair flaming over her shoulders. "Margaret loves music as much as all of us," she says. "I think these family gatherings twist a knife in her heart because her own son is exiled so far away. It must be difficult to rejoice with those who have their family around them when it has been years since you have held your own child."

Margaret sits as stiff-backed and unmoving as the carved chair she inhabits, her hands clasped tightly in her lap, as if she is forbidding herself to move with the music. Even when the rest of the gathering applauds, she casts her eyes down and does not smile.

"I know how I miss my mother," Ned says wistfully. "And she is just in London or on progress with my father."

Sad but true. Elizabeth Woodville prefers the lively company of the court and her younger son rather than the stifling structure of Ned's household. I have barely seen the queen in ten years.

He stands, straightens his jacket. "I shall go and comfort Lady Stanley. She may not have her son near, but I can talk to her about King Arthur and the book my Uncle Rivers gave me."

Threading his way through the guests, Ned stops to listen to one, clasp another on his shoulder. His manner is easy, for these are people he has known since I first had permission to bring him to Bolton when a young child. I convinced the king and queen that a brief spell with my family would do him no harm and a break from the grinding routine of the prince's household would be favourable to his happiness and health.

"He's a kind boy." Meg sips from her cup, watches Ned as he approaches Margaret and leans over to talk to her. "Your guidance over the years has brought a warmth and naturalness to his character that Lord Rivers would not have nurtured."

I have to agree. Lord Rivers is a man of great learning and greater chivalry, but he is as cold as an icicle and as much fun as a cloistered monk. "I love when Ned comes to Bolton. I feel he can see a different life, enjoy growing up being a boy here, not a prince."

"It has made him a sensitive and levelheaded young man," Meg replies. "And now he is twelve, you can relinquish more of his care to his chaplain and less as his godmother."

I'm not sure I want to hear this. Ned has been my life for the past twelve years, and I think that I am in many ways more his mother than Elizabeth Woodville ever has been. God's pardon for my blasphemy, a chaplain will never take my place.

Meg turns as her husband joins us. She shakes a disapproving finger at him. "Will Catesby, please now leave business aside and let us enjoy time with our family. You will turn us to stone if you keep us at council all day and night. Surely for once the royal family can manage without us."

She echoes my thoughts, my hope that Jack will spend more time at Bolton Castle now. He is getting too old to muster for the king, to fight to defend the border from Scottish invaders. There is no more need for war councils and skirmishes. The king rules over a peaceful land. Of course, I would never tell him he is aging. But I see the weariness that sometimes creeps upon him when he thinks I am not looking. All I want is this next turn in life's wheel, the undisturbed rhythm of betrothals and marriages, births and christenings, my healthy and happy husband at my side.

Will bows to Meg in mock respect, blond hair falling in waves over his eyes. "My love, the only council that matters is the one you rule: the Catesby family council. God forbid I would put the king or Gloucester's needs before your agenda."

Meg lifts her hand for her husband to kiss, but instead Will pulls her up into his arms and lifts her from her feet. He runs with her, dodging between the crowded tables, until he reaches the dancing space. He sets her down in the middle of the floor, a wide grin on his face. Solemnly, Meg bows and Will curtseys back, wobbling in the unaccustomed motion. They hold the pose for a few moments before falling laughing into each other's arms. Ned has been requisitioned by our falconer's daughter, and he joins them in the dance. Together they promenade across the room to the cheers of our tenants.

I take a deep breath. Duty calls. I kiss Jack's head and walk over to where my sister sits by herself again.

Margaret draws herself up into a disapproving pillar. After all these years, I can sense without her even speaking when my sister is at odds with the world. Which is often. "Jack is very familiar with his tenants. I would have expected a little more decorum from his position."

"Jack treats men as equals," I respond. "Your southern standards of formality and protocol don't belong here in Yorkshire."

"Is that why you let the heir to the throne cavort as if he is a squire's baseborn son? He has no guard, no keeper, and mingles with the peasants with no protection."

And all to his well-being. My godson has now squeezed onto the bench next to Jack and has been handed a mug of ale by one of the squires. He proudly downs it in one gulp and slams the tankard on the table. At twelve years old, keeping pace with the men is important.

I smile and shake my head in mock disapproval. "Margaret, Ned has enough rules to live with every day he is tutored by Lord Rivers. If he doesn't understand his subjects, how can you expect him to rule over them? He needs to know the people of the land in order to know the land itself. Trust me when I tell you that these times of informality are what will help him be a fine king one day."

43

My sister sniffs, wipes her eyes with an ample linen square she pulls from her sleeve.

Oh no. Here come Margaret's tears.

"If your child had been taken from you when you were just a child yourself, you would perhaps understand that trust does not come easily and safety is of the utmost importance." Margaret delivers her own life story as a reproach.

My heart twists, the small guilt-worm that lives in its chambers burrowing at my conscience. There is no doubt that Margaret's young marriage and childbirth was a difficult and damaging time for my sister. And I still regret I did not plead with our mother to postpone Edmund Tudor's indecent eagerness to impregnate his prized wife. But these were times long past, and Margaret has survived, along with her precious son.

As ever, I search for words to diffuse my sister's bitterness. "Margaret, your son will return from exile soon. Your negotiations with the king are well underway. I am sure you can depend on his fairness to forgive Henry his rebellious streak and bring him home."

"Just as I depended on our mother, who sold me to the highest bidder when I was but twelve?" Tears are running down her cheeks. In truth, Margaret's temperament flies from sanguine to melancholic in an eye's blink. "My childhood and my life with all of you at Bletsoe was happy. And then it was torn from me."

I take her kerchief and dab at Margaret's cheeks in a habit grown in our childhood and instinctively returning, even at our age. Margaret's memories are important. Those were good years before we were parted. Our whole family spoiled Margaret, all loved the little half-sister who lost her father before she turned a year.

"You were the Beaufort heiress. Our mother had no choice once the king ordered your betrothal to his half-brother." I reach for Margaret's hand, become momentarily her protector again, trying to make up the divide between us, rewrite the hurt I have caused my sister by being absent when she needed me the most. "I know how you feel, Margaret. Lord Zouche was twice my age. You know I was married to him to secure the lands next to Bletsoe."

Margaret purses her lips and pulls her hand away. The moment of tenderness has gone. "You were grown. I was a child. Zouche died. And then I encouraged your decision to marry for love. Or lust?"

"Leave Jack from this conversation, Margaret." A flush rises through my body. My sister does not know what joy a husband can bring. Margaret mistakes ambition posing as passion. That is evident from her recent marriage to Lord Stanley, a business transacted not even a year after her husband Stafford was cold in his grave. "Surely you are not here to rake over old embers."

"You could help me now, as I helped you," replies Margaret. "If I had not placed you in sanctuary and contracted you the position of godmother, you would not have thrived. You have the king's ear. Use your influence now to bring Henry home."

"I barely see the king. And when I do, it is not to ask political favours, but to discuss his own son's well-being."

Margaret turns to me then, all trace of tears gone from her cheeks. "So next time discuss *my* son's well-being. It is the least you can do."

I stand, brushing Margaret's words from my lap like crumbs from a trencher. "Do not tell me what favours to ask of the king, Sister. And leave your politics at the door, not at my table."

I leave the dais, make my way to Jack's side among the friends I have treasured these past ten years. I push away the uneasiness Margaret's demand has cast over me. Begging favours from the king for my sister's exiled son is not within my purview.

"I visit Sheriff Hutton next month, my love." Jack gestures to a page, tops up his cup and mine too.

"Oh, not again." What new orders will come from the Duke of Gloucester that take my husband away from me again?

Jack knows my heart. "Gloucester has requested Will and I attend, for he is planning an expansion of the council's power, and he wants my local knowledge and Will's fine legal brain on the drafting of the documents."

"And you don't have a mind?" I tease him. My husband hates the world of scribing and parchment.

"Not fit for clerking," he shoots back as he strokes the inside of my wrist, making me shiver.

"And what are you fit for?"

"You tell me." Jack casts a look that heats my blood. "So I must travel tomorrow to inspect lands, gather tithes and rents, meet with my men before our business with the duke. I'll return in a fortnight. And so will you come with me to the northern court, Lady Scrope, or shall I leave you here in your lonely castle turret?"

"While I pine for a chivalrous knight to rescue me?" I pretend to turn away. "Perhaps I should send a favour to Lord Rivers and beg his assistance."

"He'd be as much use to you as a broken quill." Under the cover of the table carpet, Jack's finger strokes my thigh through my gown, and I am mesmerised by his sensual mouth close to mine. "Or do you prefer a man who only writes the language of love and does not speak it?"

The music fills my ears, and the wine warms my blood. Leaving the young people dancing to the throbbing drums, we hasten like newlyweds to Jack's chamber above mine at the very top of the tower, where we bolt the door and tumble under the sheepskins before the roaring fire. Laughing, Jack reminds me that courtly love is best left on parchment, while real love is warm skin and lips and tangled limbs as I melt under his desire, falling asleep only when he gently uncurls my arms from around him and slips from the covers to ride out into the early morning.

7
Spring 1483 | Bolton Castle

"A messenger, Lady Scrope. From the Duke of Gloucester. The king's brother requests an immediate response." The castle steward hovers in the doorway.

"Bring him here, Master Ashworth. Although I am not sure I can help him." I am reading aloud to Isabel, for Jack's sister loves to hear the tale of *The Wedding of Sir Gawain* and King Arthur's quest for what women desire most. Loyalty? Love?

Or the true answer women keep hidden from men.

Sovereynté. A right to make their own decisions.

I place the well-worn parchment of the knights' tales on my chamber's limestone window ledge.

Jack respected my *sovereynté* when I chose to marry him. But I kept that it was my decision a secret. My husband's reputation was enhanced by wooing and winning the wealthy widow, not by being chosen by her.

Curious if there is an entourage with the messenger, I nudge open the narrow window to peer down the sheer curtain walls. During the Cousins' Wars, this far-reaching view from Bolton Castle secured us from the enemy. Today, the wide windswept skies arc over our peaceful lands. Sun-bright clouds chase shadows from the forested valleys to the purple hills, and sweet birdsong replaces the clashing of iron being forged in the castle armoury. The only movement in the apothecary garden below my window is the gardener pulling weeds from the lavender beds.

Spurs jangle on the spiral steps, and Isabel looks up from her embroidery; her head bobs like the narcissus in the grasses lapping Bolton's keep. An envoy strides across the solar. His murrey-and-blue livery proclaims the household of Richard Plantagenet, Duke of Gloucester.

Best to tell him his journey is wasted. "My husband is not here. Lord Scrope rides out to our farthest boundaries. He will not return for several weeks."

"The message is to both you and Lord Scrope." The rider thrusts a packet at me, crumpled and bulky, begging exploration. "The duke ordered I remain for further instruction."

How peculiar Gloucester addresses us both. I ponder whether to read it now or wait for Jack's return. The missive weighs heavy in my hands. While he is gone, he insists that although the steward governs in name, decisions about the castle are my responsibility.

But this is official business, from outside my domain, from Gloucester himself.

I run my fingernail under the edge of the seal, cracking the red wax slightly.

It is, after all, addressed to both of us.

The right to make my own decision. "Then I shall see what is so urgent from the king's brother."

Isabel joins me at the window, leans against my arm in her curiosity to see what I have received. "Should you not wait for Jack? Or ask Oliver his advice? He can ride from our home in just an hour."

"My husband trusts me, and this is not addressed to my brother."

I break open the seal with a click, and a pearl-and-ruby crucifix tumbles forth. I catch the cross just before it drops to the floor. No scribe has touched this note, for the writing is hasty, perhaps scrawled in Gloucester's own hand. His words are abrupt, a series of directions, as if he is issuing instructions for a military campaign.

I command you both to Middleham on a matter of great urgency. Jack, you must attend us immediately and bring a troop of your most trustworthy men. Elysabeth, I send the king's jewel as a reminder of your holy vow. Prince Edward is in danger. Do not delay, for each hour could cost us dearly. Prepare to travel with me to London.

The ill-fitting window shutter bangs open. A sudden cold eastern gust barges through the latch, whisking me back to the steps of the cathedral at Westminster. A November twelve years past and yet clear as day. The day I swore my sacred oath as godmother to the heir of England's throne, to protect Ned against the wrong in the world.

A second note, just a scrap, flutters from the folds. Meg's curved writing jumps from the parchment.

Come, Belle-maman, I am at Middleham with Will. You and Jack must come. Please. We are depending on you.

Blessed Virgin Mother. My vow is called. And not just by Ned's uncle, but by someone who understands my oath better than any, who lived through those tortuous days in sanctuary with me. Whatever has caused Meg to scrawl her note, she would not call upon me without reason.

"What does the letter say, Elysabeth?" I hear Isabel's words on the edge of my consciousness but cannot yet leave my thoughts.

I hand her the document. "Ned is in some kind of danger." How could this be? We had no hint of worry at Hocktide. What could have changed in a week?

Through the window, the black-and-white flash of a single magpie flies across the valley, east from Middleham. What sorrow forecast? I blink twice to repel his spell.

Sovereynté.

Jack is not here. I must make this decision now.

The messenger is waiting for my response, shuffling impatiently from foot to foot. He is eager to report back to Gloucester.

"I will travel to Middleham and on to London," I reply.

The steward sucks in his breath. He doubts I can ride three leagues to Middleham Castle by myself, let alone venture to the wicked capital. But Jack's allegiance to Gloucester is more important than our servant's disapproval. I do not know when Jack will return. I have no reason to disobey Gloucester's command and stay at Bolton.

I make my choice. "Lord Scrope would wish it so. Bring me parchment so I may leave instructions for my husband. Prepare my horse and a guard of six."

"Elysabeth, you can't go by yourself." My sister-in-law's face is a picture of surprise, round blue eyes wide open, pink mouth forming an O. Isabel is always the cautious one. She tempers my brother Oliver's hotheadedness. Gossip said it was providential that two Scropes married two St.Johns, further stitching together York and Lancaster. I know it is love, not ambition, that nurtures both marriages.

I kiss Isabel's soft cheek, smooth the worry line from her brow. "Meg and Will are with Gloucester. I won't be alone. I shall ride today. Explain to Oliver that Gloucester has called my vow. Jack can follow as soon as he receives my message. My brother may wish to ride to Middleham with Jack when he returns."

Holding the crucifix tightly in my hand, the familiar feel giving me strength, I summon my gentlewoman. "Pack my silk court gowns and sleeves, jewelry, and apothecaries. We have a journey ahead."

8

Spring 1483 | Middleham Castle

Ancient dry-stone walls direct the track easterly across the ridgelines to Middleham Castle before the pathway plunges into the forested valleys. It is a well-worn route, for we frequent Gloucester's household often, and I know the way well. My guard and I splash through fords where golden catkins dance over the becks that tumble from the high moors, the waters foaming brown and turbulent over jagged rocks. It is not far, no more than two hours, but plenty of time to ponder the urgency of the duke's command.

I touch the familiar outline of the crucifix, safely tucked inside my purse next to Gloucester's cryptic note. Just days ago, Ned was dancing at the Hocktide feast and then safely returned to the care of Lord Rivers at Ludlow. Why could he possibly now be in danger?

The late afternoon sun warms my back as the hulking stone walls of Middleham appear, soaring above the village huddled at its feet. Azure pennants displaying Gloucester's distinctive white boar emblem stream from the towers. We clatter across the drawbridge and under the massive portcullis and immediately are swept into the commotion of a household on the move. Furious banging and hammering from the smithy announce the rapid forging of weapons and horseshoes. The mingled aromas of baking breads and roasting meats are tangled in blue smoke drifting through the inner ward. Ponies are turning the giant mill wheel within the granary. And barrels of ale and flagons of wine are being precisely set into carts under the boteler's watchful eyes.

I dismount by the entrance chamber and catch the arm of an official hurrying by, a harried scribe with a great bundle of parchments stacked in his arms.

"I am here at the command of the Duke of Gloucester." My words are rushed by the urgency in the air. "Take me to him."

The man hesitates for a moment and then gestures impatiently to a youth hovering in the shadows.

"Take this lady to Lord Gloucester," he instructs. "And then return immediately. I have an errand for you."

I follow the page up the broad staircase and into the great hall. Richard, Duke of Gloucester, stands at the dais, papers and coins spread across the board and a gathering of officials before him. The rumble of men's talk brings a different timbre to the room. We are usually attending for banquets and celebrations. This feels like a military camp. Musicians and the soft laughter of the women of the castle are the sounds of the Middleham I know. Now I am beset by the clamour of armoured men and rough voices. Without Jack and his easy friendship with Gloucester, I hesitate, out of place and off-balance.

Already I am beginning to regret my hasty decision. Is Meg in the castle? Her husband, Will Catesby, stands at the high table, his lawyer's eyes skimming words on parchments.

Gloucester addresses one after another of his captains. "Make haste, make haste," he urges. "And ensure we have the supplies and resources to move our men two hundred miles south to London."

London. I don't know what I thought I would find when I arrived, but I suddenly feel unprepared for a journey on my own.

Sanding his signature and tossing the parchment to Will, Gloucester catches sight of me and waves my guards out of ears' reach. He is an elegant man, but fate has omitted even a ghost of his brother's fine physique and careless charm. Gloucester's stature is slim, and his pale complexion conceals him within the dim hall. Since I first saw him at the Tower all those years ago, he has aged. And when he is tired at the end of one of our banquets, he rises from the table slowly and stiffly, like an old man in pain. Jack never speaks of his lord's physical ailment, but there is an affliction somewhere that Gloucester stubbornly hides.

"Lady Scrope. Elysabeth." The charm flickers, and I smile back. He is one who does not need to illuminate a room when he can influence from the shadows. Jack often says his Yorkist lord has perfected that role his entire life, eclipsed by the splendour of his magnificent brothers. "And Jack is . . . ?" He peers over my shoulder, worry lines creasing his forehead.

"My lord," I curtsey deeply, forming the words I have prepared on my ride to explain my sole appearance. "I opened your letter. You summoned me urgently with a crucifix." A flush burns my cheeks, and I lift my chin up. "I came alone."

"Alone?" Gloucester clasps his hands together, rotates the ring on his little finger. "Without Jack? And with no soldiers?"

"Yes, my lord." I touch the crucifix, take comfort in its contours through the fabric of my purse.

He looks at me askance, as if to say, *What am I supposed to do with you, then?* "Jack is coming later today?"

"Jack has not received your message. He is in our eastern lands. I have sent word to find him, to ask him to return as soon as he can."

"That will be too late," Gloucester says, half under his breath. He flexes his shoulders, stares at me hard, makes a decision. "Ah well, we still need you, Elysabeth."

I am relieved and anxious all at once. "What can I do? You said in your letter that Ned is danger."

"He is. We must leave for London immediately."

"But Ned is in Ludlow, on the Welsh borders."

"Not anymore. Even now Ned rides south from Ludlow Castle under the guardianship of Lord Rivers, accompanied by an army of two thousand men."

"An army? For what reason?" I am feeling like I am going in circles. And I don't know how much more time Gloucester will spend with me now that he knows Jack is not here.

"My brother." Gloucester clears his throat, twists his ring some more. "My brother the king is dead of an apoplexy. Nigh on a week ago in Westminster."

"Sweet Jesu, God rest his soul." His words stumble me back a pace. "How could this be?" My hand flies to my chest to calm my pounding heart. "King Edward was hale, hearty, full of life when I saw him this past Christmas."

Richard's expression is unreadable, his mouth set in a thin line.

"This means . . ." I pause, struggling for the words.

"My nephew Prince Edward takes the throne. Your godson Ned, the Woodville woman's child, is King of England."

I shake my head to clear my mind. *My Ned. King. So very young.*

Gloucester looks distractedly over my shoulder.

He is courteous, but I know he is not a patient man. "You sent a crucifix to remind me of my vow. What must I do?" I ask him.

Gloucester gestures to Will, holding up his hand to say he will be with him shortly. "The king trusted you. He wished the memento be given to his heir, for his last thoughts were of his son's spiritual well-being. The queen refuses to leave London; the child is your sacred responsibility."

"She refuses?" Really, what now from this Woodville woman? "Of course I am here to assist Ned. And gladly so, my lord. My vow was to stand with my godson against danger. I promised King Edward I would always remember." That miserable winter of Westminster's sanctuary, the queen's resentment, her life-threatening labour. The king's pardon. And warning.

Gloucester's eyes glisten as the setting sun tosses a spear of light across the hall. "Elizabeth Woodville did not even notify me of my own brother's death. Will Catesby delivered me the news." He guides me to an alcove away from the bustle of the hall. "The Woodvilles plan on immediately crowning Prince Edward and thus securing their supremacy over the throne. I will stop them."

What does he mean, stop them? Stop Ned from being crowned? "You would cross the queen, my lord?"

Gloucester frowned. "I act on my brother's command."

"Surely that is to crown his son." King Edward desired family unity, not division. He intentionally included the Woodvilles in Ned's upbringing, appointed Lord Rivers his tutor and guardian.

"Under my control," avowed Gloucester. "Upon his deathbed, the king made his enemies and friends swear fealty to each other. He removed the queen as executor of his will. And in that same breath, he appointed me England's Lord Protector of the Realm. I must ensure the safety of his sons, the young princes."

Ned and Dickon. My boys. One now king, the other his heir. The world shifts, and in my heart of hearts I feel a distant pang of unease. "And so you direct the succession, not the queen and council? And the Woodvilles have agreed to this?" Surely King Edward did not intend his wife and brother to be sparring over Ned's future the moment he died.

Gloucester smiles, tilts his head. Again, that flash of charm, concealed like a pike beneath a lily pad. "The Woodvilles have no say. I am the brother and uncle of kings. I am Lord Protector of the Realm. I crown the new king. Not the upstart Woodvilles." He squints towards the dais and the soldiers waiting for his next commands. "And since his mother refuses to ride out to join us, you will accompany Ned, ensure that he understands the importance of my role."

"Of course." So here is my duty.

Gloucester takes my hand, kisses it. "Thank you, Elysabeth. I know the terrible pain of losing a father young. You will bring comfort to my beloved nephew, stay with him, and keep him safe as we negotiate with Rivers. Ned trusts you." He nods to Catesby and leaves me. "Stay with Meg tonight. And be ready to ride out before dawn," he calls over his shoulder as he rejoins his soldiers.

I have received my orders, but I am not confident I understand my role within this altered landscape. Jack knows how to negotiate these shifting alliances. Gloucester's summons demands more than the fulfillment of a godmother's vow. I have responsibility for Ned's spiritual well-being. Now it seems I am concerned with his physical safety too.

Sovereynté is already showing its dangerous face.

I sit wide-eyed at the window, sleep kept at bay by the anxiety of the morrow's journey. The dead king swore me to defend his son against his enemies. Neither of us ever considered his wife and queen, Ned's own mother, would be the foe.

Darkness clings to Middleham's parapets as shadows spawned by the blazing torches race along the stone walls. A hundred flares turn night into day, expediting Gloucester's preparations. Will and Meg's room is in a timber-framed lodge across from the main keep. The wooden bridge between the two complexes rattles and clatters with men dashing from one to another to ready their departure.

"Will has just told me some strange news," Meg says, picking at a thread in her shawl. I can see she is ill at ease.

"What now?" I'm not sure I'm ready for any more surprises tonight.

"Your kinsman the Duke of Buckingham joins us upon the road. With his own troop of three hundred men."

I try not to roll my eyes at the mention of Margaret's nephew. Buckingham has never impressed me with his manners or his intellect. "Why on earth would he suddenly appear? Harry has no loyalty to Gloucester."

Meg shrugged. "I know. Will says the same. But Harry offered his resources and his allegiance, and at this short notice Gloucester doesn't have a lot of choice."

"There must be better allies than the Duke of Buckingham. Harry's not one to trust. He is a fair-weather friend, never one to provide shelter in a storm."

"He has a powerful army. He offered two thousand men." Meg shrugs. "Will doesn't trust Harry either. He's not sure what is motivating this sudden loyalty. After all, he's married to the queen's sister. Why would he turn against them?"

"I can tell you that. Power. Land. And a chance to further his own riches. Harry's loyalty does not come free of strings."

"Enough to turn against his own brother- and sister-in-law?" Meg questions. "What kind of motivation would kindle a conflict of this magnitude within a family?"

"Harry is overflowing with avarice. Desire comes in many forms, my sweet."

And so does betrayal. Most perilously of all when one spawns the other.

A thought strikes me. "Margaret or her husband are not joining us, are they? She is close to Harry."

"Not that I have heard. But nothing would surprise me. Margaret has a nose for intrigue, and there is certainly plenty about on this journey." Meg takes a pot from the fireplace, pours hot water into two cups. A sweet fragrance steams from the brew. It is a comforting ritual, a woman's soothing act.

I shake my head slowly. One small choice to answer a letter and suddenly I am thrust into a web of conspiracy.

"Belle-maman, you made the right decision." Meg calmly offers the chamomile and lavender posset. "Jack will be with us soon. The king called on you from beyond the grave. You had no other option."

"Meg, I acted in haste. I hope I shall not regret it." How long before the messengers will find Jack? "And your note convinced me that I should not wait."

"You did what your king—and God—commanded of you. You are Ned's godmother. You are acting in his best interest. I see no wrong in that."

"Ned has come first for me so many times, Meg. You've seen how I've been ordered to Christmases at Westminster, his birthdays at

Ludlow. Even to the loss of precious time with my own family." I rest my forehead against the cool stone. "And now Gloucester paints the Woodvilles as adversaries. Lord Rivers is a faithful guardian to Ned. I've never doubted his love and loyalty."

"We all understand your duty to the royal family," Meg replies. "And frankly, we've benefitted from it. My marriage to Will, Gloucester's trust in Jack—those would not have come about without your influence."

"You make me sound like Margaret."

Meg winks. "There's no worry there. You're not on your knees enough."

The banging and shouting below our window continue. Jumping down from the sill, I tie my hair back in a hasty braid. Within hours, we ride south to challenge Lord Rivers for custody of the king. Jack will not arrive in time. I must now think of what I can do to keep Ned busy while Gloucester and Lord Rivers talk about his future.

The unnatural red glow of the torches and Gloucester's words keep me ill company through the sleepless night until my heels ache from pacing the unforgiving floor. By the time the Prime bell rings, I am mounted on my horse, the reins tight between my clenched fingers to keep the shivers at bay. Our great procession to meet the new king leaves Middleham under the faint and optimistic gleam of a new crescent moon and takes the road south.

9

Spring 1483 | Northampton

As we ride towards London, the countryside drapes smooth from the high peaks down to England's middle lands, the rolling hills flattening into forests and chase, where outlaws reign and York and Lancaster once sparred. Is Ned prepared to rule this land and keep it peaceful? I have confidence in him, for he has been tutored from birth in the ways of kings. His reign may have come without warning, but a prince is always prepared for his destiny.

Three days in the saddle and my back is stiffening like a board. Meg and I ride astride to keep pace with the men. We are not about to be relegated to the gaggle of sidesaddle women in the middle of the convoy nor trail with the baggage strumpets who follow in its dusty wake, doling hurried favours for a soldier's coin.

Gloucester drops back from the lead as we approach Northampton's boundary. He is dusty-faced, his eyes pinpoints of light. "The Duke of Buckingham's advance riders have arrived. The king and Lord Rivers left Wales two days ago. We will all meet up here." He indicates an inn set alongside the road, one of several that hosts travellers on the Great North Road. "Join us later to sup as we wait. I will send word when they have arrived."

The Talbot is shabbily thatched with yellow-green moss gluing the clumped grey reeds. Swallows' nests streak mud from the eaves to the drains. A pack of lurchers squabbles over scraps, their yelps and snarls filling the small courtyard. I shrug. I've stayed in worse.

We are crammed in tightly, for we are just the tip of the procession, and Meg and I are lucky to be in Gloucester's party. We secure a room together with a simple bed and a chair by the fire. At least it's cleaner inside than out. After settling, the evening's quiet is broken by horse hooves striking the cobbles and shouts from the ostlers. Lanterns flare a welcome, casting bumpy shadows across the wattle-and-daub walls. I push open the splintered shutter. Men swarm the courtyard—there is Lord Rivers's dark green livery and the black and red of my cousin Harry, the illustrious Duke of Buckingham. I must admit I am not looking forward to seeing him. I stand up and sit down a dozen times at a footfall on the stair, and yet no summons knocks at our door. Eventually, Meg goes in search of food, for it is evident that no invitation to sup is coming from Gloucester this evening. We are forgotten.

Meg returns with a flushed face and irate air, carrying a hasty tray of cold meats, cheeses, and coarse bread. "Gloucester meets with Lord Rivers and Buckingham in the taproom." She thumps the tray on a bench by the cold fireplace. No one has brought kindling. "The whole inn is turned upside down to serve them, for they make most merry and order the landlord to bring his best wines from the cellar. The cook is so overcome that he cannot attend to anyone else's needs."

"Thank you, Meg. That sounds like Harry. You did your best. Is Will with them too?" I nibble a corner of the dried bread.

"My darling husband will be up most of the night sending orders to London." Meg perches on a stool, cuts a hunk of cheese. "We are going to visit our sons tomorrow, for Ashby Manor is just a few miles from here. Court will demand all his time now, and it may be the last chance to see them for a while."

"How long will you stay?"

"Will for just the day. I will try to spend the week at home with them. I miss them terribly."

I sit silently. Not only is Jack still absent, now Meg is leaving. "I hope I can still see Ned tonight."

"Don't count on it, Belle-maman. If the men are talking, then the women are waiting."

"Well, not always. If Margaret were here . . ."

Meg snorts with laughter. "If Margaret were here, we'd be dining with Gloucester and Buckingham would be waiting on us."

She is, of course, right. Margaret does as she wishes. And makes sure that everyone else does what she wants too. "What do you think Margaret will say of the king's death?"

"She'll find the good in it for her, and she'll be envious of you." Meg is her usual direct self. "Yes, green with it, I'd say."

"Envious? Of me? Why?" Margaret has been approving of my role since I aligned with the House of York. Not that I had a lot of choice.

Meg leans forward, selects another piece of cheese, examines it, and flicks a speck of mold onto the floorboards. "You know her belief in fate's wheel. Once she was ascending and told by King Henry that her son was his heir." She nods at the pouch containing the crucifix, which I can't seem to put down. "No one expected King Edward to die with so much unfinished, including her precious son's pardon. It's all she lives for, to bring Henry Tudor home from exile. And now you're the king's mother."

"Godmother. And I have no influence to cause Margaret jealousy. Her marriage to Lord Stanley last year put her firmly back at the very top of the court's hierarchy."

"The dead king's hierarchy," Meg corrects me. She has picked up good political instincts from Will Catesby, and I listen to her carefully. "You will have influence because the Woodvilles are descending fate's wheel and Gloucester is protector of the new king. Especially since you have access to Ned like no other."

My daughter stands, brushes down her skirts. "It is late, Belle-maman, and you must rest. Let us try to sleep, and I will say good-bye now, for I leave early in the morning." She hugs me tightly, this wonderful girl of mine, and climbs onto the bed. "You will do marvellously, and Ned will be so relieved that you accompany him. I'll see you in London for the coronation!"

I lay on top of the threadbare cover as shadows flicker across the ceiling from the sputtering candle. So much has happened in just a few days, and I am adrift from familiar surroundings. How lost darling Ned must feel.

I pray to God to keep safe everyone I love. I think of pleasant things to send me to sleep—Jack's embrace, his steady breathing calm and familiar. Perhaps he'll catch up with us and arrive tomorrow.

Meg is sleeping deeply, her youth untroubled by circumstance. The candles melt to stubs, their flames shimmering through my eyelids. A gale of laughter drifts up through the uneven floorboards, startling me awake. Horses canter from the yard, and the inn falls quiet. I punch the lumpy straw-filled bolster and scratch a flea bite on my calf, willing myself to rest. I'll see Ned in the morning, and we'll soon be in London.

A tapping on the door and again sleep flies. I pull my robe around me and open the latch.

"Lady Scrope?" The innkeeper's skinny lad slouches on the threshold. "Them dukes want you downstairs." He sticks a thumb over his shoulder. "Now."

I leave Meg sleeping soundly and follow the boy. At the landing, I pause to feel my way, for the taproom is a pool of darkness, the banked fire disguising the figures at the table. Wine fumes mingle with dinner's leftover aroma of roasted game. My stomach grumbles. The men feasted well.

"Come, Lady Scrope," calls Gloucester. "Your kinsman waits to greet you. He insisted I bring you down tonight, even as I insisted you were sleeping."

The bench scrapes, and Harry's burly figure blocks the fire's warmth. He is as richly dressed and well-fed as ever, no doubt at the expense of Margaret's table. Why spend money on his own living when his aunt presides over one of the wealthiest households in all of England?

"Harry." I do not really want to look at him. "It has been a while."

He kisses my hand and then my cheek, his lips damp, his breath wine-sour. "Too long, Elysabeth. Much has happened since we last dined together at Aunt Margaret's home."

"How fares my sister?" I force a pleasing expression. "Does she know of the king's death?"

Harry nods importantly. "Naturally. She relies on my intelligence. She understands that with Ned's succession, the York dynasty prevails for good. She may be the last bloodline descending from Lancaster. But no one will follow a woman's challenge." He fills his goblet from a flask on the table and raises it in a mock toast. "No matter, for Margaret Beaufort holds land and wealth beyond all measure, and her son will return from France now the king has forgiven him his insurrection—"

"My brother intended to pardon Henry Tudor for his past rebellion," Gloucester interrupts. "He did not finalise the decree restoring his title and lands before he died. Lady Stanley will have to commence her bargaining over again. And not with Ned. With me."

Oh, that will not please Margaret. She knows not Gloucester. Failure is unacceptable, especially over her forfeited Tudor riches.

A grimace twists Harry's handsome face. A flash of the familiar jealousy at the mention of Henry Tudor. Truly, he cannot stand any man that threatens his own puffery.

"And my godson?" I have had enough of my sister's quandaries. "I saw Lord Rivers was here earlier. Is Prince—King Edward in his own chamber?"

Harry sits on the bench again, holds his glass up to the dying fire. He scowls at the cloudy liquid. "Lord Rivers came only to dine and to allay our concern for Edward's security. He has moved the king on to Stony Stratford, some fifteen miles south of here." He drains the goblet and shudders; his tone turns sarcastic. "One would almost think it intentional."

"You mull over Rivers's action. What mean you, Harry?" Gloucester demands.

"Rivers is advancing to London ahead of us." Harry refills the wine. "He acts as if there are no lodgings here, but for the king there is always room. This ploy will give him an advantage in the morning, and he travels lightly with Edward to London."

"He has an army," contradicts Gloucester. "He cannot move too fast."

"They will form a rearguard." Harry stretches and burps, laces his hands behind his head. "And challenge us to maneuver our way through. A delaying tactic. They will gain hours, perhaps days over us."

Gloucester thumps his fist on the table. "I refuse to play blind man's buff with the Woodvilles."

If I am just here to witness their petty jealousies, I would rather return to bed. "My Lord Gloucester, surely my godson would prefer to travel with you, his protector. I am sure now he knows you are here, he will wait for you in the morning."

Harry snorts. "Always believing the best of people, Elysabeth. Leave politics to your husband. He knows where loyalty lies. Your record is less clear."

"As the husband of the queen's sister, perhaps look to yourself first, Harry," I retort.

He flushes and turns to Gloucester. "Do as I recommend, my lord, and you will prevent the Woodville faction from seizing the throne. And while you deal with Rivers in the morning, Elysabeth will tend to Edward. He will need a godmother's comfort when he realises what is happening."

Harry's resentment follows its usual pattern. Drink. Bluster. Drink. Bully. I refuse to think that Lord Rivers can have anything but Ned's safety foremost in his mind. "Harry, Lord Gloucester, perhaps a talk with Lord Rivers—"

Gloucester clasps Harry's elbow, pulls him close. "So you suggest we take Lady Scrope with us to where Ned is held?"

"Of course." Harry's glance slips sideways with a smile that does not reach his eyes. "That's why she's here. Margaret has always said she's the helpful one in the family."

Enough of this nonsense. Harry is creating mischief yet again, for he thrives on division. Time to end this conversation now, for God only knows what they spoke of before I was called to their table. "Forgive me, my lord, for I would return to my chamber. It is late, and I am tired." I curtsey to Gloucester, nod at Harry. "Cousin."

"Take a couple of hours' rest, no more." Gloucester drains his cup. "A small party of us will leave before first light. You will ride with us to greet your godson." His voice softens as he kisses my hand; his face assumes its usual pleasing expression. "Thank you, Lady Scrope, for your loyalty. No matter what transpires, my nephew will be reassured with you by his side."

"My duty is to serve Ned. And keep him safe from those who would do him harm," I reply.

Before ascending the stairs, I glance over my shoulder. Gloucester and Harry are in deep discussion, wrapped in darkness, one figure crowned with two heads. I try to dismiss a spine chill.

Jack, what would you say, what would you do? Gloucester is your lord, and yet Harry has much power. Who is leading whom? I must remember all this to tell you as soon as you arrive.

My uneasiness keeps me from returning to bed. Perching on the stair, I clasp the splintered wood banister, until my back aches and my feet grow numb.

"She'll . . . as you predict? Lady Scrope is a woman of character, and I respect her fortitude." Gloucester's broken words rise above the murmur of their talk.

"Of course. Like any woman, once I have command, she'll be as biddable as a bitch in whelp . . ."

Bastard.

The men stand, gather their jackets. I steady myself against the rough plaster wall, tiptoe up the stairs ahead of them, open the latch. I think of waking Meg, but there is little she can do. I wish her to go and visit her sons in peace and not worry about me. I will not sleep for fear of the night mare settling upon me, for I have no doubt evil spirits are abroad tonight. I lay down fully clothed and wide-eyed for the small amount of time before I have to leave.

10

Spring 1483 | Stony Stratford

"Go to Ned's chamber, Lady Scrope. You can see for yourself—there, upstairs, with the guard on the door." Gloucester nods across the mud-rutted stable yard of the Rose and Crown in Stony Stratford. "'Struth, but this is a piss-poor place for the King of England to spend the night. But directly on the London road." He glances at Harry. "I believe you are right. Lord Rivers is preparing for a speedy departure."

"And that he will have," responds Harry. "But perhaps not in the direction he planned." He gestures at me impatiently. "Go now to the king."

I dismount and walk cautiously up the broken wooden stairs to the outer gallery. Harry's ranting increased on the brief ride from Northampton, his cursing against the Woodvilles unbearable. I just want to hold Ned, comfort him and give him courage to face the days ahead. The poor boy has lost his father. The rest is men's talk.

The guard is sleepy, his air distracted.

"I am Lady Scrope. Godmother to King Edward."

He just stares ahead.

"Let me pass."

Reluctantly, he moves to one side.

My precious boy stands in the middle of the room, quite alone. He cries in surprise and runs into my arms. Ned's thin frame is trembling like a stricken rabbit. He is now my king, but he is also my boy, a mere twelve-year-old lad guarded and alone in his chamber in this dilapidated inn.

"My father." His voice cracks like a broken reed. "Oh, Lady Scrope, I did not get to say good-bye to him."

"Hush. Hush, my Ned." His baby name slips out naturally. I hug him for the longest time, feeling his tense shoulders gradually lower. I can feel him struggling not to cry, and I must help him gather his emotions. I hold him at arm's length to look into his eyes. "Be brave, my darling, take courage. You must be strong, be true to your destiny."

"But not yet, Lady Scrope. I'm not ready yet." His eyes well with tears again. My heart breaks.

"Listen to me," I say fiercely. "Just as Arthur pulled the sword from the stone, kingship has been thrust upon you."

He looks at me, his head tilted. "And he didn't even know he would be king."

I knew I'd capture his imagination. "No, he didn't. And look how brave he was."

Ned childishly scrubs his face, a crimson flush on his fair skin. "Our favourite story. Do you think I could be a great king like Arthur?"

"Yes, my darling. Yes. For you have been schooled well in chivalry, Ned. Your father and Lord Rivers have prepared you since your birth for this moment, although it has indeed come too quickly." I gently wipe a tear from his smooth cheek. "And you have me, Lord Scrope, and your mother, Dickon, and your sisters, your family who loves you so very much, to help you."

Ned lifts his chin, sucks in a deep shuddering breath. I free the crucifix from my purse and fold it into his palms, pressing his hands around the precious relic.

"From your father, to my care." I stroke the blond hair that tufts from his damp forehead in the way it has grown since he was four years old. "So you would know he is always with you, Ned. And that he entrusts me with your well-being."

Ned kisses the jewelled cross, laces the pearl chain through his delicate fingers.

"My father sent this?" he asks, his delicate face tear-blotched in the lightening dawn.

Sweet boy. "Yes, to give to you, the last thought as he left this earth. I carried it at your baptism. You and the Duke of Gloucester are most beloved to him. And that is why he appointed his brother your Lord Protector of the Realm."

Ned's face creases into a frown. "I really don't know my Uncle Richard."

"You will come to appreciate his wisdom and his fairness." This is what Gloucester wants me to remind his nephew. "He is beloved throughout the North and well respected for his learning and justness."

"I look forward to understanding him better." Ned fiddles with the crucifix's chain, his voice low. "Lord Rivers has been both a guardian and a father to me, and his love has protected me from danger and intrigue."

"Lord Rivers will always be your beloved uncle—" A sudden thumping and shouting interrupts us. I rush to the open door, ready to stand between Ned and an intruder. Gloucester's soldiers clatter along the gallery, banging on the flimsy walls and dragging the sleepy inhabitants from within. Ned's half-brother Richard Grey is rushed towards the stairs, pushed and shoved like a commoner. Dear God. I did not even know of Grey being with Ned. And where is Lord Rivers?

Ned's wail is smothered under the men's rough tones.

Trying not to scream, I clasp his shoulders, the blades under his gown protruding like tiny angel wings.

"Traitor!" Gloucester thunders at Grey from the courtyard below, wheeling his mount in circles, careless of who is under its thrashing hooves. "You deceived the king that you and Rivers direct his coronation when you know I am Lord Protector of the Realm."

Ned shrieks. "My brother is not a traitor!"

His cry pierces my heart. What in God's name is Gloucester doing?

Richard Grey's handsome face grimaces as he half falls down the stairs and is shoved across the courtyard. *Dear God, his hands are bound behind his back like a common thief.* Bile chokes my throat; my heart thumps a frantic beat.

"Your Grace, do not fear," Grey calls up to us. "This is merely a misunderstanding. Our mother will put this to right—"

"Leave him alone. Let him go. Let him go!" Ned is sobbing now. I grab him to prevent him from breaking past the guards and running down the stairs after his brother.

Oh, Jack, what madness have I become caught up in?

"I cannot release him, Your Grace." Gloucester dismounts in one easy motion and holds up his hands to Ned, who is trembling at my side. "Your brother and Lord Rivers have betrayed you and the crown of England. They are under arrest. They are both traitors to your father's wishes."

Traitors? How can this be?

A Woodville guard breaks free and frantically runs after Grey. Harry steps in his path, draws his dagger, and plunges it into his chest. The man falls, a gush of crimson blood spouting over the mossy-green cobblestones. I retch and turn Ned from the gore, clasping him tightly within my arms.

Dear God. Harry's madness could be the death of all of us.

Harry wipes his blade on the man's coat and shoves the weapon back in its scabbard. "Take heart, Nephew, for we are loyal only to you. You remember me—your beloved Uncle Harry, Duke of Buckingham, husband to your Aunt Katherine. We are your trusted friends. And family."

How revolting he is. Beloved? After betraying his brother-in-law? Slaughtering a man in cold blood?

Ned wriggles free to face Harry. "Let my brother go!"

Harry throws his arm around Gloucester's shoulders, flouting protocol. "I cannot, Your Grace. Your Uncle Gloucester and I are bound to serve your father and you. We carry out his dying wish to see you safely on the throne of England. Others are not so honest."

"I don't know. I don't know what to do," whispers Ned, his voice breaking.

I breathe deeply, try to steady my heartbeat.

I don't know either.

What warning did I miss last night of this vicious turn against the Woodvilles? Yes, Harry and the Duke spoke of taking command of the king's welfare. It was what his dying father had requested. But not arresting Lord Rivers like a criminal and dragging Ned's brother in front of him in complete humiliation.

"Lady Scrope!" Gloucester's command slices the silence. "Bring the king here." Everyone is now looking at me.

My vow.

"Your Grace, you will do as your father directed and join his brother." *What would Jack say?* I gather strength from the unquestioning Scrope loyalty to Gloucester. "Obey the man your father appointed your protector. The Duke of Gloucester has your best interests at heart. And those of England."

But not those of Lord Rivers and Lord Grey. Gloucester may as well have locked up the queen's brother and son and thrown away the key.

Harry leads Ned's horse into the yard; his black-and-red-liveried guards surround the perimeter, menacingly silent with weapons drawn. This looks more like Buckingham has taken charge of the king rather than Gloucester. He gestures for Ned and me to come down to the courtyard.

I must obey.

Ahead is London and Ned's coronation. *Protect against all threats. Remember your vow.*

I take Ned's hand. "Come, my lord. Your mother and Dickon await your arrival. Let us join your Uncle Richard," I say, my words burying the seed of doubt deep in my heart. "For surely there was never a man more loyal to you or England's throne than the Duke of Gloucester."

11

Spring 1483 | London

"A word, Elysabeth. Now."

Harry sways over me in the cramped front room of the tavern. I have tried to avoid him thus far, but this time he has cornered me as I sit on a bench by the cold and ash-filled fireplace. His fair cheeks are flushed red; his lips glisten with spittle.

I sigh, lean away as far as I am able, and wait for his news. No doubt he's drunk all the hippocras and bedded the landlord's daughter. Or wife. One more night until we reach London and I will be done with his company. "Harry?"

"I'll make this simple for you," he slurs, the words accentuated in the way of most drunks. "The queen has taken refuge in Westminster's sanctuary. The prince must not find out. Not until we get him safely to London and our men have destroyed the last of the Woodville power base."

"Why should she take sanctuary? Her son is about to be crowned king." I lift a hand to my mouth and nose, shielding against his noxious breath.

"Lord Rivers and Grey. Our . . . intervention . . . and her failed attempt to control her son's crowning." Buckingham sniggers. "She's taken Ned's brother and sisters with her. All tucked up like mice in a hole. So make sure your godson doesn't find out."

"That's absurd. Gloucester has assured us detaining Rivers and Grey is merely a precaution." Harry really is revolting. I edge further away, but there is little room to escape. "And you think my godson should not know about his own mother?"

Across the smoky and low-ceilinged chamber at a table set aside for the royal party, Gloucester cups my boy's face in his hands and speaks seriously, his eyes crinkling at the corners with affection. Ned gazes up at him, concentrating on his uncle's words. During the three days since leaving Stony Stratford, I have held Ned close to comfort him in his grief and encouraged him to start trusting his uncle. I have no answers to Ned's questions about Lord Rivers, but I can tell him about the pleasures of life at Middleham and the respect Gloucester commands in Yorkshire.

"A pretty scene, isn't it? Such trust. Such care." Harry leans over me, and I almost fall backwards in an effort to avoid him. "It would be a pity to ruin their new friendship."

"You overstep your place, Cousin," I tell him. "For you do not order me what to say or not say to my godson."

He lays a heavy hand on my shoulder, forces my attention back to him. "I do order you when it comes to matters of state," he replies. "The queen's son Dorset has left England with half the crown jewels in his baggage, her brother tried to muster a fleet against us, and the city has turned its back on the Woodvilles and refuses to take up arms against Gloucester."

"And you would keep this from your future king?" I snap back. "Ned has a duty to know if his mother and brother are in danger."

"There is no danger except from the queen herself. The bitch suffers from hysteria and is overly preoccupied with the fate of her offspring. As usual, 'tis her womb directing her, not her mind." Harry plants his feet and places his hands on his hips, accentuating his broad shoulders and brawny physique. "The king is under our authority, not that of his mother. It is your duty to ensure he is not told of her whereabouts until he is in custody at the Bishop of Ely's Palace. He cannot change his mind and join her in sanctuary with his brother."

So this is what he really wants. "I will not lie to him. So do not ask me to disregard my vow."

"Oh, we ask nothing of you," he replies, his eyes moving to Gloucester and the king. "And everything. Keep your silence. Or you may be back in Yorkshire sooner than you think. At Sheriff Hutton with Lord Rivers."

Idiot. I jump to my feet and brush past him. Fuming, I thread my way across the crowded taproom in time to catch Gloucester's last words.

". . . a misunderstanding, I am sure, Ned." Gloucester's voice is calm, low-pitched. "Your Uncle Rivers is being treated respectfully, and no doubt he will meet us and your mother in London in time for your coronation."

Yet Harry says the opposite. And Elizabeth Woodville's action underscores her fears for her own safety. *Sanctuary*. I know well the queen's despair, the troubling fugitive existence she had just committed herself and her children to endure.

"Lord Gloucester, is everything well?" I nod towards Buckingham. "It seems there is some news from London?"

Gloucester's face bears its usual pleasant expression; his fine slender fingers rest calmly on the scored and roughened table. I can see no indication of the conflict swirling around Ned.

"Very well, Lady Scrope." Gloucester follows my gaze. "Is your cousin telling stories again?" He pauses a beat. "I am afraid sometimes his imagination gets the better of him. We would not want to worry anyone by giving them information that is not helpful to their situation." Gloucester looks meaningfully down at Ned.

I weigh who I trust more. And decide upon Gloucester. "I am relieved. I thought perhaps there were deeper concerns."

"None that cannot be resolved." Gloucester clasps Ned around his shoulders, smiles at me. "I was just telling Ned that his father would be most proud of him. His manners and learning are excellent."

Ned blushes endearingly; he still appears frail, fey almost. An infection in his jaw saps his strength, and it has flared up again and diminishes his appetite. I have been trying my best to rid the pain with lavender and clove oil ointments, but my home remedies are no match for the skills of the London apothecaries. The sooner we can get him to consult with a pharmacist, the better I will feel.

"Lord Rivers followed my father's detailed instructions for my education," Ned replies. "I hope I can continue my schooling in London."

"You will, sire." Gloucester twists the ring on his little finger, turning the ruby to flash in the candlelight. "All Christendom will want to pay homage to the new king, and learned scholars from across Europe will be eager to fill your court."

"And as my protector, you will guide me, Uncle? Help me make the right choices?"

"With all my heart. I shall be Sir Lancelot to your King Arthur." Gloucester places his hand over Ned's. Their square palms and tapered fingers matched, linking their family resemblance. "Just as your father loved the tales of the knights, so do I. We grew close when we were in exile together, and there were many times he inspired me with their stirring stories."

Ned's face grows serious. "Their friendship also destroyed the kingdom when Lancelot betrayed Arthur."

Gloucester flicks a glance at me and back to Ned. "This is our chance to create history, Ned. We can show people that the old ways are not always the best and that there is always opportunity to bring new ideas to light. I favour justice and equality, fairness and fair play. Would you agree?"

Ned nods, his face aglow with excitement. "And we can do this together?"

"Together," replies Gloucester simply. "Together until you come into your majority, and you will rule England as her most noble king."

This is why Jack is fiercely loyal to this Plantagenet. My husband admires his prowess in battle; I appreciate his gentle courtesy. Thank the Lord that Gloucester is Ned's chosen protector, not Harry.

A movement across the taproom catches my eye. Buckingham's guards have doubled at the door, I now count eight of them, and although the room appears relaxed and jovial, the soldiers are stone-faced. Through the wavy green glass of the small window, I can make out a wall of armed men across the forecourt of the inn. Ned twists and half kneels on the bench to look out.

"Those are a lot of guards," he says. "Why do we suddenly have so many? Is something wrong?"

I put my arm around him, pull him back down to the seat. Gloucester is staring pointedly at me.

"Tell us more about your favourite pastimes, Ned," I say hurriedly. "Do you enjoy archery, or do you prefer hunting?"

Ned looks up at me. "You know that, Godmother. Archery," he says tersely. "Why are there suddenly so many guards, Lady Scrope?"

Please don't ask me these direct questions, Ned. I would not lie to you.

"We will have to ask your Uncle Buckingham," I reply. "They are his men, after all."

Gloucester leans forward. "Later, Ned," he says. "I'm sure it's just Buckingham being overprotective."

"But I saw you talking to him just now, Godmother. He seemed quite intense in his conversation." Ned cocks his head. "Are you hiding

73

something from me?" He turns to Gloucester. "This is not another situation like that of Lord Rivers, is it, Uncle?"

I meet Gloucester's eyes over Ned's head. *You tell him. For I shall not lie.*

"Not that I have heard, Your Grace." Gloucester tilts his head at me. "Lady Scrope, have you anything to add?"

Don't falter, don't fall. I am back in sanctuary as if it were yesterday, the clashing of bells, the singing, the long dark winter days and freezing nights. Holding this child that I have walked around Jerusalem with, rocking him in my arms until his gripe pains fled and he fell exhausted to sleep. My promise. My holy vow.

"Ned, you will face many new challenges as king," I say softly. "Some of which you can control, others you cannot. And in each event, you will have to learn who to trust, who not to—"

"And of course you can trust your family," Gloucester interrupts smoothly.

I blink. Ned's blue eyes are wide with curiosity.

"Your family," I repeat. "Like me and Lord Scrope and your brother, Dickon . . ."

"And me," Gloucester says emphatically. "Now, enough distractions, let us plan our household, Ned."

Swiftly changing the subject, Gloucester speaks poetically of a court filled with equity, learning, and chivalry, the finest musicians, magnificent dancers, the noblest, most gentle knights. Soon the guards are forgotten, for Ned is just twelve years old and still one for stirring tales and yarn spinning. Harry sulks in the corner as Gloucester and Ned outshine each other conceiving their new household, and when I recount the tale of Sir Gawain and insist that women deserve their secret heart's desire, they laugh and charge me with ensuring *sovereynté* for all the fair maidens in the land.

"You will always be honoured at my court, Godmother," Ned cries. "Won't she, Uncle Richard?"

Gloucester smiles and lays his hand over mine. "Always," he replies. "Lady Scrope is a true friend."

I smile back at my husband's lord, yearning for the confidence that he expresses. *I wish I could say more. There may still be a moment I can talk to Ned and warn him of his mother's worries.*

The harsh scraping of Harry's chair makes us all look up. He weaves to the table with a parchment in one hand, a quill and ink in the other.

"Practice!" He grins broadly, but the smile does not reach his eyes. "I assemble here and now the new government and request our noble monarch sign his first order! Let the king practice his signature while we, his loyal uncles, bear witness!"

Ned's face breaks into a broad grin as Harry places the blank sheet before him. In block letters he carefully writes EDWARDUS QUINTUS. He hands the quill to Gloucester, who neatly signs his own name and reads aloud as he scratches his motto. "Loyaulté me lie.' *Loyalty Binds Me.* I pledge my life to Your Grace."

Ned ducks his head, embarrassed and yet obviously very pleased at his uncle's words. Harry sits down heavily at the table and pushes aside Gloucester's arm. He snatches the quill and scrawls his name, followed by a motto. I catch the challenge in his eyes as he stares belligerently across the table.

"'Souvent Me Souvene.' *Remember Me Often,*" he reads loudly, all trace of drink vanishing from his speech. "Remember me often."

I catch my breath. This is disturbing. That was John of Gaunt's motto. Combined with that of Henry VI. And Margaret Beaufort. This motto emerges from the blood of England's royal family. Typical Harry. He may as well have claimed the throne for himself, so royal in its pedigree is his new motto. Gloucester frowns, opens his mouth to say something, and then appears to think the better of it.

"And have you thought of a motto yet, Ned?" I ask quickly. "For every king has one."

Ned ponders, his sweet face serious. "I shall have to earn my personal motto," he replies. "My father's was 'Counforte et Liesse': *Comfort and Joy.* Perhaps a good wish for bringing peace to a country that has been at war for so long. But for now, I shall use the motto that accompanies my coat of arms as King of England. 'Dieu et Mon Droit.' *God and My Right.*" He stares at Buckingham. "I think you can remember that, my lord?"

So many undercurrents. One moment Ned is a boy, distracted by tales of King Arthur, the next an astute ruler sending a message to his subject. I move the paper from the table and set it aside. This is not the time to challenge Harry his conceit. But I will not forget to tell my husband of this strange interlude on my journey. Jack will be better placed than me to monitor Buckingham's arrogance.

"I am going to retire," I say. "Are you ready to rest, Ned?"

My godson stretches his arms above his head. "I will escort you," he replies. He holds up his hand to stay Buckingham and Gloucester. "No need to come with me," he stops them. "I am perfectly capable to seeing myself to my room."

Both men have half risen and then sit again at his gesture. Buckingham's eyes are boring into me, and I refuse to pay him any attention. His gaze burns between my shoulder blades as I edge my way through the taproom, Ned before me.

When we reach the foot of the narrow staircase leading to the gallery, Ned turns to the guards. "Wait here." He takes my arm, pulls me into the darkness under the wooden stair casing.

"What do you know, Godmother?" he asks urgently. "And I beg you, do not lie to me."

In that moment, I know I cannot. "Ned, I am sure this is just temporary." I take a deep breath.

"Tell me the truth. I am old enough to bear it. Why so many guards? Why is Buckingham acting this way?"

I am going against Buckingham and Gloucester, but I make my choice. My first loyalty will always be to Ned. "You mother has taken sanctuary in Westminster with your brother and sisters."

"Sanctuary? What?" Ned looks back at the guards, a menacing wall of black and red. "But why? Why, just when I am to arrive in London to be crowned?"

"I know it seems desperate," I continue hurriedly. "Your mother is prone to acting on impulse, and without your father there to guide her, I think she is just taking precautions until you get to London."

"What kind of precautions? Why would she be scared enough to take sanctuary? Why would she not ride to greet me instead?"

"That's a good question. And one I don't have an answer for." I decide that I will tell Ned only the facts that I know. Trouble will come if I try to interpret them.

"Is there anything to do with Lord Rivers being held? My brother being captured?" Ned's voice rises. "Is there something my Uncle Gloucester is doing that I should be aware of?"

I don't know. But I cannot stray into the world of supposition. And I cannot plant seeds of doubt in this young mind. "Let us do this, sweeting," I say firmly. "We will be in London tomorrow, and when you have rested, we can go to the Jerusalem Chamber in Westminster

Abbey and ask your mother directly what she is thinking. Would that be the right idea?"

Ned thinks for a moment. "I do not know her temperament well," he replies. "And if she is frightened and lonely, being under God's watch is the safest place for her."

"You are a wise king." I am relieved at his response. "Let us keep this conversation just between you and me at this moment, Ned. We would not want your uncles Buckingham and Gloucester to worry about you. And the less pressure on your mother, the better." I think of what else might soothe him and still be the truth. "The abbey is also a very quiet and holy place. Let us consider her time there as a small sojourn while she comes to terms with her beloved husband's death."

"I agree, Godmother." Ned leads me to the foot of the stairs and summons the nearest guards to accompany us to our chambers. "But promise me this."

"Anything."

"Promise you will always tell me the truth, no matter how much you are worried it might hurt me."

"Always."

London announces itself as a hazy southern sky; a thousand cooking fires plume silver into the rising sun. We crest over the last of the country hills, and spread before us is the capital, with the shining Thames threading its way through the villages and towns all the way to the city and the sea beyond. Church spires pierce the smoke, and the Westminster towers stand head and shoulder above all. I think of the queen waiting for our arrival and hope we can see her tomorrow. Ned catches my eye, and we share our secret in a quiet smile.

Gloucester's advance riders clear the road, and groups of curious travellers are pressed into the frothing hawthorn hedges, crushing and releasing the May blossoms' peppery spring scent. I dread messengers from the queen. I hope that my promise to Ned to visit her will be enough if the plea comes to join her in sanctuary. So far, I am relieved that such is the size of our procession no northbound rider can possibly breach the forces of Gloucester and Buckingham.

With each mile closer to the city, I grow as taut as a lyre string. Gloucester has to remedy this whole Woodville situation when we reach London. He has already successfully integrated some of Rivers's men into his cavalcade with no objections. As we approach the city gates, Ned rides into the lead, flanked by his black-clad uncles and himself looking delicately handsome in blue velvet on a York-white palfrey.

Still, Jack has not caught up. Perhaps the messengers have yet to intercept him; the Scrope land is wild and forsaken on its eastern borders.

The Plantagenets enter London triumphantly, for Harry and Gloucester ensure no trace of the Woodville family taints the procession into the city. In my mind's eye, I am with the queen and her children in Westminster's cramped and doleful sanctuary. How sad to be newly widowed and separated from her eldest son. I am eager to tell her how well Ned has assumed his new role. Surely Elizabeth Woodville will leave sanctuary then and join her son's coronation.

The crowds grow thick as word spreads of our arrival. My worries abate, dispersed by the cheers and good wishes from London's citizens. Along with the solemnity of the old king's passing comes the joy in the welcome of the young prince. I see the blue shadows under his eyes, the redness of his cheek where his jaw is still inflamed. His subjects see the magnificence of his grace, the undeniable power of the Dukes of Gloucester and Buckingham. I think perhaps it is my destiny to see below the surface to the reality of what lies in the depths.

We are welcomed warmly to the Bishop's Palace, with hopefully the last of the proclamations and speeches. My boy is hardly able to keep his head up, and as soon as it is polite, I insist Ned retire to his apartments. I dismiss the army of men who are to serve him, shooing them out to the privy chamber, and send for a chymist to take care of his poor aching jaw. "I am staying here within the palace and will see you on the morrow," I promise as I pull the covers over my darling Ned, smooth his hair from his damp brow. "And we shall enjoy a walk in the gardens together. Rest well, my darling."

"Good-bye, Lady Scrope. And thank you." Ned closes his eyes and turns his face to the window. I quietly shut the door behind me.

"Guard him well. And let him sleep as long as he wishes," I tell the Grooms of the Chamber. "Give him plain manchet bread and a little mulled red wine as prescribed by the chymist if he is hungry or thirsty. I will be back in the morning."

A page waits to take me to my room, but first I ask to be led to the courtyard, where Gloucester is preparing to leave for his own dwelling at Crosby Place.

"Ned is settled," I tell him. "But exhausted. I must insist that his duties are light for the next few days."

"He will have the best care in the country. He is the king," Gloucester replies with a smile. "And he has his godmother at his side. You have done well, Elysabeth. Ned was to have been crowned by the Woodvilles today, and their attempt to gain control of the throne would certainly have returned us to war." He carefully mounts his horse, the muscle in his cheek clenching as he heaves himself into the saddle. "You have seen him safely to the custody of the Bishop of Ely, secure under my guard."

"I did my duty," I reply. I do not tell him that Ned knows of his mother's situation. It would not help matters. "I am sorry the queen does not feel safe to greet her son."

"Think not of the queen," Gloucester responds quickly. "She is of little consequence now." He smiles pleasantly, although his lips are clamped tight together. "Thank you for staying here to keep Ned company."

"I shall help him settle in, ensure that he recovers his health, and then move to my home at Le Ryall to wait for Jack."

"Then we will meet again soon, for there are many festivities planned in the coming weeks to which you and Jack will be invited," he replies. "And thank you, Elysabeth, for your assistance in delivering the prince safely to London. We have much to celebrate."

12

Spring 1483 | The Bishop's Palace

"Your Grace, how are your preparations for your government?" A week has passed since our arrival in London, and I pause with Ned under the honeysuckle-scented canopy of our favourite arbor. Each day sees him a little stronger, and today he is walking the farthest he has since we arrived. The Bishop's Palace is a fertile enclave in the heart of Holborn where we can stroll together, enjoying the gardens, plucking the first tiny strawberries from their nests within the bales. I am curious to hear how his young mind grasps the importance of his position. Lord Rivers had provided calm and steady guidance. Who has supplanted him in Ned's life?

"I have met with my father's previous advisors, and Lord Hastings has been most helpful. My father trusted him more than any of his councillors, and I will do the same," Ned replies. The sunshine glistens on his golden hair, traces of Elizabeth Woodville's beauty reflected in his young features. "But most of all, I wish I could ride to Westminster and visit my mother and Dickon and my sisters. They remain in sanctuary, and my Uncle Richard insists I not visit them for fear of stirring up trouble. I don't understand."

"You will see them soon, Ned." I take his hand. "Sometimes the time of succession between rulers can be one of uncertainty." I feel this is a simple explanation, but I agree with him. I do not understand the queen's reluctance to leave sanctuary. Nor why we are prohibited from visiting her. "The Lords Gloucester and Buckingham meet with the council to confirm your coronation date and expedite preparation. I am sure your family will join us here shortly to prepare for your crowning." What mother would miss her son's elevation to the most important position in England?

A stirring across the palace grounds catches my eye. "There arrives the Duke of Buckingham now. He will have news."

80

We walk across the verdant lawns, past the shadowed cloisters, and into the great hall of the palace. Inside, cool air washes over us, and although the sky shimmers blue through the high transom windows, shade puddles around the pillars and benches, and even the jubilant spring birdsong is muted. A door clicks by the dais, and Harry strides into the hall. He is dressed for office in black velvet with silver thread; fine white silk billows through his highly fashioned slashed sleeves. The Plantagenet in him reigns handsome today.

"Your Grace." Harry drops to his knee in front of Ned, his face flushed. For a spring day, the weather has turned warm. He always sweats excessively, and I draw away from his clammy hand.

"Lord Buckingham." Ned's formality distances him from his uncle. "You appear to be heated. Is there an urgency to your visit?"

Harry removes his hat and clutches it to his chest, crumpling it between his thick fingers. "Urgency, no, Your Grace. Excitement, certainly."

Ned waits. He has learned much about caution these past days. Or perhaps his Uncle Woodville already warned him of charm's many disguises. He still speaks of Lord Rivers with great affection and longing. I have avoided answering Ned when he asks about his uncle's due arrival in London, for I have heard nothing more from Gloucester. It is as if Rivers has disappeared into the Northland completely.

"Your coronation is the twenty-fourth of June," Harry continues. "Preparations are underway."

"I thought they would have been complete, Lord Buckingham," Ned replies. "Lord Rivers told me I was to be crowned a week past. That was the reason for our haste to London. Until you stopped our journey."

Harry winces and shifts on his knees. A man of his size would be uncomfortable for any time in that position. Perchance Ned realises that.

"Those arrangements were . . . inappropriate," he replies. "Now, under your protector's direction, letters are being sent out to all the nobles across the land, inviting them to attend. You will be fitted for your robes in the next few days, rehearsed on the protocol of the coronation."

I murmur in Ned's ear, "I think you should release him now."

A smile quivers over Ned's face. "Thank you. I shall look forward to receiving the delegation to review the arrangements and to discuss the guests and ceremony." He holds his hand out to his uncle, encourages him to rise. "I am most grateful for your support."

Harry reaches his full height, looks down upon the boy. "And one more thing, Your Grace." He takes a step closer to Ned, forces the boy to crane his neck to look up at him.

"Tomorrow, you shall enter the Palace of the Tower of London."

My heart turns over. "What? Why does he leave here so soon?" He is thriving at the Bishop's Palace. I do not know what the conditions are like at the Tower.

"You are aware of this, Elysabeth. It is customary for all Kings of England to spend the period prior to their coronation in the Tower." Harry gestures expansively, as if disdaining the entire Bishop's Palace. "This may be suitable for a few days, Your Grace, but you should be housed according to your position. I suggested to the council today that we escort you to the Tower immediately. The royal apartments are waiting for you. The Duke of Gloucester has arranged this."

That ghost of unease returns, an unwanted shadow flickering at the back of my mind. The last I was in the Palace of the Tower was the morning King Henry was discovered dead in his gaol. And on that event, Ned's father consolidated his control of the throne.

"But perhaps the night before. Not a month or more before the crowning." I glance at Ned's face, now pale, his lower lip caught between his teeth. How swiftly he changes from prince to boy. "I will accompany him to the Tower?" My statement dissolves into a question.

Harry stares down at me, his face impassive. "You must accompany him, see him settled, and then depart. The time has come to assume his kingship. He will rely on his chaplain for spiritual guidance. And his household for company."

There must be other reasons to stay. I am not ready to leave his side.

"My lord—" I implore, but Harry turns his back, blocks the prince from my view.

"If this is tradition, then who am I to refuse?" Ned replies. He sidesteps Harry, reaches for my arm. "Come, Godmother, I would walk in the garden and recount the story of Sir Gawain and King Arthur once more with you. If you are to be the member of my court in charge of *sovereynté*, then we start today and discuss your role." He glances back at Harry. "Gloucester has already pledged to serve as my

Lancelot. Perhaps you will be one of my Knights of the Round Table, Lord Buckingham. A trusted advisor and friend. I will be ready to leave for the Palace of the Tower tomorrow."

13

Spring 1483 | The Palace of The Tower

Sovereynté, King Arthur's tales tell me, is what women desire the most. The power to make our own decisions. Freedom from control. More than love, more than friendship, we desire *power*. And when the power of *sovereynté* was given to me in the form of an urgent appeal and a pearl crucifix, I grabbed it with both hands. Just three weeks ago, I was at home by the hearth, the woman's natural place, my life spinning before me in the predictable warp and weft of family and friends. Today, because of my *sovereynté*, I am riding with the King of England to prepare for his coronation.

My young sovereign. A sweet play on words.

Sovereynté. His destiny. My power.

Word of our progression whispers like a summer breeze before us as we wend the narrow streets from the Bishop's Palace to the Tower. I ride in a cavalcade of a hundred royal-liveried guards led by proud Buckingham and sweet Ned, and me in the third row next to the Bishop of Ely on his high-stepping white palfrey. Gloucester has ridden ahead to welcome Ned to the Tower.

Calling and waving from the upper windows of the homes that lean across the lanes, women toss rose petals that flutter down upon Ned's slender shoulders. Men weep to see their beloved King Edward reincarnated in his golden boy. Apprentices run through the side alleys, cluster at the entryways, jump on each other's shoulders to catch a glimpse of the boy king who is no older than they are. He is the hope of all England.

I ride with joy in my heart; after a sleep broken by dreams of the Tower walls tumbling upon my head and Buckingham's words whispering in my mind, I awoke this morning to find that Jack finally sent a messenger announcing he should arrive any day. And far from chastising me for my decision to travel alone, he praised my devotion to his Lord Gloucester. His honest note dismissed the fancies that I have been imagining around Ned's moving to the Tower.

> *My sweetheart, you have served us well. I am proud of your loyalty to your king and my lord, and I know that your presence reassured Ned in his grief and rapidly changing world and convinced him of the wisdom of travelling with his Uncle Gloucester. Ned is in safekeeping with my lord, for never was a man fairer nor more devoted to his family. I long to hold you when I reach Le Ryall. Your loving husband.*

I made the right decision to ride to London.

Cresting Tower Hill, we travel triumphantly towards the Byward Gate. Upon its battlements, pennants flutter upon the easterly breeze, and trumpets blare as we are sighted by the guards. I laugh aloud; Harry gives a great shout of triumph, and even my sweet Ned, who is solemn and dignified today, lifts his arm in the air and salutes the heavens. Lining the path to the Tower entrance, armed guards stand to attention, pikes glinting in the morning sun. On the gleaming silvery river, barges and wherries crowd the water, swaying, moored cheek by jowl to witness the prince arrive. And as our horses' hooves clatter across the bridge, the sound deafening as we are funnelled into a double line through the narrow gate, my heart swells with pride.

"You have arrived, Your Grace," I call. "The Tower of London, England's greatest castle, welcomes the next King of England. Your people love you. All your citizens celebrate and count the days to your coronation."

Ned allows a small smile to light his serious countenance. He holds himself with great dignity. I know he is thinking that beyond the excitement and pageantry is the holy ceremony in Westminster Abbey, an ancient anointing of an English monarch that stretches back in time to the fabled traditions of King Arthur.

"I am honoured," Ned calls back. "Honoured and humbled."

Harry rides between us, his muscular stallion forcing us apart. "Not too humbled, Your Grace," he interrupts. "We have work to do to keep this kingdom of yours at peace. Your Uncle Gloucester will rely upon your royal prerogative to help him rule."

"Harry, do not overstate the protector's role, for it is the Duke of Gloucester who assists the prince to rule," I contradict him, wanting to dispel the shadow that crosses Ned's expression. "And only until Ned reaches his maturity at fourteen. That is a mere eighteen months from now."

"Of course." Harry urges his horse forward along the outer ward, past the water gate to the Thames, and turns to his left under a deep archway. I follow, remembering my arrival from Westminster years ago at that very gate, smelling again the stench of stagnant water, a waft of rosemary drifting from a hidden fragrant garden. Memories I hardly knew I retained, carried on scents that remain. We halt before an imposing barred entryway.

"Coldharbour Gate and the royal apartments," Harry announces. "Welcome to your palace, Your Grace."

Above my head soar the lime-washed walls of the White Tower, the centre of the entire complex. They are higher even than Bolton Castle's sheer ramparts and just as invincible. I am reminded again that this palace is also a stronghold, built to defend against and destroy its enemies.

How I had trembled the day I was last here, freed from sanctuary and yet bound to the Yorkists. My concentration was on keeping my knees from buckling under the fear of the king's judgment. Today is as different as it could possibly be. Ned rides before me, a young man strong and true, and I recognise his father in him, the king who not only pardoned my Lancastrian sympathies, but welcomed me into his family. For the first time since his death, tears fill my eyes as I suddenly mourn the loss of King Edward, remembering his kindness that gave me a new life within the royal circle.

A flight of crows arises from the ramparts, their caws ringing dissident against the cheers of the crowd gathered at the Tower's base. I wonder, fleetingly, which arrow-slit crevice was the cell of King Henry, he who died the night I stayed here last. And then I dismiss the memories in favour of a prayer to King Edward.

I have brought your son here safely. I believe those were your final wishes. I honour your memory. How proud you would be of him today.

Before me at the Coldharbour Gate, Harry and Ned have already dismounted. Of course, my cousin does not bother to assist me down in his eagerness to walk Ned into the palace, leaving a groom to help me. The guards form a line on either side of the gate, and I stride forward, half hearing Harry's long-winded welcome on behalf of the court. I catch up with them as Harry murmurs something to the head guard waiting at the entrance to the palace. The man nods.

I hesitate at the threshold of the great hall, seeing this time what fear obscured on my last visit. Marble pillars soar to support huge wooden rafters, cut like ship's joists, the ceiling's ribs floating on a sea of air. Light dazzles through clear glazed arched windows, pooling into a lake of sunshine on the shimmering flagstones. A fanfare of trumpets echoes through the stone walls, a customary greeting for the new King of England as he takes up residence in his royal palace. Harry and Ned step towards two figures on the dais at the far end of the great hall, and I follow closely behind.

The light from the clerestory windows dazzles, and I squint to see who is standing before me. There is Gloucester, unmistakable in his form. But surely that is not my sister on his right? I quicken my pace to catch up with Ned and Harry.

Dear God, it is Margaret. And looking every inch the royal Beaufort heiress in both her gown and demeanour.

My sister sweeps a deep formal curtsey as Ned approaches. "Your Grace."

Margaret's headdress is pure white; a tracery of the Beaufort portcullis is embroidered into her cloak's burgundy velvet lining. Her gown is a priceless black silk with a kirtle of silver tissue. A striking rosary of gold and rubies on a long chain hangs from her waist. She raises herself, her head bowed, ignoring my outstretched hand and half-uttered greeting.

Gloucester drops to a knee. "My nephew. My king. Welcome."

"My Lord Gloucester," Ned replies. "Uncle. I thank you for bringing me safely to London, to my people, and to the Tower to prepare me for my coronation."

Gloucester gets to his feet, his eyes fixed upon the prince's face, Margaret standing like a statue at his side. There is my sister's enigmatic smile again, one that I last saw when she condemned me to sanctuary to be housed with our York enemies. Why is Margaret in the Tower, welcoming Ned? And why has she not told me of her plans? She has had plenty of time to write to me at the Bishop's Palace.

"And my Lady Stanley." Ned holds his hand out for Margaret to kiss. "What a pleasure to be able to greet you personally. My father respected your husband as one of his most loyal lords. I hope he will serve on my council too."

"He awaits your command, Your Grace," replies Margaret. "Our family look forward to supporting you and your protector in the coming years as you take your rightful place on England's throne."

I raise an eyebrow, turn my head before my expression reveals my thoughts. Margaret's ability to negotiate these changing alliances is remarkable. Her marriage to Lord Stanley assumes today even more importance than when King Edward was alive. Now she is pledging the significant Stanley loyalty to Ned's reign. Of course, that would also include the opportunity to ask him directly to bring her own son home. Margaret's God has answered her prayers.

"Thank you, Lady Stanley." Ned reaches his hand out, but I am three paces away. "And speaking of family, your sister has taken such perfect care of me. You will be glad to hear she has guided my spiritual well-being with a mother's love. If not for her, I do not think I would have travelled so willingly to London. She comforted me in the absence of Lord Rivers and encouraged me to temper my mourning and embrace my destiny."

Margaret inclines her head but does not look at me. "I am delighted, Your Grace. And I trust my nephew Buckingham has been equally solicitous?"

Am I the only one who notices Ned's pause?

"Without fail, my lady," he quietly replies.

"Then my family has safely delivered you from your enemies who wish you harm, securely into the hands of those who love you." Margaret clasps her rosary before her chest, bows her head in a brief and silent prayer.

"I don't think the Woodvilles intend harm, nor do they not love Ned," I respond firmly. Margaret's insinuations are the last things Ned should hear at this moment. He may turn and ask for his mother to be brought to him immediately. And I have still had not heard why the queen remains in sanctuary, nor have I been able to command a messenger to Westminster to discover more.

"Sister, you may leave the prince with me now. There are conversations about our family we should have that I fear you may have overlooked." Margaret's voice is cold.

"Not overlooked, Margaret. Simply recognising there is a time and place for everything." The moment we meet again, there she goes, pushing her own priorities with little concern for others.

"You may leave."

Leave? I wonder if I have heard correctly. "I am to see Ned to his lodgings."

My sister ignores me, continues her instructions. "I shall escort him to the royal apartments. The council has requested I attend him as we prepare for the coronation." Margaret turns back to Ned. "We have a household to arrange, positions to fill. You have a lot to learn over the coming weeks as you prepare for your anointing. But it is not all business and politics. Now tell me, who do you think should be your hawk master?"

Margaret now guides Ned? The Stanleys have wasted no time in inserting themselves into the heart of the accession.

Ned steps forward as if to embrace me and hesitates.

"Lady Scrope, my thanks," he says formally. "I will see you next at my coronation."

I match his serious tone, belying the ache in my heart. For the sake of Ned, this is not the time to challenge Margaret. "I am honoured to have been part of your accession, my lord. Remember your catechism. Know I pray for you daily." Ned's hand touches his chest, where he keeps the crucifix concealed. "And be inspired by your father and King Arthur as you prepare to take the throne of England."

Ned's lip trembles, and he suddenly clings to me, his fingers fiercely gripping my arms. "I love you," he whispers. "I love you."

As I hold him close and tell him I love him too, Gloucester lays his hand on Ned's shoulder.

"Come, Edward, let us escort you to your lodgings." He politely nods to me, the informality of our ride south vanishing. "It has been quite a journey, Lady Scrope. I am deeply grateful for your care in escorting the prince to London and now the Tower."

Harry steps forward, addresses Margaret. All this time he has been watching the interplay, and I have been wondering when he was going to insert himself into the discussion. "Lady Stanley, you have been most helpful over the past weeks. And now we can jointly prepare my nephew for his coronation."

I have to say more, have to ensure Ned is nurtured as a boy, not just the new king. "Margaret, the prince still suffers from a sore jaw, an infection that lingers." I fumble in my purse for the anise pastilles, find them, and hold them out to my sister. She does not take them. "I would ask you to—"

"We will care for him, Elysabeth. He is the king in all but anointing. He has his own household now." Margaret frowns slightly at Harry, as if conveying a message. "Finish your good-byes. I will call on you later when you have settled in at Le Ryall. I am sure we will find plenty to talk about."

Racing cloud shadows scamper across the hall as Ned is escorted into the royal apartments. Gloucester places a hand on my boy's back, urging him forward. They vanish behind the great iron doors, Ned's fair head gleaming golden in a final shaft of sunlight as he disappears.

I let out my breath with a shudder. My vow is fulfilled. I have done my duty. The succession is secured. I bid a silent farewell to my boy, not just from this journey, but to his youth and his unique time with me as his godmother. I swallow a lump in my throat, am determined to be brave. Margaret is the most devoted mother to her own child; she has navigated the roughest of waters for Henry, through war and treachery, long absences and sad farewells. Margaret knows how to prepare Ned for the throne

After all, she once considered her own son a candidate.

I repeat my prayer to King Edward in heaven.

God rest your soul and know that your son is safely delivered. I have kept my vow and carried out your wish.

Doors slam shut. Bolts rattle into place.

And God protect my boy, give him strength to rule with honour, to take counsel from those whom he trusts and avoid those who might betray him.

My eyes snap open. What demon of doubt scribed that prayer?

A faint call from far above. There, at an upper gallery, Ned's pale face appears. He gestures for me to join him.

He needs me still. My heart lifts. I walk swiftly to the door, happiness springing in my heels. *I'm coming, my darling.*

The guards bar the way. Soldiers appear in each corner, at every door, double, triple deep. Their livery is a worryingly familiar black and red.

"I'm sorry, Lady Scrope. We have instructions not to let anyone through now." The guard is apologetic, embarrassed even. He witnessed our triumphant arrival just minutes before.

"On whose orders?" Surely there is a mistake.

"The Duke of Buckingham."

I stare up at Ned in the gallery. Harry looms at his side, steers him away from the rail. Ned clings to the edge for a moment, lifts his hand briefly, and then pulls a rueful face as he is led away.

"And so not even his godmother is allowed to enter?"

The guard shakes his head. "Best be going home, Lady Scrope." He changes from kindly to distant. "Best leave."

A flush of anger heats my cheeks. *"As biddable as a bitch in whelp."*

Harry used me as a mounting block on his swift ride to power. I must share this truth with Margaret, warn her to be wary of his ambition. Tomorrow. When Margaret visits Le Ryall and we talk about Ned's dreams for his future, the need to visit the queen in Sanctuary and reconcile the family.

Taking one last look at where Ned stood, I gather my skirts. Let Margaret deal with Harry tonight. I do not want to leave, but it is time to go home. Jack will be at Le Ryall shortly. I long to share my journey with him, talk with my beloved, who knows me better than any, who will put my scattered feelings into perspective.

The guards move forward, and I realise I am being escorted from the dais. Surely just a formality. I am spent, the emotion of the last week draining me.

Don't falter, don't fall.

My old creed from sanctuary bubbles up unbidden, and my footsteps echo through the cavernous hall as I leave my prince in the Tower.

14
Summer 1483 | Le Ryall

An hour from the Tower to ride to Le Ryall, and all the way I keep ill company with Buckingham's concealed threats and Margaret's curious presence. Conflicting thoughts pile upon me like lead weights balancing an apothecary's scale.

Margaret will take good care of him. She promised.

Why has Buckingham banned me from Ned's side? He has no right.

I tip towards disquiet.

Ahead, the familiar dog leg turn from broad Thames Street into Ryall Lane. Almost home. My own sanctuary. Home. Where lies my heart. Is Jack even now waiting for me?

I tip towards excitement.

Le Ryall's pointed gables rise above the narrow street, the very tops catching the last rays of sun. I seek and find the diamond-paned window that is my chamber and the painted glass casements that light the gallery with jewelled tones of amethyst and emerald. Our family home in the Vintry ward was built by my grandfather, once the mayor of Bordeaux, and it was his fortune in the wine trade that blessed us today with wealth and a fine mansion within the city walls. When he commissioned Le Ryall to be built, my very sober and clearheaded grandfather ordered craftsmen to paint the windows in the purple tones of amethyst, the stone long revered to prevent drunkenness.

This house has been my refuge since my first husband died and I emerged from that marriage no longer an innocent girl, but an older and wiser widow. Joyous family Christmases, my brother Oliver's wedding to Jack's sister, Margaret's return from Wales after she desperately bade good-bye to her son . . . all had been welcomed at our beloved home. I have not returned since my mother's death a year past. Is it still the same? Across the way, the cloth merchants outside the royal wardrobe storerooms display their precious swathes of silks and velvets. Window boxes brimming with pink-and-red Sweet Williams decorate Le Ryall's whitewashed walls. Perhaps nothing has changed except the loss of my mother's calming presence.

I dismount, hand the reins to the groom, and stumble towards the door. As I lift my hand, it swings open, and I almost fall into the shadowed interior.

"Elysabeth!"

Jack is standing in the hall, shrugging off his leather riding jacket and pushing his long dark hair back in a gesture I know as well as I know my own hand. His height fills the doorway, green eyes reflecting the light as he turns at my step and catches me in his arms.

"Jack. Oh, thank God." I blink away sudden stinging tears that came unbidden.

My husband kisses me hungrily; his mouth demanding me, wordlessly telling of his longing. His beard is rough on my cheek as he lifts me on my toes. My skin burns, and a rush of heat floods my body as I think of his nakedness upon me. I wrap my arms around his neck, trace his jaw with my fingers as I cup his face between my hands, kiss his firm lips. They are slightly rough, travel-chapped from the sun and wind. My words leave me as I lean into him, savouring the familiar sweet-saltiness of his mouth.

Home.

"My love." Jack pushes back my hood and, burying his face in my hair, removes the pins and lifts the locks to his face. "My love, I could not ride fast enough to be here. Don't ever, ever leave me again that way."

"The Duke of Gloucester commanded"—I protest—"my vow was called."

"I don't care if God commanded—" He stops me with another deep kiss. "I missed you beyond words. I respect your decision. And I'm thankful that I'm here now so you do not have to make any more choices on your own."

"My choice was simply to obey the king's dying wish. Such a journey, my love. I helped bring Ned here safely. But through strange challenges. And my heart sits uneasy." I move from the distraction of his embrace before I forget myself and untie his shirt right there in the hall, so tempting is he with the fine linen clinging damply to him. "Margaret has taken charge of Ned in the Tower. She's got a secret plan; I can tell. She says she will care for him. I cannot say exactly what

93

worries me." I take another step back as a servant appears, carrying a full tray with cups and a flagon of ale. "Then Harry. He has appeared from nowhere and asserts himself as Gloucester's chief advisor." As I speak, my anxieties rise in my throat, and I swallow them back down. I am not making sense. Especially to one such as Jack, who needs black and white and no shades of grey.

"Margaret always vexes you. I've said before, pay no heed." Jack takes a cup and downs it in one long gulp. "'Struth, I'm thirsty. And famished. Can we eat?" He grins. "After I've bathed." He pulls me close again, holds me prisoner against him with his hands locked around my waist. "I have no page with me. Do you know of anyone who may assist me?"

I lean back so I can look up into his face. Here I am troubled to have left the new King of England alone in the Tower of London under my sister's dubious care, and my husband just wants his supper and his woman. After a few moments, I laugh in spite of myself. Wasn't this moment just what I have been longing for since I left Middleham?

"I might, my lord." I send the servant running to the kitchens to prepare food and heat water. And then I take my husband upstairs to our chamber.

Later, much later, we wrap ourselves in soft silky robes and wander down to the oak-panelled parlour. A table has been laid before the bay window with cold roasted meats, fresh white bread, and a selection of cheeses. Placed on a silver tray are several flasks of Bordeaux wine and delicate Venetian glasses that reflect the candlelight on their precisely cut bevels.

I reluctantly let go of Jack's hand and heap a platter with food. I place it in front of him, dropping a kiss on his rosemary-scented hair that now curls damply on his shoulders.

"So let me understand this." Jack bites into the roasted chicken, plunges his knife into the carcass, and neatly decimates the other leg. He glances at me, his mouth full. "Sorry. I didn't stop much on the journey south. You tell me that Gloucester took control of Ned in Northampton; Grey and Lord Rivers were sent under guard to Sheriff Hutton, and Harry is at Gloucester's right hand at every turn."

"And my sister appears to be pulling on strings from her usual place in the shadows." I add.

Jack chews thoughtfully. "Do you think Gloucester made the wrong decision? It doesn't seem as though he had much choice."

"You're right," I reply. "And it all happened so swiftly. I think Gloucester just wanted to be sure the Woodvilles didn't challenge the king's dying wish that he be protector of Ned."

"Makes sense." Jack reaches across the table for my hand. "Gloucester worshipped his older brother, will take this duty very seriously. Especially since it was issued on the king's deathbed. And removing the queen from any responsibility could be construed either way. Gloucester may just have wished to save her the trouble."

"But she still sought sanctuary. She must be afraid of something. And why did Gloucester see the need to bring Harry into such a position of power?" I turn Jack's sword hand over, lightly caress the callus on his palm. "Harry was unbearable on the journey, so arrogant." I lift his hand to my lips, kiss each finger. Unbidden, the sight of Lord Rivers's servant lying gutted on the dirt slams into my mind, the man's life blood pumping into the earth from the wound rent by Buckingham's dagger.

"Elysabeth . . . Elysabeth! Where are you, my love?"

I blink. "I'm with you." How can I explain to Jack the foreboding Harry creates in me?

"You were far away."

I clench his hand tightly. "It is nothing." But I cannot unsee Harry's smile as he sheathed his weapon.

"Gloucester can handle Harry. I've seen him command an army. One arrogant duke is a piss to him. No, I think he needed a show of force, quickly, and Harry provided it." Jack takes a lock of my hair with his other hand and wraps it around our wrists, tying them loosely together with the silken strand. "Did Meg and Will travel with you? Catesby would know what's going on with Harry."

I curl my fingers around his, the tug of desire flushing my cheeks. "No. Meg has been with the boys at Ashby Manor, and Will is in council meetings every day." I couldn't leave the worry alone; it has settled under my skin like an infected bee sting. "Harry even invented a new motto for himself that bleats of his royal heritage."

"Idiot," replies Jack absently. He twirls my hair into vibrant chestnut loops, watching as it springs back straight when he lets go.

"He boasted he could control me like a bitch in whelp."

Jack looks up at me sharply. "Bastard. If he bleats and brags too loud, he will find himself with a throat cut like a slaughtered sheep at a Michaelmas fair."

"Hush, my love," I soothe. I needed to tell him of Harry's boasting, but I do not need Jack challenging Harry. My cousin is just a spoiled child with a sense of entitlement that he has never outgrown. The worry under my skin nags. Harry I can read. Margaret is oblique, her countenance carved as still as one of her stone saints, and she has always been so. I fall silent, chew my thumb.

"You always do that when you are irritated by Margaret." Jack gently moves my hand down to my lap. "I told you, ignore her."

I shrug. "She's married to Ned's senior advisor now. Ned confirmed he wanted to keep Lord Stanley on his council."

"As usual, Margaret is finding her position on Fortune's wheel." Jack leans back, closes his eyes briefly against the low afternoon light shining on the honeyed oak panelling and intricately woven Arras wall hangings. His fine cambric shirt is open at his throat, his beard trimmed and smoothed. He is at ease in the luxurious room, elegant in his confidence. Jack can travel from soldier to statesman with the ease of changing his jacket.

My husband explains gently and logically how I have prevented the Woodvilles from assuming control of Ned and ruling the country. How that would have unsettled the people, perhaps led to another war. And how I have earned the gratitude of Gloucester in demonstrating my loyalty to the king and his young heir.

I listen and then crave his arms around me. He reads my need, as he so often does, and pulls me into his lap. I tuck my head under his chin, feel his heart beat strongly. Jack draws me closer and finishes his thoughts. "With Gloucester's elevation to Lord Protector of the Realm and your godson on the throne, our destiny is powerful. Let Margaret strive for her own position; you have done your work, fulfilled your vow. You will not be needed anymore, except as a doting godmother. Your role in politics is over. All you need to think of now is the joy of Ned's coronation."

I agree, shake the doubts from my mind. My husband is right. I worry too much, let my sister annoy me without cause. "I think Margaret has every intent to pursue her son's pardon with Ned, which excuses me from pleading on her behalf. I am finally free from her demands." I kiss Jack, first lightly and then more deeply. "Of course, if there are other wishes I can fulfil . . ."

As Jack predicted, no command comes from the Palace of the Tower requiring my attendance. I hear from Margaret after three days that the prince's health is mending and that I should not be concerned about his well-being. It is a simple note, one sister to another, telling family news.

Countering the silence from the palace, Jack is sharing with me the freshest events from court, for Gloucester has surrounded himself with his loyal men of the North, and Jack and Will are trusted friends at the protector's daily council meetings. By the end of the month, Meg arrives from the country, and I command dressmakers to Le Ryall, choosing expensive fabrics in the latest fashions to wear at the celebrations. Yards of red velvet, silver tissue, and white damask are draped across the tables in Le Ryall's parlour, and we enjoy creating our finery.

Meg is proud to tell me of Will's senior position on the new council and the lands Gloucester has awarded him to adjoin his estates in the Midlands. And she shares with me snippets Will reveals of the new government taking its first steps with a bill here, a proclamation there. Even coins are minted—Meg has a purse stuffed full of gold angels with Ned's title and Gloucester's boar mark. And from the council chamber within the Tower of London, Gloucester steers the ship, his crew handpicked from those who'd served his brother well, who will transfer their loyalty to Gloucester, protect the prince from any Woodville challenges at all costs. The new regime is under full sail, and none more so than Harry, reports Jack. Wealth, land, castles, honours, titles . . . all rain down on his head in gratitude for his hasty and well-timed support. Every day Gloucester stamps his boar seal on another bequest, inks a new order with the council's clerks. Apparently, Harry's arrogance increases tenfold with every new perquisite. And there seems no end to his rewards.

Jack walks with me in the garden at Le Ryall, our custom each twilight, as he delivers the events he witnessed that day. "It is command over the Welsh Marches, and all the lordships in Gower for Buckingham," he says. "Gloucester must have reason to reward him so quickly and so generously. Perhaps the Woodvilles planned more than we know for Ned's succession."

June's new crescent moon scythes the sky like a rapier blade through velvet. London settles with the sough of a night breeze; a lute player at the house adjoining plucks at his instrument, the notes drifting and mingling with a thrush's fluid evensong. Jack tells more, his information dropping in bits and pieces as he sifts through what he thinks I will enjoy. "The coronation is progressing as planned. Commands of attendance have gone out across the country to fifty men who will be knighted at the ceremony. Margaret has ordered an acre of costly fabrics, is buying up all the merchants on Threadneedle."

"She could ask for my help. I have heard nothing from her. Nor Ned." I dislike the whine in my voice, but still I feel put out. The sweetly potent scent of lily of the valley blooms on the soft evening air. I take a deep breath to soothe myself, tamp down the ember of worry before it can flare. "It is as if I don't exist for them."

Jack kisses the inside of my wrist. "You did what was required of you, my love. Honestly, it's probably chaotic at the Tower right now. I can only imagine the demands issuing from your sister. Enjoy your life as the honoured godmother who saw the king safely to the throne." His green eyes twinkle. "Besides, would you want to be at Margaret's beck and call as she dictates the arrangements?"

In spite of my hurt feelings, he makes me laugh. Even as a child, Margaret showed an aptitude for commanding her half-brothers and sisters, and we all have stories of a horrendous scolding if we did not hasten to obey her river of orders.

"Are Oliver and Isabel here from the country soon? I saw you received messengers from Lydiard this afternoon." I hope so. My favourite brother and Jack's sister make good company, and Oliver always seems to know how to manage Margaret.

"They arrive sometime before the coronation," replies Jack. "And then we will start our celebrations in earnest. I have invited Harry along with Margaret and Lord Stanley to dine next week—"

"Harry? I would prefer not." A fluttering curdles my stomach. "He's conceited and arrogant, and I can only think what these recent rewards have done to his self-importance."

"He is also the second most powerful man in the country after Gloucester." Jack's tone is gentle but firm. "And frankly, Lord Stanley is the third. Oliver has some business he wishes to discuss with

Margaret and her husband, and your cousin Harry is an important ally. You can spend one dinner in his company."

"Then I shall seat Harry by Margaret and keep Oliver between us." I pull my shawl closer; the dew settles and chills my skin.

"Be sure to conceal your irritation with them both. You are too anxious."

"On the contrary. Better to be anxious than indifferent."

"It is important that we keep peace with them, Elysabeth."

"They can talk to each other in peace all they want. I would prefer not to listen. Nor be involved."

15
Summer 1483 | Le Ryall

Grilled eel, fish fresh that morning from Billingsgate market, a dozen pullets, marchpane fancies, and three newly slaughtered calves delivered fresh from the Lydiard farms. Our country manor always supplies the finest quality of food. I add berries and compotes, creams, and fruit cooked in hippocras to the list of dishes. A feast indeed, which even sober Margaret may find tempting and Harry might gorge until his mouth is stuffed with food instead of idle boasts. The dining hall is laid with silver plate, lavender buds sprinkled across the floorboards scent the air, and the vinegar-washed windowpanes sparkle. Great bowls of summer flowers decorate the table and mantel; we are ready for Harry and Margaret.

Jack runs downstairs, tying the final lace on his doublet and whistling. I know that sound anywhere, for it is of home and my love.

He smiles when he sees me. "Happy?"

"Yes." I straighten his collars, kiss his cheek. "Yes, I am. And hopeful for the future."

"Gloucester is one of the fairest princes in Christendom. He will guide Ned well."

"I hope so. Lord Rivers molded Ned into an extraordinary boy—"

"And Gloucester will make an exceptional warrior of him. After serving under the king and him for so many years, I know the kind of leader he is."

"Gloucester I can understand. Harry is a whole different subject," I reply. "Do you think he will continue to want a part in Ned's life?"

"He will definitely want a senior place on his council. And perhaps tonight we'll discover more of his plans for the future." Jack eyes my dress. "Speaking of which, you know I think you beautiful naked or clothed, er, but your attire . . . ."

My sweet husband. He knows my clothes are not always at the front of my thoughts. "I'm on my way to dress. Although why I bother, I know not. Margaret always makes me feel unkempt, and I'm sure tonight will be no exception."

A hammering on the doors to the street and Jack's exclamation stop me on the landing. I peer over the rail to the hall below, where my husband stands with a letter in his hands, his eyes fixed on a messenger dressed in Lord Stanley's livery.

"Are you certain?" he demands. "Now?"

The man nods. "Now. My Lady Stanley will not be coming here. You must go to her immediately."

Margaret. Blessed be. Again, demanding submission to her needs, placing her priorities over all else. "Let her come here, Jack," I call. Oliver and Isabel will be arriving shortly. "Everything is planned. I cannot cancel at this late notice."

Jack looks up at me. "We have no choice, my love. Margaret commands us to her home. She cannot leave. Lord Stanley has been arrested at the Tower of London. She fears for her husband's life. And hers."

The light has drained from the cobblestoned lanes that snake from Le Ryall to Stanley's residence in southern Vintry, turning the familiar streets into a dimly lit and hostile maze. Torches flare on corners, throwing puddles of light and deep wells of darkness. Arms linked, Jack and I weave through the congested alleys, avoiding clusters of tipsy Londoners already spilling from the overcrowded taverns. On every lane, the runnels are sluggish and stinking with the day's waste from the stalls and animal pens in the yards between the houses and shops, for the night cleaners have yet to appear. I gag at the combined heat and smell as I try to keep pace with Jack, dizzy with Margaret's news. As the quarter-hour bells peal from the city's churches, we reach the Stanley mansion.

The face of the house is blazing with torches, and a crush of horses and messengers mill in the lane. The entry doors are gaping open and flanked by guards armed with pikes and swords. A stream of people is scurrying around the gates. Jack pushes his way to the front, a firm arm keeping me close to his side. His height and bearing clear a path.

"Allow us through," Jack demands of the guards. "I am Lord Scrope, and this is the Lady Margaret's sister."

The men stand aside and immediately step together again as we pass into the hall. I am beset by a throng of liveried retainers representing half a dozen of England's most senior lords. There are the houses of Suffolk and Norfolk, the Earl of Essex's men, Northumberland's messengers entering behind me. Margaret has cast her plea to most of England's nobility. And they have responded to the Beaufort command. The hubbub of voices bays like hounds at a chase. I pause, finding my bearings in the heaving mass of people.

"There's Margaret." I grab Jack's hand and steer him through a pack of messengers in Stanley orange and green, some just arriving, others departing, and all conveying urgency. Margaret stands before the great fireplace, her hands clasped in front of her, her face impassive as she listens to the runners and dictates responses. She is in her traditional black gown with a white wimple, nun-like except for the vivid green underskirt that flashes as she turns from one messenger to the other.

We push through the crowd to her side. I tug her arm, turn my sister to face me. "Margaret, what has happened? What news of Lord Stanley?"

Margaret shakes her head rapidly. "Preposterous. Incredible. I cannot believe this is happening to me."

To you? What about your husband in the Tower? I stroke her hand, recognising how close Margaret is to tears under the bravado. "Tell us all you know. I am sure Jack can talk to Gloucester and put this right."

"Gloucester commanded it. His charges have brought shame upon us."

"What?" I glance at Jack. How can this be? Lord Stanley is one of the king's most senior councillors. And he is certainly the wealthiest and most influential.

"Gloucester accused my husband and Lord Hastings of treason at the council meeting. He even included Bishop Morton in his charges. Within the hour, my husband and the bishop were under guard. And Hastings was executed." Margaret takes a deep, shuddering sigh. "Gloucester's men threw Hastings to the ground on Tower Green, laid him across a log, and severed his head." Her voice breaks on the last words, and tears course down her cheeks.

The room's commotion falls behind me as I am drawn into my sister's fear. Margaret is frightened. Truly frightened.

"Dear God, why? How can this be?" Jack and I speak together.

Margaret's gaze flickers between us. "There's more." She snatches a missive from a messenger wearing the Buckingham livery, her pale face sanguine with two bright blood spots of colour in her cheeks.

"What can possibly be worse, Margaret?" I have not seen my sister this distraught since she last bade farewell to her son. "Oh God. Will? Catesby sits on the council. Is he—"

"Harry." The word spits from Margaret's mouth. She crumples the message and throws it unopened to the floor.

Jack stoops and picks it up, breaks the seal.

"Go on." I glance at my husband. What has Harry done now?

"Harry accused Hastings of treason. Convinced Gloucester there was a plot against him to remove him as protector, instigated by the former king's ministers." Margaret inhales deeply, her nostrils flaring. "And then stitched my husband into the story so he stands accused as a traitor."

"You've told us about your husband." I want to shake her. "What about Will?"

"Safe." Margaret almost shouts in her anxiety.

Jack looks up from the message. "Harry rides here now. He wants to explain."

"I will not have that traitor set foot in my home," Margaret hisses. "Refuse him entry."

Thoughts tumble across my mind. If Margaret alienates Harry, it will be impossible to know what his next move might be. "Best you acknowledge him, Sister." I take Margaret to one side, quietly stare down into my sister's pebble-blue eyes and force her to concentrate as I did when she was a child. "There will be a reason he did not kill your husband along with Hastings. If you don't listen to him, you will not know what he plans."

The crimson in Margaret's face gradually ebbs, and she takes a deep breath, straightening her sleeves several times until each cuff hangs exactly at the same length.

"Admit the Duke of Buckingham when he arrives," she orders her steward.

The church bells peal a quarter, and another. The room falls as quiet as a tomb as word spreads that the Duke of Buckingham is on his way. I take Margaret's hand, ice cold on this warm summer's eve. My sister allows the touch for a moment and then pulls away. Harry has entered

103

the hall, surrounded by his own guards. He wears the colours of his house, a crimson surcoat falling to the floor and edged with black fur, even on this warm night. Standing head and shoulders above most men, he seems to suck the air from the room as he marches to stand before us. I feel an instinctive repulsion, so much so that a shiver prickles the back of my neck.

Harry bows extravagantly, his surcoat flying open to reveal expensive black velvet, a gold chain of office glistening on his broad chest.

Popinjay. Peacock. I glance from his clothes to his expression. *Predator.*

"Aunt Margaret."

"My Lord Buckingham." My sister's use of his title signifies her displeasure.

Neither is willing to say more. I break the silence. "Harry. What are you thinking? Margaret's husband? You must—"

"I must do nothing," Harry snaps back at me.

Jack stirs at my side, and I feel him watching intently. He may be less than a Duke, but he will not tolerate Harry's rudeness to me.

Harry continues, half a dozen of his retainers grouped silently around him in a semicircle of brute force and power. "Aunt Margaret, your husband is accused of plotting with Hastings to put Ned back under the power of the Woodvilles. They gathered here secretly, at your home, away from the eyes of the council and Gloucester."

"There is nothing wrong with two friends meeting." Margaret's lips are white and clenched.

Dear Lord, what now is Margaret dabbling in? Friends meeting is one thing. Creating intrigue behind Gloucester's back is completely another.

Jack squeezes my elbow, warns me to keep silent.

Harry's face splits into a sneer. "There is when it's a daily occurrence. And then Hastings sent his mistress to meet with the queen in sanctuary. He as good as told the world there was a plot to bring Ned out of the Tower and into Westminster, return him to the influence of all those old men who were his father's council."

"Lord Stanley had no intention to plot treason. And you know so. Otherwise, you would have beheaded my husband this afternoon across the fallen log alongside Hastings." Margaret stands her ground. She barely reaches Buckingham's chest in height and yet commands the conversation. Gone is the tearful and frightened wife, and in her place rises a formidable courtier. "You made a mistake, Harry. You shall pay for this."

Harry laughs. "With what, Aunt? I have as much power as Stanley now. Thanks to Gloucester, I have castles and estates, land and authority to rival your husband throughout the Welsh Marches. I think more likely he can pay me for his release."

"Are you bargaining for Lord Stanley's life?" Margaret steps towards Harry. "Are you holding him hostage in the Tower, Harry?"

I hold my breath. I know the molten anger hidden within Margaret's mild words, recognise the drop in her tone that foretells a torrent of rage.

Harry puffs himself up like a pig's bladder ball. Such a sight, this powerful, handsome man, twice the size of the woman before him. And yet he drops his gaze first.

"It wasn't just me." He rounds to include Jack and me. "Catesby accused him too. He's your son-in-law. Ask him where his loyalty lies."

His bluster is despicable, always deflecting, never admitting his own culpability.

"Will Catesby is a lawyer of great repute, Harry," I respond. "And loyal to Gloucester. He may have discovered more about Hastings than you know. I think you might be clutching at his words to serve your own end."

And a dangerous end it is. If Harry continues this way, there really isn't anyone left who would counter his influence on Ned's council.

Margaret holds up her hand. We are immediately ringed by a dozen or more Stanley men, armed and fierce. Harry's guards look around and realise they are significantly outnumbered. They stand with heads bowed. Harry turns bright red, crumples his hat in his beefy fists.

Here it comes.

Margaret speaks as slowly as if he were a child.

"If you are holding my husband hostage, Harry, I would suggest you release him and bring him here now. For if you want to list armies and holdings in Wales, let me remind you that the Stanleys have ruled the borders for more than three hundred years. We own towns and families across a hundred miles who have depended on our benefice for centuries. I will assemble an army of loyal men in a day that will bury you."

I almost feel sorry for Harry. Sweat has broken out on his forehead, and a tremor starts in his right knee, shaking so hard it is visible through his hose. He opens and closes his mouth, gasping like a cod in a net. I can't recall the last time my cousin was lost for words.

Margaret takes another step forward, her voice pitched lower, almost whispering, forcing Harry to cock his head to listen. "And if you would like me to call upon Jasper Tudor and his followers, I am sure my son's uncle and the Welsh lords would be only too happy to respond. And you think you have power in Wales?" She holds out her hand towards him. It is completely steady.

Harry falls to his knees, clutches Margaret's fingers like a drowning man. "Lord Stanley's imprisonment is no doubt an error made in haste," he mutters, his chin pressed to his chest.

"I can't hear you."

Harry lifts his head, humiliation staining his expression. "A mistake. He will be released to be kept here in his home until talk quietens." He climbs to his feet, sweeps an unsteady bow.

"Insufficient." Margaret's voice is like cannon shot.

Harry freezes, stares down at his feet.

"You will find an opportunity to not only commend my husband to Gloucester, but to raise my status with him too. And I want it in front of the entire court. This incident must be eradicated from the Stanley family name."

Harry takes a deep breath, shudders like a wet dog. He kisses the air above Margaret's hand. "I will see that it is, Aunt. Extinguished. Completely."

Margaret withdraws her hand, straightens her cuffs. Her face is impassive, her spine severe.

I shrug at Jack. Once again, my sister has fought a battle of wills against a powerful man and won. "Come, my love," I say. "Let us return to Le Ryall. There is no further need to stay." Time to go home.

"One more thing, Aunt." Harry's words stop our steps.

This is a joust, not a conversation.

"I am sending Archbishop Bourchier into Westminster on Monday. He will remove Dickon from sanctuary to join Ned, for given these uncertain times and your husband's foolish actions, the boy is safer in the Tower than with the queen. As Ned's brother, he is second in line to the throne. We want no more Woodville plots to tempt your husband to stray again. Dickon and Ned should be together as the coronation plans finalise."

Am I the only one sickened by the note of triumph in Harry's voice?

"And now that Hastings is dead and Lord Stanley will remain here under observation at his house, the queen will have no one to advise her otherwise." Harry strides towards the door without looking back, throwing the words over his shoulder to land before us with a heart thump. "It is time for both princes to be guarded in the Tower."

Dickon is no more than ten. Too young to be alone in the Tower, even if his brother is there. And now Margaret is distracted by her husband's arrest. Who will care for them?

"My love?" Jack's voice breaks through my thoughts. I jump at his touch as he blots a tear from my cheek with his thumb. "Elysabeth? What's wrong? Why do you cry?"

I brush away his hand. "Nothing."

And everything. So young. And now the queen gives both boys to Gloucester.

"The boys need to spend time together. You should be happy. What better occasion than preparing for Ned's coronation? We'll go to Westminster on Monday, welcome Dickon as he leaves sanctuary. It's a joyous occasion." Jack's arm lays heavy on my shoulders as he steers me from Margaret's house. "What's worrying you now?"

"Nothing." *Everything.*

16

Summer 1483 | Westminster Palace

"Make way! Make way for Richard, Duke of York!"

The call has gone out. Dickon is arriving. Trumpets blare within Westminster Hall, shattering the still air into fragments of jubilant sound. The guards, stacked five deep around the perimeter—*Why so many?*—snap to attention; their pikes and staffs thump the ground in a resounding thunder.

Jack is happy that the two princes will be together in the Tower. I am not. If I am worried, how must the queen feel to give both her boys over to Gloucester and Harry?

She is locked in Cheyneygates, no more than a hundred yards from us. Did she part with her son gladly, I wonder, giving him up to the band of stone-faced clergy and soldiers that collected him? Or did she wail and weep as her youngest boy was torn from her arms? There is no telling, but in my heart of hearts, I think she may have sobbed.

Dickon emerges, blinking from the dark corridors leading from sanctuary, and even the wooden angels carved on the rafters smile down upon the child. He much resembles his older brother—though a sturdier, more solid version—from his bright blond hair to his sweet expression. The nobles and courtiers kneel to greet Ned's heir, for Dickon is next in the line of succession until his older brother marries and bears a son.

"Ah, Dickon," I whisper. "God bless you!"

Around me, others cheer and call out. "Welcome! Welcome, Prince Richard!"

Jack is clapping loudly, his face alight with simple joy. He is a man who deserves sons. A surprise pain pierces my heart. I thought I buried that failure a while ago. At least I have brought that joy into our family; perhaps not my own flesh and blood, but a boy in Ned for Jack to love as his own over the years.

Since we left the Stanley mansion on Friday, Jack has spent much of his time trying to convince me of the good that will come of Gloucester's protectorship and reuniting of the boys. Gloucester was close with his own brother the king, and certainly wants the same for his nephews.

"The brothers will be together and learn to love each other," my husband keeps repeating, and he says it again now as Dickon draws close.

"But now? In this way?"

"Must you always argue, Elysabeth?"

"I am just speaking my own truth." *Just because I don't agree with you, you call it an argument.*

I agree the brothers need to spend time in each other's company, for they have been brought up in different households, separate worlds. A few days snatched together at Bolton Castle in the summer and the formal court functions make them acquaintances, but not deep friends.

But the coronation is in ten days, and after that they will have all the time in the world to get to know each other. Why the urgency now, to wrench Dickon from his mother and sisters, distract Ned from all that he has to learn and rehearse for his anointing?

Why do the queen and her daughters refuse to leave Cheyneygates?

Dickon wears the pallor of sanctuary in his face, and I am thrust back into memories of my own time imprisoned within the abbot's dreary house, struggling to mourn my own child's loss so shortly before the queen's birthing of Ned.

And then the fleeting thought wings away as Jack hugs me in excitement. "Don't be so serious, Elysabeth! The boys will be together, and Ned will love Dickon's company."

I lock away the memory, the distant time gone, for who should grieve in the face of happiness? Jack has never blamed me for his lack of sons. He is such a fair man.

"Dickon looks well," I say. "His time in sanctuary has not stopped his growth. He's taller by a hand since we saw him at Christmas."

"He's a little peaked and pale," observes Jack. "But he'll soon be outside on Tower Green, shooting arrows at the butts and practicing his swordplay. Ned has the best instructors in the land, and Gloucester is determined to make soldiers of them yet!"

The prince is flanked by Archbishop Bourchier and Lord Stanley. "It didn't take long for Buckingham to make good on his promise to Margaret," I murmur. "It seems he has quickly made amends for his mistake and restored her husband to his seniority at court."

Jack glances at Stanley's smug face. "Lord Stanley comes from a long line of coat-turners," he says in a low tone. "Gloucester had best hold him closer than a friend."

Dickon walks ceremoniously through the assembled courtiers. He is wearing a surcoat of emerald velvet and fine burgundy hose. As he nears, I see his wrists poke beyond the cuffs of his coat and his hose are stretched thin to transparency around his knees. He needs new clothes, fit for the coronation. I wonder who is going to take care of those details in the Tower.

Catching sight of us, Dickon drops his dignified demeanour and grins. I wave back. Dickon's high spirits have not been subdued by his time in sanctuary nor the magnitude of today's occasion. The archbishop's red robes flutter and flap as he briskly walks Dickon towards the Star Chamber, followed by a procession of black-garbed clergy. I can no longer see Dickon for the flock of clerics surrounding him.

"I wish I could visit them," I say to Jack. I am probably the person who has spent the most time with them together. "I could help Dickon settle into his new position. I am sure the queen has done little to prepare him."

"Dickon will find his feet," Jack replies. "You know he's not shy."

"Ned, then?" I still cannot rid the resentment that I have been excluded from my godson's side at this most important time in his life. "I'd like you to ask Gloucester if I can attend Ned—"

The great north doors of Westminster Hall crash open, and as one body we all turn to see what disturbs the decorum.

Once again, Harry draws everyone's eyes to himself. His chin is tipped up with arrogance, his shoulders thrown back in self-importance. This time he has another nobleman at his side. Together, they stride the length of the hall, spurs striking the flagged floor. Ominous and imposing in their half armour, their sudden appearance casts a shadow over Dickon's welcome.

"What now from Harry?" I seem to be saying this a lot. "And who is that with him?"

"Lord Lisle." Jack frowns. "What business can he have with Harry?"

"Who is Lord Lisle?" Unlike my sister, keeping up with every member of the nobility does not fascinate me.

"John Talbot," Jack replies. "And you should remember—his mother was your mother's cousin, the other Lady Beauchamp."

Margaret would have known that in a heartbeat. "Oh, Eleanor Talbot's brother. I try not to think of them." I stand on tiptoe to get a better look at this distant cousin. "We were all concerned about her dalliance with King Edward before he married the queen. My sister was convinced Eleanor's behaviour would sully our family's reputation."

Jack grins. "I can imagine that giving Margaret a megrim. Fortunately, it didn't last long."

The men march past, and Harry squints sideways at me and then looks ahead again. They follow Dickon towards the Star Chamber.

"We should return to Le Ryall." Jack peers through the crowd towards the street. "We've welcomed Dickon, and I have other business to attend to."

My eye is caught by a man wearing Gloucester's livery hurrying through the thinning crowd towards us. He holds up his hand as he approaches.

"I think you're wanted." I nod towards the messenger. Jack turns on his heel, and the servant murmurs something.

"Come with me." Jack holds out his arm. "It seems Gloucester requests a word."

"I would love to see Dickon." My pulse quickens. *And I want a word with Gloucester.*

We weave back through the hall, walking more freely now the crowds are diminishing. I am eager to see the Star Chamber, for it is not a place for women. This ancient and hallowed room is the meeting place for the King's Council, and where not only decisions are made, but justice is dispensed.

The room is intimate after the enormous hall; its proportions are graceful and breathtakingly beautiful. Upon a white plastered ceiling, gold-bossed stars shimmer and shine with celestial grace. I can't help but spin in a circle and gaze upwards, entranced by its magic. The room is warm and convivial, with cushioned benches in window nooks and a welcoming blaze glowing in the fireplace; just the place for a young boy recently released from the gloomy abbot's house to gaze at in wonder.

And yet Dickon is not here. Nor are the clerics or archbishop. Could they have already left for the Tower?

"Jack. Elysabeth." Gloucester greets us from across the room. His face is white, his forehead creased with lines of worry. Harry is there too, his pacing distracting in a room of such calm. There is no sign of Lord Lisle either, but Will Catesby leans against a table, legs stretched before him, his ankles crossed. He appears casual, but his sharp eyes are following Harry's movements.

"Will?" I reach out as if to hug him, and he shakes his head, almost imperceptibly. I realise he is there as the king's advisor, not my son-in-law. "Where's Dickon—"

Jack interrupts me. "My Lord Gloucester, you have need of us? How can we serve you?"

"Dear God, Jack, as only you can." Gloucester's voice shakes, whether from emotion or anger, I cannot tell. He clasps hands with my husband and pulls him into an embrace, both clapping each other's back in men's awkward affection. "Last year you raised an army, fought at my side on our Scottish campaign. Today, I'm asking you to pledge your loyalty once again."

Harry cuts in. "A dreadful deception, Jack. And terrible outcomes for the princes that cannot be avoided."

I stifle a cry. "The boys—"

The men ignore me. My cheeks burn. I choke back my questions and gaze up at the stars, counting them to distract myself from interrupting and being asked to leave. I do not want to be removed from whatever is going on. Especially since it concerns the princes.

"My loyalty is yours without question. Tell me." Jack's tone is urgent. "Tell me what you need, my lord, and I swear by my life I will bring it to you."

"Men. And weapons." Gloucester paces, tosses the words like darts. "I need men from the North, from our land. Men I can trust. Men from Middleham, Bolton, Masham, York. Our countrymen. I've commanded Ratcliffe and Lovell to do the same. Join forces with my trusted councillors, I beg you."

"Who are we fighting, my lord?" Jack's military training comes to the fore. "Are you expecting an uprising? An invasion? What supplies and arms do I need to commandeer?"

This is men's talk. They are familiar with this ground, planning campaigns, mustering for battle. What can this have to do with Ned and Dickon? Through the window and across a tree-filled courtyard, a small boy scampers across the gravel. I wonder who he belongs to.

"Where's Dickon?" I demand.

"Safe," Will says briefly. "Not an invasion, Jack. But more insidious, more destructive." Our son-in-law speaks low and seriously. "We have received news that gives us great concern that the citizens of London may rebel. Before we make any announcements, I must investigate the cause, validate the truth."

"Rebellion?" I repeat. How could this morning's events have changed so suddenly? "You believe we are under attack?"

"Not yet," Will says somberly. "But we have to prepare for an uprising. And I must bring clarity to these accusations."

Jack frowns. "If there is anyone who can untangle a thread and weave a clean opinion, it is you, Will."

"Is that why Dickon is not here?" I ask. "Have you already taken him to the Tower? Rushed like a prisoner, not paraded like Ned's heir?"

"Elysabeth." Jack's voice carries the warning tone he uses when he thinks I have spoken too frankly.

"She's right, Jack," Gloucester says. He turns to me, speaks gently. "We did need to get him safely to the Tower, just as a precaution."

Harry gives a great sigh and slaps his gloves on his thighs. He is surely like a child waiting to speak before a schoolmaster. "We must act immediately, before the news spreads."

I glance at Jack. He ignores Harry's petulance, waits for Gloucester's command.

Gloucester's anxiety clenches his jaw; his mouth is tight from control. "Can you and your brother-in-law Oliver muster for Bolton and Masham, Jack?"

"Our men are faithful unto death, my lord. One word from you and they will follow you to the ends of the earth."

Gloucester looks from Will to Jack. He also ignores Harry, and I guess my cousin has already played his part in this drama. "Go now." His voice still trembles, as if some terrible demon has him by the throat. "Collect money and letters from Stanley, enough to pay a thousand men. Bring them to London. Bring as many as you can as fast as you can. Tell the men of York to come to me, for never have I

113

had more need. Do not question me, just trust that I would not ask you if it was not life or death. Take a guard of mine with you and go. Now."

Jack bows swiftly. "I am yours to command, Lord Gloucester." He takes me in his arms, kisses me. "Be safe, my love," he whispers, but I can feel his urgency. He has already left me.

"God bless you," I reply. "God keep you safe. And hurry swiftly home."

My husband strides from the room.

I turn to Gloucester and Harry, clench my fists in my skirts to give me confidence. If the boys need me, I will also go to the ends of the earth. "How can I help with the princes?"

Harry stands arms akimbo, feet planted wide. Not only does he dominate the chamber physically, Gloucester's anxiety diminishes his own authority. Harry appears the royal one, regal and stately, calm and not his usual blustering self.

"Go home, Elysabeth." Harry throws his arrogant command at me as if I were a servant, not his cousin. "There is nothing for you to do. I have taken care of everything."

Never do I despise Harry's choler more than when he is in this mood, for his smooth demeanour hides a thousand wicked thoughts.

"Have you, Harry?" I stand toe to toe with him, for I hate to see what he has done to Gloucester's confidence, what turmoil he has suddenly laid upon Ned's coronation. "It seems to me you have created havoc, not taken care of Dickon's and Ned's well-being."

Harry shrugs, turns away from me. "There are plenty of servants to take care of them."

But not to love and comfort them. They are reunited in the Tower but still mourning their father, separated from their mother.

"I'll take care of them." The words are out before I realise what I have said. "Grant me a pass, Lord Gloucester. Let me stay with them these next few days while they become reacquainted."

"It's no place for you," Gloucester says quickly. "Jack is doing enough for me."

"And I can do more. I've tended them both at Bolton Castle for many summers. I can care for them now too."

"These times are different. There is unrest in the air." Gloucester looks at Harry, who shrugs. "Besides, your sister oversees the preparations."

"And at that she is very efficient, but . . ." I do not want to make an enemy of Margaret, and so I measure my words carefully, "I am still responsible for Ned's spiritual well-being."

Harry shuffles his feet, inches impatiently towards the door. Whatever he has planned next, he is eager to get to it.

Gloucester still hesitates. "I saw how you were with Ned when we travelled together, Elysabeth. But we must be on guard. Challenges could come from any direction."

"So very different from when you challenged Lord Rivers, captured Lord Grey?" I reply. Not that I agreed with his actions. But it serves my purpose to bring this up. "You depended on me then to keep Ned steady. It sounds as if there may be need again."

"You love them very much, don't you?" Gloucester's frown lifts.

"I do. And my vow to God and the king will be in my heart always."

He smiles, and there again is the man I saw at Middleham, the loving uncle who sat with us at the roadside inn and planned Ned's court. "Are you declaring *sovereynté*, Elysabeth?" Gloucester catches my thought and teases me; then his face grows serious again. "I know the loyalty you have for both of them." He touches my arm, inclines his head in graceful thanks. "Wait here. I can write this permit now."

He walks over to Will, leaving me alone with Harry.

Time to scratch below his skin.

"Harry, why is Dickon joining Ned now? And why is the queen staying in sanctuary? Surely they should all be together now the coronation is just a few days away." I could not think why the boys were separated from their mother at this late stage. "Surely—"

"Surely yours is not to question, but to obey," Harry cuts me off. "If you are going to join them in the Tower, keep the boys together and watch over them at all times."

"So am I to be their guardian or their gaoler?"

"Yours to choose," he replies and turns away. "But not yours to question."

I bite my tongue. I dare not push Harry too far, or he may advise Gloucester I cannot go to the boys.

Will calls over as he hurries to join us, documents in his hands. "Take Meg with you. She will be good company." He hands me the passes. "I don't believe you will be there more than a few days." His smile is overshadowed by the worry lines on his brow.

I push away the worm of uncertainty that wriggles through my thoughts and prepare to return to the Tower of London.

17

Summer 1483 | The Tower of London

Within the king's private chamber adjoining the great hall at the Palace of the Tower, Ned reads aloud from a book of hours while Dickon fiddles with his dagger, the small deer he is carving tossed to one side. Ned takes seriously the red-letter words inscribed within the jewel-covered book. I know that Dickon would rather trace his finger over the cunning illustrations of wild boar, foxes, hawks, and rabbits.

I arrived on Monday, and it is now Thursday afternoon. I imagine Jack is more than halfway to Bolton Castle by now, while I am halfway to nowhere. There is a lack of news, a suspension of activity that makes the days drag. There is a dearth of servants, and the Constable of the Tower is in charge of our well-being. We may as well be in a garrison than a palace. Meg came shortly after me with a hastily assembled travelling chest of our needs, but no more news to add to my scant knowledge.

I have heard nothing since, and the frantic urgency of Monday's meeting in the Star Chamber has disappeared under a pall of boredom and uncertainty.

Harry's words caused Gloucester to prepare for battle. And yet here in the Tower, in England's military heart, Meg and I sit with two young boys and wait out the days playing interminable games of chess and cards.

The palace was once beautiful, I can see, with faded wall paintings of ancient queens and kings and mythical creatures lit by clouded and cracked windows that are no longer clear. As I walk through its empty corridors, I discover many of the rooms are closed, their floors broken and rotting, fireplaces cold and heaped with fallen bird's nests. The king's chapel within the White Tower is stacked with papers and chests and no longer used for worship. Instead, we are escorted thrice daily across the green to the church of St. Peter ad Vincula for prayers with the rest of the Tower's residents.

There are far too few retainers and far too many guards, and it is as if we are existing in a rarefied world of our own, for no tutors or chaplains serve Ned, and our meals are taken together in a small chamber off the great hall with little ceremony. Meg and I share a dormitory holding a rickety bed with moth-chewed hangings. Noxious fumes curl around us from the garderobe, which no longer drains. The entire palace is crumbling and rotting around us. What kind of portent is this for Ned's reign? I grow more furious with each new discovery of decline. My sister would not tolerate this kind of royal household, and neither will I.

"Have you lived like this since you arrived?" I ask Ned. I do not want to worry him, but these conditions are appalling. How can the future king be living in such squalour?

He looks around as if noticing through my eyes just how ramshackle our surroundings are. "No," he replies. "Until last Friday, we lived as I did at the other royal palaces, with a full retinue. But then we heard a disturbance on the green. Lady Stanley left us without warning, and after my Uncle Buckingham visited us, there was a great upheaval in the palace and our situation changed to this."

The same day Hastings was executed and Stanley arrested.

"And your Uncle Gloucester?"

"I have not seen him for a week."

This is unacceptable. If I do not hear from Jack or Gloucester by Monday, I shall simply return to Westminster and demand an audience. We must finalise our preparations for the coronation, rehearse Ned for his long and important day, and yet no one comes near us.

The boys spend much of their time within the great hall, running around the columns and playing chase across the slippery floors. Meg has persuaded one of the guards to give us his knucklebones set, and I encourage the diversion. The boys' carefree times will soon be curtailed once Ned is crowned and the real business of kingship descends on his slender shoulders. Besides, play is the best way for the brothers to build their friendship, over games and friendly competition. Dickon outstrips Ned in sport, but Ned is canny in games of skill and is teaching Dickon his own strategies in chess and tables. I also overhear him questioning Dickon about their mother and her welfare, and my heart aches that he is still not able to see her.

Wretched woman, that she has meddled in politics to the degree that she is denied access to Ned and places her own security before her son's. And his well-being. Ned's tooth is bothering him again, and despite my requests we have yet to receive a visit from a physician. I do the best I can with the herbs from the Lieutenant's Garden, but it is not enough to take away my boy's pain.

I walk with Meg around the great hall, now empty of tables and benches and echoing with our footsteps. The soaring rafters are home to a colony of nesting pigeons, and although no servant is cleaning the mess they drop on the tiled floor, I find the birds' rustling and cooing soothing in the silence.

"No news, Meg?" A stupid question, for if a messenger had been sent through to us, I would have seen him.

"No news, Belle-maman."

"Are you certain Will told you nothing before you came?" I make Meg recall again the days leading up to Dickon's release from sanctuary and her joining me in the Tower. "There must have been something to do with John Talbot, Lord Lisle. Harry brought him before Gloucester for a reason."

Meg slowly shakes her head, keeps pacing. "No. Will has been custodian of the Talbots' business ever since he was a young lawyer, for they are related. He has always advised on their family affairs. I can think of nothing different that he has said to me."

"What could possibly have prompted Gloucester to send Jack to Yorkshire to muster an army?" It is one thing to be concerned about rumours within London. There is always gossip. But to request armed men from the North?

"I cannot think." Meg links arms with me. Her familiar touch is reassuring. "We must depend on Will and Gloucester to resolve this situation. And Jack will return soon with an army of loyal Yorkshiremen. Whatever Buckingham uncovered, they will rectify."

"Will and Gloucester I trust. Harry—not at all."

The doors to the hall creak open, and, shadowed against the bright outdoors, a guard of four enters to collect the boys for their bow practice on Tower Green. Each day Ned and Dickon have the same routine, and I encourage them to go outside and exercise with the soldiers of the Tower. There are no better marksmen to teach them archery, to be sure.

Please God they will not have to use these skills in combat.

Ned may be only twelve, but princes ride to battle at this age to rouse courage in the hearts of their soldiers. I think of my nephew Henry Tudor. Margaret's son has been exiled from England and fighting alongside his Uncle Jasper since he was ten years of age. I cannot imagine her worries and fears, but I can think of her nightly prayers to keep him safe.

Please God that Jack's army is to keep the peace, not start a war.

The thought of my boy being called to fight in the coming weeks strikes fear into my heart.

The guard who has given Meg the knucklebones set lingers, standing hesitantly in the shadows, as if he has business with us.

I approach him. "Did you wish to say something?"

He looks uneasily around. "I dursen't be caught telling you this."

"Telling me what?" I question. "What do you know?"

"We've been ordered to double our guard. We're to be on the lookout for any strangers without permission entering the Tower, restrict passage to just the Byward Gate."

"Go on."

The guard glances up, his face red under a thatch of straw coloured hair. "I'm loyal to the king's lad," he says. "I fought for his father at Barnet. I'd lay down me life for his son."

"We know you would," replies Meg gently. "What can you tell us?"

"Gloucester has delayed Prince Edward's coronation. The council worries there be unrest in the city."

"What? That's impossible." As his words register, I see through the open doors that Ned is being marched to the green by the guards, and my pulse quickens. *Nonsense. This is just his archery lesson.* "The coronation delayed? What more have you heard?"

"Nowt. I've said too much." The guard clamps his mouth shut, bows abruptly, and backs away.

"Come back!" My world is spinning, I can barely speak to call after him, but he has gone, and the expanse and silence of the great hall settles back into its foundations. A sick feeling comes over me. "Meg, that's why Gloucester sent Jack to raise an army."

On the green, Dickon and Ned take up position at the butts. They both shoot their arrows into the centre of the targets. From here, they appear athletic and talented recruits, not boys playing at lessons. They look fully capable of leading a troop into battle.

Meg looks at me with dawning horror. "If Londoners hear that the coronation has been delayed, they will rise up against the council."

"Get word to Will immediately," I say urgently. This news is startling, more so because I have heard this through a guard, not officially from Gloucester. "We have to know what is happening. And why we don't have more guards to protect us if the Tower is locking down."

"I shall send a messenger, Belle-maman." Meg's tone is calm, but her face is worried.

As Ned's little party disappears from sight, another guard marches from the direction of the river gate. The unpleasantly familiar livery of red and black jumps out at me. Harry's guards stride in tight formation. They are tall and well-built and fully armed.

They march straight into the great hall and stop before Meg and me.

"We are here to escort the princes," the captain says.

"Escort them where?" I demand. Dear God, what now on the heels of the coronation news? "What command do you have that permits you to take them?"

"My Lord Buckingham orders you to prepare their personal items to move them from here," the captain replies. "Where are the princes?"

"Yours to find." I have no intention of aiding Harry on whatever this next event is that he has instigated.

The soldier turns to the other five men. "Go and search the Liberty. They cannot be far. And as soon as you find them, bring them to Coldharbour Gate."

"Where are you taking them?" I demand. "We have no notice from the protector."

"None needed," says the captain. "The Duke of Buckingham has been appointed Chief Constable of England. Lord Gloucester has delegated security to him. Lord Buckingham has ordered they be moved for their own protection into a safer location."

"More secure than inside the Tower of London?" I laugh in my nervousness. "There is no place more secure in all of England."

"They are to be moved from the palace to the Garden Tower."

"Into a prison?" I am shocked. "I cannot allow this."

The guard sets his mouth. "You have no choice, Lady Scrope."

I glance at Meg. My worst fear is that of Gloucester commanding the boys to ride out and lead an army. And now, without warning, I am told they are to be relocated from palace to gaol. Both are frightening choices. If they are choices.

"I am here at the direction of Lord Gloucester, Protector of all England. I am responsible for the well-being of the prince," I protest. I do not want to jeopardise their safety. But why has nothing been said to me?

"And I am here at the command of the Constable of all England. I am responsible for their safety and security. His word has precedence," the captain replies.

"But a gaol?" I cry. "Why a gaol? Why not to St. Thomas's Tower, the private royal apartments?"

"Security," the captain says. "St. Thomas's Tower sits on the river. We cannot seal entries." And with that, he takes a step back to his men, forming a block of imposing guards. "Their personal items, Lady Scrope?"

Meg shakes her head. "I think we must do as he says, Belle-maman."

I make the choice that is no choice. "I shall send a note with yours to Will and tell Gloucester that once again Harry takes things too far."

Together, we walk back to the small chamber behind the dais and gather up the boys' books and papers, a chess set, and a lute. I slip Dickon's carved deer into my pocket to keep it safe.

"To the Garden Tower, then," Meg says. "We can stay in the Lieutenant's House across the garden. I am sure this is just temporary."

The guard does not comment, simply leads us from the palace, through Coldharbour Gate, and down the slope towards the river. The sun feels good on my cheeks, and a fresh breeze blows from the river, which runs on a cleansing high tide. The wind delivers a hint of the fragrant orchards on the south bank. After the rotting and musty palace, it is a welcome relief.

The Garden Tower catches the warmth of the sun and is hewn from the same golden stone as the rest of the walls. It is not white-washed like the White Tower, and it sits tucked into the land that runs down to the river from Coldharbor Gate. The inner ward wall joins its western face, and from here the Lieutenant's Garden unravels like a beautifully woven carpet to its feet, fresh with flowers and herbs. To the west, nestled in the gardens, the gabled Lieutenant's House is well-built and in good repair, looking just like a knight's manor. If I do not turn and see the White Tower behind me, I could be in the Suffolk countryside.

We walk under the hefty iron portcullis that spans the Garden Tower and past the massive ropes and pulleys. The gate is retracted into the stonework, creating an open archway that leads to a chamber.

The captain waves to a servant by the door. "Take the princes' items," he says. "Lady Scrope will not be needed any further."

"What?" I whirl round. "What? You did not say this!"

The captain stands blank-faced.

Meg and I are to be dismissed?

"You cannot be right. I demand an explanation." Something is slipping away from me, and I must insist I remain with Ned. "Lord Gloucester appointed me to look after the boys, stay with them while in the palace."

"Since they are no longer in the palace, your services are not needed," replies the captain.

"On whose authority?" But with a sinking heart I know the answer, for all roads are now leading to his command.

"Lord Buckingham's." The guard shifts, looks towards the green. "And now, if you will excuse me Lady Scrope, I have a duty to escort the princes here."

I root my feet. "I am not leaving without seeing their chambers, ensure their new lodgings are appropriate, however temporary they may be." *Palace? Or gaol?*

The guard stares straight ahead, his face crimson.

"I understand why there may be concern for their security." I brush past the servant into the low-ceilinged chamber. A heady scent of roses fills the room from a door propped open to the gardens. "It's just the way this is being handled."

"What else did you expect of Harry?" Meg follows behind me.

"I know. I know." I try to calm down, see the situation from another view. "I suppose Gloucester wants them closely guarded until whatever is causing the delay is resolved and the new coronation date is set."

Meg walks over to a large desk that is placed under a wide and sunlit window, examines the books and writing equipment that are neatly laid out upon its polished surface. "Ned will like this," she says. "These are stories of knights and damsels, good quality parchment, and a fine set of pens. That's all he needs to be happy."

Someone at least has planned for Ned's comfort. And I have to admit the room is spotlessly clean, with rich hangings on the walls, an elegant set of plate on the board. In its own way, this neat and organised room is much more welcoming than the dilapidated chambers of the palace.

I look through the doorway into the bright sunshine. The gardens are full of birdsong and fruit trees, winding paths, and shrubs to play hide and seek amongst. If I ignore the guards patrolling the fence and standing at the wicket gate, it looks like the walled garden at Lydiard. "At least they can go outside safely here without a guard marching them everywhere." The defensive walls of the inner ward run all the way to the Lieutenant's House. No likelihood of anyone penetrating this area.

"Dickon will love the henhouse." Meg joins me. "And there is grass for them to kick a ball on."

"It's still a gaol, Meg."

"It's safe, Belle-maman. And until we know that Jack is back and the unrest in the city quelled, don't you think we should do what Gloucester and Buckingham think best for the boys?"

The Garden Tower does not have the grandeur of the royal apartments, nor the furnishings of St. Thomas's Tower. It has a history of being a holding place for those who have incurred the king's displeasure. But for two young boys, it will be like ruling over their own private castle.

Making my choice that is not a choice, I nod. "It is secure, and I am sure it's just for a few days—until this unrest calms down."

"They will think it an adventure," Meg says. "A time for fun before they are back in the royal household and assuming their roles as princes of the realm again."

"And our dismissal?" I cannot help feeling that Harry has again achieved something that I am not privy to.

"They are taking precautions. The last thing they need is to look after us too," Meg replies. "The unrest will calm down. Especially since Jack is bringing more men in from the North to provide security at the coronation." Meg's political learnings from Will make perfect sense. "I believe Gloucester only postponed the date to allow time for them to arrive."

"I can understand Gloucester wanting his own men around him. I know Jack will march them at a fast pace. They will be here as quickly as he can lead them south." Away from Westminster's intrigues, my fears seem overwrought. This is a safety issue, no more. "Harry is just ensuring that the boys are watched more closely. The palace is almost impossible to keep safe. That's why he orders the boys moved into a more secure lodging." As I say it aloud, it makes more sense. I just wish I had received this command from someone other than Harry.

"And after Hastings's execution, there are probably more rumours flying around London right now than gossips chattering at a seven-month birthing," Meg replies. "And you know Harry. He always overdramatises things and overemphasises the importance of his role. This will get resolved quickly, I am sure."

"Lady Scrope?" The captain is waiting at the door. "Is there anything else? I must ask you to leave."

"I would see them settled and ensure they are not in any discomfort in the next few days." I try to prolong the moments before I leave with good cause. "And the king requires a physician to treat his jaw. Please be sure you attend to this immediately. I am accountable for Ned's well-being. I must know how he will be treated this time. I will not permit a repeat of the neglect I witnessed at the palace.

There is a screen at the far end of the room, and I check behind to see what other accommodation is within the chamber. A large posted bed stands in the middle of the floor, draped in decent tawny velvet hangings, fresh linen sheets upon the mattress. Another wide window lets in the afternoon sun, its lead panes and clear glass casting a shimmering diamond pattern across the golden oak floorboards.

"Lady Scrope," calls the guard.

I am still not ready to leave. *Not yet. Not yet.*

I unlatch the casement and lean out. The boys are running around on Tower Green, picking their arrows from the targets and gathering up their bows. A puppy gambols around Dickon's ankles, and the boy's high laughter floats over the freshly mowed grass and through the open window. Harry's guards are watching them, chuckling at their antics, and making no move to surround them or force them to leave their practice.

"I must insist, Lady Scrope . . ." The guard is now standing in the chamber with me, and I cannot put off my departure any longer.

A shrill cry from the green whips my head around. Ned has tripped and fallen, and Dickon runs to help him. He crouches on the grass beside his brother. I lean farther from the window, call out to the boys, but I am too distant for them to hear me. The wall of guards stands immobile.

Dickon hauls his brother to his feet and bows. Ned picks grass blades from his hair, thumps his brother on his arm. They both dissolve into giggles.

I let out my breath. "It's not such a bad place," I admit, "for a few days." I shoo away the crow that perches on the wall below the window, and it flaps away with a hoarse caw.

18

Summer 1483 | St. Paul's Cathedral

Out of the protected world of the Tower and back in the heart of London at Le Ryall, I feel the difference that only a few days' absence has wrought. The city trembles like an eager terrier at a warren, ready to flush rabbits. Its citizens congregate on street corners, whisper in taverns; the merchants' wives stock extra supplies for their pantries, surety against whatever supposed uprising is eddying under the relentless June sun.

Questions flood the streets and refuse to ebb. I am bombarded with worries from my cook, the steward, the stable master. And I cannot answer them. Why did Gloucester execute the late king's most trusted friend? Why does the queen remain in sanctuary? Why was Dickon taken to the Tower? Why are twenty thousand armed men marching towards London?

Is Lord Scrope leading an army to dispel unrest or create it?

I add my own concerns to the swirling rumours. Is Jack's troop from Bolton Castle going to reawaken London's loathing for York? And now an urgent message from Will before I hardly have time to remove my cloak.

Stay at Le Ryall, both of you, he commands from Gloucester's council chamber. *Do not leave, and especially do not travel to the Tower to visit the princes.*

The less I know, the more I imagine.

I was tricked into leaving the Tower.

Harry wants no one but himself responsible for the princes.

The boys will be commanded to join Jack's army against the London rebels.

It is like being back in sanctuary, for I am as much a prisoner in my own home as I ever was at the abbey.

The merchants close their shops, board their precious windows. They know better than to stay open when unrest roams the streets. There is a shortage of flour and meat, and the steward at Le Ryall requires extra coin to fill the larders; I send to Lydiard for beef and poultry.

The days drag by with no trustworthy news. No permission arrives from Will to visit the boys. My son-in-law does not come back to Le Ryall, but lodges in Westminster by Gloucester's side. A week has passed since I left the Tower and no word of Jack's arrival or the new coronation date. I hear nothing from Margaret; Meg receives only ten-word notes from Will, warning us to remain at home. We are remote from knowledge, floating like an island in an unchartered sea.

Where is my sovereynté now?

All the praise I received from Jack, the warm blush of independence, the endorsement of my decision—all has vanished. Now, as always, the women are defined by their husbands' actions. Our men remain tied to Gloucester's dictates; Lord Stanley is forgiven but still under watch; Jack is somewhere in the Midlands, riding south at the head of an army of loyal Yorkshiremen.

Meg says Will shadows Gloucester, barely sleeping through the demands to bring his legal thinking to avert a disaster. "It's something to do with the late king and Eleanor Talbot," she tells me. "More than that, Will refuses to say."

Sovereynté. Once again, I contemplate the irony of my wish. I have no power. My voice is no more use than a broken reed in a musician's pipe. And just as soundless.

I sit by the parlour window as a messenger in Stanley colours picks his way through the crowd. There is no purpose to the people milling on Ryall Lane, but more they would rather be outside than in, waiting for unknown news. Surely there is nothing more unsettling than waiting for unknown news.

At last, perhaps Margaret is sending me the new coronation date. She would make it her business to be the first to know, the first to tell.

I count to fifty, knowing that the door will open and the messenger walk in on the beat of fifty-one. The command he brings from Margaret is unexpected, raises my curiosity.

Meet me at St. Paul's Cross at noon, my sister writes. *Bring a discreet attendant. And disguise yourself in a servant's robe, for we must not be recognised. There is a sermon we must hear.*

Not what I was expecting, but a welcome distraction. It takes but a heartbeat to fathom Margaret's instructions and another to act, for if I am forced to stay inside any longer, I will go mad. Will may have forbidden me to visit the Tower, but surely he does not include listening to a sermon with my sister in that curfew. To avoid explaining, I slip from a side door when Meg is in the kitchens and take a sturdy groom with me. Act first, apologise later.

With a sense of disquiet, I walk east to St. Paul's. What sermon could Margaret want me to hear? Certes, there are a thousand other people who have the same idea. Word must be out that news is coming. Delivery by sermon makes it irrefutably validated by God's representatives on earth.

I learn to push through the crowds with elbows out and a ready curse, following my groom, who knows how to navigate the tensions and shouting. He takes it all in his stride, where I am as skittish as a fallow deer surrounded by a pack of hounds.

St. Paul's Cross is set in the fore of the great cathedral and is a popular place to hear sermons. Today, with the uneasy air and voices shrill with tension, a hubbub surrounds me, the crowd heaving with dissention like a monster in the deep. With the groom protecting me, I push my way to the side of the square under the overhang of the cloisters, where we can hear and see the preacher but not be hemmed in by the crowd. It is airless within the space, for no river breeze trickles in from the Thames on this stifling June day, and the hot breath of a thousand citizens stokes the fires of uncertainty. A touch at my elbow and Margaret stands by me; our servants take a position on my other side.

"Sister." She looks her usual self; I see no excitement in her calm demeanour.

"What news?" I demand. "Why are we here?"

Margaret stares at the cross as a portly cleric climbs the stairs to the preacher's box and lifts his hands for quiet.

"Doctor Shaw is delivering a sermon from which there is no return," my sister murmurs, half to me, half to herself. She fixes on the clergyman, who appears to float above the people from his place on the dais. "We must listen for ourselves and then be prepared to leave ahead of the crowd."

The preacher begins to speak. We fall quiet. He says he has words that we must pay heed to. Words that will change our thinking, challenge our loyalties. Most of all, words that must be obeyed or risk the wrath of God in heaven. I glance at Margaret. What kind of sermon is this? Why does she bring me here? I open my mouth to say something, but she pinches my arm.

"Shh," she whispers. "Here it comes."

I stare at the preacher. From where I stand, I see his sharp teeth and fat red lips. A dribble of saliva trickles from the corner of his mouth. Sweat stains seep under his arms as he lifts his hands to the heavens, invoking God's mercy in the name of the Duke of Gloucester.

"Why is he saying all this?" I have not heard a sermon preached with such vehemence in all my days.

"Listen," says Margaret.

"Secret wedding . . . Illegitimate . . . Bastard slips shall not take root." Shaw thunders Ecclesiastes from his pulpit. A torrent of words floods over us. He tells of a marriage pre-contract between Lady Eleanor Talbot and King Edward the Fourth. He whispers and rants about how Elizabeth Woodville was deceived into marriage with the king. Even raises doubt of the dead king's legitimacy, accusing his mother of adultery.

"Margaret, what does he mean?" I hiss, shocked beyond measure at the man's rancour.

Every damning word strikes us with relentless clarity. With each new revelation, the crowd gasps until the groans and cries evoke purgatory itself on one of London's holiest sites.

"Shaw is preaching the truth. Harry says he has proof," Margaret whispers.

Sour bile scorches my gut, burns in my chest. "Proof of what?"

"King Edward was betrothed to Eleanor Talbot before marrying the queen."

"Dear Mother of God." I am jostled by a bellowing bull of a man, almost swept from my feet.

"The Woodville marriage is not legal," Margaret shouts through the clamour.

Not legal? I freeze; the world has shrunk to Margaret's words. "And so?"

Margaret is now shoved up close to me by the crowds, can barely turn to face me. When she does, a curious smile plays upon her lips.

"Think, Elysabeth, think. If the Woodville marriage is illegal, then the princes . . ."

". . . the princes are illegitimate," I croak, horror clawing my throat.

Margaret bares her teeth in a wide grin that mingles triumph and tragedy. Such an odd expression, I think. So odd.

"And if Ned is illegitimate . . ." My hands fly unbidden to my mouth, try to force the words back inside me.

". . . he cannot inherit the throne."

Margaret's appalling statement falls like an axe blow upon my head. *Bastard.*

My beautiful godson is a bastard and cannot be king.

Bastard. Bastards. The Woodville boys are bastards.

"Bastards. They are both bastards." Shaw's words pelt London's citizenry. Margaret is trembling at my side.

I blurt a question. "What happens now, Sister?"

Margaret's eyes shine bright with tears. "Happens? I believe the throne stands vacant, Elysabeth. And although Gloucester thinks it his, there is another who has equal or greater claim. Another who is closer to you even than your godson."

"Don't speak, Margaret," I shout at her, my words barely registering over the catcalls and sobbing of the people ringing us. *Don't say it, for saying it will make it true. Bury your ambition.* "Do not speak his name."

But Margaret is caught up in the moment, in the fervor of Shaw's rhetoric, the promise of the vista that is now thrown wide before her. She is not reckless enough to say more than one word. But that one word whispers more than the entire Shaw sermon.

"Henry."

19

Summer 1483 | Le Ryall

I can only think in one-word bursts. Jack. Gloucester. Harry. Henry. Ned. Dickon. *Bastards.*

Led by our servants, Margaret and I force our way against the tide of citizens who surge through the city streets. Holding hands tightly, we hug the buildings to avoid the filth in the runnels and shelter in doorways and under awnings when the rough characters stagger past. From St. Paul's to Le Ryall is less than a half hour's stroll, and yet today it is the stuff of nightmares, for the people will not disperse. Like an unfed beast, the crowd rumbles and roars, confined between the narrow alleys and shops. Faces appear and disappear, red gap-toothed mouths shouting profanities, stinking bodies lurching arm in arm through the narrow lanes. As the crowd surges along Knight Ryder Street, we escape down Garlick Hill and are washed up on the doorstep of Le Ryall.

And all the way, the dreadful words keep ringing in my mind, dictating my pace, tolling with the city bells that are pealing from every church steeple in alarm.

Bastards. Bastards. Bastards.

"You cannot go back out. Stay here," I say to Margaret as we reel into the safety of our home. My sister cannot navigate these streets alone. "London will rise. We wait for Jack."

Margaret's eyes are blazing fierce blue in the dark hall. "I must get a letter to Henry," she says. "Send me your clerk—now. I must write to my son." We walk to the parlour and stop on the threshold. Will and Meg stand in the quiet room, the ancient walls soundproofing the running feet and shouts that are clamouring through the streets.

"You've heard, Belle-maman?" Fear widens Meg's eyes. "I looked for you, and you were gone. You went to St. Paul's?"

I am mute. I am spinning from the news, the crush of the crowds, this tumbling down of all I love. If I open my mouth, I know what will come out.

Bastards. Bastards. Bastards.

"Are you hurt?" Will's calm voice soothes as he leads Margaret and me to the window chairs, pours wine for each of us from the cut-glass carafe. His gesture is so familiar. Yet so foreign in this new world that envelops me.

"Are you hurt?" he repeats.

"No." I sip from my cup. "Why are you here?"

Margaret bounces up again as if she has been bitten. "Summon me a clerk," she orders Meg. "I must write a letter to my son."

Will kneels on the floor next to me, his tired eyes kind. "I wanted to tell you myself," he replies. "I knew how devastated you would be. I did not think you would endanger yourself and go to hear the sermon."

"Did you know? Did Jack?" I am wavering between anguish and anger, and anger is winning. "How could this be true?" Now that the words are flowing, they gush like a ruptured pipe into a rain barrel. "And Gloucester believes this? And refuses to overturn these dreadful lies? And Harry? Harry revealed this? That's why he brought Eleanor Talbot's brother to Westminster. What other harm, Will, could they both possibly do?"

My son-in-law stills, bows his head. The bright light beyond the windows casts Will's face in darkness, and I shudder. A terrible and dark premonition creeps over me, racing my heart, slowing my movements except for a trembling in my shoulders that seems to belong to someone else. There is more?

The clerk enters, and Margaret moves swiftly to the table, seating herself and opening the writing box. Soon her quill scratches furiously over parchment, obliterating Will's silence.

"What more?" I hear my own voice as if from a great distance. I put down the wine; it is burning my throat and souring in my stomach as I swallow.

Meg presses a tisane into my hands. I smell valerian and sloe berries to calm nerves and restore strength. *Good girl.*

"Lord Rivers," replies Will. Margaret's scratching stops abruptly.

I am silenced at this. I was thinking of Ned and Dickon. Why would Will speak of their uncle?

133

I clasp the tisane and let my other hand drift up to hold Meg's.

"He has been found guilty of treason." Will walks to the window and looks out. His back is set, his shoulders rigid. "He conspired with the Woodvilles to remove the allies of Gloucester who sit on the council. He was plotting on taking control of Ned. He will be beheaded tomorrow at Pontefract." He turns, his face impassive, his formal lawyer's expression in place. When Margaret cries out, his mask cracks for a moment and then re-establishes itself. "He names me executor of his will."

"Beheaded for treason?" Margaret and I speak in accord. How can this noble and righteous man be a blood enemy of his beloved nephew?

"Along with the queen's son Sir Richard Grey," Will continues. "As long as they live, there will be uprisings to support Ned. They have already attempted an escape from Sheriff Hutton when they were held there. It would only be a matter of time before they try again."

I cannot see sense, find it impossible to logic the way Will does. "It is Ned's throne, Will. Ned is the rightful king. Lord Rivers is only doing what is right, acknowledging his Woodville family!" My words end on a shout, and I bite back my tongue.

I drop the tisane, and its crimson liquid spills across the oak floorboards, spreading quickly across the golden wood, trickling through the joins. No one moves.

"Ned is the rightful king." My anger swings to anguish "He is! He is . . . he . . ." Tears spurt from my eyes. "Harry!" I recall the long-ago joust in Westminster, his words at the inn at Stony Stratford, his envy of Lord Rivers. "Harry did this, didn't he?"

"You cannot be sure." Margaret's voice cracks. She and Lord Rivers are close, sharing their common love of learning, their joy in the new printings of Caxton. "You cannot blame Harry."

"Even as he prepares his speech for the Guildhall tomorrow?" interrupts Meg. She is on fire too, and for a moment I feel sorry for Will, surrounded by all these opinionated women. "Harry is quick to be kingmaker. He may have failed with Ned, but he will pledge support to Gloucester, announce him as the true king, and London will follow."

"Gloucester becomes king? Just like that? Is this true?" I round on Will. "Oh God, preserve me from the men who twist facts and fate to achieve their unholy ambitions." I dash Meg's arm away. "And why did Rivers think he could safeguard his family by appointing you executor of his will?"

Will takes a long, shuddering breath, slowly meets my eyes. "Because he trusts me," he says softly. "Because he knows I kept the secret as long as anyone. That I did everything I could to protect the boys."

"Secret?" This time we speak in unison, Margaret, Meg, and me.

Will pushes back his hair, and I see that he has not been barbered for several days. "I knew of the pre-contract with Eleanor Talbot. She was my father's cousin."

I try to speak. He holds up his hand.

"My family knew, but with Eleanor's death and the passing of time, it did not matter," Will says, as if speaking to a jury. Which he is. "With the king's robust health and his fine strong sons, it did not matter. But when he died, when the king died and left a child to inherit the throne, history returned to devour us all."

"But why?" I cry. "Why, Will? Gloucester can continue as protector. He can bring an act before Parliament legitimising Ned, making him king, surely?"

"Not soon enough, Elysabeth. And there will be challenges from opponents that they are still bastards. Look at what happened to Hastings when he tried to enforce Ned's father's council upon Gloucester." Will resumes his lawyer's tone, speaks calmly, slowly, deliberately. "More importantly, there are others who can raise a more legitimate claim to the throne than Gloucester. Such as Harry Stafford. And others."

Margaret is white-faced, her hand on her throat.

Will continues his explanation. Is this how he speaks in the Star Chamber? Maybe he already has. "Yes, Margaret. Even Henry Tudor could convince people of the legality of his place in the succession."

Oh God, Will sees her ambition as plain as day.

"And as these men fight over the throne like a pack of starving dogs," he continues, "England would be plunged into war again."

Margaret turns abruptly away and walks to the desk. Soon the scratching resumes, serrating my nerves as she continues her letter.

Wrapping his case, Will kneels again by my side, takes my hands. "And when others make that inevitable claim to England's throne, they will stop at nothing to permanently remove the princes to prevent retaliation. Nothing. Gloucester cannot risk their lives."

"So you choose to publicly declare my godson a bastard and murder his uncle," I whisper, as spent and dead as an empty snail shell picked clean by a crow. "Now you tell me that you are doing this to save Ned's life?"

"I choose publicly to save England, keep the princes from harm," replies Will. "I am simply doing what Gloucester commands of me. And what the law dictates."

God damn the law.

And God damn Richard, Duke of Gloucester.

20

Summer 1483 | The Tower of London

When Will leaves for Lord Gloucester and the chaos of Westminster Palace, I hurry Meg to my private chamber, away from Margaret's incessant letter writing. Fractured thoughts race through my mind, and I must talk to someone I can trust.

"I have to go to Ned," I say simply. "He needs me more than any time in his life before."

Meg leans back against the door, keeping it shut. "It's too dangerous."

"I don't care." Nothing in heaven or on earth can stop me. Whatever his fate, Ned will not face it alone. "I must find out what Richard and Harry have told the princes. And warn Ned to be on the alert for changes in his captivity." Suddenly, he is an inconvenient former king. Just as Henry VI was after Ned's father retook the throne.

"Then I'm coming with you," Meg says. "We'll go now. Before curfew makes the city even more dangerous."

Already I am tugging on my sturdy brown leather street shoes, fastening my skirt clips in place. "No, Meg. I'm not going to risk you coming with me."

An inconvenient king. The horrible reality of my words repeat in my mind, crowding out any other thoughts.

"You don't have a choice," Meg says in her voice that I know means she will not budge.

I dig in my casket for the passes Gloucester issued, for God only knows how I will get beyond the guards at the Tower. With Meg's eyes upon me, I hesitate and then pull out both of them. "Thank you."

Maybe these will work. I have no other solution if the Tower is locked down.

We hurry back down the stairs and into the aromatic corridor that leads to the kitchens. Meat is roasting, bread is baking; for my household, it is a normal day. For me, my wheel of destiny has come loose from its axel and run away out of control. I pick up my cloak, hand a shawl to Meg, check my purse for coin. Enough to get us to Tower Wharf. And more to slip into a palm if needed. "We'll go by barge. It's safer and quicker."

Stepping into the alley that runs alongside Le Ryall, we descend Garlick Hill. The crowds are still milling like sheep driven to St. Swithin's Fair, the shock of Shaw's sermon keeping people outside, straining for more news. Just the few streets from Le Ryall down to the riverbank are frantic with armed soldiers hunting for food and a bed, merchants hawking pies at triple price, and foolish apprentices running in gangs, creating havoc with their antics. There are guards on every corner now, slippery-eyed and watchful. They are a mismatch of liveries, some Gloucester, some Buckingham, some Stanley. There are more I don't recognise from other noble households. Someone in the heart of Westminster is coordinating this, planning for an uprising.

Bastards.

I am preoccupied with Will's explanation, his lawyer's concise reckoning of the wanton, lustful, and reckless behaviour of the king that has jeopardised England's throne and threatens his sons' lives.

Bastard. Dear God. What does the queen know?

"Meg, did Will say? Is the queen party to this deception? Did she know of the Talbot pre-contract?"

Meg's reply is scattered between the shoving of the crowds and our haste to the river pier at Blackfriars. "How could she not know?" She flinches as a fat flour-dusted baker treads on her foot. "Was it that much of a secret?"

"So the Woodville woman stays in sanctuary to save her own skin from being complicit in this?" We bump up against a crush of people on the wharf; the boats are rowing in and barely stopping at the wooden jetty before they bob out to the river again, full to the brim and dangerously low in the water.

"I have not heard of her leaving," Meg calls back.

So she hides still in sanctuary after she gives up both sons to her husband's loyal brother, the man the king named protector as he lay dying. Yet so broken is the trust that she cannot deal with Richard directly in this time of crisis. And the news of Lord Rivers's and her son's execution will surely drive her to madness.

"Get in, my ladies," the bargeman shouts at us. "I got no time for dallying. Plenty more custom behind you."

Everyone around us is talking about my boy and Dickon.

Bastards.

I am so grateful for Meg's company as we are rowed downstream to the Tower. Convention does not permit me to travel alone, and I will draw unwanted attention to myself as a single woman of noble class. I clench my purse tightly on my lap, the precious passes folded inside.

What are the options for how I will present myself at the Tower to gain entry? The royal godmother, Baron Scrope's wife, the Countess of Richmond's sister, the Duke of Buckingham's cousin? I bite the inside of my cheek to stifle a bitter laugh at these identities. Where is Elysabeth St.John in all these? I am all and nothing. But like a chameleon, I will assume the role that helps my true intent to gain entry to the Tower and comfort Ned.

Our barge sails on the ebbing tide, past the steelyard and Coldharbor, past a man watering his horses, a woman fishing, her skirts tucked up around her plump white thighs. I grip the rough wooden bench as we glide through the pontoons of the bridge, but today there are no rapids; in contrast to the frenzy on land, the silvery Thames slides indolently out to sea with all the time in the world.

As we draw closer to the Tower, I consider what I need to accomplish. This river journey has given me time to think more deeply. Simply comforting Ned is not enough. I need to convince him that he is now facing the biggest threat of his young life.

"What concerns you the most, Belle-maman?" Meg reads my thoughts, breaks my silence. "I can help explain your fears to Will, advise him what we think is best for the boys."

"I don't even know where to start," I reply. "But there is such dread in my heart that I know I must warn Ned to be vigilant."

"Dread? When we know Richard only wishes what is best for his nephews?"

"We think those are his wishes, Meg. I have not seen proof."

An inconvenient king. Those who are closest to Ned are those he must hold the farthest arm's length away. How tragic that between both his uncles, I cannot tell which to trust, Richard or Harry.

At the wharf, we disembark with those who have permission to visit the Tower; some to serve in the bakehouses and kitchens, others arriving to work at the mint or the armory. I pull out the passes and grip them tightly. As we inch towards the Byward Gate, we follow behind a crowd of country women carrying baskets of berries and produce. Even in times of crisis, the Tower must still eat.

I dip into my purse, pull out a handful of coin. One is the newly minted angel with Ned's likeness on it. "For luck," I whisper to myself, "for luck."

"Here." I thrust the money at the woman standing next to me holding a panier of fragrant wild strawberries nesting in hay. "I'll take your berries. For this."

She gawps at me, and I know I am overpaying. But at what cost comes access?

"Give them to me," I command.

The woman shuts her mouth and hands me her basket. We are at the Byward Gate. I take Meg's arm.

"Your business?" The guard is taller than me by a foot, with shoulders as wide as the gate, it seems.

"We are taking a gift of berries to the princes," I say, my throat dry.

"From who?" The guard demands. "And where are your passes?"

"From their uncle, the Duke of Gloucester." I thrust the papers at him, hold the basket close.

"They ain't allowed visitors."

"We are not visitors," I snap back. "We are family."

The guard snatches the paper, mouths each word carefully. "Godmother, eh?"

"Godmother," I reply firmly.

He eyes us both. Meg smiles winningly. I grip the panier so tightly my knuckles turn white, and I have to loosen my fingers. If I don't see Ned now, I don't know when I will get this close to him again.

We are holding up the crowd behind us, and I am teetering in the yes-or-no balance of the guard's thinking.

Let. Me. Pass.

"Go on."

We are through. We walk under the portcullis, and a bubble of glee rises in my chest and threatens to burst from my mouth in laughter. I swallow it back. I also remember another time I entered through this gate, parading on horseback with Harry and Ned as I triumphantly delivered my godson into the Tower to prepare for his coronation. Pride before a fall, I tell myself. Pride before a fall.

"This way," I say to Meg. We trudge up the cobblestoned slope to the entry by the Garden Tower, and there are more guards, yet we are not stopped. If we were allowed through the Byward Gate, we must have permission to have come this far. It is an advantage to be a woman. For we are not questioned when we are serving such a menial purpose as bringing food to prisoners. Or perhaps there is no more need to guard a bastard king without prospects or throne.

At the path's turn to Tower Green, I know Meg and I both thinking the same thing.

"The garden." Meg points to a wicket gate leading into the Lieutenant's orchard.

I agree. "Knowing those boys, they'll be out to tease the chicks before long."

How simple. The men put guards on doors and bar up the windows, clutch swords and brandish daggers. It takes a woman to know where boys play, even when they are young men. In the end, I come into the Tower of London as plain Elysabeth, godmother.

Slipping through the gate, Meg and I walk under a fragrant canopy of fruit trees. The peaches are ripe and the branches laden, hosting wasps drunk on juice oozing from the splitting skins.

"We can wait here," I say. "No one will bother us." I sit on a shaded bench by the henhouse, and a dove takes up an insistent cooing in the cote overlooking the herb garden. There is silence and peace, and the fragrance of lavender and rosemary scenting the air adds a dreamlike quality. It is a strange contrast against the city's frantic streets.

Within in the refuge of the peaceful gardens, it is possible to think of Ned leaving and none of us ever returning. As the country and Parliament comes to terms with his new station in life, he will be awarded manors and country estates of his own to enjoy. His life under Richard will be a pleasant one as he grows into manhood—a trusted nephew, born on the wrong side of the blanket but still trained in royal protocol and courtly ways. The shock of this morning's announcement is turning into pondering the opportunities that lie ahead for the boys. And the life I can help make for them. As soon as I can get him out of the Tower.

"We could be at home at Bletsoe," I say to Meg, feeling a sense of peace stealing over me with the fragrance of the roses and lilac surrounding us. "I feel like a girl again. And it would be a lovely life for the boys."

Meg closes her eyes. She shares the same peaceful memories, for it was my family home that we would escape when Lord Zouche became too ill-tempered and I longed for the comfort of childhood again.

"Godmother!"

Before me stands Ned, Dickon beside him, both grinning. "Why are you here?" They are grubby, their faces shining red and perspiring. The puppy sits at Dickon's heels, and both of Ned's knees have scraped holes in his hose.

"I miss you," I say carefully. "And so Meg and I decided to visit the Tower and see how you are."

Ned shrugs. "A bit bored, but we are fine. It is quiet, though. We have been on our own all day. I am surprised there is not more activity since my coronation is just a day away."

I shiver as a shadow races across the sun. *Surely not. Surely he doesn't think* . . . Suddenly, the buzzing of the bees sounds discordant, louder, more aggressive. *Surely not.*

"Has no one been to visit you?" I ask. "Your uncles Harry or Gloucester?"

"No." Ned shades his eyes, peers around the garden. "And I still have yet to hear from Lord Rivers. It is most unlike him. I'd have thought by now he would be here with me on the eve of my crowning. He promised he would see me to the throne when we first left Ludlow." With the short attention of a youth, he swats at a wasp, jumps up and down as he avoids the sting. "Dickon, should we search the patch by the back door? We haven't looked there yet."

Ned turns his gaze back to me. "Treasure," he says happily. "We're hunting for lost treasure."

My heart is beating so fast blood pounds in my ears as I am caught in a net of indecision. Should I be the one to tell the prince of all that is happening? It is not my place. And yet . . . how will he be told by Harry or Gloucester? Certainly not with a mother's tenderness. The queen has shown no sign of leaving sanctuary. She will not be available to hold Ned close, tell him the terrible truths about his beloved father. Nor warn him about the conflict that lurks just over the horizon.

I thought I was coming to comfort Ned, help him deal with his new position. Instead, I am the one to break the news to him. That alone tells me that Richard cares little for Ned's happiness.

"Sit here next to me, Ned." I keep my voice steady and low. "Meg will take Dickon to look for the treasure."

My daughter knows what she has to do and leaves with the ten-year-old boy who is no longer his brother's heir. His telling will be easier. I am the one who has to warn the king that one uncle has declared him a bastard and the other has stolen his throne.

I take Ned's hands. They are roughened even since I last held them. He is playing hard at his sports and recreation. "My darling," I begin. "I need you to be brave again."

His eyes light up. "Like King Arthur?"

I pause, let the garden tranquility steady me, knowing that how I speak will do terrible damage whichever way I tell the story.

"Ned, there are matters that have come to light that will affect your future." I take a deep breath. "In the simplest of terms, there is a legal issue which cannot be changed."

He turns serious, his young face solemn. And still his jaw is reddened and swollen. Do these wretched physicians neglect him? A few drops of myrrh are needed to soothe.

"Continue, Lady Scrope," he replies. His use of my formal name grants us both the distance we need.

I grip his fingers. "There was a contract. A betrothal between your father and Lady Eleanor Talbot. Long before he met your mother, even longer before you were born."

He is attentive, quiet.

"The contract means that he was not legally allowed to marry your mother." Is this sufficient? Does he know what comes next?

"Go on," he commands. He is not shy to hear the truth.

"And because he was not allowed to marry your mother, when he did, that marriage was invalid."

"That is not true." Ned turns his head away, tries to withdraw his hands.

I do not let him. "Ned, my darling, do you know what this means?"

Softly, so softly under his breath that I am not sure he has spoken aloud or if I am sharing his thoughts, my godson whispers, "I am a bastard."

Then cries aloud, "I am a bastard."

Bastard.

He snatches back his hands. Stands straight like a man, not slump-shouldered like a boy. Across the verdant and humming garden, Dickon waves at us. Meg catches his wrist, kneels before him to look into his face, and begins talking.

Ned lifts his chin. "A bastard cannot reign."

"No."

"I will not be crowned king."

"No, my darling, you will not."

"And my Uncle Richard inherits the throne, then?"

I take his hand, stand by his side, shoulder to shoulder as he looks up at the great White Tower, across to the Royal Palace, over towards the Lieutenant's House. I see his eyes dart from one to another, and I know that the familiar buildings are no longer the same, for they no longer belong to him. These are the times when I would rush to fill silence like water racing over a sluice gate. But for the true knowledge to sink in, for my boy to understand how much has changed and has been taken away from him, I cannot coat the truth with shallow words of cold comfort.

The Bell Tower peals a quarter hour. Curfew approaches. The sun drops behind the great inner walls, and a sudden chill falls upon the garden, releasing a sharp scent of damp earth and cold stone. It is no longer a comforting place to sit.

"I do not know what will happen today or tomorrow, Ned," I say as gently as I can. I must warn him and not frighten him. "I do not know who will visit you or send for you or take you far away."

He looks at me, startled. "Send me away?"

"I will not let them," I rush now to comfort, without knowing how I can possibly make good on this promise.

Even as I speak, guards approach us, marching like an ant line across the grass and around the bushes. There must be at least a dozen strong men, bearing pikes and swords and stern expressions.

"These are my guard," Ned says. "They have done this the last three nights. I thought it was because of the coronation approaching, but . . ." his voice trails off.

I cannot risk staying and being discovered. It is one thing to visit as Elysabeth St.John. But Richard of Gloucester cannot be told that Lady Scrope, the wife of his favourite loyal lord, is whispering secrets with the bastard prince.

"I must leave, my darling," I say. "Be most prudent in your actions, stay close to the Garden Tower, and do not believe all who come to your side." I waver for a moment, go with the feeling that is deep in my heart. "And if your Uncle Harry comes for you, pretend you are too ill to travel, that your cheek is hurting too much, so you must take to your bed."

"And then?" Ned looks at me calmly, and I realise again he is a prince of the realm, that he is versed in the stories of betrayal and intrigue that have plagued his family for generations. He is not frightened. Even still, it breaks my heart to be the one who destroys his innocence.

"I will come for you. I will come back, I promise." Meg is hurrying towards me, and I know she has heard the curfew warning. I must leave, with hollow words and impulsive promises.

God damn you, Richard of Gloucester.

"Did he know this, Godmother?" His voice cracks, wavering between man and youth. "Did my Uncle Richard know this when we wrote our names together in that inn and he swore loyalty to me forever?"

Tears now spill from my eyes, for I can no longer hold them at bay. And still I wonder why it is me telling Ned of his future, me telling him of his uncles' betrayal. "No, Ned, I cannot believe he did."

Ned looks around the orchard, the Garden Tower, and back again to the great White Tower looming over the wall. "And so where do I go now?" he asks. "Where do I go?"

"I do not know," I reply. "But I will come back for you."

21
Summer 1483 | Le Ryall

"I had to tell my godson," I spit the words at Jack, ignoring his white face, the lines of exhaustion filled with dust from the road. He arrived at Le Ryall just after I returned from the Tower, expecting a hero's welcome, no doubt.

Think again, Husband.

"I had to tell Ned of his father's disgrace, his mother's betrayal, his own bastard birth."

Jack shakes his head, rubs his eyes wearily. "I am sorry, Elysabeth. I got here as soon as I could. It was not my intent that you should bear this alone."

"I could not tell him the worst. I could not tell him of his other losses. Lord Rivers? His half-brother Grey?" I bite down to keep the burning vomit from rising in my throat. "Gloucester executed them. Executed the queen's brother and son!"

"They were planning an uprising. So goes war. Besides, Catesby looked out for Rivers. He is an executor of his will. He will see his family is provided for."

"These are the times I do not know you."

"You know, like you, I am loyal to peace in England."

"I know nothing," I shout. "And now you ride into London at the head of a force of northerners, celebrating the ascent of your precious Richard of Gloucester to the throne? Was that the plan all along? You were bringing an army to celebrate victory, not one to quell unease."

The parlour at Le Ryall is too small to hold my rage, and I run from the room to seek a wider horizon, slamming the door behind me. Grabbing my shawl from the peg, I leave the house, ignoring convention, safety, and Londoners unleashing their evening's entertainment at the city's inns.

146

The sun has dropped behind the topsy-turvy roofs, and I crave open space. Garlick Hill sends me down to the Thames. Although rubbish has washed up on the river's mud banks and gravelly shores, the breeze ripples from the east, carrying the call of sea on white gull wings. I stoop beneath a weeping willow and catch my breath, searching beyond the river's curve for the distant horizon, where the boys lie behind bars in the Garden Tower and Richard of Gloucester lies in the royal palace with the crown dancing before his eyes.

I am not melancholy that my godson is prevented from taking the throne. It makes no difference to my love for Ned whether he is king or bastard. I am not a born courtier. I care not to scratch and claw my way into favour or spend sleepless nights fretting the name of my next betrayer.

No, I am beside myself with fear that these boys will be the alchemy of insurrection, pawns in the battle for England's throne. For surely men true to King Edward, whose memory is still so fresh among them, will never allow his brother to usurp the beloved young heir and steal the throne.

The inconvenient king. When I was pardoned by Ned's father, the king he had just defeated in battle was locked in the Tower, just yards from where we celebrated. The next morning he was dead. Some even whispered it was at Gloucester's hand, but I could never believe that. At the time.

Now, I wonder. Wonder what lies ahead for Ned. Wonder what I must do.

I haven't even dared think about what lurks in the darkest chambers of Margaret's heart, ambition for her son crawling like a maggot through the carcass of lost dreams.

Dear Mother Mary, all I desire is peace. And all men crave is war.

The river is churning with fishermen hauling nets from the running tide, water drops sparkling in the red westerly sun. The gulls wheel overhead, calling others to join them in the bounty. Women stand gossiping on the banks, ready to sort the catch. They are living their lives oblivious to which king rules. Perhaps that is the ultimate power.

A touch on my waist and I swing around.

"You must believe that Gloucester only wants what's best for Ned and Dickon." Jack has followed me, his face full of concern.

"And himself." I cannot reconcile. I refuse to agree.

"And the country. Will must have explained to you the reasons he had to act so quickly."

I stride from the dappled shade of the grieving willow, follow the river's path east. I need the breeze on my cheeks, the sun warming my back. Anything to prove life can still hold simple pleasure. I want to walk all the way to the Tower and confront the man who told my boy he would always be faithful, who signed his name next to Ned's with his motto under it.

Loyaulté me lie.

A damned lie, indeed.

Jack's footfall is behind me. I do not turn. I cannot bear to see him. I shout into the wind, the words flying back over my shoulder for my husband to catch as he wishes. "And Harry? Why is Harry so eager to turn Gloucester into a king? He started this, raked up Talbot's old story, convinced Shaw to preach the sermon, persuaded the city to declare their willingness to accept him as king."

"It's for stability, Elysabeth. He knows the price of families at war. Just as water rushes in to fill an empty vessel, so would enemies shipwreck a kingdom with a bastard child king." Jack strides before me, blocks my path. "It is not the boys you should be worrying about," he says.

I cannot go around him without walking into a patch of nettles. The track is narrow; the river laps at my feet, staining my indoor slippers.

"What do you mean?"

My husband rubs his beard, squares his shoulders. "This opens old wounds and new ambitions. We can predict what Harry Stafford wants, and Gloucester is keeping him satisfied with a steady stream of land and revenues. My Lord Gloucester will take care of King Edward's children, the girls included, for all are now bastards because of the Talbot pre-contract." Jack's narrowed green eyes reflect the western radiance, and I dread his next words, for this is an old argument we rake over in times of stress. It burrows deep into our York and Lancaster roots, lops any shoots of reconciliation.

I save him the trouble of invoking my sister's name. "Margaret. She will re-assert Henry's Tudor claim."

He nods. "Not immediately, for she is too cunning for that. But at some point. And you must be clever and quick on your feet, Elysabeth, that she does not drag you with her into challenging the rightful new King Richard and attempting to put her own son on the throne."

148

There is an inevitability about the next days, where time passes with each quarter-hour peal from London's churches. I remember the dark indelible November nights of sanctuary, time measured by bells tolling. There is no stopping them, and I hear far too many. They peal through the hot July nights, where despite the evil humours that creep into the city after sundown, our windows are open and the bells of St. Michael Paternoster and St. John the Baptist and St. Thomas the Apostle crash across my hot and sweat-drenched pillow.

I still cannot look at Jack without seeing betrayal, and fortunately he is in lodgings at Westminster Palace, drilling his troops and preparing for whatever insurrection they think is coming. I say "fortunately" because I cannot share a bed with him while this shroud of anger binds me.

On the sixth day of July, we stand together for the first time since we walked by the river. We are before the doors of Westminster Abbey, and London's cheers crash over my head like a tempest as Gloucester and his meek little Neville wife approach. As the about-to-be-anointed king, he spent last night in the Palace of the Tower. The Tower! Did he visit Ned and Dickon? Did he go on bended knee as before or make Ned bow to him? Bestow a Judas kiss on his cheek?

How betrayed my boys must feel.

My heart drowns in sorrow's well. Here I am, encircled by all the nobles of the land while Ned and Dickon lie abandoned in a cold stone room surrounded, not by knights and pages and heralds, but by guards. Are they to protect the princes or prevent escape? I blink away a tear of anger, fracturing the day in a prism of colours, for spread upon the ground are costly fabrics and red-and-white striped carpets, and above our heads are canopies twinkling with gold-threaded stars.

All this was created for Ned. All now is grabbed by Gloucester.

"Here they come!" Jack's voice thrums with excitement. His face is alive with joy; he believes Gloucester's—*and Harry, for he is the face of the kingmakers*—solution a good one, a fateful destiny on the turn of Fortune's wheel.

Richard, Duke of Gloucester, and his wife—for I cannot think of them as the king and queen—arrive and walk barefoot past us, a sign of humility. Hypocrites! Jack and I fall into place behind them in the procession. Jack is so proud of his lord's elevation, and I am so miserable at my boys' descent.

And there, in the highest position of state, walks Margaret and Lord Stanley, she carrying Anne Neville's train; Stanley, the Chamberlain's mace. Their allegiances twist in the wind like vanes upon a church tower. Charlatans.

At the high altar, Richard and Anne appear in their specially crafted undergarments designed to portray humility, their heads bare. How long have the seamstresses been preparing these clothes? Richard presents his pale and muscular back, one shoulder lower, his hip tilted to the right, as if he is casually waiting for a sign from God. My sign from God would be to strike him dead, for I cannot reconcile this man who tearfully pledged loyalty to Ned at that roadside inn with the traitorous uncle who has stolen the crown.

"We are preserving the monarchy, my love, preventing anarchy." Jack joins with Will's defence and repeats this legal excuse over and over until he sounds like a stumbling student of law reciting his primer.

"Save your verses, Jack. And leave the legal opinions to Will. They do not sit well on you." I despise every word they utter. Gloucester has the power to deny Shaw's sermon, ride over the claims put forth, even declare the bastardy an untruth, for God was the only other witness. He seizes a different opportunity.

The ceremony is over.

The blessing sticks in my throat. I cannot wish King Richard the Third of England a long life.

Jack takes my hand. "Come, love," he whispers, his voice cracking with embarrassment. "Your face is thunder. For all of our sakes, do not show your wrath so plainly. King Richard has done no wrong. He is a good and kind and fair uncle."

Another lie I am asked to perpetrate. I smack his hand away, hug my arms around myself, and march on ahead, caring not who whispers that the Lord and Lady Scrope are in dispute.

The richly woven carpet leads from the abbey to the great hall of Westminster. Jack, along with Catesby, is seated at the barons' table close by Richard, and I find my place with Meg.

My daughter kisses my cheek, holds me tightly. "Belle-maman, sit with me," she whispers. "You cannot change this day, and so please accept your place and support your husband."

"And who is supporting my godson and his brother?" I hiss back. "Who is looking out for them? If I break my godmother's oath and ignore their plight, will Jack say prayers to release me from purgatory?"

"Will says the king will take care of Ned and Dickon. They have already had discussions as to where the boys can best be brought up. Richard's bastards are housed comfortably at Sheriff Hutton. It is a luxurious home, surrounded by forests and hunting—all two boys could wish for." Meg presses me onto the bench. "Have something to drink. Eat. The boys will be fine."

"They are not just bastards. Ned is the rightful King of England, Dickon his heir," I say. Does no one think as I do? Meg's practical words rip at my heart. "Your husband takes care of Richard's needs first. The princes have no one to speak for them."

A blare of trumpets and drunken shouts echo from the walls and rafters as the doors are thrown open. The King's Champion, seated on a huge black destrier resplendent with trappings of gold, red, and white silk, gallops into the hall. The knight throws down his gauntlet to challenge any man who opposes King Richard. I half rise to my feet— *I do*—and Meg pulls me down again before I can open my mouth.

Jack scowls from his position of honour. We have never been in such discord. My husband is Richard's man through and through and does not see the wrong. In my heart, I cry for those years when Jack rejoiced in Ned's company, looked upon him as his own son. All tossed on the midden heap of King Edward IV's duplicity and betrayal.

Harry presides at the king's right hand, and Margaret serves the queen her courses in a position of great honour. From the proud set of her shoulders, she relishes her role.

Hypocrite. I wonder at your ability to swing in the winds of fate so swiftly.

As the abbey bells crash above our heads, I remember Cheyneygates and Elizabeth Woodville on that November night of Ned's birth. How fares she today, locked again in sanctuary, just yards away, now alone with her daughters, her two sons captive in the Tower? I bow my head, but no prayers come. I cannot but think the queen brought this upon herself, complicitly and secretly, thinking her bone-bred witchery above fate. I confronted her upon my arrival, a cuckoo in her York nest, a godmother thrust upon her with no option to accept me. Perhaps I should visit her in sanctuary again tomorrow and demand we discuss a solution. After all, Ned is our son.

I blink and return to the feast, where course after course of fantastic foods on gold and silver platters parade before us, and I am so heartsick I cannot force one bite down my throat as I think of the princes eating mutton from pewter in the loneliness of their guarded tower.

Jack and Catesby and Harry and Stanley sit elevated at the high table, laughing and drinking together, while I am left with the cold company of my bitter thoughts.

This day should have been Ned's.

Where will he go now?

And how can I protect him?

Without question, my vow at his birth is more important than it has ever been in his short life.

22

Summer 1483 | Westminster

"Tell me once more why you have decided you cannot leave London?" Jack flings his challenge as soon as we reach our chamber within Le Ryall, for after the feast he returned to our home, but was silent the entire ride from Westminster. "Not only do you sit with a face like thunder through the entire coronation, you decide now to snub the king and make a fool of me by not travelling with us? Meg and Will leave by week's end. Why not you?"

Richard is setting out on a grand progress across his newly stolen realm. Jack says I must call him the king; in my mind, he will always be Gloucester. He has ordered Jack and Lord Stanley to accompany him as he shows his newfound force around the country. He invites Jack because he trusts him, commands Stanley because he doesn't.

I turn my back, pick up my surcoat where I have dropped it on a bench. "I have commitments here that are more important." I throw the fabric over my shoulders, pull it tight, more for comfort because the July night is still warm.

"More important than honouring your king?" Jack explodes. "And where are you going?"

"I *am* honouring my king," I snap. "The true king. I have heard nothing these past days that assures me that Richard has any plan for the boys, any thought other than keeping them locked in the Tower under watch." I push past him, leave him standing in our chamber. If I have to sleep alone tonight, I will, even with him here and standing before me, for I still cannot bring myself to lie with him. "I have nothing more to say to you. Go on your progress, build your precious Richard's reputation across the country. I'll consider joining you at the end of the month at Minster Lovell, once I have assured myself that Ned and Dickon are in good hands and are treated with the respect and care they are due."

"Don't bother sending any messengers to tell me of your arrival," Jack retorts. "I shall not be looking for you."

I ignore his words and the hurt in his eyes and leave, closing the door deliberately with a soft click that speaks much more than if I had slammed it.

Immediately upon our husbands' departure, I send Margaret a message to meet me at Westminster. If anyone can help me persuade the queen that she must lobby Gloucester for the boys' release, it is Margaret, and so I walk with my sister in the privy gardens, where the palace boundaries meet those of the abbey. Those ladies who have not gone on progress drift through the scented gardens, sipping cordials and chattering like sparrows in the hidden arbours. A fountain splashes rainbow drops onto a glistening granite stone, and beneath a cool fern-lined ledge a frog croaks his rhythmic litany.

"The coronation went smoothly," Margaret's bland statement hangs in the still summer air, and I look at her sharply. She is not one for idle talk, so she is leading somewhere with this remark. "And I am delighted that my husband enjoyed a place of honour with the king."

Hold your friend close and your enemy closer. The king has his reasons, Sister.

As she prattles without waiting for me to respond, the ladies surrounding us gradually fall out of step until we are left alone. Margaret quietens. I am distracted more by her silence than her words.

"Margaret, I asked you to join me for a specific reason," I say bluntly. "I have no desire to talk about the coronation or Richard or how effectively you manipulated Harry to secure the position of honour in the procession."

"You must admit Lord Stanley has recovered admirably from his recent fall from grace," she says demurely. "Helped, of course, by me."

"I would not doubt for one moment that you did not have a hand in your and Lord Stanley's reinstatement," I reply. "Which is why I need you here now. You have spent more time with the queen than I have these past years, and you will open the door to Cheyneygates for me now."

"How intriguing," she says lightly. I take her arm and lead her away from the ladies of the court, away from the knot gardens and lavender beds. "And what brings on this urgency?" She looks at me shrewdly. "Is it the princes?"

"Get me before the queen," I repeat. I can see her thoughts as if they are written across her forehead. She is looking for how this will benefit her. I am looking for how she can help me.

"As you wish." She grabs a handful of sage plant that spreads across the paving, and the spicy aroma is trapped in our skirts and scents our steps. Now we are alone, and I lead my sister to a narrow path hidden between glossy privet hedges. This snakes round to the side of the abbey, by the abbot's house. I know it well, for this is where I directed the scullion boy to pick nettles for the queen's confinement.

Unlatching the scullery door to Cheyneygates, I take her hand and slip into the shaded room. The kitchens have not changed since I sat on the fireplace bench so many years ago with Meg, and I know in the dark and with my eyes closed I could find my way to the boteler's pantry, the birthing chamber we created together.

At our sudden appearance, the abbot's steward pauses in his discussions with the cook, and Margaret is all charm.

"Master Harris," she purrs. "Excuse my informal appearance, but I did not want to call attention to our presence. My physician, Dr. Carleon, suggested that my sister and I should visit the queen to discuss her health." She reverently placed the sage on the table as if offering a priceless curative from a London apothecary. "Women's matters. And of course, you are aware Lady Scrope attended her in childbirth."

The man flushes and ducks his head back to his inventory lists. These things are not discussed in male company.

Margaret pulls me through to the service passage, obviously familiar with the layout of the warren of rooms. It is not the first time she has visited the queen in sanctuary. For me, it is a strangely disconnected return to a dark period in my life.

When we enter the Jerusalem Chamber, the abbey bells strike, my past and present connect, and I relive my first meeting with the queen. Today feels the same and yet so very different.

Even in the dim light, Elizabeth Woodville is haggard, a crone compared to the sleekly ripe and beautiful woman I first met in this room twelve years ago. The surroundings have not altered, the tapestries still drape the walls, the window still faces out to the gargoyle and abbey, but the queen is almost unrecognisable. In a strange parody of my first encounter, her daughters sit at her feet, only now there are

155

two more, and the eldest, Bess, has grown into a pretty lass of sixteen or seventeen summers.

"Lady Stanley. Lady Scrope." The queen hardly seems surprised, and I suspect she has fallen into a fugue. She motions at the princesses, and they leave except for Bess, who stays at her mother's side and clasps her hands between her own, softly stroking them. Margaret stands before the queen, her face calm, almost beatific.

"Your Grace," she replies. "God be with you. And bless you in these difficult times."

"My greatest sympathy, Your Grace," I add. "Your pain must be terrible."

As the younger girls leave, the queen weeps aloud, pulls at her gold-grey hair. "I made such a terrible mistake," she cries. "I should never have released Dickon. Richard told me it was to reunite my sons, to rejoice in the crowning. Now I know it was to imprison them together and usurp the throne."

So she thinks the same as me. "A shocking event," I reply. "And one that we must remedy as quickly as possible."

"I am not sure Richard intended this to happen," Margaret says. "But now we must accept that the boys are under Richard's care."

The queen starts from her chair, paces the chamber. "Richard's *care*? The same care that executed my brother and son, usurped the throne, elevated the madman Buckingham to the highest guard in the land?"

"Care?" I have to bitterly agree. "I have seen no proof of care."

"Are they hurt, Lady Scrope?" The queen turns to me swiftly. "Please God, tell me my boys are not in pain?"

"No, no," I soothe. "Far from it, Your Grace. They are in fine health and spirits. I saw them myself just a few days ago."

Margaret chooses to ignore the queen's list of injuries to her family and instead picks out her words against Harry. "My nephew Buckingham is now Chief Constable of all England. We may find that he is of more use than you think."

"Buckingham is also my brother-in-law. And yet his loyalty to his Woodville family is highly questionable." The queen turns to me, her mouth ugly with pain. "Lady Scrope, a word. In private."

Ignoring Margaret's indignant indrawn breath, for she assisted my entry here and surely does not want to be excluded from any conversation, I follow the queen to the tall west window. I can almost see my footprints on the floor, in this familiar place where I had spent each night in sanctuary walking with Ned in my arms, each morning imploring God for Jack's safety and my own release.

And now I couldn't pray for Jack to leave me fast enough. A tangled web indeed. Did this queen have a witch premonition all those years ago?

"You saw my son at Stony Stratford before he was captured by Buckingham," Elizabeth Woodville whispers. "Before this nightmare began. How was he when Gloucester arrested him? Was he brave?"

So much loss, this woman has suffered, so much grief. I may be angry at the queen for taking sanctuary, but I cannot censure the mother in her.

"Yes, my lady," I reply. "He was not only brave, but thought first of Ned, not his own circumstance. He was at pains to reassure him that he was safe, that it was simply a mistake." I want to give her more, ease her anguish. "Your son could not have been nobler nor more dignified."

Elizabeth Woodville clasps her hands in prayer. "God rest his soul." The tears stream down her face. "And that of my brother Anthony, whose only fault was that he was too perfect for this earth."

I bow my head under the weight of the queen's anguish. Margaret is staring furiously at me, cocking her head as if to ask what the queen is telling me. Disregarding my sister's agitation, I venture to touch the queen softly on her shoulder. After all, she is Ned's mother on earth. And I am Ned's mother in God's presence.

"Your Grace, about Ned and Dickon," I say gently. "As soon as I heard the news, I went to the Tower to comfort them."

The queen places her hand over mine and clings tightly. "My boys?" she asks. "No one will tell me when they come back here. Or when I can take them away from London and retire to the country."

I hide my dismay. *Oh, surely this queen does not think it is that simple.*

"It may take a while," I say carefully, not wanting to reveal my own anxiety. "My husband says that the king has thought that Sheriff Hutton may be the best place for them."

"In with his brood of bastards?" the queen spits, suddenly animated. "Never. When will I ever see them? For two princes of the royal blood to rot in some northern keep is not in their best interests."

"We will not let that happen, Your Grace," I reply, relieved to now see her emotions again.

"You promise me, Lady Scrope?" She scrabbles at my hand, pulls me close to her face. "Remember the night Ned was born? I know what happened. I know you saved his life. Now, for the sake of the bond we have between us, you must save his life again."

I have no choice. He is my boy too.

She draws me away from the window, sits at the massive table, and beckons Margaret to join us. The tears have gone, and in their place a queen speaks. "All my children must be taken to safety. Now. London is quiet. Everyone is with Richard."

All her children? I just wish to take the boys from the Tower. Now she wants to remove her daughters from sanctuary as well?

"I don't—" I begin.

"I agree," interrupts Margaret. She bows her head as if thinking deeply. Or praying. In the quiet of sanctuary, only the rustling of the doves perched on the window ledge disturb our silence. And the clicking of my sister's rosary beads. "The girls should be free."

Seven. Eight. Nine. Ten.

Jack's words flood into my thoughts. *Beware your sister,* he said. *Beware that she does not pull you into her web of intrigue.*

The queen grasps at my sleeve, her fingers like claws, the nails bitten to the quicks. "Elysabeth, you must seize this time to take back control of Ned. And bring Dickon too. It's just until Richard returns and I can negotiate a proper and lasting arrangement." A light comes over her face, and she grips my arm more tightly. "We could send them to their aunt in Burgundy. You and the Duchess have known each other well for many years since you were in her bridal party. You could escort them."

"No, no, Your Grace, I cannot—" I shake my head to clear my mind. *This is madness.* It would be impossible for me to escort the princes to Burgundy. Jack already is furious that I have defied him to stay in London. Even thinking of leaving England without telling him would be a disaster for our marriage.

Click. Click. Click. Margaret's beads are still marking time.

"An excellent idea. Simple. Effective." My sister counts her beads a little faster now. "And, Your Grace, we could arrange for men loyal to your beloved husband here in London to escort them. It would not be unusual for the boys to spend some time with their aunt. And Richard was sent by his own mother to Burgundy for safety when he was their age." Two spots of colour appear in her cheeks. "It sounds very simple to me."

"Simple? Are you mad? You are considering sending them from the country?" I glance at the queen. She is hanging on Margaret's words. "Without Richard's permission?" This situation is running away from me faster than a bolting horse. I regret that I brought Margaret here at all, for she has now taken control.

"We can tell him after the fact." Margaret turns to the queen. "After all, we are simply sending them to his sister, to a royal court where they can be treated as even he would think fit."

I shake my head. "It is not a bad idea. But to do so without his permission?"

Margaret shrugs. "He is no longer the protector, for Ned is no longer the heir. It is a simple family decision that the boys' mother is making on behalf of her sons."

"I don't think Richard would see it that way," I persist. Although the idea of my boys living at the magnificent Burgundian court with the Duchess of Burgundy is an appealing one. Their mother is correct. I served under the duchess in my youth, and she is a devout and educated woman. Richard could not fault the way his sister would care for the boys.

Margaret sniffs. "He would agree if Harry and my husband put this to him. After the fact. After all, what harm is done?"

"How soon could you take them, Margaret?" the queen asks eagerly. I have the sense that a decision has been made, with or without my agreement.

"You know people here who are loyal to the deceased king, who would form a network of guards and protect your sons?" Margaret asks.

Elizabeth Woodville drums her fingers on the polished table with rising rapidity. "There are many here in London who were in King Edward's household. They would be honoured to form an escort."

Margaret leans across the table to me. Those telltale spots of colour rise in her cheeks. "We will appoint our half-brother John Welles to head the delegation, for he is familiar with the Burgundian Court and can provide a guard. A couple of extra young pages in his retinue would not be noticed."

"You say move them without permission, disguised in Welles's household? Margaret, how would you ever carry this off?" I am simultaneously horrified and intrigued with the prospect. "But the

159

Duchess of Burgundy would certainly provide an appropriate court environment for the boys—"

"It is best to act with confidence and while Richard is distracted with the first days of his reign," Margaret says briskly. "Yes. Their aunt would be happy to take them for a few months. They'll be safe there. The girls can spend the rest of the year in the country here in England, and by December the queen can leave sanctuary and join them. By then, people will have forgotten these few weeks of indecision and confusion."

So there is Margaret's plan, laid out like an intricate tapestry of dreams before us. I see the boys hunting and hawking at the Burgundian court, welcomed as the young princes they are. I see the princesses regaining their strength in the quiet and healing of an English manor.

Elizabeth Woodville smiles for the first time since we entered the room. "My sister-in-law would be delighted to take care of my sons in Burgundy. Thank you, Margaret and Elysabeth. Your help is most appreciated."

I shake my head to make the pleasing vision disappear. "Margaret, please, slow your thinking. Yes, taking the boys to their aunt is an option, but . . ." *Taking charge of the princes? Smuggling them from the country? Stanley and Harry may handle the king. How will I explain this to Jack?* I dig my thumbnail into my forefinger to hold my temper. "We can't just open the Tower gates and escort them out!"

"We cannot. But Buckingham can as Constable of England. I am sure he will exert his authority over the Constable of the Tower." Margaret dismisses my concerns as if talking about a children's outing to a country fair. "Harry will be most helpful in supporting our mission of moving the boys into a neutral, safe place. He knows that will ensure his continued loyalty to me and his wife's family, and caring for Richard's nephews will be politically highly regarded. I will talk to him immediately. And send a message to our brother Welles to meet us at Le Ryall to discuss the arrangements."

Margaret has thought of everything.

The queen turns to Bess, the princess sitting so quietly and calmly I almost forgot she is with us. "See, my sweeting, Lady Scrope and Lady Stanley will help us. They will take care of your brothers. And you and your sisters will enjoy some peace as well."

160

Bess smiles with a sweet beauty that illuminates her pale face. "Thank you both. I am most grateful for your assistance. It will put my mother's mind at rest to know they are safe with my aunt. And don't worry about my sisters and me, for we do not want to leave my mother alone."

Margaret returns the smile, looks her up and down appraisingly. "A simple solution, and one that we can all agree is right for everyone. Best not to have the princes remain in view right now as reminders of the king's controversial claim," she says. "And perhaps best you and your sisters stay concealed here with your mother in sanctuary a little while longer until we take care of your brothers."

Jack's warning about Margaret's conniving character enters my thoughts again. Fair enough to remove the boys from the Tower. Harry could do that under his watch with little suspicion. But to send them overseas? Yet the Burgundian court would be a perfect place for them to recover from the trauma of this summer. Surely Margaret has no ulterior motive. Why would it be an advantage to aid this powerless queen? She makes no reference to her own son's exile, and I am not going to invoke Henry Tudor's name at this time.

"Whatever you deem is right, Lady Stanley, for I respect your wisdom." Bess takes her mother's hand again, sits her tenderly on the window bench. "Mother, may I bring you a posset? Or perhaps I could read to you while you lay down."

The queen's head droops towards her daughter. How much she relies on her eldest child, I think. "That would be most welcome, my darling."

Bess looks up at Margaret and me. "Thank you, Lady Stanley and Lady Scrope, for your help. With your assistance, my brothers will be safe with their aunt, and my mother will rest peacefully."

Our hint to leave.

As we ride our horses through London's streets to Le Ryall, all I can think about is the conversation we will have to have with Harry, asking him to remove the princes from the Tower. And Jack. When will I tell Jack? Thank God he has already left with Richard, for I will not have to face him in a lie when I return to Le Ryall this afternoon. Best to tell him after the fact, when the Burgundian court celebrates the arrival of the young princes and Richard is riding high on his successful progress through his new realm. The absence of the boys from the Tower will be a few days' worth of gossip, nothing more.

I let Margaret's excited chatter wash over me. While I am rehearsing in my mind exactly what I will say to Jack, all my sister can talk about is what a fine young woman Bess has grown up to be. The very image of her father, the York king.

23

Summer 1483 | The Tower of London

"I will handle Harry," says Margaret. "Come with me so you can take measure of his response, but don't speak more than you need. You two are like oil and water."

Although I would prefer to not only speak to Harry, but give him a piece of my mind, I let Margaret think I agree to silence. Especially if it means I am invited inside the Tower and can see the boys.

Accompanied by a small retinue of trusted servants, Margaret and I ride from Le Ryall to the Tower of London through a sudden thunderstorm, slipping and sliding on the slick cobbles. The city is quiet, for the northern army left with the king, and London breathes a sigh of relief now that the drama of the last few weeks is over. But I know how these men of York and Lancaster ebb and flow. Under the smooth surface of a peaceful transition of power lurks a tempest that is yet to be tamed, waiting for the next gale to whip up the storm. My boys must not be the wind in the sails of rebellion. I am here with Margaret to secure Buckingham's agreement to help move them to the court at Burgundy.

At the Byward Gate, the guards wave us through when they see the Stanley livery, for Margaret and her husband are back at the top of Fortune's wheel again. We proceed along the inner ward. The rain is hammering on the leaves of the chestnut trees, and I hope this storm will break the stifling heat of the last weeks. Margaret is muffled in her great cape, and as she dismounts she clutches at the reins and almost slips, her cloak weighing her down with its soaked and muddy hem. She furiously brushes at her clothes, smearing the soil even more, and I stifle a nervous urge to laugh aloud at the disgust in her face.

"Follow me, my ladies," the guard steps forward. We are not led towards the palace, but instead to St. Thomas's Tower, the royal residence built over the iron-barred river gate. How surprising.

163

"These are the private apartments of the king." I pause at the corner of Mint Lane. "We are here to dine with the Duke of Buckingham."

The guard makes no reply but continues along the slick cobbles, and we follow up him up the stairs into the hall of St. Thomas's Tower.

A fire burns in the painted stone fireplace to dismiss the rain's chill and the damp from the river that splashes the tower's feet. The chamber is lavishly furnished with embroidered hangings and upholstered chairs, and aromas of spiced wines and cloves mingle with expensive scents of myrrh and the cleansing qualities of lavender and rosemary.

Why were my boys not housed here rather than the Garden Tower?

Harry stands before the windows overlooking the river; beyond the panes, the Stafford gold-painted barge is moored at the wharf where the king's is usually tethered. My cousin appears to have made himself quite at home.

He orders the server to pour us a cup of Rhenish and then dismisses him to wait outside in the entry porch. We are quite alone in the king's chamber, drinking the royal wine, eating the king's sweetmeats. A spatter of rain and wind rattles the windows overlooking the inner ward. A light wavers in the Garden Tower across the way. Are the boys eating their supper, saying their night's prayers?

"You are certainly taking full advantage of your position as constable, Harry." Margaret settles herself on a bench by the window, disdaining both the luxury of a cushioned bench and the warmth of the fireplace. "It is gratifying to see the honour the king pays you in allowing use of his private apartments."

Harry gestures with his cup, his sweeping movement taking in the entire room. "I make my own use," he replies. "As a prince of royal blood, I am deserving of this. As Constable of England, all chambers are open to me."

Will's words haunt me. *There are others who can raise a more legitimate claim to the throne than Gloucester.*

"A prince of the blood?" I mutter disbelievingly. "Convenient that you should remember that now, Cousin."

Margaret frowns and talks over me. "And Brackenbury does not question your move? There has always been a tradition that no one is above the Constable of the Tower within these walls."

"He does as I say," replies Harry. "Everyone does."

I swallow my revulsion. I've heard his boast of his descent from John of Gaunt before. But never while standing in a royal palace, drinking the king's wine. "Certes, you are a man of great influence. Which is why we are here, Harry."

He lifts an eyebrow. "Such haste, Elysabeth. Why not enjoy some refreshments, avail yourself of the king's and my hospitality?"

"I would rather speak of my godson and his treatment."

Margaret sips on her own wine, as delicately as if tasting Christ's blood at the altar. "Harry, you have managed matters exceedingly well during this . . . transition. What are your future plans?"

"I will consider joining the king on progress until he leaves for the North. And then tour my new properties in the Welsh Marches."

I fidget, look out upon the inner ward again, willing Ned or Dickon to come to the window across the way that I might see them.

"You must stay with us at Lathom Park," Margaret says. "We have much to discuss of the future of our family, and I would welcome your wise counsel."

I almost choke. Harry has no more sense than the master of the revels at Twelfth Night. He only repeats what he hears and acts upon command.

Harry puffs his chest, drinks again. "I would enjoy that, Aunt. It is important to me that I manage our family advancements."

Margaret tilts her head encouragingly. "I must tell you of my son's latest news," she replies. "And the visit I had recently with your sister-in-law, the dowager queen."

What about the boys? I want to shout.

As if hearing my thoughts, Margaret continues. "After we have dined, Harry, perhaps we may visit the boys for a few minutes. I know I long to see them."

Harry shrugs. "As you wish. I believe they are in good spirits. I haven't seen them for a while. They are just across the lane. You may call on your way home."

"So you do not visit them often?" My anger, not far below the surface, rises again. "Do you not think they may be afraid, lonely?"

Buckingham belches, drinks again. "They are well cared for. And besides, I will have little to do with them once they are moved to Sheriff Hutton. They are no longer of any importance to me."

"Unless they represent opposition to Richard," Margaret says softly. "And if enough people rally to return Ned to the throne,

Gloucester's seizing of power could be challenged. As will your role as kingmaker. In the streets and taverns of London, Richard is already being called the usurper. Such rumours will undermine his authority. And those of any associated with him."

Where is all this coming from? I thought we were to talk to Harry about the boys. Margaret is going off on a tangent I have no interest in. Time to steer the conversation back to our reason for seeing Harry. I don't need him distracted with Margaret's insinuations. I try to temper my sister's rhetoric. "If the boys were to be . . . removed . . . out of the public's mind for a few months, the anger at King Richard will diminish. Distractions will be lessened. His rule and his councillors will be accepted."

"And you will be credited with restoring his good graces with the people," Margaret adds. "If the boys are moved to Sheriff Hutton, they are exchanging one of Richard's prisons for another. Should they be sent abroad, say to their loving aunt in Burgundy, then whomever arranged that would immediately deserve reward for changing opinion in England favourably to Richard."

I have to stifle a laugh as Harry purses his mouth and nods sagely. "I was thinking that way myself," he says. "The idea has much merit. To the king. And to me. I will be appointed to the King's Council when I meet with him later this month and will then be consulted frequently on these kinds of matters. Perhaps after I have returned from Wales later this year, we can speak again."

Margaret lifts a delicately arched eyebrow. "The King's Council, eh? How strange, my husband made no mention when he left with the king on his progress."

"After all I have done these past months to secure Richard on the throne, it is my right." Harry tips himself more wine.

"I'd have thought so too," agrees Margaret. "But Richard's northern allies close around him like collies around a stray sheep—"

"That is a strong statement," I interrupt. What is Margaret playing at now, teasing Harry by sowing doubt into his already-clouded mind? "I am sure Harry will be admitted. I saw how the king relied upon him on our journey south."

"Relied upon Harry's army and influence." Margaret draws a finger across raindrops that are running down a leaking windowpane, blocking one and letting the other run on. Outside, the Thames flows dark, no bobbing lanterns glinting on the ripples. Few craft are abroad on such a night.

"I am already appointed to Constable of England," protests Harry, his voice rising in uncertainty. "The king needs me. I am his ally."

"But not his blood. Nor his friend." Margaret stands then, brushes the tips of her fingers together delicately, as if dismissing Harry's role. "You may think wisely, Nephew, of whether 'tis better to be the friend of a usurper king or the uncle of the rightful heir. My son."

"Margaret!" I exclaim. "You must stop this talk of Henry. For your own sake and those who love you."

Dear God. Where does she think she is going with this kind of talk?

Harry thumps his cup down, missing the table and staggering slightly. He recovers his balance, wipes his mouth with his sleeve. "Are you saying I backed the wrong horse, Margaret?"

"What Margaret means is"—I rush to distract—"perhaps not the wrong horse, Harry. But maybe not the winning one." I grab Margaret's arm, walk her to the door before she can do more damage. "Now, please send us with guard over to *your nephews* so we may talk to them about preparing for their departure."

Was I mistaken, or did Harry wince at my emphasis on his relationship to the princes?

He turns his back and shouts impatiently for a guard to escort us from the palace. Within minutes, Sir Robert Brackenbury, the Constable of the Tower, arrives, a tall, pleasingly countenanced man with a calm manner. "My Lord Buckingham?" His voice is questioning, polite.

"Take my aunt and her sister to the boys," Buckingham throws the command at him without turning from the window.

Brackenbury pauses. "As Constable of the Tower, my orders regarding the princes come from the king."

Buckingham whirls, rests his hand on his sword pommel. "As Constable of England, my orders ARE the king's. I have precedence. And as I have told you before, my nephews are under my care."

My concern about Margaret's words disappears under my worry that we may be prevented from seeing the boys. The two men stand feet apart, two dogs at bay, until Brackenbury speaks through tightened lips. "As you wish," he says quietly.

Buckingham laughs. "See, Aunt. The Tower is mine."

Brackenbury pins him with a look and lets silence speak for him. Eventually, he turns to Margaret and me. "This way, my ladies." And without bowing, or any gesture of deference, he leads us from the room.

From the king's apartment, the boys are just a few steps away; we hurry through another rain shower that slicks the path and weighs down our cloaks. There is no chance to chastise Margaret for her baiting of Harry, question why she introduced her son into the conversation. With Brackenbury leading, we are waved into the Garden Tower with no questions.

The Constable stands to one side as we squeeze through the narrow door. As I pass, he touches my arm to hold me back. "Lady Scrope," he says in a low tone. "I am relieved you have found reason to visit your godson. As you have observed, the duke has taken upon himself to command their well-being. There is little I can do." He pauses as if there is more but remains silent, bows, and leaves. My heart is fluttering as we rapidly climb the narrow spiral staircase, past the massive iron bars of the portcullis, and enter the low-ceilinged chamber.

Dickon sits alone, whittling as usual. He turns at the sound of our entry, and his face lights up. "Lady Scrope!" He runs to hug me and then hesitates as he sees Margaret.

"You remember my sister, Dickon," I assure him. "She just wants to visit you too."

He gives Margaret a wide grin and holds out the little animal he is carving. Margaret bends over it, and I see the mother in her then, the fleeting longing as she cups her hands around his to admire the carving.

"It's a unicorn," says Dickon. "Just like in Ned's favourite King Arthur story, where the unicorn looks after the lost child when his mother neglects him. I'm making one to look after him."

Margaret's expression crumples. Her heartache at missing so much of her own child's life shadows her face. In that moment, I forgive her earlier mention of Henry. I have only been separated from Ned for a few weeks, and it is grieving me. Margaret has been apart from her son for years, and that kind of absence would cut my heart out.

"Dickon, my darling, where is Ned?" I ask.

"Over there," says Dickon. Behind the screen, a whimpering that I have mistaken to be Dickon's puppy grows louder.

Sweet Ned is lying on disheveled covers, and as I lift him in my arms, he groans in pain.

"My darling boy, what has happened to you?" In the dim light, I cannot see any colour in his face, and his jaw is swollen as if he holds an apple in his cheek. Behind me a gasp, and it is Margaret, her eyes full of concern.

"Let me die," Ned mumbles. "Let me die."

He is perspiring and shivering. His pillow is sweat-soaked and dirty. There is no watered wine, no sustenance that I can see to soothe his fever. I am so furious with Harry, with Gloucester, with these men who move armies around the country without a thought and cannot care for one sick child. Margaret takes her cloak and, turning the damp to the outside, wraps it around Ned, the silver embroidery glinting in the flickering candlelight.

Dickon joins us, still clutching the little unicorn.

"How long has your brother been like this?" I ask.

"Days," replies Dickon, "but no one will pay attention to me, for they think I am making up how ill he is, and no one comes to play with us anymore, and they took away my puppy, and we're not allowed outside."

"I am so sorry, sweetheart." I smooth Ned's hair back from his brow, carefully turn over the pillow to try to find a cool spot, and draw Margaret over to the narrow window.

"It is worse than we thought," Margaret murmurs. "And yet there is hope while Harry is acting king here in the Tower that we can take advantage of his preoccupation with power and persuade him to move the boys."

"Margaret, you heard him tonight. His thoughts lie only with his own rewards for elevating Richard to the throne. And you distract him with your talk of Henry." I glance over at St. Thomas's Tower, where now a hundred candles are lighting the night and the sound of merry instruments and song lilt across the inner ward. "Buckingham knows from us now that the boys should be moved. We just need to do as we promised the queen and hope we can achieve this before Ned becomes sicker."

A gale of laughter followed by loud cheers and Buckingham's shouts makes Ned wince in pain.

169

A guard raps on the door. "Time to move on, my ladies. His Lordship just gave permission for you to see the children, not tarry long with them."

"One moment more," I call and turn to whisper to Dickon. "We have to leave now. We have to leave, but we will return."

"When?" asks Dickon.

"Very soon. And I have to ask you to be strong, my darling, and help me look after your brother."

"I don't know how," Dickon replies miserably.

I hug him. "I shall arrange for fresh bedding and food and wine to be brought in immediately. See if you can help him eat and drink, just a little at a time."

"I can do that."

"It won't be for long." I hesitate and decide not to tell him any more about our moving them from these conditions. It is not right to burden a child with keeping secrets.

Margaret tries to take her cloak, but Ned is hunched tight in it, and so she leaves him that small comfort. Kissing both boys, we hurry down the stairs together and out into the cool night. As I wrap my own cloak around Margaret, I embrace her slight figure.

"They cannot stay there, Margaret. You heard; they are barely attended to. And Ned is the worst I have seen him yet." Over Margaret's shoulder, the White Tower rises to the storm clouds, and rain gusts on the wind. The only lights I can see are in Buckingham's rooms, flaring like a beacon on a cold dark sea. The rest of the fortress is black and silent. Alone. We are so alone.

"We cannot do it alone," Margaret says, mirroring my thoughts. "And I cannot risk bringing Stanley men into this. As we said to the queen, we will call on our brother Welles to help." She looks to St. Thomas's Tower. "Let Harry follow his own conclusions, for it will take a few days for his mind to grasp all that is at stake. In the meantime, I have a plan."

I shiver. Which path is worse? Trusting Harry and leaving the princes in the Tower under his guardianship? Or removing them and facing Jack's wrath at my defiance, the king's shock at our presumption? Either way, I am going to be challenged by the outcome; and I cannot rely on Margaret to think of the results beyond her own agenda.

I put my head down into the wind and march forward, bringing Margaret along with me under my cloak. "I'll listen to your plan, Sister. But I will decide which is best, not you."

24

Summer 1483 | The Tower of London

Margaret and I wait in the parlour at Le Ryall. Our brother has been summoned to the family home, and although he is the youngest of all of us, he has grown up to have useful connections—and a deep resentment that he was on the losing side of the Cousins' Wars.

"Welles is a Lancastrian to the bone," my sister explains, for she is much closer to him than I am and has stayed in touch with him throughout the wars.

"So why is he helping the York cause?" I know little of this young half-brother who was born after I left Bletsoe to marry Lord Zouche.

Margaret looks at me as if I know nothing. And I probably don't. Politics are not my strong point. "Welles will risk much to avenge his family's losses during the wars. Do not take anything I say to him to heart. It is only the means to get our brother to agree to this simple request."

"I don't think it's that simple," I argue. "Removing the princes from the Tower while they are under the custody of Brackenbury is flying in the face of the king's orders."

Margaret shrugs. "That won't deter our brother. Welles can handle the practicalities. Harry can manage any displeasure from the king. He has proven that he can ask for anything and be given it." She gives me a glimpse into the workings of her mind. "Buckingham's wealth and power is best wielded in peace-keeping for Richard. And if Harry tells the king it was a decision he made to ensure the well-being of their precious nephews, then our action is justified by the second most powerful man in the land."

"And our brother Welles? Is he such a Lancastrian that he cares not what happens to the princes? Will he look after them on the journey to Burgundy?" In other words, can he be trusted with my precious boys?

"He will care for them as if they are his own when I show him that he has the opportunity to regain his attainted lands and title," Margaret counters. "When his father and brother were executed for their opposition to York, all their wealth was stripped from them. If Welles proves himself willing to help King Richard now by taking the boys to Burgundy, he will have the right to ask for his title and lands back."

This seems warped logic to me, but I have to trust Margaret. She is my key to a successful plan.

The parlour door opens, and Welles is admitted. My reunion with him is stilted at first, for we do not have much in common except our mother's bloodline and Margaret as a sister. But he is an affable man, and one who seems eager to please. Margaret knows how to manage him, and he eagerly receives her suggestion that helping us now will give him the access and ability to ask the king to restore his family lands and title.

"I know King Edward's wardrobe master," Welles says as he sprawls in the chair by the window. I stand, too anxious to sit still. "He still has unquestioned access to the Tower, and he has other friends who could join him in escorting the princes from there."

"The thing is, Welles," Margaret says quietly, "we can't make this a formal leaving."

"It's more a quiet removal," I add. "We don't want a big fuss nor Brackenbury really involved—"

"It's more under Harry's jurisdiction as Constable of England," finishes Margaret.

Welles ponders. "So should I provide some kind of distraction while they are smuggled out?"

I hesitate at the word *smuggle*, and then commit. "Yes."

"I can't be seen there myself," Welles says. "I'm still not exactly welcome in a Yorkist stronghold. But I can create a diversion." Our brother sits straighter, starts waving his arms around. He has the excitement of an apprentice on his Sunday afternoon off. "If my friends can walk them from the Garden Tower just a few yards to the water gate, we can meet the boys at the wharf, transfer them to a barge, and row downriver to a ship. Then I sail with them for Burgundy." Welles pauses, furrows his brow. "But how will I get them through Calais?"

I am torn. On the one hand, Welles has reduced this plan to a simple outing on the river. On the other, I am proposing removing the once King of England from the Tower of London and smuggling him to the Continent. Same decision, rather different perspectives.

"Elysabeth?" Margaret prompts.

I have an answer to Welles's concern. And am now involving another family member. "My stepson Sir John Zouche is married to John Dynham's sister. As Lieutenant of Calais, Lord Dynham guards the port." I reply. "I will give you a letter to take with you that confirms from me, as godmother of the prince, that you have permission to take Ned to his aunt for his education. It is only natural that Dickon goes with him to keep him company. Dynham will respect my instructions, especially with my stepson's endorsement."

How odd fate has turned in this unexpected direction. And how provident that my marriage to Lord Zouche has given me loving stepchildren in Meg and John who are in positions of power at this very time I need them most. Welles can present his letter of credence in Calais to get the boys through to Burgundy; Meg can ask Will to help the king understand why I have taken this action.

Simple.

And with Welles's contacts within the Tower, something that can be accomplished quickly and easily. I will be able to get the boys on their way to their aunt and still join Jack on progress in Minster Lovell, reconcile with him, for we both have now cause to celebrate. Together with Meg and Will, I can tell the king of the solution I chose to take care of the boys. After all, I am simply living by my oath.

I will protect him from evil, show him the light, and prevent those who would hurt him from ever doing so.

"Margaret, you will manage Harry," I say. "He has already told us that he overrules any orders from Sir Robert Brackenbury, the Constable of the Tower. Play to his conceit and flatter him to meet our needs to slip the boys away. Surely he can encourage the boys to be lightly guarded when we decide it's the right time."

Margaret nods, tugs at her sleeves to even them up, and addresses our brother. "It may be best to conceal the boys as pages within your household, Welles. You will need to travel swiftly, and keeping them hidden will speed your journey."

"And bring a physician with you," I add. "Ned is not well, and he must be treated for his inflamed jaw."

"Will I be in trouble?" A worried frown wrinkles Welles's broad face. "I cannot afford to further offend the king. I don't want to suffer the same fate as my brother and father."

"No," Margaret hurries to reassure him. "The Zouche name will protect you if you are stopped and questioned once you reach France."

"I will travel to Minster Lovell to tell the king at the end of the week, once the boys are on the Continent," I continue. "I am sure Jack will understand our urgency. And that we have acted in everyone's best interests. I will be able to tell King Richard of your kindness and help in safeguarding his nephews, Welles. He is bound to reward you and restore your lands and family title. After all, he only wants the best for them. They are of his blood."

Three nights later, I am hunched on a barge tethered just upriver from Tower Wharf. The heated summer thunderstorms that have lashed London for a week still sweep across the city, shattering roof tiles to the ground and striking chimneys ablaze. I perch in a boat with no livery and guards bearing no emblems, for it is best that there is no indication of who is escorting the boys. Not that anyone can really see farther than their nose in this teeming rain.

"I will meet them on the river while you stay at home," I ordered Margaret. She becomes even more demanding when she's anxious, and I do not need her nerves infecting mine. "Best you remain at arm's length, especially given Lord Stanley's recent arrest. You are only just back in favour. The boys need to see me. They may make a fuss and refuse to go if they don't know anyone. They will trust me."

The slapping of water rocks my barge as a larger vessel passes by, and I jump as the Bell Tower clock strikes seven and the church bells of All Hallows and St Peter ad Vincula toll for Compline. This is the signal that Welles's distraction is about to begin. Moments later, an updraft of embers signals where fires are sparking on Tower Hill, Cheapside, The Yarde, and the meadows all around the Tower. My heart leaps in response, and I adjust my skirt clips to make sure my feet are free so I can move quickly out of the way. The boys will arrive any moment. While the Tower guards are skeltering across the land to extinguish the fires, Welles's men will bring them through the water gate to the river and me.

The wind picks up, and a squall churns the black water, the rain fracturing the smooth surface into rings within rings. My bargemen dip their oars as a deluge sweeps across them. They are poised to row forward at the first sign of the boys.

I pull my hood farther down my brow and swiftly run through our plans again. I am to accompany them as far as Deptford, where Welles's ship takes the boys to Calais. Lord Dynham sees them safely into France. From there, they travel across land to Dijon and the Burgundian court. Margaret has set up all of the stages and the money to smooth Welles's way. How she has pulled this together in three days is remarkable; it is a sign of the hidden depths of Beaufort power that she can act so swiftly and with such discreet and loyal followers. Of course, I am sure she enlisted some help from the queen, where a whispered request to a loyal follower of the old king would be instantly obeyed.

Welles's distracting bonfires flare, their orange flames glowing faintly under the storm clouds. Soon there will be fifty such fires blazing around the Tower precincts.

It is time.

"Row forward to the wharf," I command the oarsmen. The boys cannot wait for one moment.

On the jetty, a man quickly unties our rope and tosses it into the boat, where it smacks and coils wetly at my feet. The four bargemen heave together. The vessel shoots forward into the shadows of the Tower's walls. I grip the side and lean to the left, peering into the curling mist as we approach the water gate. The wharf looms before us, empty and appearing much larger from the water than it does by land.

I glance back over my shoulder to the shore. The fires are faintly flickering.

Dear God, they are taking a while to catch. A milkmaid could extinguish the embers by All Hallows Church with a pail of cow's milk. What is taking so long?

We slide downstream. The wharf blocks my view. Any moment the flames will leap to the sky, and I will hear the watchmen's shouts as panic spreads.

The only sound is the slapping of water against the wharf and the grunts of the oarsmen.

Now smoke plumes into the mist in ghostly ribbons as one by one the fires are extinguished before they can fully catch. As my barge rocks up against the wharf, the rain tamps the struggling flames better than any fire watchman can.

This can't be happening.

The watch is silent. The fires have died. I clutch the slippery wet stones of the wharf with my hands, straining to keep the barge next to the wharf.

Now, my darlings, come now!

Clattering footsteps tells me there is still time.

By the light of the mist-swathed yellow lanterns pinned high upon the stone walls, I peer into the darkness for a glimpse of Ned's golden hair, Dickon's stocky shoulders. The barge bumps alongside the wharf, but there is no one to grab the rope, keep it stable to pick up its passengers.

"Wait!" I command the bargemen. "Wait, for they come."

Shadows race, and then a dozen, two dozen yeoman warders run across the stones with drawn swords and brutal pikes, and thunder rolls down the Thames and lightning sears the sky above the White Tower.

Where are the boys? There are no boys.

No boys.

No boys!

"Row on!" I shout urgently to the men. "Row on. Row on now!"

The oarsmen crash their oars, and we shoot past the wharf out to the choppy mid-river water and head down the Thames to lose ourselves in a flotilla of anonymous river traffic. My arms are empty, and my heart is hollow. I weep into the driving rain, for once more I have left my princes in the Tower.

25

Summer 1483 | Westminster Sanctuary

This is the worst of all outcomes. Brackenbury conceals the boys deep within the Tower Liberty, where they can no longer be seen playing in the gardens. They have disappeared from sight. When I attempt to visit them, I am turned away at the gate, even with my pass. No one is permitted within. Ned's jaw has to be causing him agony. Sleepless with worry, I furiously order Margaret to accompany me again to Elizabeth Woodville. Surely a mother's wrath can spark the flame to release them, and the dowager queen could demand that her brother-in-law provide proper care.

I meet my sister again in the kitchen gardens, by the path to the back door of Cheyneygates.

"What went wrong?" I demand. "The plan was so simple. Why did it fail?" I push ahead of Margaret, impatient to talk to the queen, tell her to demand of Richard the boys' release.

"The rainstorm. Timing. And a miscalculation of how many guards would be standing by the boys' lodging." Margaret hesitates. "Welles is worried he may have been betrayed."

"I can't think of that now," I snap. "It seems to me that he did not have the loyalty he thought from his friends. And endangered all of us in the process." I whirl around, my skirts catching on a pungent rosemary bush before I tug them free. "Did Harry not realise how important this was?"

My sister is silent.

"Margaret?"

"I didn't specifically discuss our venture with him," she says. "It wasn't necessary to beg his permission. It would have put me in his debt—"

"Not necessary? What were you thinking, in God's name? Are you saying you are not concerned about the boys?" I march forward, furious at Margaret's falseness. This is my sister at her conniving best, rolling wheels within wheels and staying clear of blame. "And that you were not prepared to even talk to Harry about moving them?"

"In good time," murmurs Margaret. "I have more significant issues I am discussing with Harry than just the princes." And she shuts her mouth like a trap.

I push open the door into the stillroom and pause on the threshold. A guard is standing at the door leading to the corridor, and although he appears relaxed, his eyes follow me as we pass the table.

"You have permission to be here?" he asks.

"Of course," I reply. "As before, we are here on women's matters to visit the queen."

He shakes his head. "Dame Grey has been prohibited visitors."

Dame Grey? When did that demotion happen?

Margaret steps forward. "This is nonsense. I am Lady Stanley. On the authority of my husband, I demand you let me pass."

The guard is resolute. "She is prohibited visitors."

I draw myself up. "I am Lady Scrope. I am godmother to the queen's son. I have full permission to visit . . . Dame Grey . . . and bring her news of him."

A flicker crosses the guard's face. "I have no warning of you coming here."

Was that a softening of his expression?

"The prince is not faring well in the Tower," I say quietly.

The guard looks at his feet.

I sense a shift in his mood and press on. "He needs his mother's care. And without news of his well-being, she cannot act on his behalf. I carry that news."

A clash of bells to ring Compline and the guard stands aside. "For the prince's sake," he mutters. "Dame Grey is only allowed visits from her physicians. This is the only time you will be allowed into sanctuary." As he waves us through, he says softly, "God save King Edward."

Pushing Margaret ahead of me, I hurry past him before he can change his mind.

The dowager queen sits gripping her claw-armed chair in the Jerusalem Chamber. Before I can express to her my anger and remorse at the failed attempt, Margaret speaks. "You have heard, no doubt, of our testing of the security of the Tower, Your Grace?"

179

The queen looks as startled as I feel. "Testing?" she repeats.

"We engaged my brother Welles to see how closely the boys are guarded, in order to prepare the way for their smooth removal," Margaret continues. "And did so without Harry's knowledge, so he would not be implicated in any unfortunate misunderstanding."

God in heaven, she's good.

"And your conclusion?" The queen jumps up and paces, her feet tracing the knife edge of her nerves. Bess joins her from the bench by the fireplace and puts arm around her waist to still her mother's restless steps. "What next, Margaret? For surely, we have no hope now of bringing my sons from the Tower."

"We don't," Margaret replies.

The queen stifles a cry. As do I.

"But Harry does," my sister continues. "He does not know I instigated this breach, for I intentionally did not seek his permission on this occasion."

I inwardly shake my head. Whatever road Margaret is on, she had better bring it to a conclusion. The boys are still in the Tower, and I have yet to help them to Burgundy or reconcile with Jack on the king's progress. We are in a worse position than even a week ago. I am torn between frustration with Margaret and my loyalty to her in front of the queen.

"What exactly do you propose, Sister?" I ask. "And this time I hope it is a real venture, and not one designed to test." I take Bess's hand, for the girl is softly weeping. "Can you tell us where the boys go next? You can see Bess is distraught at her brothers' captivity."

Margaret glares at me, continues speaking. "I have confirmed that Buckingham has instructed Brackenbury to responsibly relocate the boys out of the Garden Tower, away from any danger or further rescue attempts." She speaks as if reading from one of her books of household instructions. I can hear her issuing the orders to Harry in this tone.

"We know that, Margaret. How do we remove them from the Tower now?" I ask. The dowager queen appears beyond speech, so heavy flow her tears.

"We don't. Under Harry's direction, they will gradually disappear from public view. Fade from memory. The king will return from his progress, his son will be named Prince of Wales and next in succession, and the boys will have been quietly moved to Burgundy by Harry."

Oh, God forbid we are now under the control of Harry. Why is Margaret playing into his hands? "Go on," I say. "And then what happens?"

"We shall give credit to Harry and his clever planning, removing the boys from any more attempts to take control of them. King Richard will award him a seat on the council in gratitude, where he will be privy to all the inner workings of the kingdom. And everyone is fulfilling their destiny."

At your design.

Margaret touches the book of hours at her girdle, fiddles with the clasp. It suddenly springs open, and a piece of parchment flutters to the floor. I catch sight of the signature before Margaret swiftly picks it up and returns it to her book, snapping shut the clasp.

Henry Tudor.

Margaret ignores my gasp. "Better now a gradual disappearance than a kidnapping that could trigger an uprising," she says.

The queen dismisses Bess to the distant window bay, and Margaret's eyes follow the girl across the room.

"You are able to control this plan?" The queen speaks in a hushed tone. She stands before Margaret like a rabbit fascinated by a ferret.

"Let me explain," Margaret replies, glancing at Bess and back at the queen. Her hand strays to her girdle book again, and her fingers whiten as they tighten around it. "I cannot make your bastards legitimate again. But I can ensure that Harry gets them safely away so that they will never know the threat of death or fear a rebellion in their name. In return . . ."

And here comes Margaret's next move. For certainly, my sister is never going to agree to a one-sided bargain. The boys' safety is all I want. But what price is my sister demanding now?

". . . and in return," Margaret continues, "you will give permission for Bess to marry my son, and one day their children will aspire to the throne, for once Henry was named a king's successor, and his right is equal to—even greater than—Gloucester's."

Dear God. Her ambition will get us all killed. "Margaret! You go to far."

She ignores me as she speaks of her son, the holy truth she believes that her child's destiny is the crown. "The future hope of England lies with the women who breed, not the men who fight," Margaret says. "Once he is restored to his English titles, Henry can claim succession in his own right. And it will secure his cause to sire sons with the beloved King Edward's heiress."

"Margaret! Excuse us, Your Grace." I pull my sister away, stand between her and the dowager queen so my words cannot be heard. "Are you out of your mind? This is sedition, Margaret, planning to marry your son to the queen's daughter."

My sister is immobile except for a small muscle twitching on her eyelid. She twists her arm free and, sidestepping me, goes to Bess sitting in the window seat, gazing at the world outside sanctuary.

"You cannot keep them here forever, Your Grace." Margaret strokes Bess's golden hair, smooths it back from her brow, revealing the purity of her beauty. "And you do not want Richard to marry Bess to a northern baron with nothing but wild lands and no couth. A betrothal to my son would pre-empt his doing so."

Bess gazes up at her, tears swimming in her luminescent blue eyes. "And will this help my brothers, Lady Stanley, if I marry Henry Tudor?"

Margaret simply inclines her head.

Bess turns her eyes to me. "My earliest memory is of standing with you in the abbey, when you swore your oath as Ned's godmother to always protect him. You have not forgotten that oath, have you, Lady Scrope? And that is why you and your sister are helping us now?"

My throat constricts. "I will always stand by my vow before God."

Even if Margaret is leading me to a pact with the devil.

"You ask a lot of me," Elizabeth Woodville breaks in. "But you have recognised my strength too. The women are the hope of our line. My mother was descended from kings of England and Luxembourg. Her blood flows through me into my daughter's veins." She pauses, gathers Bess in her arms. "We will rise again."

I cross my fingers against the name of the queen's mother. It is a superstition that will always be with me, that will always cloud Elizabeth Woodville. Her mother, Jacquetta of Luxembourg, was accused of witchcraft. Hearing the queen call upon the old magic of her ancestors disturbs me nearly as much as Margaret's ambition. Both stink of dark arts and secret desires.

The queen continues, her voice growing in strength. "Yes, yes, I will consent, if Henry makes a public declaration to marry my daughter. Not immediately, but in good time, when the boys are safe and the country has forgotten this summer and my husband's memory is golden again." The queen sounds almost as if she is convincing herself.

Margaret now has tears running down her face. In truth, my sister's emotions play like an April sky, sun and rain together. "You could retire to a convent, live a quiet life. Bess will still be illegitimate. When Henry marries her, he will bring respectability to her and her sisters. They could all make good marriages."

The queen holds out her hands to Margaret, and they embrace. "But before we talk of grandchildren," she says, "together, our children will have a strong claim, Lady Stanley. Be sure you know what you are asking for."

Margaret takes her girdle book in both hands and raises it slightly before them in a benediction, as if to say, *My work is done.*

Oh God, Margaret, what conditions are you putting upon the lives of Ned and Dickon?

My sister has just accomplished in a few minutes what would have taken diplomats and ambassadors six months to negotiate. A royal marriage. Even if the groom is in exile and the bride a bastard.

And yet neither the queen nor Margaret have mentioned that in order for Henry and Bess or their children to reach the throne, King Richard needs to be removed. With this agreement, Margaret has shuffled the princes out of the way and placed her son one man's life away from the crown.

Jack's warning of Margaret's duplicity flashes into my mind. Along with my husband's sensible, forthright character and dependable ways. I have strayed far from his counsel, and in doing so I am now privy to intrigue I have no desire to pursue or be party to. I must leave, rejoin Jack. Forget Margaret's ruthless marriage negotiations. King Richard will never agree, and Henry will never be allowed to return to England to marry Bess.

"About the boys . . ." I want to be well rid of Margaret and court and intrigue. There are more important, immediate issues.

"About my boys," the dowager queen speaks simultaneously. "If one day my daughters are legitimised, my sons would be too. Why would they not rise again and reclaim their father's throne?"

"And plunge England into another Cousins' War by tearing apart your family?" Margaret shakes her head. "It is the women who can heal the country, Your Grace, and your daughter has the power to do so. Leave your sons safely out of the country. Let them live full and happy lives. And let Bess become the woman she deserves to be—your heiress, your mother's promise, Queen of England."

"And Harry? Why would Harry be part of securing the boys' freedom?" I demand, drawn in against my will, struggling to bring the conversation back to the boys. "He has nothing to gain."

"He was kingmaker once, to Richard. And he can be so again. Especially with a seat on the council and the information he will have access to."

I am done. "We leave now, Sister. We must secure the boys. That is what you should be thinking of. You must talk with Harry about moving them, and I will explain to Jack and Will. I am late already to join the king's progress, and I cannot delay further. I would like to know the boys are safe before I leave."

"I will talk to Harry and engage his support. We know he is eager to be seated on the council alongside Lovell, Catesby, and Ratcliffe. With the rumours growing that Richard does not deserve the throne, that he acted in haste to bastardise his own nephew, Harry will be rewarded for making the boys quietly disappear."

"How quickly, Margaret?" I ask. My sister must see to the needs of the boys first, her own ambition second. "I wish to join the king's progress. I can pave the way for Harry's elevation to the council as soon as you have spoken to him."

Margaret straightens her cuffs, tucks up the chain on her girdle book so it's tight around her waist. "Leave this with me. I will secure Harry's agreement immediately."

We say our good-byes to the queen, Margaret's curtsey perhaps not as deep or as reverent as when we arrived. After all, she has advanced in her mind from Lady Stanley to the king's mother during this conversation.

The queen returns to her chair and calls to Bess, who kneels at her feet and rubs her mother's hands.

"Good-bye, my dear," Margaret says sweetly to the princess, appraising her as if she is a broodmare. "You are such a good girl to look after your mother with such kindness. It bodes well for your future."

We leave the Jerusalem Chamber, and I am struck by how my wheel of destiny has turned full circle in thirteen years. According to Margaret's steering, I am now to be not only the godmother of a prince, but one day the aunt of a king.

"You have great ambitions for your son," I say. "At first, you wanted his lands restored, his title secured. Now you dream of the throne for him."

In the darkness of the cloister, Margaret's face is in shadow, but there is no missing the excitement in her voice.

"My son has been named successor to the throne before," she replies. "And these years of exile and separation have been a sacrifice we have both endured, knowing that one day God will guide us back together again. If it is to be, then it will be."

With your guidance. God is but a passenger on your journey. "This is treason, Margaret."

"This is destiny, Elysabeth."

26
Summer 1483 | Minster Lovell

Shaking off the taint of Margaret's ambition, I resolve to join Jack before rumours outrun me to the king's ear. He must know from me the reason the princes have been again moved within the Tower. God only knows what tendrils of gossip will slither between alehouses on the road to Oxford, and undoing hearsay is much harder than presenting truth. Jack and I have not been at odds like this ever before. I must now share my heart and true feelings, for I know him well enough that evasion will only worsen his mistrust.

Leaving Le Ryall with a small escort, I head west from London towards Oxford and Minster Lovell. The king's progress is wending across the placid dales and wolds of England, for although the London barons respect the king and his northern men love him, between them a vast swath of England knows not this son of York. Now he visits the great country homes of his southern allies, and he holds Francis Lovell and Will Catesby close as he links their support, stringing a garland of loyalty across peaceful summer meadows. Richard is a statesman through and through. I give him that. But how I struggle to reconcile the fair and just protector with the man who has usurped my godson. I wish with all my heart that my solution to give the boys the future they deserve in Burgundy is the start of forgiveness and healing.

Urging my horse ever forward, I follow the court's progression along the curving Thames into the deep countryside. When they pause at Oxford, to satisfy the king's desire to prove his learnings, and at Woodstock, to sate his urge to hunt and spill blood, I stop only at Thame Abbey to pass a restless night before continuing on to Minster Lovell.

With God and equity on my side, I can tell my husband the truth of the boys' circumstances, convince Catesby that my and Margaret's actions are best for their well-being. Perhaps I can even present the dowager queen's desire for a quiet life in a convent once Elizabeth Woodville is assured her children are safe.

I dread Jack's anger, yet I long to reconcile and resume our life together in harmony.

Francis Lovell's home is a newly renovated manor house that is grand enough to host a king. The Lovells have lived here for many years, and the bosky woodlands and buttercup meadows surrounding the house conceal the true beauty of their home until my very last step. Exhausted from the nervous tension of the past days and my hurried departure, I ride wearily into the manor grounds.

The courtyard is hushed, lurchers dozing, twitching in the summer sun. As I dismount and flex my spine, the burbling of a river drifts over the walls. Across the meadow, doves coo from the cote, their sighs joining the sloughing of the beech leaves.

A servant approaches. "My lady?"

"I am Lady Scrope. My husband travels with the king. Have they not yet arrived?"

"They are out hunting in the Wychwood Forest. If you would like to wait in the solar?" The servant gestures towards a gracious hall standing in the dappled shade of the woods.

"Thank you. I would rather walk out my journey." I pat my mare's neck and, lured by the sound of the Windrush, follow a path through grasses and musky cow parsley to the river. The gentle air is a balm to my heated thoughts, and I think of Jack as I search for the healing words to reunite with him.

At the riverbank, yellow water iris illuminate the pebbled depths, and in the clear waters trout flicker through the lily pads, their rainbow scales reflecting the sky. After the exhausting and worrisome days since the coronation, this countryside comforts. I sit on the bank and lean back against a sturdy beech tree, closing my eyes. Here is the old heart of England, untouched by war or dissent, betrayal or intrigue.

Jack has been fighting for so long too. Surely he desires peace, can see the importance of moving the boys away from dissention and challenges to the throne. They deserve a tranquil life too.

I must have dozed, for when I open my eyes next, the shadows have stretched and the air grown cooler. With the changing light comes shouts and barking hounds. The king and his hunting party have returned, and it is time to find Jack and tell him all that has transpired.

Or at least as much as I feel he can cope with. He is a man who only understands black and white, no shadows, no grey.

As I thread my way back through the crowded and noisy grounds, I am suddenly grabbed by the elbow. I swiftly turn, and my heart leaps as it always does when I see my husband after any time apart.

"Jack." I smile, hold my arms out, lean forward to kiss him.

"Not now." He turns his cheek. Keeping a tight grip on my arm, Jack pulls me through the courtyard to the main house and pushes me ahead of him up a flight of stone stairs. I trip over the height of the steps, try to gather my skirts to prevent treading on them in Jack's furious pace. He propels me into a chamber, and slamming the door behind us, leans against it, his face white with anger. My heart is thumping from the exertion and anxiety. What could have happened?

"Mother of God, Elysabeth, what have you done?" The golden oak floor planks stretch between us like an abyss. His voice raises. "What the hell have you done?"

I take a step back from the force of his anger.

Jack slams his fist on the wall, spins on his heel. "I have just left the king, who is dictating an urgent letter to his chamberlain to arrest four men who attempted to kidnap the princes from the tower."

Oh God, help me.

"And as I listened to his words, Catesby pulled me aside and whispered far worse." Jack strides to stand before me, quivering with the intensity of his feelings. "Do you know what he revealed, Elysabeth? DO YOU?"

I dare not speak. I know that if I add fuel to Jack's fire, the combustion will scorch beyond repair.

"John Welles." The words I dread hearing sting as if he had slapped me. Jack reaches as if to shake me and then folds his arms tightly against his chest. "Your brother John Welles rallied the old king's loyalists, stirred them to action. He has been declared a traitor and a rebel—"

"NO!"

Jack shouts over my protest. "And it's no stretch for me to connect him to Margaret. And you."

"And I am here to tell you the truth," I try to reason, but Jack's fire is still raging.

"Would you have told me anything if I had not spoken first?" His voice is full of contempt. "You were eager enough to greet me when you arrived. Was that your plan? To bed me and then whisper your intrigue in pillow talk?"

My temper rises to match his. "The boys are being neglected. Ned's tooth is causing him agony. I just want them away from the Tower so they can be cared for properly."

"That's all? And you did not think to simply send a message to me, request that of the king?" Jack demands. "Oh, that's right. You do not even acknowledge Richard as your king yet, do you?"

I look down, blink hard to prevent the hot tears that threaten to flow. This was all so wrong, so unfair.

"And Margaret? Does Margaret have the same concern?" Jack runs his fingers through his hair, takes a deep breath. "She must have been the one to bring Welles into the mix, for you barely know him. Did you stop to think that your and your sister's motives may not be the same?"

My mind flashes back a couple of days to Westminster sanctuary, Margaret's dreams of grandeur with the captive dowager queen.

"I see you thinking," Jack pounces on my pause. "There is more, isn't there?"

"Not really."

"Tell me."

"Margaret and I saw the queen in sanctuary—"

"Dear God, how in the hell did you manage to penetrate those walls? Never mind. What came of that?"

"Only that we talked about bringing the boys out of the Tower and into a place where they could be happy again, live freely as they should." How more reasonable could that be?

"What else?"

"Just how Harry could help achieve that with his power as Constable of England."

"What else?" Jack is relentless in his questioning.

My temper flashes again. "And future family arrangements. Their children, Henry, Bess." There. That's all I am going to tell him. I can't wage this battle on more than one front. Right now, the princes matter most.

Jack paces again, his furious marching turning the guest chamber into a battlefield.

"Let me lay that to rest. It will never happen. Your sister is blinded by her ambition. If you think Margaret has any hope of being allowed to marry her son to King Edward's heiress, you are deluded. You had best forget you heard any of these foolish fancies about your nephew. Say nothing more of this, for it is dangerous speculation." He grasps his head with both hands, pushes his hair back from his face impatiently. "Jesu, this women's conniving drives me to the edge of madness. Give me a man with a sword and a charger to ride into battle any day."

"I just—"

"I haven't finished." Jack takes a deep breath. "And back to Margaret's convenient truth of wanting to remove the boys to safety: You didn't stop to think that once they were out of the walls of the Tower they could be taken anywhere, controlled by anyone—including Margaret and Lord Stanley?"

"I just want what is best for them," I cry out. The extent of Margaret's scheming seems so transparent now that Jack spreads it before me, the layers of my sister's deviousness peeling away like flayed skin.

I suspected her, and it is true. Margaret manipulated me.

"Sweet Lord Jesus, woman. You are too trusting, too willing to think the best of everyone. Have all these years at court taught you nothing? When will you learn that your sister is manipulating you along with everyone else?" Jack's rage turns from white hot to ice cold. "And your cousin Buckingham. He is the instigator of all this? Do I have a nest of conspirators within my family?"

"Harry does not know of Welles's attempt. He agreed that the boys would be better off out of the Tower, but he was in no hurry to move them."

"Because he realises that this would need permission and planning and thought. Not just a bonfire and a barge on a whim."

I feel sick. Jack knows everything. So much for telling my story first. "What are you going to do with the princes?"

"ENOUGH!" Jack's temper explodes again. "The princes are under Richard's watch. And always will be. You have nothing more to do with them. Do you understand? NOTHING!"

The force of his words knocks the breath from me, so I have to sit suddenly on the bed, clasping the post until my knuckles turn white. The sounds of the household flow into our silence; a hawk screeches; the wind shivers through the beech trees.

"There is one more thing." My husband now stands before me, casting a shadow across my lap. "You will tell the king of all that you have done, lay the truth open to clear up the deception. They are your family. Margaret is your blood sister. The traitor Tudor is your nephew. This is your responsibility. You have a choice to make, Elysabeth— although in some eyes you have already made it."

A trumpet blows from the courtyard, followed by another and another, discordantly drowning the soft bubbling of the Windrush beneath our windows.

"The king requires us at the banquet." Jack turns abruptly, stands back by the door with his arms folded, his gaze stony. "Wash your face. Change your gown. Immediately the feast is over, we shall talk to Will. Hurry. Your presence has been missed. I cannot forgive the danger you have brought to us. Stay by my side as we uncover what harm you have caused our family."

"I did this *for* our family," I say, miserable that I am so misunderstood, helpless to contradict Jack's accusations, so woven together are fact and fiction.

My husband just stares back at me, his eyes blank. "I don't know you anymore. I don't know where your loyalty lies. And right now, I am not letting you from my sight."

27

Summer 1483 | Minster Lovell

Messengers arrive while we dine upon roast swan and fresh carp, dishes raised high as they are presented to loud cheers and applause. King Richard does not eat much, and after a mouthful here and there, he opens a dispatch and frowns, passing the document to Will, who then shows it to Jack. At the end of the high table, Lord Stanley watches them closely, his lizard eyes slithering sideways and darting around the hall. Margaret has not yet arrived, and he sits by himself, saying nothing but observing everything. His gaze lands on me, and he smiles slyly, lifting his glass in a toast.

Something is happening, but no one is telling me anything.

Jack is frowning at me. I hurriedly turn to Meg.

Talk. Eat. Act as if nothing is wrong, as if my marriage is not crumbling beneath my feet.

"Meg, did you enjoy your time at Oxford?" I ask. "Were the college plays entertaining?"

Meg nods eagerly. "I loved them all."

Stanley is still staring at me. Has Margaret sent him a message?

I shake my head to rid the image of his expression. "What was your favourite?"

"Without a doubt, the performance at Merton—" Meg breaks off as Jack appears at our table.

"What did you mean when you said Harry was helping you?" He leans over as if to kiss me but murmurs in my ear instead. "The king just received news that London has become restless under Harry's watch, and there are new and disquieting rumours circulating about his nephews."

Not just nephews. Princes.

I lift my face to his, murmur back between tight lips. "I told you. Harry pledged to help take the boys to safety. What rumours?"

Jack frowns. "And I told you. The boys are already safe. They have been secured within the Tower. There is no need for them to go anywhere until the king has prepared Sheriff Hutton for them. We won't be there for another fortnight." Jack places his finger under my chin. To anyone watching, he is about to kiss me. I know he is not.

"What are the messages, Jack?" I ask.

"I'm surprised you don't know, given it's your family again. Harry has abruptly left London. We hear he is riding for his estates at Brecknock without joining us here first. King Richard is sending Lovell in the morning to intercept him and bring him to meet us in Gloucester." Jack glances up at the dais, where the king is watching both of us, his hazel eyes narrowed. "And what else exactly were you going to tell me about Harry?"

"Simply that Margaret is meeting with Harry in London, that she has every intention of keeping him fixed on pleasing the king—"

We are interrupted again by a trumpet as Richard and Francis Lovell leave the head table. Will joins us, leans between Meg and me to speak urgently. "The king wants to meet. He has heard that Buckingham may be acting beyond his station, countering the king's orders for the security of the princes. Brackenbury has sent an urgent message from the Tower."

So much is happening that Jack assumes I have no information about. And yet was it my and Margaret's ill-fated attempt to move the boys to Burgundy that set these wheels in motion?

Will puts his hand on Meg's shoulder, and she leans towards him. He looks directly at me when he speaks. "There are those in London who are challenging King Richard's rule, saying that it was planned well in advance of the declaration of bastardy. And a disturbing rumour about the boys has started to circulate behind closed doors." He turns his mouth ruefully. "It will be a long night."

"I need to bring Elysabeth with me to speak to the king." Jack takes my hand, but not lovingly, more to keep me at his side. "She has news from London that will be of interest."

"Quickly, then. The king is on edge with the news of the attempt on the Tower's security—by his own brother's followers." Will kisses Meg. "It will be a long night, sweeting. Richard is wakeful and wants his trusted allies around him. Do not wait for me."

Lovell has given up his own luxurious chamber to the king while he stays, for they have been friends for a long time, and they are brothers in arms, always close. When Jack and I are escorted in with Will, Lovell and the king sit by the open window, a chessboard before them. Outside, the last twilight of August blurs the trees to join the sky, and the fragrance of the Windrush blends with the strumming of a musician's lyre from the courtyard below. The king has thrown aside his richly embroidered jacket and sits with his loose linen shirt open at the neck, the sleeves pushed back. Lovell has done the same, and this, I think, this is the king's confidence in his old friendships to keep him steady. Yes, he has a council of state to give him direction, but this trusted group of loyal friends—he can talk to as equals.

"Come in, Will." The king beckons to a chair, and Will sits by him, leaving Jack awkwardly standing. I am sorry for the uncertainty in my husband, for he should be by Richard with the other men were I not at his side. I am an anchor to the past, dragging his progress.

"Lady Scrope." Richard moves his bishop across the board, looking at the game, not at me. "I have heard that your brother Welles has been overly concerned with the fate of my nephews."

I am used to the directness of the northerners by now, am not surprised at Richard's statement. "Yes, Your Grace." I will not volunteer more than is asked for by him, though.

"And from what I know, John Welles has neither the brains nor the balls to act on his own."

Lovell chortles. "I know someone who does, though. Well perhaps not the balls—Lord Stanley would have to tell us what his wife really has under her hair shirt."

Will and Richard join his laughter. Jack shifts uncomfortably. I know he wants to laugh but is conscious they are talking of his sister-in-law. And that Margaret's inclusion in the conversation extends to me too.

"Lady Scrope?" The king keeps me standing, relies on protocol to unbalance me.

"Your Grace, when I last visited the boys . . ." Suddenly, my planned words change, and my frustration leaps to the fore. "I was horrified at their condition. Ned is desperately ill, Dickon is exhausted under the burden of trying to care for him, and Brackenbury does little except allow Dr Argentine to attend them. And frankly, the doctor is not doing any good at all."

"And you thought you could do better?"

"It couldn't be much worse."

Richard's lips twitch, and he turns back to the chessboard. Lovell jumps his knight out of the bishop's path, and Richard swiftly moves his queen to threaten the piece. "And you would risk my wrath, even accusations of treason, to kidnap the boys from under my care?"

"There was no plan of kidnapping." I feel Jack quiver beside me.

He steps quickly forward. "Your Grace, if I may speak, my wife does not—"

"Your wife does not fear reprisal when she follows her heart?" Richard stands up, walks to my side. We are of almost the same height, and I am drawn again to the memory of our ride south together—*Was it just in May?*—the shared jokes and excitement of caring for Ned. The lines of worry in his forehead have faded, the set of his mouth is not so fierce.

"Elysabeth," Richard says softly as he takes my hand. "Elysabeth, you must not act outside of my command like that. You will create enemies that I cannot protect you from. You joust in an arena that is way beyond your skills. The Woodvilles, Margaret, Buckingham—they compete in a sport that is not for you."

I hold his gaze, keep my head high. It is hard to resist his charm, and yet the voice inside my head still drums. *Why? Why? Why bastards?*

"You must not interfere again with the fate of the princes," he continues, his tone hardening. "And in the morning, you will ride and tell Margaret the same."

"My sister was just trying to help the boys, Your Grace. There is really no need to bring her to account for anything." The last thing I want to do is see Margaret alone again.

The king ignores me. "I do not know why she felt she needed to meddle with the princes' well-being," he says. "But your sister does nothing without a reason behind it. She treads on thin ice between her ambition for her son and her husband, and I will be watching closely where her loyalties lie. I have not forgotten that Henry Tudor waits in France for his time to return. And I know that is a homecoming that Margaret welcomes."

I bow my head, recall the conversation with the dowager queen in sanctuary. Have I already left it too late to tell of that conversation?

195

"We leave for the cathedral at Gloucester tomorrow. I shall expect Margaret to join us on our progress by then." The king drops my hand, and the moment of intimacy dissolves. He gestures to a desk in the corner of the room. "Will, send a message to Lady Stanley on Lady Scrope's behalf asking to see her tomorrow, privately. Lord Stanley tells me she is in Oxford, on her way to join us. A meeting in a close-by town would be best, out of the influence of the court—and Stanley."

I take a deep breath. It seems I have no choice but to meet with Margaret. "What would you have me tell my sister, Your Grace?"

"Tell her I am watching her. And to do as I do. Hold her friends close. And hold her enemies closer. If she cannot distinguish one from the other, that will be her downfall."

28

Summer 1483 | Burford

After a near sleepless night in my lonely bed, I leave the court with four Scrope guards and a heart heavy with dread. Jack and I have never been this estranged, and I feel as if my skin is flayed from our discord. He was absent from my chamber all night, and I am told he has left to go hunting when I enquire of his whereabouts this morning.

The softly rolling Cotswold hills and fragrant lanes fail to sooth my churning stomach. Across the valley, a church spire pierces the morning mist like a needle poking through fabric, and copses of moss-green trees cling to the sides of the wolds, dark and mysterious. I am travelling on Margaret's command—her response to Will's message arrived this morning. We are to meet in Burford, just a few miles from Oxford. Only too quickly do I ride down the long hill into the town.

It isn't hard to find my sister, for at the Highway Inn her entourage spreads across the forecourt and blocks the narrow archway to the stables. The same Margaret. She travels with a retinue as grand as if she is already the king's mother. I pick my way through a sea of orange, tawny, and green livery. There is no mistaking the magnificence of the Stanley household.

A groom appears, catches my horse's bridle. "This way, Lady Scrope," he says and, cutting a swath through the retainers, leads me away from the inn and towards the church. Guards stand at the entrance to the lane. There waits Margaret, and I can see from her expression she is already impatient. I dismount, hurry towards her.

"Elysabeth," Margaret calls. "We have just arrived. I don't know why this couldn't wait until I joined the court. The message demanded you needed to talk now." Margaret walks from the confusion with her lady at her side towards the church at the end of the lane. "You ask for news. It is very simple. I spoke to Buckingham again. He is in agreement that he will now move the boys earlier than he had originally planned. That is all there is to it."

"Margaret, before you say more, please listen to me." I have to unburden myself, set straight this part of the conflict in my life. Passing on the king's warning is to save my sister from further intrigue, not betray her. "I have a specific message from King Richard to share with you in private."

"Soon enough." Margaret pats my arm. "There is a splinter of the true cross within the church. I will say my prayers and join you shortly." She continues past the row of golden stone-built almshouses and the sentinel at the gates, disappearing through the great arched church doors. When Margaret has an appointment with God, everyone else can wait.

I turn back to the inn. Here I can pause in some privacy, tell Margaret of the king's warning, and ride on to Gloucester Cathedral to meet up with the court. No need to eat or take refreshment. The sooner I can leave, the sooner I can tell Jack I have done as commanded. My sister will be equally abstinent; I have never known Margaret to sit long for a meal unless required by the king or politics.

And then I am brought up short. Across the narrow stone bridge at the bottom of the hill, another mass of riders approaches. Black-and-red livery. Buckingham. They collide with the Stanley faction, and the mingling of the two retinues creates a clash of colours that makes my head ache.

Surrounded by an escort of guards—*Really, in a small market town on a peaceful Tuesday morning?*—my cousin strides towards me.

"Elysabeth? A surprise indeed." Harry surveys the crush of Margaret's retainers and back to me with a question on his face. "Why are you here? And Margaret too? What a strange coincidence we should all meet on the road like this."

I bite my cheek. There is motive behind this chance encounter. Harry may be surprised, but I have no doubt Margaret has planned this. My sister creates accidents of the universe as if she is the Almighty herself.

"I was at Minster Lovell," I say quickly, "and received word that Margaret was passing close by. I wanted to see her before I left for the North." Harry seems his usual anxious self, his forehead sweaty under his cap. "She has gone to prayer."

"Then I will wait with you." Harry glances at the inn. "This looks as good a place as any."

Reluctantly, I follow him. Already my plan to speak to Margaret privately is upturned.

We command the low-ceilinged parlour and sit at the table in front of the oriel window. The room is quiet, a blessed respite from the chaos outside. The landlord rushes to serve ale, bowing and scraping and clearly delighted at this sudden and unexpected patronage. Harry quickly counters ale for wine, even this early in the morning.

"You tallied a while in London after we saw you in July, Cousin," I observe, and Harry reddens, his thick neck bulging over his jacket collar. "I would have thought you would have been at the king's side on his progress." I can't resist digging at him. "After all, you have been like his lapdog since you broke the news of the bastardy."

"I had business," he mutters. "A service to King Richard that was best done in quiet."

"What service?" I ask. I long for the latest news of the boys. But best to wait for Margaret so my sister puts her request to Harry simultaneously.

Harry throws back his wine in one gulp and refills his glass. He leans forward, his face flushed. "I had meetings with Brackenbury. He needed to learn a lesson or two about his chain of command. And loyalty. I enjoyed teaching him," he boasts. "Now that you have thrown your lot in with your sister—For why else would you be here?—you may as well know. You served your purpose well, and your sorry attempt to remove the princes from the tower was perfectly timed."

I try to control my temper. As usual, Harry raises my hackles with his arrogance. "I do not understand your words, Cousin. Throwing my lot? Serving my purpose? You speak in riddles." *Steady,* I tell myself. I do not know yet what Margaret has asked of him. "We just want the boys to be back with their family and to be well-cared for," I continue. "Something perhaps you had overlooked."

"Ah, you are mistaken. I want them secure too," replies Harry. "Until their time comes." He drinks deeply again and examines a ring on his thumb that is embedded below his fat knuckle.

I wish Margaret would return. There is only so much I can stand of Harry, and his clumsy mysteries are annoying beyond measure.

"Margaret will be back shortly. I have things to say to her—"

"And so do I, now that I am here." He drinks again, gestures to the hovering landlord for more. "Besides, it serves her as well as it serves me. Our family unites again, and this time I am in charge of our destiny."

"You are not in charge of my destiny, Harry."

He ignores me. "You all seem to overlook that I am married to the dowager queen's sister. The princes are my nephews. Ned deserves his rightful role in governing England."

What on earth is Harry saying? What rightful role?

"What do you mean? You were the instigator in his removal from the throne." Surely Harry is lying. He cannot have turned his coat this rapidly. And for what reason?

"Margaret has her eye on future greatness, and so do I."

"You will achieve greatness through your support of Richard," I tell him. "You clearly removed Ned from the succession. What do you mean, Ned's role in governing England?"

"Always good to have a contingency," Harry replies.

A cold finger of fear tingles my spine. This chance meeting has turned the morning topsy-turvy. Part of me wants to run from the room. My loyalty to Jack and promise to the king makes me stay. "Harry, you are talking in riddles. You were instrumental in assisting Richard to the throne. Why should you now talk of elevating the princes, returning Ned to his rightful place?"

Harry simply stares into his cup of wine as if he does not hear me.

Stepping into our silence, Margaret appears at the table. The cloying scent of incense drifts from her pale blue wimple, and a beatific smile lights her face. Truly, she is pious, for no matter my sister's conceit, I cannot dispute her relationship with God.

"Harry." Margaret sits across from him, folds her hands on the table. "What a fortuitous turn of fate. How surprising and delightful to see you. And delightful timing, with Elysabeth here too. Let us speak before we go on our way."

"Did you plan this coincidence, Margaret?" I ask.

She regards me with wide eyes. "You sent the message you wanted to talk to me. I can only assume you have met with the king at Minster Lovell and told him of Harry's excellent suggestion to move the princes."

"Harry's suggestion?" So has Margaret already planted the seed and is watering now with her praise?

"Of course." She smiles. "Harry, it behooves you to hear Elysabeth's words too." The landlord brings his finest white bread to the table, and Margaret crushes a small piece between her finger and thumb, kneading it into a pellet before signaling to the servant for a cup of watered Rhenish. "And are you joining the king on progress?" she asks Harry. "I do not know why else you would be on this road."

I am witnessing my sister at her best. Margaret is fooling Harry into thinking this meeting is fate. My sister favours the power of destiny— but only as far as she can control it.

"I did not plan to ride to the king," Harry mutters. "I have my own responsibilities. Richard can wait. I must hasten to my lands in Brecon, collect the Welsh dues owed to me as constable. And ensure that Bishop Morton is being well looked after."

I remain silent, watching Margaret and Harry closely, tamping down my feelings of discomfort. While Lovell is out searching for Harry to bring him to the king's presence for questioning, we are sitting talking to him at an inn as if we are merchants' wives resting our feet on market day.

"Ah, you still keep Bishop Morton under surveillance. He was lucky to escape execution for his plotting against Richard. Your prisoner is a brilliant man," Margaret says smoothly.

I wish Jack were here to understand all these undertones. I do know that Margaret's relationship with Morton was one that stretched back to their fierce Lancastrian loyalties. With Harry's talk of restoring Ned to his rightful place, this is not an appropriate time for Margaret to recall that alliance.

My sister sips her wine. "Unfortunate that he is held under lock and key," she continues. "But I am confident he is still full of wisdom. He writes to me quite frequently."

"I take no exception with his words," Harry agrees, "and we have enjoyed many fruitful discussions. But he should be more discreet with his correspondence. Especially to those in high places."

Margaret avoids my gaze. "I shall remember your caution, Harry," she says quietly.

"Harry has something to tell you. He speaks in riddles that perhaps you will understand." I am eager to give Margaret the warning, leave Harry to his dreams of grandeur.

"Tell us of your words with the king first, Elysabeth." Margaret shifts along the bench next to me, leans her shoulder against mine as she used to when she was a child. Her familiar touch encourages me, for I am reluctant to speak before Harry.

"There have been . . . developments," I start carefully, searching for the words I have rehearsed on my ride this morning. Harry stares out of the window as if disinterested, but Margaret pays me heed. "Yesterday the king wrote to Chamberlain Shaw in London, ordering the arrest of the men who lit fires and breached the Tower. This includes our brother John Welles—" I continue in spite of Margaret's sharp intake of breath. "There is suspicion he was behind the attempt to rescue the princes."

"Rescue? Or kidnap?" sneers Buckingham, his large head now swiveling around so his bloodshot eyes fix on me.

"Go on." Margaret ignores him, stops crumbling the bread.

"These men who will be arrested were those servants to King Edward, the loyalists Welles recruited within the household who have not embraced Richard's rule." I take a breath. Here come the words I was told to say. And given Harry's newly declared loyalty, ones that are appropriate for him to hear too. "King Richard is going to take the princes to safety. He thinks there may be further attempts to remove them from within the Tower. Or that the people he holds close are scheming elsewhere. That includes you, Margaret." *And now you too, Harry.*

Outside, the commotion of the two combined retinues continues. Inside, Margaret remains completely still. This I recognise; the trait of stepping back and viewing from a distance is an ability we share.

Buckingham slams his wine cup on the table. "And who is supervising their removal? I have heard nothing." His raised voice causes Margaret's guards to shift their feet, but she holds up her hand to stop them from advancing. "Is it that idiot Brackenbury?"

"As the king has said, Brackenbury is the Constable of the Tower. They are under his watch," I say carefully. My instructions were to warn Margaret, not engage with Harry in a conversation about the reach and boundaries of his powers.

"It doesn't matter, Harry," Margaret cuts across his bluster. "If Richard is indeed removing his nephews now, then our opportunity to take control of them has passed."

"They are my nephews too." Harry's face is red with anger. "And I am his trusted councillor and constable. He should have told me of his decision. They are under my protection."

I watch my sister's face closely, hold her gaze. "Margaret, are you not concerned for the safety of our brother Welles?"

Harry sneers. "And what that could mean for both of you?"

Margaret sits back from the table, folds her hands calmly in her lap before taking her rosary and counting the next decade of beads.

"John Welles will keep his mouth closed, and there is no trace of intrigue between us. We were most careful. I am not concerned that his interrogation will lead to anything nor that his arrest will be prolonged," she says quietly.

"I hope you are right," I reply. "But what of the princes?"

Margaret continues. "We will not be able to reach the boys anymore. And your role has been diminished, it seems, Harry. Brackenbury is a longtime supporter of the king. Once again, Richard turns to his loyal northerners and not his newfound fair-weather friends. It seems you are the last to hear of this latest development. And Richard waits until you have left London to carry it out."

Her words are designed to cut through Harry's fogged brain, and I can see his growing anger that the king has not consulted him.

Margaret stands then and tugs at her sleeves, straightening the lengths until they are identical. "Elysabeth, thank you for your news. It is time for me to join my dearest husband, Lord Stanley, on the progress. I miss his steady presence, his loyalty." Her voice is firm, authoritative. The unspoken words *and make my peace with the king* hang in the air. "And, Harry, if you know what's good for you, you will be sure to meet with the king before you go to Wales."

I rise too. I have nothing more to say to Harry. But there is one more thing I must say to Margaret. Alone. "I'll walk out with you."

As we reach the street, I pull Margaret into a dank and rancid passageway, hosting the stink of drunks' piss and dreck from the inn. Beyond the alley is a sunlit garden overflowing with orange and gold summer flowers. It's my life, I think. Dark and full of hidden secrets with Margaret that taint my whole world. I long to return to the light.

"I have one more thing to tell you," I say. "From the mouth of King Richard to your ear."

Margaret looks startled. "How dramatic. And this is something he could not say to me directly when I arrive?"

I shrug. "Perhaps he does not care to. His words are simple, Margaret. He is watching you. And your son. There is a line you shall not cross. Hold your enemies close. And your friends and family closer."

"What does he mean?"

"I think you know." I glance over to where Harry is now striding from the inn towards his own convoy. "I think you know exactly what he means."

29

Summer 1483 | Gloucester

I push Jack's guards hard as our small party gallops the westerly ways to reach the city of Gloucester ahead of both Harry and Margaret. While their respective retinues jostle for precedence on the road, I take pilgrims' routes and drovers' tracks and soon leave them behind. It is a day's ride to reach the town, and I need every moment to myself to sort my thoughts and think of my life ahead. The warnings from Jack and the king are clear—as is my position. Now I have done as they bid, passed on their words, and maintained my loyalty to both King Richard and my sister.

I do not know what lies in Harry's addled mind. But I hope now I have given Margaret the message from the king that she will not encourage Harry to challenge Richard's position nor that of Ned.

As my mind clears and the fresh breeze on my cheeks gives me energy, my heart lightens. The boys will be cared for at Sheriff Hutton. Richard will see to that. It is his favourite dwelling, set in beautiful rolling hills and deep forests, with some of the best hunting and entertainment in Yorkshire. Margaret must realise that her desire of joining Elizabeth with Henry Tudor is simply a dream—a fleeting thought troubles me that I did not share my sister's ambition with the king—and will not come to fruition.

And Harry?

Whatever he is planning, I am not going to stand in his way—or catch him if he falls.

Across the rolling plains, the tower of Gloucester Cathedral comes into view, and within the hour, just as the sun casts its last glowing beams across the golden fields, I enter the city. Will and Jack will be arriving with the king at any time, and I want to be sure I give them my full account of Margaret's understanding and acceptance of the king's warning.

And Harry?

Harry can take care of himself.

At the Abbot's House in the shadow of the cathedral, the building is spilling over with the king's household, and from the jumble of retinues in the courtyard I can tell that Scrope men are already there . . . along with Buckingham's. Harry must have galloped along the roads with a small group of followers, riding carelessly over any innocent carter in his way, to arrive ahead of me. Pushing through the crowded corridors, I make my way to the abbot's inner chamber, where I am stopped by the guards.

"I'm here to see King Richard," I say.

"No one is permitted entry," one replies. "Not until he says so."

"Is Lord Scrope with him?" I recognise the guard. He is from Middleham, one of the king's loyal Yorkshire personal bodyguards. "You know us, from your visits to Bolton Castle. Please, could you let my husband know I am here? I wouldn't trouble him, but I have important news."

The guard stares at me, and I smile at him, willing him to accept my command.

"Stay here." He nods at the other guard and slips into the room. Within a minute, he returns. "Wait."

"Thank you." The antechamber is crowded with others seeking the king's audience, and I hope the guard was able to let Jack know I am here. I squeeze onto the end of a narrow bench by the door. A sudden bang echoes from inside the room, as if someone has slammed their fist on a table.

"They are my nephews too!" Harry Stafford's angry words fly from beyond the closed chamber door. "You think I don't care for their well-being? Don't know how important they are to you?"

In the anteroom, I stare at my hands clenched in my lap.

The door flies open, and Jack appears. He beckons to me, and I hurry forward with him into the chamber. The king is there, sitting in a large carved chair with his back to the window. Will stands at his side.

Harry swivels when he hears the door click shut, and his face grows crimson.

"Why are you inviting her to our meeting?" he demands. "There is no need to include your wife, Lord Scrope. She has nothing to add here."

"That is your opinion, Harry. Not mine," I say. Jack coughs, and I know he is hiding a smile. That small gesture bodes well for us, and confidence grows in my heart.

"Elysabeth witnessed firsthand the condition of the boys," replies Richard. "Since you claim such a high regard for your nephews, perhaps you can tell us why she is so concerned for their safety—and Ned's health."

Harry purses his lips and folds his arms. "I invited you and your sister to dine," he says to me abruptly, "not take a tour of the Tower."

"We didn't," I retort. "Besides, permission to walk through the Tower is Brackenbury's to give, not yours."

"Not so," snaps Harry.

"But I wanted to see my godson," I continue. "That I am entitled to. And I was appalled to see the condition in which they are both being held."

"Harry," interrupts the king. "I asked you to secure them in my absence, not gaol them. I understand they have not been seen for many days, that they are not even allowed outside to play?"

"That is all Brackenbury's doing." Harry is suddenly quick to give up his superior rank. "They were housed in the Garden Tower to make way for your stay in the palace, and after the coronation he insisted they be restricted on their movements. And then, after Elysabeth's attempt to kidnap them, it was his idea to transfer them into a more secure location."

Kidnap? Dear God, Harry.

"I was not—" I begin.

"Thank you, Elysabeth," Richard silences me. He turns back to Harry. "Where they remain today?"

"Yes." Harry waves his hand in dismissal. "They are under observation. We do not have to be concerned about their welfare. I have this all under my control. And if anyone should be held in contempt, it's Brackenbury. He should be removed."

The king stares at Harry, his face expressionless. Will is writing on a stack of parchments. Jack now sits on the windowsill, turning a chess piece over and over in his hand. A door clicks. Francis Lovell walks in, with my brother-in-law Dick Ratcliffe. The king's loyal pack surrounds him.

Harry inclines his head slightly, a smile fixed on his face as he changes the topic of conversation. "Ah, my friends from the North. And how goes the progress? Is there any assistance I may provide from my lands as you ride towards the Welsh borders? Are you content with the reception you are receiving?" His voice trails off.

Lovell flickers a glance at him. "Well enough," he says and leans forward to whisper a word to Will.

Harry scowls and then turns to my brother-in-law. "Dick Ratcliffe! We must share a drink tonight, you, me, and Jack. After all, we are all cousins together here. And are you staying with the king as far as York?"

Ratcliffe nods. He is a pleasant man, and although I don't see him often, I am happy he has made a love match with Jack's sister Agnes from their time spent together at Middleham. "As far as Sheriff Hutton, my lord, to hold our first Council of the North under the king's governance."

Harry blinks slowly. "The Council of the North?" He takes a step towards the king and then stops. "I did not receive notice, Your Grace."

"None was given. To you." Will speaks for the first time, walks to stand slightly in front of the king. Ratcliffe joins him. Richard remains in his chair, palms resting lightly on the carved swan's-head arms.

Harry looks from one to the other. "I was given to   understand . . ."

Neither says a word.

This is an interesting situation. And just as Margaret foretold when we met in Burford. Harry may think he is the most important man in the kingdom, but he does not appear to have the king's trust.

Harry swallows and stutters. "M-m-my seat on the council . . ."

"Was never planned," replies Will. "We are most grateful for your generous support. Your sudden appearance on the ascension of Prince Edward was appreciated. And in return, you have been given many rewards, my lord. Constable of England. Chamberlain of the Welsh Marches. The Bohun lands are about to be yours. Most men would be grateful for such recognition of your loyalty."

"Have you not been well-thanked, Harry?" Richard's tone is mild, but underneath I can hear a steeliness.

"Land. And wealth. That I have plenty of," Harry replies, his voice rising. He takes one step forward. Will and Dick move closer to Richard, who remains seated. Harry spreads out his arms as if to embrace the king. "My lord, I pledged you my personal support; I swore to you my honor and loyalty when I joined you in Northampton. When I brought my army to support yours in Stony Stratford. When I removed Lord Rivers from Ned's side. When I took Ned to London. When I put him in the Tower—"

My throat suddenly closes. All these events I have been a part of. All of them acting in Ned's best interests. For the king. For his dead father. For the safety of the kingdom. And now Harry is somehow turning these events of the succession into proof of his loyalty to Richard. *What does that make me?*

"When I brought you Talbot and his account of his sister's pre-contract to your brother . . ."

The king's face is impassive.

". . . it was me who discovered the loophole, who found the opening to the throne. The opening for you. Not me. You."

Lovell and Ratcliff, Will and Jack move as one to flank the king. These men resemble battle formation now, protecting their lord against this blustering, arrogant, misguided fool. Harry is stringing himself up with his own rope. And I can only watch as he tightens the noose around his own neck.

Harry doesn't know when to shut up. He continues his tirade. ". . . and encouraged Margaret Beaufort's ambitions for her own son while she pretended to care about the princes—"

Richard rises slowly to his feet. "What about Margaret's ambitions, Harry?"

Oh God, shut up, Harry.

Harry ignores his question, spewing the words now, a torrent bursting from his mouth. "And when I declared Ned a bastard and you king, when I stood before all of London and swore loyalty to you"— his voice rises, and his leg starts trembling—"you think I did that for . . . for money?"

"What did you do it for, Harry?" the king asks quietly.

Harry gives a great roar. Jack drops his hand to his sword pommel.

"I DID IT FOR YOU!" His voice breaks as he stumbles forward. In two strides, Jack puts himself between the king and Harry and draws his sword. Lovell flings open the door, the two guards who are standing outside run in and flank Harry.

He pushes them away, his physical strength taking them off-balance, before turning back to the king. "I did it for you. For what I could be with you. For how we could rule England together. I removed the only obstacle from your path by declaring the princes bastards. You have failed me. *Loyaulté me lie?* Loyalty binds you? Well, it does not bind me. God's wounds, you know not the meaning of loyalty. And you no longer deserve mine." His face purple with rage, his stride almost running, Harry bursts from the room.

In the silence that follows, we all look at each other. I think we are all a bit shaken by the vehemence of Harry's anger, his daring to express himself so to the king. He may as well have declared himself equal in claim to the throne, such was the shock of his outburst.

"Shall I fetch him back, Your Grace?" Jack finally asks.

The king clasps his brow, closes his eyes. "Leave him be," he says softly. "Leave him be. He has shown his true colours. And I fear this may be just the beginning. I must first deal with the unfortunate conditions he has left my nephews in." He pushes himself out of the chair stiffly, wincing a little as he straightens, and takes a goblet of wine from Lovell. "Jack, select your most trusted guards and leave early tomorrow morning for London. John Welles has been taken to the Tower. Verify what he knows of Margaret's scheming, both against the princes and on behalf of her son. And how far the network of dissension amongst my brother's old retainers spreads." He turns to me. "And be grateful I entrusted your brother to Jack, and not someone who has no interest in his welfare."

Jack flicks a glance at me and then looks away when I meet his eyes. The moment of connection has gone. He will always be the king's man first.

"Elysabeth."

Here it comes. I lift my chin as the king's words call upon me. Jack is motionless beside him.

"I'm sorry to say I must discover if Harry's words of Margaret's ambitions are true or bluff. She meddles with the princes. And still dreams of a pardon for her son. I hope for your sake that this is the end of your sister's challenges to me," Richard says quietly. "If you know what is right for you, you will assist your husband in his mission, tell him all that you know, not just what is convenient to you."

Jack's eyes bore into me as if stripping bare every thought in my mind. I stare back at him, frustration burning my cheeks. And I thought I had served the king, put these questions to bed.

Richard gestures to Will to seat himself again at the writing table, pushes a blank parchment towards him. "Immediately inform Brackenbury of Buckingham's mood. I don't trust Harry. On my authority, give Lord Scrope a permit to bring the boys north. Keep their whereabouts secret, move them with as little fuss as possible. God forbid anything should happen to them and people suspect I am trying to hide them away." His mouth is tight again, pain etched around his eyes. "Will, this incident with my brother's servants remaining loyal to his children is worrisome. I am greatly concerned that those who are necessary in this land to support us are not as many as we imagined. Send Tyrell to London to collect gowns and jewels from the Wardrobe. When we arrive in my city of York, there will be an investiture of my son and heir as Prince of Wales to demonstrate the power of my line. This throne is a fragile vessel, and there are many who wish to drink it dry. And one who has the greatest thirst is Harry."

We are lodged at the Sunne Inn, a pleasant and cleanly tavern away from the distractions of the court. I finally have Jack to myself, for there is no room for him at the Abbots House and the king has retired early. In our shared bed, the gulf yawns between us, wider than ever. As our neighbours settle down around us, I stare up at the embroidered canopy, feeling Jack's wakefulness next to me.

"I have left word for Margaret to not stop at Gloucester more than one night and to go straight to her home at Lathom Park," I venture. "I think it better that she not provoke the king more by returning to court."

Jack does not respond.

"I believe she will now repent of her ambition, both for the princes and her son," I continue. "She will see how close she has come to landing in serious trouble. The king has made that perfectly clear. And I am sure he will hold her husband accountable for keeping her out of sight now." I know Jack is listening, but he still refuses to speak to me.

I turn on my side to face him, pillow my cheek in my palm. "Jack, we cannot continue like this. I am sorry I acted so thoughtlessly. I am sorry it placed you in a difficult position. I was just trying to do what was best by my vow and my loyalty to the boys."

"You placed a question in the king's mind of my own loyalty." Jack's words hang between us. Still, he does not turn to me. "And your own allegiance must be to King Richard, not his bastard nephews and your ambitious, treacherous sister."

His words pierce my heart, twist the knife deeper. "You cannot say these terrible words."

"'Tis the truth." I feel the bed shift as Jack turns to me. "And the sooner the boys are at Sheriff Hutton, and Margaret is silenced, the sooner Richard can put these distractions behind him."

"I understand," I reply. Through our window, the abbey bell tolls midnight. The strokes seem never ending, but give me time to plan my next words. "I'm coming with you to London."

"No." Jack sits, tosses the cover from us.

I kneel before him on the bed, pull his reluctant hands into mine. "I must prove my loyalty to you." The faint starlight through the window glints in his eyes. They are wary. "Jack, I've been thinking. Lydiard is just a few miles from here on the way to London. Oliver and Isabel are there all summer. My brother has a closer relationship to John Welles than any of us. And he can manage Margaret. Let us stop at Lydiard on the way, tell him of all that has transpired. Once you and Oliver have talked to Welles at the Tower, assured yourself that he meant no ill intent to the king, we can all return to the North together." Jack doesn't remove his hands, and I feel him listening. "We can stop at Lathom Park on our way back and visit Margaret. Remind her of Richard's eyes on her and how critical it is she remain out of sight."

And I want to see the boys again, check on Ned's health, I silently add. *This gets me back to London.* Best not to say that aloud.

Jack is mute, but I can catch his thoughts, feel the vibration in his heart. He is open to help.

"Oliver loves you like a brother, Jack. Let him share this responsibility of dealing with Welles and Margaret with you."

I take his silence as an assent. Thanks be to God, I have found a way to involve my brother into remedying Margaret's hazard from the king's displeasure. Oliver will know how to make the danger clear to our sister, keep her out of the way. And our beloved brother will also be able to point out to Margaret the folly of considering a marriage with Bess of York to Henry Tudor. The sooner Margaret puts that ambition aside, the safer we will all be.

"You can come," Jack says finally. "But only because you may be useful in getting information out of Welles. And do not expect me to show you any favours."

30
Summer 1483 | Lydiard Park

Lydiard Park is a recent addition to the St.John family estates, though it has been with my mother's Beauchamp ancestors for many centuries. It is a charming manor, about a thousand acres, with a pleasing dwelling and a church that sits within arm's length of the main house. When I was a child, my mother used to bring us here for the summers, for she loved the easy country life and time spent away from court. Oliver and I made it our own special place, where we grew close in the shared lazy July days.

This is the first time I have returned to Lydiard since my mother's death, but the fact that she gave it to Oliver before she died is a sign of the importance she placed on this manor. Oliver's marriage to Jack's sister Isabel meant both the Scropes and the St.John families would always think of Lydiard as our home and not just another piece of property in a long list of assets left in a will. Oliver and Isabel continue the tradition of returning to Lydiard every summer and bringing their little girls, Lizzie and Eleanor, with them. I am eager to be with my family, where there are no judgments or divisions, just simple love and acceptance.

Although our ride from Gloucester has been mostly in silence, I know that Jack will be polite for Oliver's sake, for he cares deeply for his brother-in-law and will not want our personal discord to spill over into their friendship.

We ride along the familiar hollow way, the path below the beech trees fetlock deep in dust. Our summer has been dry, and the meadows stretching either side of the track are parched. As we approach the house, the church and massive oaks guard its northern face, and only the peaks of the gabled roof and chimneys reveal the hidden dwelling. The cattle stand swishing their tails under the shade of the trees, coming to the fence in curiosity as we trot past them and clatter into the cobblestoned stable yard.

My brother runs from the house, his rugged face worried as he sees us. Jack swings down from his mount and holds his hand out to help me. I sway a little as I touch the ground, my legs cramping from the long day's ride. Jack holds me close, closer for a second longer than necessary, and then steadies me and lets me go.

"Dear God, Jack, Elysabeth, what brings you unannounced and in haste?" Oliver hurries us into Lydiard's great hall, shouting at the barking dogs and sending servants to bring ale, meat. "And with the king's guard? What in hell is going on?"

"We have little time." Jack takes an ale from a servant, drains it one long gulp. "You must ride with us to London and then on to Yorkshire to meet with the king."

"What? Well, of course . . . but why? And in such a hurry? Is the king healthy?"

"Fine. Richard commands us," Jack replies. "Your brother John Welles is in the Tower, accused of attempting to kidnap the princes. I must find out from him the extent of the network that he employed. With you in the room, he may give us more information. Willingly." Jack avoids my eyes. "Otherwise . . ."

"Oh, good God." Oliver runs his hands through his hair. "Welles is not the brightest of men. Who on earth persuaded him to do that?"

Oh, Welles. I convinced you to do this. Forgive me

"It was a foolish act that Margaret and I undertook," I admit. "And if I could take it back, I would with all my heart." I wonder at Jack's calling them the princes. Suddenly, their status had been elevated again. They were, after all, just one act of Parliament away from being the legal heirs to the throne.

"What? You tried to kidnap the princes?" Oliver looks at me in horror. "With Margaret's assistance?"

A chance to tell my truth. Perhaps my brother will help convince Jack of my innocence of a threat to the king's rule. "Oliver, there was no malice, no intent to kidnap. We were just concerned for Ned's health."

"Could you not have notified the king?"

I shake my head. "It's not that simple. Margaret was supposed to let Harry know. He had the authority, as Constable of England, to help us."

"This gets better and better." Oliver is white. "No wonder you are in such a hurry to find the truth," he says to Jack. "What happened?"

"Margaret decided not to tell Harry. And then the attempt failed."

Oliver is struggling to make sense of all this, I can see. "Why did Margaret not tell Harry, if he was the key to the success of the venture?"

"She has other plans," I say. "And as a result, Harry has been blamed for the incident and the conditions the boys were kept in. He has challenged the king, revealed that he is not as loyal as Richard thought. Richard fears he may jeopardise the princes in order to achieve his own ambitions."

"Ambitions that may include the throne of England," adds Jack grimly.

Oliver storms to the window, and by the set of his shoulders he is so angry he does not wish to face me. "Harry is an idiot." He slams his fist to the wood frame around the window. "That two-faced bastard. Playing kingmaker to Gloucester, elevating himself to second in the land, and now eyeing the throne for himself, no doubt."

"He is certainly conflicted," I reply. "And completely unpredictable."

Oliver's next words hammer forth. "Where is Margaret?"

"On her way to Lathom Park." I join him, stare out across the familiar expanse of the deer park. "Oliver, she had an indirect hand in Buckingham's audacity, even encouraged him to think he could aim higher, but I do not believe she wants to harm the boys. She longs to bring her own son home and restore his titles." A flash of colour in the gardens and Oliver's daughters run through the flowers. They wear daisy crowns on their heads and are barefoot. Such sweet innocence. I bring myself back to our conversation. "Since Richard procrastinated on honouring the negotiations she had underway, challenging Richard's claim to the throne would have been a lever to bring him to the table again. Who knows, she may even think she can promise an ally in Henry. She is playing a complicated game."

Oliver's anger turns to calculation. "Do we need to safeguard Margaret?"

The girls are holding hands, skipping along the grassy paths. They stop by the pond, dip their hands, and swirl the green weed to find the fish below. I think of the times I held baby Margaret in my arms as she reached into the cool water, giggling as I squeezed her tight to stop her from falling headlong into the tempting pool. My little sister was never afraid of exploring the unknown. "She will be secure under Stanley's protection. She promises to distance herself from Harry."

Jack slams his ale on the table, bringing me back to the present and the woman Margaret has grown up to be. "Enough!" he barks. "I am tired of this woman's constant meddling. Do something to silence your sister . . . or I will."

Oliver and I glance at each other. We can't let Margaret be a target for Jack—or subsequently the king.

"Step outside with me, Elysabeth." Oliver holds out his arm. "Jack, perhaps you could check with the grooms and ensure we have enough horses and supplies to set out early in the morning."

Leaving Jack in his temper, Oliver and I walk from the house. Together, we sit on the wall overlooking the bowling green, warmed by the setting sun threading an orange glow through the woodlands. We can speak freely here, for no one will disturb us. It is our old favourite haunt, where we whispered secrets together as children. Not much has changed, and yet all is different. Lydiard remains the same. We are grown with children of our own, who enjoy the times we once loved here. But Margaret has thrown a stone in the pool of our lives, and we are rocked with the ripples disturbing the calm surface.

"I wish I knew what her real intent is." Oliver watches a flight of ducks winging across the sky, his eyes on the distant heavens as they disappear towards the lake. "One moment she's all for King Richard and Queen Anne, proud as a peacock with her position of honour at the coronation just a month ago. And now she'd just as soon see them dethroned and Ned or Harry wear the crown."

"Not quite." I kick a stone that has dislodged from the wall. There is a little cavity beneath where Oliver and I used to hide secret signs for the other to find: a snail shell, the first chestnut of autumn. Now it is empty. "It is not Ned she wishes to see on the throne nor Harry, but our nephew Henry. Harry and the princes are just a bluff, I believe."

Oliver looks at me in disbelief. "She cannot think England will rise to greet her exiled son. No one even knows who he is."

"No, but they will if she uses her combined power with the Stanleys to give him credibility." Now I must tell Oliver my secret. I pick up the stone for the strength of all the secrets shared in our past. Jack may have dismissed the Woodville conversation, but Oliver and I know Margaret's determination once she gets an idea in her head. "Margaret may be encouraging Harry to defy the king, put thoughts in his mind to challenge the throne, but at the same time she extracted a promise from the dowager queen to wed her eldest daughter to Henry Tudor."

"Oh, good God." Oliver falls silent. A deer ventures out from the distant copse and bends its neck to graze. "She is playing two games of chess at the same time," he says finally. "And will choose the best board for herself."

"Exactly." I knew Oliver would see this so clearly. "With the princes taken out of the succession, Margaret can summon Henry Tudor to walk right into the heart of England with an army of French mercenaries, challenge Richard for the throne, and marry Edward IV's heiress."

Oliver throws back his head, looks to the heavens as he thinks. "Henry can claim the throne in his own right as the last Lancastrian blood through Margaret. And then his marriage with Bess will win the hearts of the people."

I agree. Margaret has always been proud of her royal blood, which now flows in her son. "But Bess is illegitimate. Henry will not marry a bastard."

The sun sinks below the far woods, leaving an orange glow in the sky. A fire is burning somewhere in the fields, and smoke drifts across, adding to the haze. I cough as the plume winds around us.

"Henry could have that reversed if he becomes king," Oliver says slowly.

I can't believe I am even having this conversation.

Oliver continues, voicing Margaret's plan detail by detail. "But then he'd reverse the boys' illegitimacy too. And Ned would have his full claim to the throne again."

"If Henry doesn't get to him first." I voice my biggest fear.

There is a tiny piece of moss growing on the wall beside me. I pick at it with my fingernail, concentrating on prising it from the crack in the mortar.

"Our sister plays a dangerous game indeed," I speak to break Oliver's silence. I know he is as worried as I am. The chance to say this all aloud clarifies my thoughts. The sun disappears, and suddenly the gloaming surrounds us, the smoke turning silvery against a darkening sky. "Margaret is fixated on reuniting with her son. And since Richard is not intending to welcome Henry Tudor to   England . . ."

218

". . . his return can only be by an invasion, supported by an uprising."

I brush the moss to the ground, jump down from the wall. "We can't wait, Oliver. We have to find out from Welles how genuine the effort is to restore Ned to the throne. And now that Harry has turned his back on the king, who knows what his next move will be. Three now vie for England's throne: Harry, Henry, or Ned under Harry's control. And all will wish the other dead before this is over."

31

Summer 1483 | Tower of London

Once again, I reach Le Ryall with my destiny tied to Ned, but this time it is not the arrival that I am looking forward to, but the departure. The sooner we can leave again, the faster we can take the boys north, to Richard's territory, away from any threats of Harry's foolish ambitions or Margaret's aspirations for Henry Tudor.

London's streets are quiet this early in the morning as Oliver, Jack, and I set out for the Tower, for with the king away and the city at ease, there is simply the daily commerce of the markets and merchants to busy the lanes. Jack is silent in his own thoughts, and as I ride alongside the Thames, I am preoccupied with the journey ahead. I bid farewell to the landmarks that have become so familiar this summer. Enough of London and its travails, I am eager to leave for the peace of Bolton Castle and not return for a long time. I gather my reins tighter as the White Tower appears between the buildings, and my palfrey skitters a few paces as she senses my nerves.

Pausing at the Byward Gate, Jack shows the warders our passes from Will, complete with the king's seal. "Take us to Sir Robert Brackenbury," he orders. "Immediately."

Today, the Tower appears neither a royal palace nor a political prison, but simply a benign fortress and a crowded liberty stretching from the wharf to East Smithfield, Tower Hill down to the moat. Hammering from the mint, a herd of a dozen cattle being guided along the wharf, the cries of fish-sellers and oyster-shuckers . . . all is humming and busy and ignorant of the reason my heart is pounding. These citizens are going about their daily business. My work is yet to be done.

This is Oliver's first visit to the Tower, and he is looking around, fascinated at the commotion that is going on. I understand, for many people think of it as a gloomy prison or an elite royal palace. But it is its own small city, and it is apparent that all the business that comprises the liberty is out in full today.

Overlooking Tower Green, the Lieutenant's House takes up most of the southwest corner of the buildings, and once we are through the Garden Tower archway, I lead Jack and Oliver swiftly across the orchard. It takes everything I have not to look around, search the narrow windows of the keep, run to the Garden Tower calling for Ned and Dickon. I am here on king's business, and I must ensure it is swift and impersonal.

Sir Robert Brackenbury greets us from the steps of his residence, filling the door with his burly frame. His eyes widen as he recognises me. He beckons us inside and leads us through a corridor to an office that overlooks the green. Taking the papers that Jack holds out to him, he breaks the seal and reads the first quickly.

"Welles," he says shortly. "He is installed in the Beauchamp chambers. You can meet with him at any time. Let me know if you need a guard to . . . enforce . . . your discussions."

"That won't be necessary," says Oliver quickly. "He is my brother. I think I can encourage him to share his information with me."

Brackenbury lifts an eyebrow. Taking the second document, he scans it and remains staring at Will's writing, as if seeking hidden words between the lines. "The princes, eh?"

Now it is my turn. "How is Ned, Sir Robert?"

He looks at me with a question in his eyes. I know why, and I try to make my expression concerned, friendly. The last time Brackenbury saw me I was being entertained by Buckingham, and I witnessed his humiliating power play over Sir Robert, claiming precedence over the boys. Am I enemy or friend?

"No better, no worse," Brackenbury replies. "I have ordered Dr. Argentine to come daily. He does, and says that his curatives will not work when the boy is fearful, worried for his life."

I've heard enough. "Go to your business with John Welles," I chivy Jack and Oliver. "He will be glad to see you and is sure to tell you all you wish to hear. There is nothing I can add."

"And what are you to do?" Jack demands. "You are here to observe, no more."

Brackenbury is watching me closely. "What will you do?" he repeats.

"Plan the boys' departure," I respond tartly. "Read the king's command, Sir Robert. While my husband chases echoes of the old king's regime, I must assess the boys' condition, ensure they can survive the strain of the journey ahead of them."

Jack looks from me to Oliver. "I cannot do both. I must talk to Welles; the king has charged me with finding out all that lies behind his ill-planned breach. I cannot see the princes at the same time."

Suddenly, I feel sorry for him. Jack's single-minded sense of purpose sometimes hinders him in seeing beyond the immediate.

"I am not asking you to do both. I can assess how best to move the princes," I say. "I am sure Sir Robert is offering his full cooperation. Go to my brother Welles."

Jack hesitates.

"Come, Jack." Oliver has already turned to the door. "I don't think our interview with Welles will be long. And the sooner we can speak with him, the sooner I am sure we can clear up any suspicion that his actions were more than just a misadventure."

I agree. "I will be here with Sir Robert. You go to Welles."

My brother and my husband leave, and I am so relieved that Oliver is with us, for his levelheaded thinking will confirm Welles's innocence and secure his freedom.

Brackenbury puts Richard's missive on a desk, his face expressionless, and waits.

Does he accept me as a protector of the boys or mistrust me as a relative of Buckingham?

From the window facing out upon Tower Green, a commotion catches my eye. A drayman has overturned his cart and is shouting at his apprentices, horses, and the small crowd that has gathered around him. Others pass by, ignoring the upset, flowing around the blocked path as a river would surge past a tumble of boulders. Jack and Oliver happen upon the chaos as they walk towards the Beauchamp chambers. They sidestep the mess, ignoring the citizens and the argument that is brewing.

"About the princes, Sir Robert." I turn, assuming my right to speak on behalf of the king.

"King Richard says you have his permission to remove them from their lodgings." Brackenbury purses his lips. "The last we met, you were in company that was not conducive to the well-being of the boys. How do I know you have been honest with the king?

"And yet you allowed me to see them on that occasion."

"The duke commanded me." I could see how much it cost him to say that.

"And now the king commands you." I point to the document. "It seems I have the right authority at the right time, Sir Robert." I take a step closer to him, reminding myself to keep a blank face. *How would Margaret do this? Put him on the defensive.* "Do you have something to hide? Or do you serve another master other than the king?"

A tic twitches in Brackenbury's cheek. "I would die for the king. He knows the depth of my loyalty."

"Then prove it," I retort. "Save his nephews from the threats that surround them. Give them to my custody, as the king commands."

I glance past his shoulder through the window again. The White Tower stands silently, implacable in its smooth face. I force myself to stay still, disguise the pumping of my heart, the sudden rush of blood to my cheeks.

Sovereynté.

Sir Robert shifts first. "Best leave with them at sundown, Lady Scrope." He pulls a large key from the desk, hands it to me. Opening a metal strongbox within a drawer, he places the letter inside and shoves it closed again.

The key weights down my hand. Freedom. Finally.

"I moved them within the newly appointed royal apartment in the Lanthorn Tower," Brackenbury continues. "It has been both secure and comfortable for them. We have had to keep them inside for many days, for Ned's illness has stolen him from his normal play, and Dickon refuses to leave his brother on his own."

"Thank you, Sir Robert. I am worried about Ned's strength. He is a frail child, and this ordeal has been very difficult for him." A lump rises in my throat as I think of all he has been through since his father died. And then I take myself in hand. This is not the time for emotion.

Brackenbury joins me at the window and surveys the scene for a few minutes. "You will have to walk them from the Lanthorn Tower, through the palace, and to Coldharbor Gate. An hour before curfew is when the most people are leaving the precincts. There will be a crowd at the gates and at the wharf. I may be otherwise occupied, but I will be sure that my guards will not hinder you."

"You believe this is the right time to take them from the Tower? We will not be stopped or followed?"

"Not immediately. My guards can be trusted to keep the doors closed to the Lanthorn Tower overnight. But I cannot promise Lord Buckingham will not pursue them."

Harry. Always Harry. The sooner I can remove them from his influence, the better. "Won't people wonder why the boys are leaving?"

Brackenbury continues to watch from the window. "They have not been seen for a while. People's memories are short. They will not even notice. Especially if it is you leading the way. Who would think a woman would have that kind of responsibility?" He waves his hand to the window, beyond which there must have been a hundred people milling around on the green. Anyone would be hard to spot in the crowd. "And sometimes the things that are hidden in plain sight are the hardest to find."

With the help of a couple of sturdy warders, the drayman finally rights his cart, cuffs his apprentice, and calls to his wife to ride up next to him. He snaps the reins, and his pony pulls away. Gradually, the crowd thins as people return to their normal routines. Minutes later, it is as if the accident has never happened; the drayman has long disappeared.

"Hidden in plain sight," I repeat. My eyes meet Sir Robert's. He stares back at me, his face expressionless.

The Constable of the Tower, the keeper of England's most secure and feared prison, is giving me permission to defy Harry, to remove the boys, to do as his king commands.

32

Summer 1483 | Tower of London

In the stables at Le Ryall, Oliver works rapidly to muster a motley collection of carts and mismatched ponies, along with half a dozen of our loyal guard. Jack cannot believe that I have persuaded Brackenbury to let us leave under such simple circumstances; I think my husband was planning an armed troop, a procession, a show for the Londoners that the princes were officially leaving the Tower, being proudly escorted to live with their generous and affectionate Uncle Richard.

"Elysabeth and Brackenbury are correct," Oliver says. "With Buckingham so unpredictable, and Margaret with her heart set on Henry's return at any cost, there is no need to draw more attention to the princes nor ourselves. We don't want to meet with an accident on the road like Lord Woodville in Stony Stratford."

Jack listens to Oliver, but just until he has finished talking. "But I must come with you," my husband protests. "You cannot do this alone." He is not a diplomat, he is a soldier. Plain and simple. He relies on force, not subtlety.

"Jack, you are too well-known," I look at my handsome husband, tall, muscular and immediately recognisable. "People would wonder why you are there. They would remember you."

"I could disguise myself," he replies.

"Not well enough, my friend." Oliver claps him on the shoulder. "Wait here for us, have everything prepared for our journey north. Elysabeth and I will blend easily, and we will be there and back before you know it. Be ready for us when we arrive at Le Ryall with the boys, and we'll head north together."

Jack eventually agrees. He has just seen firsthand how skilfully Oliver led Welles to explain his role in our misadventure, carefully guided him to reveal that it was simply an ill-conceived whim that he saw offered him the chance to reclaim his lands and title. I know how kind and deliberate Oliver was in his questioning, and at the end of the interview Jack was satisfied that there was no greater plot, no grand scheme to kidnap the princes and restore Ned to the throne. And grateful that no interrogation was needed to make Welles talk.

My husband could recommend to the king that John Welles be set free, that no harm was intended. At the same time, he could record that Lady Scrope had simply mentioned in passing that the boys would enjoy a visit to their aunt in Burgundy. There would be no reference to Margaret at all.

One matter resolved. Now the princes.

I am so glad Oliver is by my side.

As our little procession rumbles under the Byward Gate, a peal rings out from the Bell Tower signifying Nones, the afternoon prayer. Holding on tightly to the shuddering cart, I pull my tippet over my head and recite the familiar words, feeling a tremor through my body as Oliver murmurs the closing words with me. "Deliver us from evil," I whisper, Harry's angry face imprinted on my closed eyelids.

Oliver pulls the cart piled with vegetables and bales of cloth to a stop before Coldharbour Gate and remains sitting stoically in place while the hubbub of people streams around him. There are other carts, as well as grooms and attendants holding the horses of visitors to the palace. I take three of our guards with me, their disguises as countrymen easily helping them blend in with the other visitors.

I take a deep breath and swallow. We are on our way.

We walk through Coldharbour and turn towards the river, weaving our way past the row of gabled lodgings and down through the service quarters towards the royal palace. It seems impossible that just a few weeks ago Meg and I were playing with the boys in the great hall, waiting for news. I have no time to think of all that has passed. I need to concentrate on what is happening now.

Just as Sir Robert forecast, the paths are thick with people, and as I approach the Lanthorn Tower, I dip my hand in my pocket and touch the bulky key. The tower is two stories with a light embrasure at its crown, and two large oak trees flank it. At the entry, two guards stare straight ahead and remain so, ignoring my hesitation. Ignoring me altogether.

I walk under the archway and come face-to-face with a heavy wooden door clasped in iron and with bolts top and bottom. Glancing back, I see the guards still stand facing forward towards the activity around the Tower. In fact, they have moved slightly closer together, concealing the doorway from outside eyes. I gesture to two of my guards to take up a position inside the entrance, motion the other to follow me, and slip the key into the door and turn the well-oiled lock.

A child sits alone looking through the window.

My heart pounds. One boy. Where is the other?

"Dickon," I whisper, wanting to shout. "Dickon!" I hiss until his bright eyes meet mine and widen in surprise. I place a finger upon my lips and beckon him, and like a sleepwalker he leaves his perch by the window, stretches, and casually ambles forward.

"Lady Scrope?" he asks, and I clasp his sturdy shoulders, inhaling the boy scent of his hair.

"Dickon," I whisper. "Where is Ned? We are leaving the Tower. If he needs help, take me to him, for we do not have much time."

Dickon guides me to a small circular stairwell in the corner of the room. "He is up here, sleeping," he says. "Do you know this is called the Lanthorn Tower, Lady Scrope?"

I smile down at his eager little face peering up at me. He looks none the worse for his ordeal, as cheerful and bright-eyed as always.

"There's a lantern in the roof that steers the ships safely on the Thames," he continues. "At night, when I say my prayers, I ask God to steer a ship with my mother on board to remove us from here and take us home. But she has not come yet."

"I'm here, my darling." I swallow the lump in my throat that his words created. "And we are going to go to my home at Bolton Castle. Are you ready to help me?"

He nods. "Yes. Because Ned isn't well. I will need to help him."

Ned is huddled under a cover, and I recognise Margaret's cloak from when we visited during our dinner with Harry. I carefully pull it back to the end of the bed and gently shake his shoulder. At first, his eyes are bleary. Then, when he recognises me, he holds out his arms. "Godmother."

I hold him tightly, rock him gently. His forehead is burning with fever, his jaw still red and swollen. "Shh, my darling," I whisper. "I've come to take you home. Can you walk?"

He nods. "A little. If Dickon can help me."

Dickon reaches out his arms and helps his brother from the bed, easing on his jacket. My guard picks up Ned as if he weighs nothing

227

and carefully carries him down the stairs. As I watch his bright head bobbing on the man's shoulder, I call to him. "Wait!"

Taking a handful of ashes from the fireplace, I smear them over Ned's hair and then on Dickon's, dulling the gold and streaking their faces with grime. For good measure, I dust more over their jackets and glance down at their feet. "Do you have your shoes for playing outside?" I ask. Their ornate footwear will betray their provenance. Dickon kicks off his slippers and pulls on his shoes and does same for Ned.

"Ready?" I ask and walk us casually past the guards, who step aside as we pass. We head outside and across the yard as if we have all the business in the world doing this. Looking around to see if any are watching, I grab the reins of a fat mare tied by the water trough and walk her between Dickon and the palace windows. My guard carries Ned on his back as if he is any yeoman giving his son a ride at the end of a long day. Ned's head lolls across the guard's broad shoulder, his eyes closed. Pale lavender circles like bruises are under his eyes, and in the light his inflamed cheek is horribly misshapen.

Mother Mary, please help me, please keep watch over us.

The other two guards stroll behind, jostling and teasing, drawing attention away from the boys. Between my shoulders at the back of my neck, I feel as though a hundred eyes are burning, a thousand arrows poised to shoot. But in reality, folks want to be home for their supper, and no one pauses to look at a plainly dressed woman and a young boy ambling across the cobbles.

Once in the shelter of the passageway to Coldharbor Gate, I tether the horse and pull Dickon into my arms.

"Dickon, listen to me, listen," I say as I crouch down before him. "We must move quickly. You are both in some danger, and if we don't leave now, the bad men will be after you. Can you look after Ned, keep him quiet if he cries, be brave, be strong? For Ned's sake?"

He wipes his nose on his sleeve. "Yes," he whispers. "Yes, I can."

We hurry through the dark passageway to where Oliver is waiting by the gate. I help Dickon scramble up to the back of the wagon and then gently place Ned next to him and pull blankets around both of them.

Oliver clicks his tongue. "Forward," he cries.

The pony pulls the cart around to join the queue of people leaving the Tower. I reach back my hand and clasp Ned's while Dickon hums tunelessly to himself. The crowd shuffles forward, and soon we are under the gatehouse and on the final path to Tower Hill and the liberty boundary. We ride into the setting sun in a cloud of summer dust, leaving the Tower of London with two more lives in our party than when we arrived.

33

Summer 1483 | Lathom Park

The sheltered stable yard at Le Ryall hides our preparations from the road, for the watch may be in the pay of Harry, and I cannot risk anyone following us north. The boys are huddled on the bench in the kitchen by the ash-tamped fire, waiting for us to leave. I do not want them outside until the last possible moment. Harry's spies could be anywhere, even during curfew. I walk into the dewy yard and peer up at the sky, eager for the eastern grey that foretells the dawn. As soon as Lauds rings, we will leave London. Pale wisps of clouds streak across a quarter moon.

"Are you sure you do not want to join the king on our way north?" Oliver asks as he is checking girths and packs by the light of a single lantern. "Do you still not think it safer to ride within his progress?"

Jack takes the reins from the stable boy, loops them over his horse's head. "The king is adamant that we go to Bolton Castle, stay away from court."

"Until he can really understand what Buckingham plans, he is fearful that his own entourage may still carry loyalists to the princes and their father," I add. "Buckingham's outburst did nothing to allay those fears."

Is that a paling of the sky? I ache to hear the first bell ring the dawn.

"I can understand that, when we question even our own sister. When we get near to Lathom Park, it would be best if you stay away with both boys," replies Oliver grimly. "There is an abbey nearby where you can rest. I am sorry to say I trust not Margaret's ambitions until I see her face."

We are ready and stand whispering under the porch, waiting for the moment to mount up and leave.

"Are you sure it is wise to stop at Lathom, Oliver?" I have my own reasons for seeing Margaret; I need to ensure my sister realises the import of dropping her plan to marry her son to Bess. If Henry Tudor makes that announcement, there will be no doubt where Margaret's loyalty lies. But I am conflicted, seeing how ill Ned is. "Ned is weak, and I fear for his health every day we may delay on our journey."

"We will make it brief. There is little to converse about," Jack replies tersely. He looks at the sky and opens the door to bring the boys out. The stable lad helps me onto my mare. Lauds rings out from St. Michael Paternoster, always the first church to wake in the morning. Jack mounts up, tenderly holding Ned in his arms, steadying the boy's head to prevent his poor cheek from being knocked. I pray the clove-and-honey electuary I have massaged on his gums will keep the pain at bay until our first stop, when I can give him a sleep potion. If I can just get him home to Bolton Castle, I can nurse him back to health.

"Lathom is not far out of our way if we ride swiftly and do not tally long," my brother says curtly. "As sure as I am here, we must stand before Margaret to enforce our warning. She could too easily dismiss a letter." He swings into his own saddle, reaches down a strong arm, and pulls Dickon up before him. "Now we must leave."

What a tangled web, to be sure. The queen's long-ago prediction in sanctuary of my family conflict rings in my ears. Dear God, am I still caught wrestling between my blood loyalty and my marriage vows? Margaret's betrothal pact with Elizabeth Woodville will either never come to pass or it will tear us all apart.

Skirting towns and cantering straight through villages that cluster the way, we ride north. There are old roads left from the Romans, carters' tracks from market to market, and drovers' paths from the high hills down to the valleys. Once we pass Worcester, I can breathe more easily, for we hear the king progressed this way just days before, heading away from us easterly, and with each mile we also draw farther from Buckingham's lands and closer to Lord Stanley's protection.

Oliver has made this journey many a time, between his new inheritance of Lydiard and his home in Yorkshire, and so he can recite the towns and guide us by the markers. Evesham, Wolverhampton, Stoke. Each town guides our direction north, and yet we veer into the deep country before we arrive at the town boundaries. We follow paths to more isolated settlements, where we can stay quietly at an abbey without causing attention.

At each stop, I invoke the aid of the hospitallers, who offer their own remedies for Ned's pain. And after three days, I am noticing a change in him—his eyes are brighter and his smile returns. Jack never lets go of him, and the two of them together, Ned poised before Jack on the great horse, become the image of this journey. Before my eyes, Ned is growing stronger and stronger, and I want to melt with the tenderness of Jack's care.

As the days blur together, the countryside changes, becomes more barren, wilder as we head north, and by the time we approach Manchester, a steady drizzle creeps in from the west and a grey shroud drapes the landscape. As we near the town, the track becomes clogged with groups of travellers. With disturbing frequency, those walking are scattered to the hedges and forced to jump the walls when small bands of armed riders gallop upon us.

"I don't like this," mutters Oliver after the fourth band forces us to crush up against a dilapidated barn siding, startling the pigs inside, who set up an almighty squealing. "There is too much activity, and all riding south towards Harry's lands."

Jack shifts Ned into a more comfortable resting place on his chest, for the boy has dozed off during the last few miles. "If I didn't know better, I'd say they are mustering," he replies.

"Mustering?" I tap my mare forward as the track clears. "For what?" A jolt of recollection drops like a rock into my stomach. "Surely Harry isn't going to challenge the king."

"I don't know," replies Oliver. "And hopefully, neither does Margaret. We are almost at Lathom Park. Let us hope we can get her to speak plainly for once."

Oliver and I leave Jack and the boys with the guard at Burscough Priory. This is a family matter to discuss, and one that we must keep close. It is not that I mistrust Jack, but he is in the king's inner circle, and he is still furious with Margaret's duplicity. He doesn't need to hear words firsthand from Margaret that he would be forced by his conscience to share with the king.

And my husband's loyalty? His duty is first to the princes and last to Margaret. "Be sure to get the truth from her," he tells me, his face set hard as it always is now when he speaks of my sister. "And do not think to conceal it from me. Ever again."

Lathom House is surrounded by a far-reaching deer park, and Oliver and I carefully make our way across the undulating ground, conscious that at a distance the guards could take us for poachers. The countryside is watchful, and there is no welcome as we approach the sprawling wooden fortress that is Margaret's Lancashire home. There is no moat or drawbridge, but the imposing set of iron-clad doors are firmly bolted, and only when Oliver demands of the guard that we be admitted and invokes the name of Lord Stanley are we escorted into the courtyard. We are held outside in the damp chill until the steward returns, obviously having verified our identity.

"This way," he commands and leads us through the great hall and up a twisting stairway into a solar. The room is well proportioned, with high narrow windows and torches flaring to dismiss the gloom. On every wall, paintings glow with vibrant reds and blues, deep greens and golds, all scenes of religious import. The paint is fresh, untarnished by the ages or wood smoke.

"Margaret has made herself at home here," I murmur to Oliver. "She has the company of those she treasures the most—the saints and apostles."

He grimaces. "I would warrant she prefers them to any other. Her conversations with the Lord are frequent and long. No doubt they advise her more so than her husband."

A panel by the fireplace opens, and as Margaret steps through, she reveals a glimpse of a candlelit inner sanctum, a small private chapel with a prie-dieu and a shelf of books.

"I did not expect both of you," she says. Her eyes are red-rimmed, her cheeks tearstained. She moves stiffly, as if she has been on her knees for hours. "How did you hear the news from London so quickly?"

What news? I catch Oliver's eye, a quick shift to each other and back to Margaret, followed by a silent warning to each other to let her speak first.

"A welcome would be nice, Sister," Oliver replies. He throws his gloves down on a bench and sits with his hands clasped. "And a glass of wine would not go amiss."

Margaret blinks, as if she has not even thought of offering any sustenance.

Oliver waves his hand before her. "Perhaps you could order refreshments, Margaret. You may be fasting, but we have had a long journey and are tired and thirsty."

She opens the door of the solar and speaks quietly to the servant standing outside. Within minutes, wine and sweetmeats arrive, the servant is dismissed, and Oliver pours me a glass of Bordeaux.

"The news. You have more information? When did you leave the Tower?" Margaret reaches for wine too, her hand trembling. "This is devastating. I am sorry for your loss. I am praying for their souls."

"The Tower? Souls?" I pause. "John Welles is to be released, Margaret. Oliver met with him and Jack. There is nothing more to be said about the incident."

"How did the king get orders to London so quickly? I heard Brackenbury refused. And then his lackey Tyrell took over." Margaret speaks in riddles, looks disdainfully at the food, drinks more wine.

"What are you saying, Margaret?" Oliver takes another mouthful of food. "Heard from whom? And what orders?"

"I heard from Bishop Morton." She stares at him blankly. "The princes are dead."

Dead?

I stumble to a chair, sit, gripping my arms across my body, pinching my elbows tightly to keep the denial locked inside my mouth.

"Dead?" I croak. We left them safe with Jack and a guard at the abbey. How could they be dead?

Margaret's voice comes from a distant place at the edge of my consciousness. "Murdered by Tyrell and then buried within the Tower."

"Murdered?" There is a worn thread in the carpet. A spider creeps along its web, strung between the table legs. I concentrate grimly on every mesmerising throw of its silk. Anything to avoid looking at Margaret.

Oliver walks to me, lays his hand lightly on my shoulder as if to comfort. Instead, he squeezes a warning. "And you heard this when, Margaret?" he asks carefully.

"A messenger arrived last night, carrying letters from Bishop Morton and Harry. Reporting directly from a trusted source in London." Margaret noisily starts to weep again and pulls her rosary forth. The beads click through the storm of thoughts in my mind. Is she praying for the dead boys' souls or her son's well-being?

"Can I see the messages?" Oliver asks.

"I burned them. News like that is not to be kept where spies may find it." Margaret pauses and closes her eyes, her lips moving in an Ave Maria. When done, the clicking of the next decade of beads begins again.

Oliver squeezes my shoulder tighter. "Elysabeth, I am devastated for you." He hands me a kerchief, pushes it over my face. "Take this to stem your tears."

I realise I must react with grief, for this would indeed be terrible news if I did not know the boys are tucked up in the safety of an abbey dormitory not ten miles from where we are sitting.

"My boys, my boys," I moan. "My boys . . . are . . . dead." And in truth, it doesn't take much for me to cry too, in fear for what might have happened had we not taken them when we did.

My sobs render me speechless, allowing Oliver to question Margaret. "And Harry? What does he say happened?"

Under my moans, I am so steady, conjuring my ability to detach. I feel as though I am watching myself.

"Richard killed them."

I choke on her words, cry more to cover my surprise.

"Richard?" Oliver questions.

Margaret starts another round of her beads. "He could no longer stand the threat they posed, and our attempt to free them with his brother's servants pushed him to the only possible outcome." Click. Click. Click. "They were removed. And in the removal, they perished." Click. Click. "The poor children are at peace at last. You must not mourn them, for they are with both their earthly father and their heavenly father now."

Oliver squeezes my shoulder again, and I start to sniffle, mopping my eyes. "You said m-m-murdered by Tyrell?" I ask.

"After Brackenbury refused," confirms Margaret. "Harry tells me so. He always suspected that Brackenbury would do anything for the king. He may not have wanted blood on his hands, but he left the door unlocked, stood down his guard."

That whisper of truth puts a bolt of fear into my heart. "What else, Margaret?"

Was I seen?

"Harry says already the accusations against Richard's men are being whispered around London." Margaret drops her rosary back to her breast, straightens her sleeves, picks up a wafer and munches on it.

I need to see this conversation to its inevitable outcome, hear Margaret's inner thoughts spoken aloud. "You show little sorrow or remorse, Sister."

My sister crosses herself, touches the book of hours at her waist. "It is a dreadful crime. But not one on my conscience," she replies. "You and I tried to rescue them, not murder them. This is all the king's doing."

I lean forward, keeping hold of Oliver's hand on my shoulder.

"And what does Harry intend to do now?" I ask. God forbid he is riding back to the court to confront Richard.

"I wait to hear more," Margaret replies. She stands now, looks from the window, as if she is impatient with our company. Or seeking a distant horizon. "But if Harry no longer has the princes to put back on the throne, I anticipate he will look to another."

"Himself?" Oliver and I speak in unison.

Margaret smiles, shakes her head. "Harry knows he can't rule. But he is an effective kingmaker, with his resources and standing army. And if given the right encouragement will eagerly do so again—and this time for the real reward he seeks. Power. Respect. And a seat at Henry Tudor's right hand."

I knew it. In my heart of hearts, I knew that my sister would never give up on her child. Nor the role she believes he is born to inherit.

"Margaret." Oliver's tone is quiet but firm. "Margaret, there is a rightfully crowned king on England's throne. And he has his own son and heir. You witnessed the coronation—damn it, you and your husband played a key role in it. You cannot usurp God's holy consecration."

Her face is as implacable as always, but her eyes are fiercely blue, and as she stands surrounded by the painted walls of saints, Margaret merges with the figures and becomes one with the religious fervour that shines from the cunning portraits. "If the throne was obtained through deception, how true is the king? And if the throne is kept by the murder of infants, would God look favourably upon such a sovereign?"

Now here is the heart of the matter, Margaret's justification. "You think your son is more honourable than the consecrated king is fit to

236

rule England?" I am used to Margaret's fervor, but even I am taken aback by her passion. "And that gives your son the right to challenge the throne?"

"My son stands for God and honour and what is good in this world." Margaret sweeps an arm around the chamber as if summoning the very saints down from their pedestals. "My son will lead a holy army to claim England's throne and bring God back to our people."

"You are so terribly wrong, Margaret," I say. "Grief must have addled your senses."

I gather Oliver's gloves and hand them to him. "I think we should leave, Oliver." I want no more of Margaret's treason. And I do not need to sit and listen to her weave her web any longer. "I am overcome with sorrow, and I just want to go home."

"Stay with me, Elysabeth." Margaret holds out her hand, smiles sweetly, and suddenly she is the child again, the sister I should have protected all those years ago from the Tudor marriage. Little did I know that the son she birthed at twelve years old would cause such dissension between us.

"I cannot. I must go home. Margaret, I beg you, do not engage any further with Harry or Bishop Morton. Leave this sad business alone. This is the end of your journey. Stay quietly here at Lathom under the protection of your husband's name."

I pray you, Margaret. Stop this now.

"I do not need Stanley's protection," she announces. "The Beaufort name is strong enough."

I take her hands, notice the palms are red and raw from the rope of her rosary. "You may wish for security. I don't trust Harry. And until you know which way Harry turns his coat, remember he knows of your involvement in our plan to remove the boys from the Tower. He may still tie you to their murder."

It costs me everything I have to stop from shaking Margaret, screaming at her that I have the boys safe, that they are alive. But to do so would be a double betrayal of Jack, the boys, even Richard since he planned this disappearance. All I can do is to try and isolate Margaret until the king deals with Harry and his terrible rumour-mongering. "Stay here, give your time to your charitable deeds, and do not draw attention to yourself."

Margaret pulls her hands away and seats herself at her desk. "I will let Henry know all that has happened," she says, more to herself than

Oliver and me. "He understands me; he knows how pure the throne must be." She pulls a parchment towards her, dips her quill in the ink jar. The familiar sound of scratching pen on paper fills the room. Oliver and I kiss her bowed head and leave her alone with her letter to her son.

On our ride back to the abbey, Oliver and I agree we will share with the king the strange twist of Harry and Bishop Morton's message of the rumour of the boys' deaths. But until Harry makes his next move, we cannot reveal Margaret's reaction, for it would instantly brand her a traitor.

34

Autumn 1483 | Bolton Castle

Heavy-hearted from the dreadful story and even more appalling reaction of my sister, I take the ride back to shake off Margaret's influence. When I am this close to her, it is as if I have been pulled into a mire of swirling emotions that are so foreign to me, and when I leave her, I cannot remove the layer of intrigue fast enough, like casting a familiar but worn cloak into a trunk and locking it away.

How is the king going to deal with the accusation that he murdered his nephews? And was it our own taking of the boys that has prompted Harry to spread this tale like an old woman prattling at the hearth? If so, he is playing with fire, for Richard will not tolerate the blasphemy that he is a child-killer. It is one thing for Harry to challenge the king's right to appoint his council, to accuse him of unfairness. And a completely different provocation to accuse him of murdering the princes.

This rumour must be stifled immediately.

There are ways to stop Harry; the king will exact punishment on him swiftly. But Margaret? All I can do is pray that my sister does not join her word with his and rise up against Richard in the name of her son.

When Oliver and I arrive back at Burscough Priory, so incongruous is the scene before me that I halt in the doorway, wondering if this is my family before me. So deep in thought am I over the rumours of the boys' death that it takes me a moment to clear my mind, for I am still living in Margaret's world of intrigue and murder.

Jack has Ned and Dickon seated on a bench in the dining hall, where a great platter of roasted meats and flagons of ale are piled on the board. At their feet lie half a dozen assorted dogs, from a couple of wolfhounds to a skinny lurcher, all eager to receive a scrap or two

239

if it lands their way. Jack has his feet propped up on the fire fender, with a brimming mug of ale in one hand and a chicken leg in the other. Both Ned and Dickon sprawl on the bench, kicking each other in jest and clutching their own half-pint mugs.

"What ARE you doing?" I shake my head in despair. "And what have you done to their hair?"

"Cut it. And teaching them to be men," Jack says through a mouthful of roast fowl.

"Cut it? More like shorn them like sheep!"

"Shorn like a bloody sheep," repeats Dickon delightedly.

"Like a bloody sheep," chortles Ned, adding for good measure, "God's blood, in truth we are."

I whirl around. "What did you say?"

Both boys fall quiet and gulp mouthfuls of their ale, wide eyes looking at me merrily over the mug.

"Jack? Jack." I suppress my laughter. "What are you doing?"

My husband stands lithely to his feet and bows. "Meet Ned and Dickon Pole," he announces. "Sons of your dear sister Edith who will be boarding with us at Bolton Castle to practice their skills as young knights."

"Damn right, my lady," says Ned as he bows.

"Bloody sheep." Dickon giggles and drains his mug.

I look down quickly to conceal a smile. "You both have quickly forgotten your manners," I scold. And then relent. "But I think this might be for the best."

Ned's face grows suddenly serious. "Lord Scrope advises so," he says quietly. "It seems that we were in even more peril than I feared in the Tower. Thank you for rescuing us from harm, Godmother. We promise we will not betray our true identities until you tell us it is safe to do so."

He takes Dickon's hand and holds him close. "And my brother and I will never reveal your role in our escape. We know how dangerous the world remains for us."

I look over their heads to Jack. "Can we talk privately? We found more news than we were expecting at Margaret's." I glance meaningfully at the boys. "And the sooner we can get to Bolton Castle, the safer we will be."

From Lathom Park to Bolton Castle is another two days' ride, and the last few miles are almost the hardest as familiar landmarks come into sight, so eager am I to be home. The land grows wilder and the hills higher until all we can follow are the rough tracks and the occasional lane edged by familiar dry-stone walls. Reaching the Aysgarth Falls, we carefully cross the ford, leading our horses across the flat rocks. The stones are pitted in places, with green weeds clinging to them, and will prove lethal to a horse's legs if a hoof catches in haste.

The familiar rushing water splashing over the falls sounds like home. Even in this dry month of August, the water thunders through, and Dickon's excitement brightens us all. His rosy-cheeked face shines in front of Oliver's brown leather jacket. Even Ned opens his eyes and sits straighter against Jack's chest, clutching his protective arm. I hope that finally his health is turning. He just needs to be away from the Tower, away from the terrible traumas of this summer of bloodshed and betrayal that have plagued his spirit.

"We'll come back and visit, play in the water and fish," I promise them. "For we are almost at Bolton Castle."

Through the single-track village street and stone houses and over the brow of the last hill, there lies the great sweep of the valley, the rolling hills and a blue sky doming over the land. A hawk hovers beside me, its call piercing the firmament, and the soft bleating of sheep tumbles down from the high fields.

Home. Strange how absence, even in the most familiar of surroundings, can engender a love that secretly grew in my heart. I am coming home.

About two miles away, commanding a view over the broad valley, the castle stands sentinel, as it has done for so many centuries, a stronghold, a refuge for the Scrope family.

And so it is again, this time for my precious godson and his brother.

The keep gleams in the sun, a stone fortress hewn from the land and yet shining like a beacon of hope. I cannot urge on my tired mare faster; I have not the heart to demand speed now after such a challenging journey. Our bedraggled group slowly walks the last two miles home, wending up the final hills and always drawing closer, united in a silent relief of knowing we are safely home with our secret intact.

As we approach the portcullis, the guards start hauling the massive iron gate open, and by the time we ride into the courtyard, our steward is waiting to greet us.

"My lord, messengers have been arriving since yesterday morning. The king is in York. He is asking for your presence there immediately." His eyes flicker over the boys before he hands papers to Jack.

"My nephews Dickon and Ned Pole," Jack says shortly. "Board them with the other boys and see they are equipped for their time in training here."

The steward bows. "And is there a message back to the king, my lord?"

Jack glances at me. "Can you ride farther?"

I nod. "We have no choice."

"I'll stay here for a few days." Oliver dismounts, tosses his reins to a waiting stable hand. "Just to make sure my nephews are settling into their new lives."

I smile at him gratefully. "Thank you. They will be glad of your company." I stretch my back, roll my shoulders. "Let me wash, change, and pack some items," I continue. "I can be ready to ride on to York in an hour."

Upon our arrival at the Bishop of York's Palace, Jack and I are shown to Will and Meg's rooms. It is late, and yet they are still fully dressed and waiting for us.

"The king has been so impatient to welcome you back." Will embraces Jack as Meg hugs me. "Are the boys well? Your journey uneventful?"

Jack's face is grim. "Ned was still ill when we left London, but he has gathered strength during our travel, and I think with less on his mind and more exercise outdoors, he will continue to thrive." He takes my hand, and I am grateful for his touch, for this is a moment I am dreading. "However, we have some disturbing news from Lady Stanley. Elysabeth and Oliver stopped at Lathom Park on our way north. Margaret is corresponding with Bishop Morton and Buckingham. And she appears to be in thick with both of them. There are terrible rumours starting to circulate in London. I think it best we meet immediately with the king."

242

"Now?" Will takes a step back and then sees the seriousness of Jack's expression. "Now," he confirms. "This way. Tell me as we go."

We slip through the corridors of the palace, along a gallery lined with biblical scenes lit by a harvest moon rising over the river. I feel I am hurrying past a crowded land of distant people, for so real are they it is like looking through a window into another world. I pause before King Solomon as his soldier threatens to cut a baby in half with a sword and shudder away from the dead child on the ground. The worst of this tale of the princes' murder? Margaret's cool reaction to news of the princes' death.

Between puddles of dark and light, I enter a suspended sense of being, for once we speak to the king, I know the wheel of destiny will turn once more. Whether I ascend with Jack or descend with Margaret is not my destiny to control.

We reach the king's chambers as evidenced by the guard. But here in the North, there is no need of an army of retainers, yeoman warders, or a troop of liveried and armed soldiers. Two stout and plain-dressed Yorkshiremen stand before the doors, and at seeing Will and Jack they doff their caps and wave us through into the bishop's own personal chamber. This is where Richard and his queen are lodging. A hundred candles enhance the moon's beaming and the room swims in molten gold, the flames shimmering and reflecting from honeyed-oak panelling. Richard sits before the unlit fireplace with Anne Neville next to him. A minstrel leans against the window seat and plucks softly at his instrument, the notes melding into the fragrant night air and wrapping the room in harmony.

Richard looks up, a pleasant smile on his face. In the gentle moonlight, no worry lines mar his forehead, and his hazel eyes are soft and happy. I wish myself anywhere but here at this moment, for I am truly exhausted by Margaret's plotting, whipped by my sister's intrigues that always seemed to bring mayhem to those in her path.

"My friends, thank you for your service. I want to hear how the boys fare, how your journey was. Come, enjoy the last of the day with us." Richard waves to the bench, and we sit as if we are neighbours visiting on a Sunday afternoon. "The queen and I were just reflecting on the success of our progress and talking of our son's happiness. It will be good for all the cousins to be together. What brings you here so late in the evening?"

243

I look at Will, who is about to shatter the king's calm, deliver betrayal into this peaceful room. My son-in-law bows his head in momentary thought and then utters his damning words clearly and softly, in northern plain speak, not in the language of a southern courtier.

"Your Grace, Elysabeth and Jack carry troubling news. There continues to be unrest in London; and now the Duke of Buckingham spreads word against you."

Richard's hand seeks Anne's, and they draw closer together. No longer are they king and queen, but two people who have loved each other for a long time and share strength in adversity. Richard's face hardens. "Go on."

"The boys are at Bolton Castle. But Harry . . . Harry has kindled rumours in London that they have been murdered. On your command."

Richard blanches, his lips tighten, while Anne cries out. "What? And how?"

"It is whispered within the Tower; we do not have all the information. But we believe Buckingham has implicated Brackenbury and Tyrell."

Will glances at me. This is my cue to take up the story.

"We heard this news two days ago," I continue, emulating Will's clear talking, swallowing the pain in my throat. I owe the king a clear accounting. "They are reported as rumours behind doors for now."

Richard starts up, making us all jump. "Rumours? Heard from whom? What is this?"

He appeals to Jack and Will, his trusted councillors.

Jack picks up where I left off. "My lord, Elysabeth and Oliver passed by their sister's home at Lathom Park after we left London. Margaret told her of this strange and terrible event. She had just received a messenger from Buckingham."

There is so much more to tell. I glance at Will.

Richard lifts his face, now taut with anger. "Dear God, is this Harry's resentment from his outburst in Gloucester? Such a foolish man. He has proven once more that he cannot be relied upon in a position of authority, for his brain is addled with his own importance."

Anne interrupts him, her voice piercingly high. "And the boys? They are unharmed? Do they know of these dreadful tales?"

"Safe at Bolton, Your Grace, unaware of any of this." Will shakes his head slightly at me, cautioning me not to speak. There are more immediate matters still to talk of than Ned's and Dickon's well-being.

"What was Harry thinking?" The king draws himself up, wincing as he braces his shoulders. Shock is giving way to anger. "Where in God's name is he going with this?"

Will nods to me. *Go forward again.*

"Removing the obstacles to the throne, Your Grace," I say quietly.

"WHAT?"

"When we met in Burford, before he saw you in Gloucester, he was speaking in riddles, telling me these strange ideas of his. He sees the princes as obstacles that will always tarnish the throne. Hearing that they are no longer in plain sight in the Tower and spreading the rumour that you have killed them removes them from men's ambition to return them to the throne."

"They are proven bastards; their claim is already revoked." Richard smacks his hand on his thigh in frustration. "Harry has concocted this in order to blacken me. This makes no sense. From the moment they were declared illegitimate, they were no longer my obstacles to kingship."

Will said the words we have agreed together, laying the full weight of Harry's plans before the king. "But they are his."

The four words that herald Harry's betrayal hang in the air. No one speaks or moves until we see how Richard responds. Does he realise at this moment that the man who six months ago was almost unknown to him, who brought his army to Stony Stratford, who put the princes in the Tower, who declared Richard king, who had the position of honour at his coronation, does he realise the extent of his betrayal . . . and his ambition?

And must I tell the king of Margaret too?

He is quick, catches my thought and reels it in. "Elysabeth, when you were meeting with your sister when you left the court, back at Minster Lovell. Did she also see Buckingham?"

"Yes."

"And does she know as much as you?"

"Yes, my lord."

"And she did not dare come to tell me of this betrayal?" Richard paces now, his hands clenched by his sides. His walk is uneven; he grimaces as he twists suddenly and leans into my face. "Where is Margaret now?"

"She is still at Lathom Park, my lord."

"Doing what? Why did she not return to court with you?"

The king is not stupid. He knows of Margaret's dreams. I can feel Jack's anxiety, know that Richard's reaction has widened the abyss between us again.

I look back into Richard's eyes. How strange that at all these defining moments, it narrows to he and I discussing the princes. "She had matters to attend, my lord. I think it would best be asked of Lord Stanley what his wife aspires to."

I cannot speak of my sister's letter writing, her fervour, her incantation of her son's name. I will not tell him of the light in Margaret's eyes when she heard of Harry's deed. I will not utter the words that will accuse my sister of treason.

But Jack does not hesitate. "Best keep a close watch on her, Your Grace," he says, avoiding my eyes as he lays open my sister's ambition. "Harry's obstacles are her obstacles. By starting a rumour that you have murdered the princes, he has helped her son's cause as well as his own."

"Dear Jesus. Henry Tudor enters into this too? This is a rat's nest of betrayal." Richard runs his hands through his hair. "Catesby, you must have thoughts. What do we do?"

Will is waiting for this question. I know his lawyer mind has already planned the motion for defence. "The boys are safe. No need to give life to Harry's gossip-mongering by acknowledging that you are worried by him. Unfed, these rumours will die a natural death. Your more immediate concern is if Harry is going to remain in Wales or raise up against you and attempt to take the throne." Will pauses, looking at Jack for confirmation. "It is very early in your reign, my lord, and there are many in the southern lands who believe you usurped the throne. Harry could very well channel their discontent into an uprising."

The king throws back his head and lets loose a long and terrible shout. From the depths of his being starts a trembling, and he pulls his dagger and slashes at the precious tapestry hanging by the fireplace. Such is his violence that great welts sever the heads of the apostles. "God save me from this deceitful and untrue creature. I will hunt him down like the vermin he is," he yells. "Like a fox, I will run him to ground and kill him."

35

Autumn 1483 | York

The king meets with Jack and Will throughout the endless night. When they eventually return to our room to splash water on their faces and make themselves presentable, it is to leave again to meet with the king's full council. I do not envy Jack that task, for he will bear witness to Lord Stanley's humiliation. In front of everyone, for I know well his style, the king will publicly question Stanley's ability to control his wife. After all, although Margaret is the richest woman in the kingdom, she is still Lady Stanley, and he is responsible for his own wife's behaviour.

During the day, I sit by the chamber window, peering through the diamond panes as messengers gallop forth from the bishop's palace. As the sun arched and sank into the reeds by the riverbank, I have counted more than twenty dispatched in all directions. I long to leave too, back to Bolton Castle, to the boys, to the security of home. And then I want to travel to Lathom, to warn Margaret to keep silent, keep her own counsel—as if my repetition will change her mind, for have I not been telling her this for weeks? And most of all, I want to stay here, at Jack's side, repair the damage to our marriage, be once more a baron's lady concerned only about the people in our estates, managing my household. I want my old life back. *Sovereynté* at home, not in England's royal palaces. Just as the horsemen gallop in all directions, so does my heart leap to the four winds, leaving me an empty vessel becalmed on a sea of indecision.

In the end, Jack solves my dilemma when he returns late that evening.

"The king requires you to return to Lathom Park," he says bluntly. He stands across the room, the distance between us still a chasm of politics and loyalties. "You will watch Margaret and report to us any concerns you have that she is in contact with Harry. And Henry Tudor."

And so it is the east wind that blows me to Lathom, a bitter and cold wind that heralds swift change and storms.

"You command me to spy on my own sister?" I ask. "That I will not do."

My husband folds his arms against his chest. Is it to stop from holding me? I walk to him, take his hand. The healing stitches of our ride with the boys have frayed again, for he quickly untangles my fingers from his. "She will trust you more than anyone else," Jack says. "And this will prove where your own loyalty lies too."

"Did you suggest this to the king? Is this your own way of testing my fidelity?" I slash open the wound of mistrust between us, for I am not always the one to receive the cuts. "Choose my sister's ambition or yours?"

He has the grace to look uncomfortable then. "It is Will's idea," he says quietly. "To save Stanley's dignity. He is, after all, the king's most powerful ally."

"And so you expect me to betray my sister to reveal Harry's intrigues?" I am sickened that Jack thinks I would do such a thing.

"If Margaret is wrapped up with Harry's plotting, you must disclose her part," Jack replies. "Your duty is to your king."

Yes. And to my family.

"I will not betray her," I say fiercely. "But I may be able to save her. If I find evidence of Harry's conspiracy and I share with you secrets from Margaret, you will owe me much."

"What are you bargaining for, Elysabeth?" Jack sounds suddenly weary, and I press my advantage. He is a soldier, not a courtier, and I know when he tires of words.

"Margaret's life."

"I cannot promise that."

"You will find a way," I retort. "I will look for evidence of Harry's betrayal. But I will destroy any connection with Margaret unless you tell me she will not be executed for treason."

"That is not mine to decide."

"You have influence. You and Catesby." I am playing Margaret's own game of partiality. Educated woman that she is, she would find the irony in this.

"I will do my best." Jack unfolds his arms, lets his hands loose at his sides. He looks like a lost boy.

I press home. "Swear to me."

"I swear."

His face is sad, and I know it reflects my own. For this is what our marriage has come to, the negotiations between two adversaries, and I am both angry and cut to the heart at these circumstances that has caused our love to flee. I meet his eyes, and I see behind the hurt and anger a fleeting spark of hope. Jack takes a step towards me, tilts his head in a question. Perhaps he will now speak of love, remember us, not put his king first.

"When this is over, Elysabeth, when you have secured the information the king requests . . ."

"Yes? What? When?" I trip over my words in my eagerness. Does he think beyond now to a future for us that is not contaminated with Margaret's ill humours?

"I may be sent south to the west country," he says. "The king is concerned about securing the coast against invasion."

I shake my head. A soldier first. Always a soldier first. It is what I hate. . . and love about this man.

I walk away from him then, before he sees my hurt. A soldier's wife never shows him the pain of parting. "Before I go to Margaret, I travel first to Bolton Castle," I say shortly. "The least I can do is see the boys before you exile me to Lathom."

Jack's voice hardens. "Then say farewell to them. The king is establishing Sheriff Hutton as a royal residence. There are plans for them to be moved there in secrecy for safekeeping with the other royal bastards until we discover Harry's true intent and the king feels they and he are secure. Then we can make an announcement."

"A nursery of deposed heirs. How convenient," I retort. "And when does the King's Council plan to openly investigate the rumours of Ned's and Dickon's deaths and call Harry to account?"

Jack's eyes flicker to the door and windows, and his voice drops. "The council does not know. We are keeping this between Catesby, Lovell, and Ratcliffe only. Until we bring Buckingham before us, prove his part in this, we do not want to stoke the rumours further. Word that the princes are dead by Richard's hand will be a touchstone for rebellion to support Harry. Or invite Henry to invade. And proof that they are alive will increase attempts to kill them, for Harry has stoked a fire that still burns in England's southern towns and threatens to consume Richard."

So no word that the boys are with us, that they are already in the North? Much as I despise his secrecy, I understand Richard's reasoning. For until he can truly assess the likelihood of any uprising, why add more fuel to the fire? And all the while, Harry hides in his Welsh fortress, stoking insurrection, writing letters of intrigue to my sister, inciting her to think her support of his cause will bring Henry Tudor home.

And what of Margaret's pledge to Elizabeth Woodville? How will the queen react when she hears the rumours of her sons' deaths in the Tower? Will this push her into Margaret Beaufort's camp, forever against Richard?

A horrible thought hits me like a rock. Does Margaret intend to fan the flames of the stories of Richard's murderous deeds? By doing so, she could certainly permanently turn Elizabeth Woodville away from Richard and towards Henry Tudor and the marriage with Bess.

My fury at Margaret brings a metal tang in my throat, a sickness at how often I thought to protect my sister, putting her well-being before my own. And at the same time, fear licks my limbs. Always, it has been this way between us, and there is no relief now. How suddenly I am keeping secrets from everyone. And what secrets are being kept from me?

Leaving York, I can spend no more than a night at Bolton Castle, as the king's guard waits to escort me on to Lathom Park. Will rides with me to verify that Ned and Dickon are safely concealed and to confirm that Oliver will stay by their sides until the king sends for them to be moved to Sheriff Hutton. My guard are not even permitted within the castle courtyard for fear the boys would be recognised by a follower loyal to the old King Edward. It would not take much to take control of Ned and dispatch Richard from the throne. It troubles me still that the legal complexity of their bastardy is still one that continues to ring untrue, for truly, why can't they be made legitimate? Will never wishes to speak of this again, he tells me, for what's done is done.

The boys are hidden in plain sight, just as when we left the Tower. And as we arrive home and I look up at Bolton's sheer walls, I know that they will be safe here for the next few weeks.

"I must spend some time with my sister," I explain to them as I gently unwrap Ned's arms from around my waist. Already, the fresh Yorkshire air and Oliver's exercises are bringing roses to his cheeks and encouraging an appetite as strong as any other country squire, the toothache no longer even mentioned. "You will continue to spend your time with the other boys here, and soon your uncle will send an escort to take you to his castle near York. You will be with your cousins, and perhaps even your sisters will visit you."

"We do not know whether your mother will leave sanctuary," Will continues. "But when she does, the king will take good care of her and make sure your sisters are treated with the respect they deserve."

Dickon walks with me to the portcullis gate, his little face serious. He pulls something from his pocket. "I was making this for Ned, as a surprise," he whispers. "For he told me when he turned fourteen, he would rule England as an independent king, and not with our uncle the protector." He opens his grubby hand, and there in his palm lies an exquisite little carved lion, his paws rampant. "I suppose giving him this now would hurt his feelings. And put him in danger."

"England's symbol of royalty." I kiss his warm head, the hair now growing in darker than before; shearing his locks vanquished his blond baby curls. "He will still love the care with which you have carved this, Dickon."

"Perhaps one day he may still be king," he continues hopefully, looking up at me with bright eyes. "For once you are born with royal blood, they cannot drain it from you, can they?"

The anger in my throat thickens my voice. Taking the little lion from Dickon's hand, I kiss its beautifully carved mane. "No, Dickon, they can never remove your birthright. And always remember you too are the son of a king." I slip the little creature in my pocket. "I will take care of this for you. For now, you must forget your heritage, to be safe. But one day you will be reunited with your sisters and recognised that once, your brother was king of England, and you his heir."

I leave abruptly before my anger speaks more, for I must not worry Dickon; the child has been through enough these recent months. But I cannot rid the image of Ned lying ill in the Tower, Dickon trying desperately to keep his brother alive. Whatever it takes, on God's holy word, I will see that Harry pays for what he has done . . . to the prince who once was king and his brother who was his heir.

36
Winter 1483 | Lathom Park

I ride to Lathom Park on the billowing breast of a storm, fitting for this moment when my own heart is lightning-seared by the deception that lays ahead. On the second day, as we descend down from the dales and gallop across the valleys, the badge of the White Boar on my guards' hats clears travellers from our path. We are riding on the king's business, and no man dare delay us. Thunder rumbles and bounces across the surrounding hilltops, and by the time we take refuge at Lathom Park, the witches are sweeping boulders down the escarpments, so loud crashes the storm. As we race into the castle grounds, a spear of lightning rents the sky, and the shouts of the guard drown in the first fat drops of rain pummelling the thirsty ground.

This time no supercilious steward keeps me waiting, and I sense a change in his attitude towards me. He shows more respect when I am returning with the king's guard.

Margaret is, of course, at prayer in her private chapel, and I am forced to pace within the room of the saints while she finishes her bargaining with God. In truth, Margaret is the most pious of women, and I wonder at her multi-chambered heart, dedicated to God and conniving to man. It is hard for me not to think that Margaret's prayers, her own personal prayers, not those repeated from her books, must resemble a negotiation rather than a plea for forgiveness of her sins.

"You have returned. And you are alone?" Margaret leaves her prie-dieu, and the door remains open. Candles flicker in the draft raised by the storm. "Why do you come?" She loses interest and sits on a bench, opening the book of hours she always carries with her.

"The king has ordered me so. I will stay here while he investigates Harry."

She looks up sharply then. "What reason does he have to question Harry? What concerns him?"

"I had no choice but to tell the king of our encounter at Burford."

A flicker of anxiety crosses Margaret's face as another flash of lightning rips the sky. "You repeated our private conversation to the king?"

"Not directly of your words." I join her on the bench. "But more of Harry's riddles. The king has vowed to find the truth of Harry's loyalty and bring him to account for his actions."

And hunt him down if he has proven disloyal.

Margaret fumbles for her rosary and falls silent, her lips moving as she fingers her beads.

I wait. What will she do?

"The king should have appreciated Harry more," Margaret says finally, "given him the respect his bloodline warrants." Her eyes shift to a casket on her writing desk. It is a good size, shaped like a coffin of smoothly polished elm. More significantly, it is large and could contain many documents. "And now, if you will excuse me, I shall ask you to leave me in private. I have business to attend to, and Reginald Bray will be here shortly to meet with me."

And I would prefer not to stay. By the time I return later that evening to sup with Margaret and play a game of chess, there is no sign of the casket, and our only company for supper is Margaret's trusted friend, Reginald Bray.

Messengers arrive daily at Lathom Park carrying letters from Jack and Meg, notes from Will, and a quick missive from Oliver. These are merely excuses to keep open communication between us, for it would be odd for me to write to them daily, but I can answer their letters with a return by messenger. For a week, I have nothing to write about other than news of the weather and the simple walks I take daily within Lathom's sprawling grounds. I do not question Margaret deeply, for I have decided that I will tread carefully between the weft and weave of close family and distant cousins. I cannot probe for damaging rumours of Henry Tudor, for Margaret has always had her ambitions for him, and he is of my own flesh and blood.

Instead, I seek clues of Harry's treachery.

On Saturday, the entire household assembles on Castle Fields to celebrate the gathering of the crops festival, for the full harvest moon has risen, and it is has been a bountiful year. After an intense period of reaping and winnowing, the people are ready to enjoy the fruits of their labour. Margaret knows the importance of keeping her tenants happy, and she sits on the chair of state in the pavilion on the grass, tapping her foot to the sound of the gitterns and drums. Her own musicians are some of the best in the land, and her wheat-gold gown is of the richest velvet and satin. Margaret may wear a hair shirt for penance on holy days, but she grew up with me in our mother's home, where luxury was prized and adornment a way of life. My sister loves rich fabrics and talented musicians.

The tent is crammed full with neighbours from miles around who join the celebration, and soon I am able to slip into the crowds and leave the dancing and feasting behind. The moon again lights my way, just as it did a few weeks ago at the Bishop's Palace. Tonight, I seek the written evidence of Harry's scheming, and I can only do so when I know Margaret is excused from her meetings with God upon her private prie-dieu.

Under the disapproving stares of the painted saints trapped on the walls of Margaret's hallowed chamber, I search her moonlit room. The casket is not on her desk, but it has to be somewhere close by. I take a deep breath and enter her private prayer room, apologising to Margaret's God and asking permission from mine.

This is to protect the boys, I explain in my silent prayer. For if I find the evidence that Harry is planning an uprising and intends to take the throne, Richard will stop him, and this whole episode in their lives will be over.

There is just one high window in this tiny octagonal room, and I find a flint and light candles to help my search. There are many books on the shelves, but no elm coffin-box of letters. I look carefully at the cloth that drapes her prie-dieu, and when I pull aside the heavy fabric, there is the casket. I sit on the floor and place it before me. As I expected, the box is stuffed with papers, and I carefully lift each from its hiding place and spread the parchments before me. Under the first few inventories and contracts, warrants and letters of credit, I come across a bundle of letters and notes tied with a green braided ribbon. Henry's. I refrain from pulling the knot, for these are not my business, and Margaret's son's letters are for his mother alone.

A sudden click and the outer door to Margaret's chamber creaks open. I freeze, my fingers buried in the letters, others strewn around my skirts. I cannot move for fear of making a noise. Footsteps click across the floorboards.

Oh God, don't let Margaret be back already.

I swallow, furiously thinking of reasons that I would be rifling through my sister's private letters.

A clink of metal and a scrape of wood against wood. I shift slightly, and my knee pops, deafening to me.

In Margaret's solar, the sounds of logs being added, a fire being poked, a chair dragged closer. Footsteps again, this time fading away. Through the opening, the room now glows with an orange light, the flames bringing a welcoming cheer to the room, readying for Margaret's return.

Moving speedily now, I set aside parchments with the Woodville seals on them, digging my fingers through the mass of papers. Below them are another, smaller bundle, a tiny seal with the Stafford knot cracked on one of them. I open the first, and Harry's writing jumps out at me. *A copy,* he scrawls, *"of the request I have sent to your son. We are ready. We are united. He must set sail and join us on 18th October. The rising has begun."* The breath punches from my lungs; I crawl closer to the window and the pale moonlight, try to read a scribbled note at the bottom. *Do not betray me. If you do, I will bury you with the princes.* God only knows how Harry means to carry out this threat to my sister. But there is no doubt he thinks the princes dead.

I clutch the letter, send a prayer to the heavens, for here is the proof. Harry is rebelling. His death warrant is in my hands. I must send it to Jack. And ensure that he upholds our bargain that by revealing these plans, it is not Margaret's execution sentence too.

37

Winter 1483 | Lathom Park

Concealed within an innocent missive from me, Harry's fated letter travels to the king on the last Scrope messenger to leave Lathom before fierce autumn storms isolate us from the world. Since the fine harvest festival, a rain has set in that has yet to lift, and after five days we peer from the castle over fields of water. The river burst its banks, and Lathom floats like an island surrounded by an endless moat that keeps us safe within—and everyone else away. When the rain pauses and the sheets of water part, the view from the solar is bleak. Debris pushes against the walls; dead sheep wash up against the stone, felled trees stretch and claw bare branches to the sky, and one day a drowned child is trapped in the jetsam of the storm. Margaret offers a prayer to save its soul from purgatory, and I send the steward to risk his own life to bring the little girl into the castle to be prepared for a decent burial. I cannot let the poor babe stay outside by herself in a watery grave.

We burn candles all day to lift the heavy midday skies, and our eyes are reddened and strained by the dim light. Margaret prays for hours at a time, and I simply sit on the seat by the window, embroidery useless on my lap, and stare out into the unremitting grey.

Where is my letter now? Is this enough to convict Harry, bring about his downfall? I have no wish for another's blood on my hands, and yet my act has set in motion his end. I pray it is not my sister's outcome too.

From within Margaret's chapel comes a loud exclamation, and her door flies open.

"Have you been in my private papers?" Margaret has lost weight, and her eyes are huge in her thin face. They burn a feverish blue, like the inner heart of a flame. "Are you such a wretch that you steal from your own flesh and blood and betray your own nephew?"

So now we are here at this moment of truth. "I have not touched your letters from Henry. But yes, I have sent Harry's message to the king."

"And in so doing, you have betrayed Henry. He is named within. He is implicated in Harry's rebellion." Margaret steadies herself against the stout wall of the window embrasure, trembling. "Oh, Elysabeth, what have you done?"

"I have not shared any of Henry's letters. I have neither touched them nor read them. They are yours and yours alone. But from the documents I saw, you have left a trail across half of England with the money and men you are raising to support his return." I draw my sister down on the seat next to me. "I know Henry is your life. I know he is everything in the world to you. But you commit treason, Margaret, by helping him return to England, for the only reason he returns now is to challenge the throne."

"That is Harry's ambition," she replies. Her trembling ceases; deep lines draw her mouth down. "Harry will challenge the king, lead a rebellion, leave the way open for Henry's destiny. The work is all Stafford's. I arranged it so."

Another gust of rain pelts the window, and the wind blows so hard it sends a draft into the chimney, blowing acrid smoke into the room from the fireplace, making my eyes water. The storm outside reflects the tempest within our family. Soon my nephew will be crossing the channel from France. What are Henry's chances of even landing in England? It is a perilous voyage on a calm day. With these storms, the worse in living memory, it is a death wish.

I try to convince Margaret to see the danger she is in. "You join your cause with Stafford's so that Henry may ultimately claim the crown." My simple statement holds the weight of my sister's ambition. "At what point were you going to tell Harry that he fights not for his own ambition, but to put your son on the throne? That you have misled him all this time?"

"He may think of it as a betrayal. But I know what's best for both of them. Harry would never be capable of being king, only a kingmaker. My son always comes first." Margaret shrugs my arm from her, slowly stands. "And now it is your choice, Elysabeth. Your godson is dead, you have no connection to the throne, and yet you still choose your York husband over the bloodline and destiny of your own family."

"And you can say that with such ice in your heart, Margaret. Have you no pity for the lives you are destroying in your ambition?" I have to hear for myself her words, convince myself that my choice is right.

"The princes were a casualty of war," she replies. "Tragic, yes. But inevitable. And Richard must have thought the same."

"You believe he murdered them?"

"They died under his watch. I believe they were an obstacle to his keeping the throne. For as long as they were alive, men would find reason to challenge him."

"Yet you are the one to challenge him now?"

She shakes her head, laughs at me in my naiveté. "I don't challenge him. Harry does."

"You have set Harry up to be the face of the rebellion," I say. "Yet your ambition is for your son."

She shrugs. "Harry can choose to believe whatever he wants. But Henry is going to win the throne. Remember, when he does, that he is your nephew. Ask me then if blood is thicker than the water in your veins."

A silence wraps like a winding cloth around us, binding our ties, lashing us to the fate we are both born to, a destiny that finally cleaves us apart.

My heart breaking, I tell her my true feelings. "You will always be my sister, Margaret. I just don't know if you will always be my ally."

Your son will never reach the throne when Harry is captured and the princes are revealed as alive. This is the final parting of our ways.

In truth, when I receive word that the arrests have begun, I am relieved that my guardianship is over. Enough. Enough of this dreadful halter of sisterhood around my neck, unfairly yoked together. I am exhausted. Yet I have the strength for one last effort to save my sister. I tear up the scrawled note from Jack and break open one from Meg. Jack's warning is true. Meg reaffirms his hurried words. The arrests have begun. And Margaret will be named. I run into Margaret's private chapel, almost knocking her from her knees.

"Burn them now!" I shake my sister by the shoulders, pushing her headdress askew. "Destroy the evidence of your plotting, Sister!

Whatever letters you have from Grey, Woodville, Bray, Morton, burn them immediately."

Margaret crosses herself hastily and rises awkwardly from her prie-dieu. "I will not. I have nothing to hide—"

"And everything to lose." I hold out my hands. "Give me the casket. The Woodvilles are being called to account. Dorset and Lionel Woodville are being hunted like foxes. Others have already been arrested. Buckingham has been condemned as a traitor; there is a bounty on his head. There is no doubt Harry will name you as his co-conspirator." I wave Meg's letter, telling the story straight from my daughter's heart, not couched in men's politicking. "The rebellion will fail, Margaret. And you are so bound up in the fate of these men that there is little I can do to extract you. Give me the casket. NOW."

Margaret's eyes flicker to a chest under the window, and I pull out robes and linen garments and embroidered tunics made for a man. It is Margaret's hope chest, hope that one day she will put these shirts over her son's head and sit by him at his coronation banquet with a coronet on her head and a crown on his. At the bottom, my fingers touch the unyielding lid of the casket, and I heave it from its hiding place. Throwing open the lid, I pull out every document that has the names of the rebels.

Margaret yanks at my hands, crying as her arthritic swollen fingers scratch and claw at mine. She sobs a torrent, wailing with tears pouring down her cheeks. "Not Henry's letters. Not my son's words." She stuffs both hands to her mouth and stifles a scream. "Where is he? Has he landed? I have heard nothing. Have you? Have you?"

"Nothing. We must fight this first, Margaret. I cannot help Henry right now. But I can diminish your risk." I toss the bound packet of Henry's letters to her and grab the other documents, running to the solar and feeding them to the fire. "Where else, Margaret? Where else have you hidden evidence that will incriminate you? I cannot bring back all that you have sent out in the world, but I can at least destroy all that returned to you."

Blessed God, help me destroy any mention of my name linked with yours or Harry's.

Margaret's weeping is stilled as she realises the danger. She pulls documents from secret drawers, hidden compartments, a loose panel. There is a pile two hands high by the time she has given me everything, and I rapidly feed the fire, sate it with my sister's traitorous evidence.

At last, there is nothing but black greasy ash in the fireplace and the acrid smell of burnt vellum polluting the air. Margaret still clutches Henry's letters as if holding a baby, tears freshly rolling down her face. She weeps easily for one so strong, and I let her. She is descending with Fortune again, and this time there is no clue when the wheel will stop rolling.

I rock her, hold my little sister close as she cries. "Hush." I comfort Margaret as when she was a child with a scraped knee. "Hush, my darling. I'm here. I will not leave you. I will not let you go by yourself again." Margaret's weeping continues for a while until darkness falls again and a tumult of hooves echoes through the courtyard. We run to the window, peer down into the dim heart of Lathom Park. This time the king's messenger is accompanied by a guard of twenty, and Margaret looks at me, her eyes red and fearful. The reckoning has come.

So many intersections of fate. Isolated at Lathom Park, I am forgotten, designated a convenient minder of the woman who stirs rebellion, while we wait for men to decree our fate. How strange that while life continues in its tedious sameness for us, others are living under the daily threat of death, fighting across England's land again. The rains still fall, we have the king's guard now surrounding us, and there is nothing I can do but light candles and pray.

Margaret swears that Harry has his rebellion coordinated across all of England, with men rising in the south and east to join him. He will unite England under his leadership, she says, unite her son's kingdom to welcome his return. When Henry lands on the south coast, they will march together to challenge Richard the Usurper—not with the intent to restore Ned to the throne, for he is conveniently dead, but to place Henry Tudor in power.

I cannot meet her eyes when she repeats this plan over and over for fear that some spark of knowledge will reveal my truth. When I pray, I keep my head dutifully bowed. As my sister implores God for a safe passage from France for her son, I plead for God to keep the boys safe and hidden. For if Harry or Henry were to discover they are alive, they would be removed permanently from this earth, ensuring no challenge to Henry Tudor remains.

I will always protect you.

My godmother's oath mocks me. I am powerless to do anything but pray that Bolton's walls keep Ned and Dickon secure.

Margaret paces the chamber, pausing every few minutes to gaze from the window. What does she expect to see? Henry Tudor riding triumphantly home to his mother, red Welsh dragon banners flying above his head?

She gasps, brings her hand to her throat.

Who has she seen? I rush to the window. It is not Henry Tudor, but our brother Oliver riding into the courtyard. Alone except for a Scrope guard of four.

Standing as if she is to be sentenced, Margaret takes a position by the fireplace. I cannot wait and fly to the door, trip halfway down the stairs until I meet Oliver on his way up. He holds me close and feels reassuringly solid. "Say nothing," he whispers as he leads me back to Margaret.

The three of us stand close together, for after all, we are family. Oliver takes each of our hands, forming our little circle. We used to play with Margaret this way when she was a child, a nursery dance that she loved to supervise. I wonder if she remembers as I see the fear bleached across her face.

"I thought you should know that Harry Stafford died three days ago in Salisbury." Oliver grips our hands tightly, speaks directly to Margaret. "He died crying out his lies and screaming the names of others who rebelled with him, believing that the king would forgive him."

"And Henry?" All the blood has drained from Margaret's face, and it is as white as the wimple that holds her captive.

"He never landed. He came within sight of the English coast and turned back to France. I think he realised that Harry's was a lost cause."

Margaret slumps but still grips our hands.

Oliver turns to me. "I know you will not pray for Harry's soul, but perhaps there is some justice that the man who conspired to remove Ned from the throne has been executed."

And on the 2nd of November, the day Ned was born. Justice indeed.

Margaret asks through tight lips, "Did he reveal his plans with Henry?"

"Not on the block," Oliver replies. "What he may have said while in prison, I have no idea." He walks to the door, calls for wine. "Sit here, Margaret, and rest. Your son is safe. For now."

I help Margaret to the bench, caress her hand until the server arrives with the wine. She takes a sip, and a little colour returns to her cheeks. She rises again, looks through the window into the courtyard as she walks to her private prayer room. "I long for freedom," she whispers. The king's guards stand sentinel at the gates. Margaret is not officially under arrest, but it is perfectly clear that she cannot leave.

"Now that Harry has died, this may all go away," I reply. "We have heard no more about your involvement. Henry has fled to Brittany. Perhaps now we may return to our normal lives."

"Perhaps." Margaret hands me a shawl. "Go and take some fresh air with Oliver. You look as pale as death yourself."

I do not need much persuading, and we descend the stairs and walk out into the courtyard and through the gates to the castle grounds. Oliver is silent, and I know he does not wish to say anything until we are well out of the confines of the house. The earth is still muddy, but someone has thrown gravel on the paths, and I can step without sinking. The air is misty, and a watery sun bleeds from the sky. It is not a fine afternoon for walking, but I am outside and can breathe deeply again.

"The boys?" As soon as we are alone, I turn to Oliver, search his eyes for the truth.

"Safe," he replies. "Safe still hidden at Bolton Castle, for the king is still leery of the conspiracies that are the aftermath of Harry's uprising."

"Thank God." I lift my face to the sky, take what feels like my first deep breath in days. "But surely with Harry's death, there is no more rebellion, no more danger to them?'

Oliver stops walking, gazes out over the flat lands and the shadow of rising northlands on the horizon. "It may be hard to surprise Bolton Castle with an attack," he replies.

"And Jack?" I ask in a small voice. "Does he stay and defend Bolton?"

"For now," answers Oliver, his voice kindly. My brother suspects that all is not well between us but would not dare intrude on my private affairs. "But Henry is amassing a great army in France and has the support of the French king."

"He still pursues the crown? Dear God, when will this cease?" I am so tired of war.

"When one of them is dead," replies Oliver grimly. "When Richard or Henry is dead."

Surely it is time for me to return to Bolton Castle, for what else can be done at Lathom? Oliver tells us that the king rides to London, and I long to return home, to leave this life sentence with Margaret that fate has thrust upon me. When he departs, I send a special hug with Oliver to share with the boys and make him promise that he will send for me as soon as he has obtained permission for me to go home.

I continue my walks in the parklands, and a couple of days after Oliver's departure, as I trudge back to the castle, something disturbs me in the gloom. Daylight is now fading and the mist drawing in. A figure slips from the rear gate and darts across the path. A horse whickers, and hoofbeats thrum into the mist, disappearing as quickly as they start. My pulse quickens, for is this a ghost or a real messenger? And why not through the main castle gates? I realise I am directly under Margaret's solar. My sister stands framed at the window, a candle in her hand as she gazes down to where the messenger disappeared.

I groan, pick up my skirts, and run to the chamber, a red veil of anger blurring my path. I stumble on the steps, the worn treads sending my balance backwards, graze my palm on the rough stone wall of the stairwell, and fly on bruised feet into Margaret's sanctuary.

"You cannot—you must not—tell me you have not written secretly again." I choke. "You selfish bitch!"

Margaret stands very still, her chest rising and falling under her tunic. Her only motion is a tightening of her lips.

I grab her by the shoulders, furiously shake her. The beads wrapped around Margaret's fingers clatter and drop to the floor, overly loud in breaking my sister's silence. "You will have us both killed, Margaret. I will never forgive you for this. Do you understand the peril you put us in?"

Margaret smiles, smacks my hands from her. "Do you think I can simply watch and not act? Do you think I would desert my son?"

"He deserted you, Margaret. He never landed in England. He never came to support Harry," I shout.

She ignores my outburst. "You remember the promise the queen made to me. You remember that when the time comes, she will announce Henry's marriage to her daughter."

"You cannot bring that up again, Margaret. If you are not imprisoned for treason for your part in Harry's rebellion, you will be now if you broker a marriage to Bess of York."

"I disagree. Henry has never been more powerful. The princes are dead. Harry is dead. The time has come, Elysabeth."

I want to shout at her that the princes are alive. I want to tell her that she is making decisions based on Richard's subterfuge. But I cannot tell her without betraying Jack or endangering the princes' lives. Such a web I am tangled in now that I see no escape.

Margaret picks up a parchment that is lying open on her desk. "I have received a note from our brother John Welles that he escaped the rebellion and is safe in Paris with Henry."

Welles? After all this time, he has now grown balls and fights in a battle? I am shocked our half brother has the backbone to do so.

My sister reads the letter again, looks up at me. "All those with influence who followed Harry Stafford have left England and set up an entire court in exile with Henry."

"A rival court? Is he mad?"

"Tonight, I sent word to the queen," Margaret continues, "that Henry will announce his marriage to her daughter Elizabeth of York on Christmas Day."

"Dear God, Margaret you dice with death. That is high treason."
And this time she has my soul clutched in her fist, ready to throw me away on the next roll.

"Henry will join the supporters of York and Lancaster with this marriage," Margaret continues. "Unite England. Establish a dynasty with a fertile queen and a peaceful throne. It is not the Plantagenets who are England's future. It is the Tudors. And one day, you see, he will rule England is his own right as a royal prince of the blood."

38
Winter 1483 | Le Ryall

Margaret and I co-exist in a frozen silence, avoiding time together, eating our meals alone, and only once a day do I check to see if my sister is still in her chamber. As far as I can tell, there is no changing her mind in her mission to advance her son. She is now as a nun in a convent, for she rarely strays from her rooms. No doubt she prays numerous times a day, fasts, and wears her hair shirt, her faith and her devotion to God keeping her company. I fear the clouds that wrapped around Lathom for so many weeks have settled in her brain and affect her judgment. Still, she writes her letters, and messengers appear and disappear across her lands. Hardly any come for me except the occasional note from Oliver, saying that all is well at Bolton.

Just after All Saints Day, I receive the news I am to join Jack for Christmas in London with the court, and this fills me with dread and joy combined. Perhaps finally my own exile is ending, and yet I wish I could return to Bolton and not the confines and intrigue of the court. There is a Parliament planned, and the king is determined to bring all those who rebelled against him that remain in England to trial.

Jack's men ride down to Lathom with baggage carts and an escort of the king's guard. Margaret is not permitted to accompany me, for she is considered a prisoner and is still confined to Lathom Park until the king decides otherwise.

"I am to meet Jack at Le Ryall," I tell her. "The king has called his first Parliament for late January. They will all be there: Catesby, Lovell, Ratcliffe . . . and your husband. I know it irks you, but the guard continues to keep you here, out of sight at Lathom. The longer you are absent, perhaps the more your conniving with Harry will be forgotten."

Margaret shrugs. "I cannot be kept here forever," she replies. "Go with God, Elysabeth, and wish my husband good health. Tell him how you leave me, devout in my prayers, loyal unto God and my son. And wish him to be the same."

I shake my head. "You know I cannot say that to Lord Stanley. Those words alone are treasonous. I will give him your blessing. And leave the rest to his imagination."

After so many weeks of solitude and quiet, London crashes with a wave of sights and sounds that leaves me dizzy. It is the same feeling I had leaving sanctuary; and yet then optimism quickly replaced my fear. Today, I don't know what lies ahead. The bells peal across the city and the streets heave with people, visitors and locals alike. Processions of black-garbed clerics, apprentices kicking a pig's bladder, a clutch of merchants' wives pushing the limits of the sumptuary laws . . . and always the beggars, the destitute, the wounded and diseased men. All of life gathers here, and I clutch my clove-studded pomander to my nose while inhaling the chaos of its streets. Fortunately, I stay at Le Ryall, away from the crowds around Westminster and yet close enough to spend time at the palace when called. For called I will be, I have no doubt, to testify about Margaret's role in the rebellion.

I sink into the familiar comfort of my family home, sit quietly in the parlour in solitude as the thick walls shelter me. This ancient house had seen much in its time, both war and healing. Away from Margaret's scheming and the troubles of the court, I am gradually shedding the ill-humour of intrigue and feel cleansed, strengthened. More than anything, I have the time to reflect on Jack, to think of all that has happened in this short year. Never has so much occurred in my life, and never have I felt such a welter of emotions. I am so wrapped up in anticipating his arrival that when the click of the street door intrudes upon my thoughts, he is here before I can prepare my face for another rejection.

Jack stands framed in the doorway, as hesitant as me to cross the abyss. He looks younger somehow, and for a moment I see the man I first fell in love with, for I realise although the years have burdened us, he has not changed. Meeting his eyes, I see they are clear, the protective clouds gone. He must see the same in me, for he steps forward, holds out his arms.

The two months of purgatory in Margaret's presence have served my penance for betrayal. I am forgiven. In turn, I forgive him for his priorities. We may have travelled upon opposing wheels, but in the end we have arrived at the same destination. Each other.

At first, there are no words, just joy in a familiar embrace. I lay my cheek against Jack's chest, his surcoat of fur tickling my skin. His breathing is steady, and he knows just to hold me, that words will follow in good time. He seeks my mouth with his, kisses me softly and then deeply and without pause, mingling our breath, forming our own unique bond.

Eventually, he leads me to the familiar chair by the window in the parlour. He leans back against the window seat, keeping his leg pressed against mine. A flagon of wine is on the small table, along with wafers, and he pours a glass for each of us. His silence is calming, unhurried, and I lovingly reconcile both faces of this man: the soldier who is quick to fight and the husband who is patient to listen.

"Were you there?" I finally ask. "Were you there when Harry was executed?"

Jack draws his eyes from where he has been staring out of the window. A gentle dusting of powdery snow is settling on the roofs of the merchants' houses, and those who are on the street are hurrying home, bundled up in winter furs and dun-coloured woolens. "Yes. Do you want to hear of his death?"

"Yes." I do not need to know every word, but I want to hear that he suffered as my boys have suffered. That his life was taken from him as he robbed them of their future.

"Buckingham was betrayed by one of his own," Jack continues. "The men he raised melted away with the rains. The armies never came; the counties never united. And when he realised the failure, he hid in a common hovel until his own servant turned him in, and he was dragged to the prison in Salisbury."

It is ungodly to rejoice in revenge, but I am glad to think of him stripped of his position, his attitude, his very identity. No longer was he the uncle of kings, a kingmaker himself. He was a rat in a trap.

"His downfall was complete when the king refused to see him. And within hours, he was taken to the square in Salisbury and his head struck from his body."

Jack reaches for me, kisses the lines of blue veins on the inside of my wrist. "On Ned's birthday."

I cup his hand around my cheek. "Fitting."

"Yes."

There is more in Jack's eyes, something he has to say.

"My sister?" I know I must ask, that he must tell me the inevitable outcome of her actions. I hesitate to name her, to bring her discord back between us.

"The king will hear everyone's part in the rebellion when Parliament opens. Will is drafting the bills against them, along with the king's other business. The Bishop of Ely, the Woodvilles, Dorset . . . and Margaret."

Her name, among the list of traitors.

"She will be tried for treason?"

"Yes."

"And no special exemption?"

"No. As soon as court convenes in January, her case will be heard."

"You promised me that she would not be put to death." I remind Jack of our bargain.

"The Plantagenets do not execute women," he replies.

I mouth the words, imagined the herald's announcement.

Margaret Beaufort. Traitor.

I start to weep, the tears burning my cheeks, shuddering at the thought of Margaret's attainder, desperate to think how she might avoid it. As I bow my head, the conflict becomes overbearing, and I slip from the chair to the ground and lay my head across my arms, weeping. No matter how far we travel in life, no matter what hurt done, Margaret will always be my eleven-year-old little sister sobbing in my arms as she was torn from our family, sold to the Tudor bidder, violated to bear the Tudor heir. Jack kneels with me, pulls me close to his chest, tucking my head under his chin. He says nothing, but everything is in his embrace, his love for me, his steadfastness, his understanding.

"Cry, my love," he whispers softly, "there is no disgrace in weeping for Margaret. She is lost, and I do not know what will become of her. But know that I will be at your side, whatever may happen, whatever the verdict and punishment."

The following afternoon, I turn the corner past the empty jousting structure of Westminster Palace and pause under the winter-stripped chestnut tree. I steady myself against the broad trunk as a hundred memories fly into my mind. As the crows roost on the branches above me, cawing their prediction of death, so do I think of watching those two warriors, Buckingham and Rivers, who had met in a parody of battle here just a few years ago. A joust to celebrate Dickon's betrothal, at five years old, to the little Mowbray heiress. Now Dickon is in hiding, his child bride dead, and Harry Stafford and Anthony Woodville are no more. They may have thought their end would come on a distant battlefield, defending English honour against the French or ridding the infidel from the holy lands.

Instead, they were killed by ambition and King Richard.

Their ghosts linger close this winter's day, and I find room in my heart to pray even for Harry, for in fuelling his ambition was many a life laid waste; his uprising brought men from their hearths, fields left fallow and women made widows as the rebellion's followers were imprisoned or exiled for life.

Still the boys are hidden at Bolton Castle. I hear from Oliver regularly that they have settled into their lives with the ease of youth and are growing strong and brave as they learn warfare as young squires. They are still called the Poles. There is no clue that they are the princes, for the rumours of their death put about by Harry have stuck on Richard's legacy.

And the queen and her beautiful daughters are sheltering in sanctuary.

What is it all for?

A gentle touch on my arm and I look into Meg's sweet face.

"Are you remembering, Belle-maman?" she asks softly. "I let you walk ahead, for I felt your thoughts were heavy."

I nod, my heart too full to speak.

"I know you want to go to the abbey, attend Mass," Meg continues. "But I have a pass authorised from Will. For us to visit the dowager queen in Cheyneygates."

"Why?" This is not what I expected to hear.

Meg pushes back her hood, and a few flakes of snow settle on her flaming hair. "King Richard would like to bring them forth from sanctuary, arrange an amnesty, care for the girls."

"And what does that mean for the princes?"

Meg smiles. "I knew that would be your first thought. The king wants to reunite them, bring all the children to Sheriff Hutton."

"He's been saying that for months," I reply. "And yet I see no action."

"Harry put a stop to any move, for it would not have been safe to reveal them while insurrection stalked across England," Meg says. "Once the trials are over and the rebels punished, Will thinks it might be safe for them again."

I will believe that when I see it. I know Richard to be a cautious man, but this vigilance is wearying.

"Why do we visit the queen in sanctuary? What does Will want me to do?" I am so tired of these political games. I feel as much a pawn on the chessboard of England as I did when I first met the queen all those years ago.

"Prepare the queen to receive Richard's offer of release. Show her the path forward to peace. For if she accepts the king's friendship, she sends a sign to her dead husband's supporters that there is no more reason to fight against Richard."

Meg brings up an interesting situation. By encouraging this alliance, I would remove Bess of York from Margaret's influence too. No longer would Henry dare pledge his marriage if she is under King Richard's care.

On my left, the Palace of Westminster, the warmth of the yule festivities.

Ahead, God's healing grace within the ancient abbey.

On my right, the bleak sanctuary and a queen in waiting.

I turn and trace a path through the fast-settling snow towards Cheyneygates. If today is the day to confront ghosts, then I may as well challenge my own past, revisit where this all began. I take a deep breath as I plan how I will explain to the queen that the reports of her sons' deaths are not true.

Waved through on the strength of Will's pass, once more Meg and I walk towards the Jerusalem Chamber, and this time the once-princess Cecily greets us at the door. The girl has grown into a beautiful young woman, and despite some many months in captivity, she has a dimpled smile about her face and an expression of sweetness that is lacking in

Bess. I kiss her cheeks and hold her hand. Cecily has always been my favourite.

"Lady Scrope?" she asks, a question in her voice. "I do not remember when you were in sanctuary with us, but I am saddened to meet you back here."

"I hope for just a short time more," I reply. "Is your mother resting?"

Cecily glances back over her shoulder. "You will find her much changed, I am afraid," she whispers. "My brothers' deaths weigh heavily upon her."

I clasp Cecily close, smooth her shining hair. "I know, my darling, I know."

Cecily stands aside and leads us to the familiar bench by the fireplace. A huge yule log has been felled and wedged into the space, and garlands of greenery hang from the mantel. This small attempt at festivity brightens the gloom; it seems that sanctuary is not as deprived as it once was. From her position by the large west window, the queen turns to meet us.

Elizabeth Woodville still wears the mantle of sovereignty, but her gait is stiff, and she no longer moves with the grace and litheness of youth. Lines across her forehead and loose skin around her neck tell more of the ravages of age, and as she takes her own seat in the claw-armed chair, silver hair glints more brightly than gold under her coif.

"Elysabeth," she greets me. "Such sad and terrible times. I did not think to see you here again."

"I am at Westminster for Parliament's opening." I reply. "I have been at Lathom Park."

"Ah, with Margaret." The queen pauses as if assessing my mood. "The secret power behind Buckingham's ill-judged rising." A tear slides down her face. "And the woman who got her wish. The final removal of my sons."

"Your Grace." Margaret is a distraction I do not need this moment. "Your Grace, the king has suggested I speak with you on a timely matter—" I glance at Meg, who nods in encouragement. "King Richard would like to see you leave sanctuary, bring your daughters to court."

The queen turns white, clutches at her breast. "That murderer? The man who ordered the death of my sons, who had them brutally killed in their sleep and then secretly buried within the Tower walls?"

"Your Grace—"

"He has the gall to think I would entrust my daughters to his care?" The queen's voice rises to the verge of hysteria, and Cecily runs to her side. Across the chamber, Bess lifts her head, watches us closely. "The accounts describe clearly of his part in my boys' murders. Therein lies the truth of Richard's evil."

"There is more than one truth to the rumours," I say softly, hoping to calm her with my own stillness. "And even more untruths. You remember my godmother's oath?"

The queen brushes the tears from her eyes. "I remember both your oath and your actions on the night Ned was born." Her face crumples again, and I see the lines that are tear tracks from her sorrow. "But even you failed to protect my son this time."

From one mother to another, I cannot let her suffer more. I am taking an enormous risk, but I cannot let this woman believe her sons to be dead. "Your Grace, sometimes rumours are just those. It was politically beneficial for Harry to accuse the king of murder, twist truth to clear the path for his own ambition—"

"What are you saying, Elysabeth? What truth do you conceal?" The queen clutches the arms of the chairs, leans forward until I can count the lines on her forehead. Still, her silvery cat eyes have the power to penetrate my thoughts.

I must approach obliquely, remember what Will has asked me to secure. "If you were to leave sanctuary, my lady, what kind of assurances would you wish from the king?"

The queen refuses to be diverted. "What rumours, Elysabeth? What truths and untruths do you unpick from your web?" Cecily places her hand on her mother's shoulder; Bess now walks from the across the chamber and stands on her right. The three women stare at me with shock and disbelief on their faces.

I continue. "Assurances, my lady?"

Bess addresses me. "I shall tell you, Lady Scrope," she replies for her mother. "I shall tell you the conditions for our release."

The dowager queen bows her head as her eldest daughter holds up her hand and ticks from her fingers.

"Item. That we be given into safe custody, that no harm will come to us. Item. That Richard will pledge personally to stand for our security."

Bess is queen-like, such is the authority in her voice.

"Item," she continues. "One that bears no negotiation. That we will never be taken to the Tower."

In the silence that followed Bess's conditions we are all remembering Dickon's last day as he left sanctuary.

The dowager queen takes a great shuddering sigh. "Lady Scrope, I implore you, if you have news—"

"I cannot say more, my lady, except that I believe the king will pledge his word to your list of assurances." I stand, my official business done. Now I can speak as one mother to another. "And if you were to find a way to agree to Richard's terms, it would be little trouble to reunite *all* of your children." I look at Bess and Cecily and repeat for their benefit. "All of you."

Tears pour down Elizabeth Woodville's face, and her shoulders shake with sobs. "My boys, my boys," she whispers.

Bess steps forward. "I will see to it that my mother will consider the king's assurances," she says, her chin tilted up, her bearing more regal than her mother's. "Deliver them to us in written form within the week, and we will consider his pledge."

She has grown into a formidable young woman. The news of the deaths of her brothers assigned her the role of King Edward's heir. I see a replica of her father in her. With the canniness of her mother.

"Thank you, Bess," I say. "I think you will find it advantageous to find agreement."

Bess steps before her mother, blocks her from my view. She walks forward to me, takes my arm as if in intimate conversation, and walks with me to the door. "You may not have heard this news, Lady Scrope, for the messengers just arrived here an hour ago. Your nephew Henry Tudor declared his betrothal to me on Christmas Day at Rennes Cathedral, in front of five hundred loyal supporters." She smiles with more than a hint of steel. "So, Aunt, if Richard does anything to harm us or goes back on his word, my husband will invade England immediately and kill him in battle."

Oh God.

Margaret Beaufort. Traitor.

Henry Tudor. Traitor.

And what must I do now to escape the malign influence of my family's stars?

39

Winter 1483 | Westminster

Meg and I squeeze into a window ledge in an enclave by the Painted Chamber. Richard's first Parliament opens this brittle cold morning, and I begged Will to let us be close to hear of Margaret's sentence. My sister is not here, still incarcerated at Lathom Park. I picture her praying, pacing, praying, pacing, staring from the window across the blank park pastures to the south, willing an envoy to escort her to London. But to no avail. This is not a hearing that requires her appearance. This is a meeting of the anointed king's court to pass a sentence none could challenge.

I want to be the one to send messengers racing to Lathom first to tell her to repent and save her mortal soul. Better a family retainer arrives to break the news before the king's guard comes to arrest her.

"Will has been appointed Speaker of the House." Meg's prayer book lies unopened on her lap. "He has been working with the king on the bills of attainder and a law that confirms the king's royal title to the throne."

"Will is trusted by all," I reply. "You must be very proud of him, Meg. He is a fine man, a loving husband and father, and a wise lawyer. He has risen high in power these past months."

Meg traces the jewels on the cover of her little book. It is a most precious object, another sign of their wealth. "He believes in the king and the right of his succession."

"And the princes?" I ask, for they are never far from my mind, especially in the Palace of Westminster. "Harry's wicked rumours persist that Richard murdered them. Will the boys be named in this document of his right to reign and be presented in public to quench the ill-speak of Richard once and for all? Is that part of his assurances to the queen?"

My daughter looks down, shakes her head. "Belle-maman, the king is not yet ready," she replies softly. "Will says there are insurgents throughout Kent and the West Country that have not fled to France and are still talking of rebellion. They muster for Henry Tudor. Until the king has eradicated the rebels' threat, he is concerned the boys will be a beacon for them to rally around. Or kill, to attain the throne."

"And so he would rather people think he murdered them?" I am horrified. Surely this warped logic cannot be true.

Meg takes my hand. "Perhaps. If you were about to rise up against the crown, would you think twice if the man you were challenging had killed his nephews with little or no conscience? In some ways, the king is letting these rumours build a fear of his ruthlessness that would not be present any other way."

"At the expense of his own reputation?"

"We know they are safe. He knows they are secure. A few more months, when the throne is stable and Henry Tudor's threat is finally crushed, Richard will bring them back to London, honour them with their place at court."

A clutch of black-robed clerics walked by, and I tuck my feet under the bench to avoid their dusty gowns. The clergy pay no attention, for we are invisible women in this world of men.

"He has more to concern himself now than old wives' gossip," Meg continues. "Much was lost in the last years of King Edward's reign. He spent his time on lechery and lewd acts, neglecting his subjects and their welfare. King Richard wants nothing but to establish a fair rule and a kingdom of peace, where the memory of his brother's reign is golden again, unblemished by his reckless pursuit of women."

I am praying for Richard's sense of justice to rule over Margaret's verdict. "I have always found Richard to be a fair man," I say.

"He has advanced ideas that will make this a better country for everyone," Meg replies. "Will and he talk long about the new laws and governance he will bring to reform our world."

A lump rises in my throat. "That was his vision when we first travelled south with Ned," I say, a sudden poignant memory arising of the inn, our laughter and shared dreams. "A court of beauty and chivalry, where the finest minds and the most gifted artists would flourish. And fairness and equity reign. Camelot. How long ago and far away that seems now."

"Would this be so, Belle-maman. It is still possible. And I think he means to show his intent in his treatment of Margaret."

"You have heard something from Will?" my voice is suddenly loud in the small antechamber, and I lower it immediately.

"The Plantagenets don't execute women." Meg's words slice through the air like a sword blade, repeating Jack's pledge to me.

There is a movement at the door, and Jack appears from inside the Painted Chamber. Meg and I clasp hands. My knees are trembling, so I do not stand.

"She is attainted," he announces. "Stripped of her estates, her land, her wealth—"

"That will devastate her," Meg says.

"—but not imprisoned. She is to live under house arrest indefinitely, under the protection of her husband." Jack takes my face between his hands, keeps my gaze on his until I draw strength from his confidence. "It is the best possible solution for her, Elysabeth. She is not imprisoned in the Tower. Her husband retains all her property. Her freedom may be impaired, but she is alive and in her own home."

I sag with relief, and yet in a strange and curious way, I almost ache with the lightness of Margaret's sentence. I do not agree with my sister's destruction, and yet is this really a punishment? How could this stop Margaret's ambition, vanquish her dream to place her son on the throne? And will she cease her plotting? I doubt it.

I wonder aloud. "Why was the king so lenient? Imprisonment under her own husband's watch? Surely he realises that is hardly to be enforced."

Jack drops his hands. "Politics," he says contemptuously. "Lord Stanley is the king's strongest ally, the largest landowner, can muster the mightiest army. Richard does not want to make an enemy of him too. Now, with Margaret's sentence and transferring her assets to her husband, the king has bought Stanley's loyalty."

He looks back over his shoulder to where the doors to the Painted Chamber are closing again. "I must go back inside. Go to Le Ryall, Elysabeth, and prepare to travel home to Bolton Castle." Jack checks the antechamber; it is empty except for us. "Be with the boys. And hopefully by the spring, the queen and her daughters will join you in the North at Richard's court at Middleham or Sheriff Hutton. The worst is over. There is no more need for you to be here."

Our family returns to the welcome embrace of Le Ryall this evening. Jack and Will have been relieved from court attendance, and my brother Oliver and his wife, Isabel, made the journey down from Yorkshire to join us. I am eager to catch up on the news of the boys as we enjoy the peace and privacy of our own home. Within the safety of our trusted four walls, we are able to finally talk openly, and I am free to share my thoughts about Margaret and my visit to the queen in sanctuary.

"I know that Margaret will be furious that her possessions have been turned over to Stanley," Will says with a wry smile on his face. "But perhaps in time she will consider the alternatives and realise that she was treated with more respect than she was ever due."

"Or Stanley was," remarks Jack.

"I don't trust that bastard." Oliver's voice is gruff. "I have warned the king about his cunning and sly ways. Showing too much leniency is not the way to hold a man's loyalty."

"At least now we have a peaceful prospect ahead of us." I reach for Jack's hand, resting on the cloth between us. "We can return to Yorkshire, bring the boys to Sheriff Hutton, and prepare to welcome the dowager queen and her daughters to our northern court." I caress his wrist in our own secret signal. "Right, my love?"

Jack clears his throat; I can see from his eyes he has been miles away. Will and Oliver exchange a quick glance and then both drink their wine.

"What?" I ask sharply. "What was that look?"

My husband kisses my fingers, holds my hand close to his mouth. "I love you," he says. "You see through pretence like a hawk hunting a rabbit."

A shiver raises gooseflesh on my arm. It is not just desire from his touch, but a tremor of apprehension.

"Why should you lie to me?" I ask. Surely these games are not starting again.

"No lies," Jack hastens to reassure me. Will and Oliver look down at their plates. Isabel and Meg are quietly listening. "But I may not be leaving for Bolton with you."

"Why not? Your work here is done. We need you back home."

Will takes a sip of his wine, mops his mouth with his napkin. "Unfortunately, Elysabeth, the king needs him more. Jack has been given a signification promotion in his responsibilities—"

"To what?" I interrupt, my temper rising. Our service is complete. The rebellion is quelled. Buckingham is dead. Margaret is attainted. There can be no more for my family. "What does *significant promotion* mean?"

Jack tosses down his napkin, scrapes back his chair. "There is no easy way to say this, my love. The West Country is still not at peace. Uprising stirs. The southern ports are on a high state of alarm in case Henry Tudor decides an invasion attempt again."

"What Jack is saying," Will says, his clear lawyer's voice cutting through my distress, "is that he has been appointed to root out and remove any remaining rebels and to set up the defences to protect our southern coast."

I stare miserably at my husband. *We have just reconciled. Now we are to be torn apart again?* "For how long?"

My soldier speaks, my lover gone. "Until there is no more threat. At home or abroad. Henry Tudor must be crushed once and for all. The king sends me to defend our vulnerable lands in the west. We have not seen the last of Tudor. He now has the support of the King of France. He calls himself King of England. He will invade again. The sooner we can lure him back so he can be slaughtered on English soil, the better."

Later, much later, as the candles dwindle to a mere glow and our chamber is love-warmed, I curl up against Jack's chest, his breathing calm now, passion spent.

"I love you," I murmur, my limbs warm and languid from our lovemaking. "I know it is hard for you to leave. I never want you to feel I will prevent you from serving your country and your king, no matter what history has been before us."

Jack lazily traces a pattern on my bare arm, caressing me from wrist to elbow. "I never doubt you. I just want to you to be safe, away from the intrigues and plotting that Margaret always draws you into."

I lay my palm flat on his chest, feel the steady beat of his heart under the powerful soldier's muscles. "I trust you," I say. "I trust you will always do what is right for me, for the boys, for our family."

"Always," he replies. "Keep my truth in your heart, Elysabeth, no matter what you hear, what news comes from Margaret.

"What could Margaret send me? She is without power, without lands, money—"

"She is never without power. Even as her husband pretends to guard her, I have no doubt she is doubling her efforts to secure support for Henry Tudor in England."

"And why would she call on me?"

"You have access to Elizabeth Woodville. Bess. If the princesses are to be brought under Richard's supervision, she will find a way to get to you, sway their loyalty. She will call on your blood relationship to Henry."

"I will never defer to her again. You are first, my love." I lift my mouth, kiss his beautiful lips, push my hands into his long hair, and draw his body over mine.

"As you are to me, my love," Jack murmurs, his arms tightening around me, his elbows lifting him over me. "You foremost, always and forever."

40

Spring 1484 | Bolton Castle

I leave my love at Le Ryall. We part with lingering kisses as I cup Jack's face between my hands and say goodbye, keeping his likeness remembered in my palms. I know he is not riding to war, simply to keep order, but for us to be so newly reconciled and now parted again is painful.

My darling Oliver and Isabel travel with me to Bolton Castle and I am glad of their company. The journey is uneventful, and as we approach the turning for Lathom Park, I glance west but ride on. I do not wish to visit Margaret in her dismal solitude when the joy of reuniting with the boys calls me onward.

Snow crystals encrust my cloak and gloves as we ride under the great iron portcullis and into Bolton's keep in a swirl of white on a dusky January afternoon. Its great walls wrap around me with a protective embrace, flaring torches throwing heat and light into the courtyard and turning the thickly descending flakes tawny and gold.

Home.

The doors to the west tower are thrown open, and Ned and Dickon race across the cobbles, slipping and sliding on the settling snow, their fair hair sunbeams in the wintry shadows. I scramble down from my mount and hold my arms out, and they run to me like puppies, almost knocking me over in their excitement.

"My boys," I cry, tears warm on my cheeks. "I have missed you so much." They have grown in the six months we have been apart, stronger and taller, character emerging in their faces, and I see the men they will become.

"We have missed you too." Ned puts his arm around my waist, carefully guides me across the icy courtyard. "And now you are home to stay."

"To stay," I agree as we walk into the welcoming warmth of the castle entry, climb the stairs to the hall, where a huge fire is blazing in the hearth and the dogs are dozing in a circle on the heated stones. "I am here to stay."

The winter is a harsh one, colder and darker than I remember in a long time. But within our castle walls, our little community flourishes. Completely at home as my Pole nephews, Dickon and Ned are part of our extended family of cousins, and the routine that Oliver established for them when they first arrived has served them well. We play games, sing songs, tell stories, and walk outside when the weather permits. These times are so precious, and I treasure every day.

February ice and March gales keeps us isolated, and only when the tracks are packed with dry snow or a thaw comes does Oliver travel back and forth between our lands. It is a comfort to have him close. Ned especially loves my brother; Oliver's patience and discipline have brought a maturity to his character. No longer are the princes children, but they are growing fast into young men, and with Oliver's fine guidance Ned has become an excellent horseman. We may not have the book learning that Lord Rivers was so fond of, but Oliver's tutoring in life's practicalities and the boys' opportunity to be treated as equals to the other squires have taught them invaluable lessons in understanding men and their ways.

All that is missing is my husband's presence, and I pray daily for his safety and return to Bolton. As far as I can tell, Jack is keeping the West Country under watch and preventing any further uprisings. Letters from him are scarce. Sometimes a whole packet arrives, declaring his devotion, turning me flushed with his love-words; other times I wait for weeks, only to receive a request for more arms or men—or both—to support his assignment. I revert back to my role as a military man's wife, praying to God nightly for his safety and running the business of the castle during the days.

After Henry's Christmas Day announcement of his betrothal to Bess, the king has commissioned arrays across the country. I think he is being overly cautious in raising arms, for surely Margaret's son has seen the futility of his attempts to invade England. But Oliver reminds me that there are many around Henry Tudor, including the King of

France, who would see him king instead of Richard, especially those who once embraced the Lancastrian cause. Stockpiling weapons and keeping men trained for the king's defence is a sensible precaution.

The messenger arrives from Middleham in early April, an echo of twelve months previous. Such an evocative reminder of all that has happened in just a year. This time, as I sit in the steward's quarters working on inventory lists, I laugh to myself at the difference time and *sovereynté* can bring. Last year I was reading the romance of King Arthur to Isabel. This year my studies of crop yields and sheep counts are significantly more useful than that of foolish fancies. I naturally open the letter, this time feeling no hesitance, for Jack is far away and the decision is mine.

> *Come to Middleham*, the king dictates. *Queen Anne and I are on our way north from Cambridge. Jack has brought peace to the West Country, and I am assured the land is quiet now. Bring Dickon and Ned, for it is time the cousins were united. They can stay a while with our son, Prince Edward, for we have much to entertain the boys, and then ride on to Sheriff Hutton and take up their permanent home.*

I drop the news into my lap and walk across to the deep window embrasure. Down in the field below the castle keep, where the narcissus sprinkle their white faces like fallen stars in the grass, Ned and Dickon are flying their hawks. I watch as they masterfully train their birds, both confident and assured as they toss the creatures to the sky and let them circle before luring them back with bloody rabbit meat in their gloved hands.

Time for you to fly. Time to leave me and assume your rightful place with your family.

It is bittersweet, but are not all departures? For although the sorrow at their leaving is uppermost in my mind, pride in the young men they have become, and my role in keeping them safe, is a happy reward.

"Tell the king we shall see him at Middleham," I reply to the messenger. "We will be there by week's end."

Meg is in the Midlands at her home at Ashby Manor with her boys, and only Oliver is at Bolton. "I'll ride with you," he confirms when I tell him the news. He knows the sad happiness I am feeling, and as always, he is my rock. "I can stay until the king leaves for Sheriff Hutton. Then I'll return to Masham. Isabel and my girls are asking when I will return to them, and with the boys back with the king, I can spend more of my time with them."

"You've been like a second father to the princes, Oliver," I reply. I am so grateful for my brother's devotion, for in Jack's absence he has been a steady presence every day. "They love you very much."

"I love them too," he says and clears his throat noisily. I smile, for I know it takes a lot for my gruff and restrained brother to state those words. His duties have mellowed him.

I send word to Jack that we are leaving for Middleham, not knowing if or when it will reach him clear across the country. I say little more, for letters can be intercepted, and even at this time I do not want the boys' identity revealed until they are safe under Richard's protection. They are excited to travel to Middleham, and Ned especially is curious to see his uncle again. I think he wants to hear directly from Richard all of the actions and decisions that have led to this point. Who better than his father's brother to tell him the truth of his family and his inheritance.

On Friday morning, I find Ned and Dickon in the courtyard, packing their own saddlebags. Dickon tucks in his whittling blade and his treasured pieces of oak that he found at the lightning-struck tree by Aysgarth Falls. He catches me looking and grins. "To remind me of Bolton Castle," he says. "For I have been happier here, Lady Scrope, than anywhere else I can remember."

"You will be just as happy at Sheriff Hutton," I reply. "Especially when the king brings your sisters to visit. You will be together again, as the family you once were under your father."

"But not as a royal family nor Ned as king," he says wistfully. "Never Ned."

I embrace him, hold him tightly, willing him to accept his new life. "You will always have royal blood in you, my darling."

Dickon hugs me back. "You have his lion I carved? Perhaps one day he will like it."

"I will keep it safe," I promise.

A clatter of hooves behind us and we both turn as Ned mounts his spirited black stallion and, putting him on a tight rein, walks him a few paces backwards and then halts and commands the creature to bend a knee. We applaud his beautiful manoeuvre, and Ned flushes with pride. I pull my kerchief from my sleeve and walk to him. Reaching up, I tie the scrap of fabric to his sleeve. My beautiful godson straightens on his stallion, controlling the giant beast with the invisible pressure of his legs. Beneath Ned's rosy cheeks and serious eyes, I glimpse young stubble on his chin. My boy is becoming a man.

"You will always be my champion," I say. "Always my courageous and truly noble knight."

Just as I did a year ago, I marvel at the subtle beauty of a northern spring. The clouds drift by on the brisk April breezes, and lambs frolic in the fields, little gangs of them chasing each other up and down the ridges. "You'll be like that with your cousin and your sisters," I call to Dickon, who grimaces with embarrassment and kicks his horse on to ride with Oliver and Ned. I laugh.

No more than a mile from Middleham, two messengers wearing the white boar mark gallop past, driving us towards the lane's ditch. It is most unusual for the king's guards to behave so ill mannerly. As we travel through the village and approach the castle, a prickle rises on the back of my neck. More messengers are galloping from the drawbridge, a stream of riders heading to the four winds, all leaving, none arriving. Our little party from Bolton Castle enters the courtyard and into a crowd of people, all strangely subdued.

Leaving the boys with a Scrope guard, I run up the stairs into the great hall, closely followed by Oliver. Will is standing right inside, as if he is looking out for us. His face is white, bleached, taut with anxiety.

"Will," I gasp, for I have not seen this expression on his face since the day the boys were declared bastards. "Why are you here? Have you just arrived? What is going on?"

He pulls us aside from the crush of people, into perhaps even the same enclave that Gloucester spoke to me within a year ago. "A terrible, terrible thing." He brushes his hand over his mouth, wipes his forehead.

"What has happened?" Oliver glances across the crush of people, who appear to be in great grief. "Good God, is it the king?"

Will shakes his head. "I believe him safe. But his son and only heir, Edward, has died here, two nights ago."

"Oh Jesus." Oliver turns white. "Oh God, protect us all."

Another child lost. Tears well in my eyes. "I am so desperately sorry for him and the queen," I whisper. "No one should lose a child—"

"Dear Mother of God," Oliver interrupts me. "The boys."

Will hurries us back down the stairs. "Are they here with you?"

"Just arrived." Oliver briefly grips Will's arm. "Steady, man. Save your worries for Richard. I'll take them back to Bolton immediately. Elysabeth, follow with a guard as soon as you can. Will can arrange." And he is gone.

I stare after him, hardly believing what is happening. "The king commanded us here. Why now do we leave?"

Will halts me. People under the mantle of great grief flow around us, the shuffling of footsteps and keening sending a shiver through me. "He has not just lost a child," my son-in-law replies. "He has lost a kingdom."

"How?" I cannot fathom Will's words. "How can this be?"

Meg's husband, King Richard's chief advisor, the kingdom's chancellor, speaks carefully to me. "He has no other legitimate children, Elysabeth. And with Anne's health, he is unlikely to sire more. He has no nephew who is a legal heir, except possibly John de la Pole, and no one will accept him." He wipes his brow again. "He is a king without an heir. The end of the York dynasty. Except—"

"Except Ned and Dickon," I reply. Once more, they are thrust into the cauldron of politics and war.

One act of Parliament to make them bastards. One further act to legitimise them again.

"Ned is in grave danger, for his father's loyalists will fight to oust the king and seize Ned for the throne, or other men will kill him before he can be legitimised and crowned."

The horror in me grows until I can barely speak; my throat is so constricted. "It is not *other men* you speak of. It is one man. My nephew. Henry Tudor."

Will nods grimly. "Now that Richard has no heir, there has never been a clearer path to the throne for Henry. And Margaret will know this the minute she hears of Prince Edward's death."

"What will you do? Does the king know?"

"He does not know yet. We have sent messengers to find him. He is somewhere between Cambridge and Nottingham." Sorrow shadows Will's brow.

"He will be devastated," I say softly. We both fall silent as we think of the parents who are this moment joyful about returning to Middleham to be with their boy, could even in the next hour be shattered when told their only child is dead. "Oliver will ensure the boys remain hidden. Fortunately, in this chaos I don't think anyone noticed they were here. I'll return to Bolton Castle now."

Will takes my hands. "I am afraid not, Elysabeth."

"Why? I am of no use here."

"Not here," Will says. "But I must ask you to go to Lathom Park again. You are the only one who can truly gauge Margaret's intent. Take the Scrope guard, ride directly there, and write to me immediately of her actions."

41

Summer 1484 | Lathom Park

I find Margaret on the battlements, gazing over the fields and forests towards the Welsh borderlands. As delicate as a butterfly, both of her hands lightly rest upon the stone crenellations, and the sky-blue veil from her hennin ascends to the heavens and ripples behind her on the breeze. She is fluid, at one with the air, and I know immediately that no prison will ever keep her spirit captive.

She turns and holds out her arms. "Elysabeth, how lovely to see you." She kisses my forehead as if a benediction, and I hold my little sister close.

"You have found peace, Margaret." We stroll the battlements, the April sun dappling through the scudding clouds, creating shadows across the pastures far below, racing like ship's sails upon the German Sea.

"My son is safe. He escaped Harry's disastrous uprising. He is betrothed to the king's daughter. Bess will make him a splendid wife. Life is good."

"And yet you are captive here?" I bide time to speak the news that will change my sister's destiny yet again.

"Perhaps. Although I welcome the tranquility, the quiet. I can walk here and travel anywhere in my thoughts. And I can pray for as long as I wish with no disturbances." Margaret pauses, her eyes on the distant horizon. "It is a simple life now, Elysabeth. Almost as when we were children at Bletsoe. I am cared for, protected, immured from life's travails. I have no decisions to make, no choices to worry over. It is not such a bad life."

"And Henry? Do you not regret that you may never see him again?"

"What makes you say that?" There is genuine surprise in her voice.

"You are confined to house arrest. He is exiled with no hope of being invited back."

Margaret guides me to the stairs, leading the way back to her solar. "There are many rotations on Fortune's wheel; some we see, some we are only aware of when the wheel has passed us by." Her voice drifts up the spiral staircase that twists down to her room. Inside, the painted saints stand vigil; the rich tapestries decorate her table.

"Are you staying long, Elysabeth?"

"For a while." I sit with my sister in the window seat, as we have so many times before. "I have something to tell you."

Margaret folds her hands in her lap and waits patiently. The wild bird on the battlements is back in her cage, and she knows the merits of endurance.

"I have been sent here to tell you that the king's son is dead. I come from Middleham, and I have seen for myself. Edward is dead."

The saints behind her do not blink, but tears form in Margaret's eyes until they brim and overflow, streaming down her cheeks.

"Edward is dead?" she whispers. Tears spring from her eyes, roll down her cheeks.

I take her folded hands and feel her grip tighten. "Yes. I am sorry it grieves you so deeply. It is indeed most tragic for the king and queen."

Margaret gently removes her hands from mine and crosses to her writing desk. She pulls a parchment towards her, dipping her quill in the inkwell.

"I will have one of my guards take your letter," I say. "I know you are not permitted to correspond with anyone."

Margaret looks puzzled. "Why would your guard take my letter?" she asks, a frown on her face.

"I can arrange for your condolences to be sent to Middleham."

She smiles then, a true Margaret smile. "I am not writing to Richard," she says softly. "I am writing to the rightful king. My son. Henry Tudor."

Her quill scratches across the page in that familiar sound I always associate with Margaret. "The road to Westminster Palace is wide open now," Margaret continues. "And you, Elysabeth, are no longer godmother to a prince. You are aunt to a king."

I grab her pen and snap it in half, throwing it down on the parchment in a spatter of ink. "Do not dare to implicate me in your treason, Margaret."

She steadily pushes the broken halves together to the back of her desk, blots the spilled ink. "It is not treason when Henry is the true king."

"Henry will never be the true king!" I shout. "If there is any true king, it is Ned."

"The dead bastard?" Margaret crosses herself. "A tragedy indeed. But hardly one that I can change. Or regret. Except, of course, to pray for the soul of the murdered innocent himself." She looks up at me, searches my eyes. "You are remarkably loyal to a lost child, Sister."

I bite my tongue, count to ten to control my temper, prevent myself from revealing more.

"Nothing to say?" My sister picks a fresh quill, turns over the parchment.

I clench her hand, still her writing. "If you persist in your ambition to put Henry on the throne, I shall have to report to the king that you are flouting the terms of your attainder."

"Do you think I really care?" Margaret replies. "The wheel is turning too fast to stop it now, Elysabeth. Be careful you and your precious King Richard are not crushed beneath it."

We exist in solitude, yoked together and yet pulling in different directions. I only talk about necessities, and even then in the shortest possible conversations. She chatters constantly about Henry. My time with Margaret has stretched into summer, for with each week comes just enough news of Henry's growing power, just enough intelligence to keep me harnessed to Margaret's side. So confident is my sister of her son's strength that she barely conceals anything from me and takes great delight in sharing the news of his influence. A commitment from the King of France. Financing from noblemen across England. And a court in Brittany that rivals that of King Richard.

There are days that my anxiety bleeds into every moment, bowing my head and aching across my neck and shoulders. On others, that I am sure my husband and Richard know exactly what they are doing, their long military experience preparing for the inevitable conflict that

289

lies ahead. I hope that my secondhand news conveys some information, for if I did not think I was helping, I would go mad with frustration. Even so, trapped with Margaret at Lathom Park, I feel as if my very being is reduced to words on a page, my life bound by the incessant scratching of a goose quill on parchment.

In June, around midsummer, a sudden running of footsteps on the stairs to Margaret's solar startles us. The door flies open, and Jack strides into the room. I spring up from the window seat, my embroidery spilling to the floor.

"My love!" I hardly dare believe he is here, what his arrival may mean to my own captivity.

Jack pulls me into his arms and kisses my mouth, my neck, holds me so tightly I feel my heart will be squeezed from my breast. "Elysabeth." The way he breathes my name, I know he has come for me.

"You arrive unannounced." Margaret's voice has the sourness of lemons in its tang. "What reason, Jack?"

He bows at her, always the courteous one. "To collect my wife."

Margaret blinks. "Why now? I thought you were remaining in the West Country for an unspecified time." She smiles humourlessly. "If Henry allows you that luxury."

Jack ignores her baiting, turns to me. "The western lands are quiet, and I have some happy news at last," he says. "The queen has left sanctuary, along with her daughters. They want to visit family, spend time in the country, gather their strength. Cecily chooses to see you, Elysabeth. She travels with me. She is in my guard and waits at the abbey an hour from here. And that's why we have come for you."

A flush of excitement runs through me. "Cecily? How wonderful. Is she on her way to Sheriff Hutton?"

Jack grinned. "Not quite. More like Bolton Castle."

I stare at him. "Bolton? Is that wise?"

Jack nods, smiles. "Trust me."

He looks at Margaret and this time does not bow. He pauses in thought, as if balancing his words. "I do not plan on seeing you again, Margaret. Live well. Live in the present turn of your life's wheel, for God himself only knows what the future holds."

"What do you mean? What do you know?" Margaret straightens her back, tugs on her sleeves.

"Only that your son's destiny is descending rapidly. We have never been so strongly armed, so ready to fight. If Henry returns to England, he will be slaughtered by Richard's army. And if he stays in France, he will die a lonely old man, for you will never be able to travel to him again." He kisses Margaret's hand, walks to the door. "Say your good-byes, Elysabeth. We leave now."

I blanch at Jack's honesty, and yet I know he speaks from his own integrity and kindness.

Alone with my sister, I fold my hands around Margaret's, holding them between my own. I truly feel I may not see her again for a long time, if ever. Our roads have diverged too widely, and there is nothing to keep us together. The most significant parting I can give Margaret is my blessing.

I close my eyes. The time-honoured prayer of Thomas à Kempis comes unbidden into my mouth. "Pray with me, Margaret. Let forgiveness flow into your heart . . .

"'For all those also whom, at any time, I may have
vexed, troubled, burdened, and scandalised, by words
or deeds, knowingly or in ignorance; that Thou
wouldst grant us all equally pardon for our offences
against each other.'"

I peep under my lashes. Margaret's eyes are squeezed shut, her lips reverently mouthing the words. I see the little girl in her quiet face and swallow back my tears. This is a blessing and a goodbye.

"'Take away from our hearts, O Lord, all
suspiciousness, indignation, wrath, and contention,
and whatsoever may hurt charity, and lessen brotherly
love. Have mercy, O Lord, have mercy, Amen.'"

"Amen," responds Margaret. "And God bless and keep my son, Henry Tudor, King of England."

I sadly release my sister's hands, leave her standing alone, surrounded by her painted saints. It is time to leave, leave her with the intrigue and ambition, the secrets and betrayals. I touch my pocket and feel the wooden lion of England that I keep with me as a love token.

Carved by Dickon for Ned.

Meant for a king. But never to be given to one.

I place the little talisman on Margaret's desk. It is just a crudely carved piece of wood, a child's dream that vanished under Richard's authority, that I now pass to my sister. A reminder that any fantasy can disappear.

"Henry will never be king, Margaret."

There is nothing more to say.

42

Autumn 1484 | Bolton Castle

Cecily trembles like a captive bird as we stand by my chamber's window and stretch our eyes as far as we can see over the forests of the valley. We have arrived at Bolton when the boys are at hunt and now have had to pass the final hours of our journey longing for the horns heralding their return. Her legs are shaking the draping woollen of her skirts, and I draw her to stillness in my arms. She is delicate; her bones feel hollow.

"Hush, little one, hush," I soothe. "Just a while longer."

She stiffens at a clattering of hooves below, and a cry escapes her lips as she twists free. "Ned. Dickon." She runs to the door and stops. "They are here."

Jack is waiting in the courtyard to bring the Pole brothers directly to my chamber. We are cautious; we have not yet received permission for the boys to be officially recognised in our home, although the rumours ebb that Richard murdered them. No conveniently matching boys' bodies have ever been found, no telling-tale witnesses produced.

Just as Will predicted. A fire that is deprived of air will burn itself out.

A step on the stair, a burst of boyish laughter, a door flung open.

Ned stops first, Dickon bumps into him, and both boys' eyes widen and mouths gape.

"Oh, blessed Father in heaven," cries Cecily and runs the final three paces to her brothers, sobbing and laughing and pulling them into her arms. They sink to the floor like a tumble of puppies, blond hair mingling.

"Cecily," Ned and Dickon chant. "Cecily Sisily, sister Cecily, Sisily, Sisily." Their nickname for her harmonises with tears and rough joy.

Jack is grinning from ear to ear, and I slip from my chamber with him. We close the door behind us and, stationing a guard on the spiral stair, leave them to their blessed reunion.

The impact of Bess and Cecily leaving sanctuary under Richard's sworn statement of protection is helpful for the boys. What mother, asks everyone, would deliver her daughters into the arms of the man accused of murdering their brothers? No mother would. Another flame of Harry's dreadful lie doused.

Soon Richard will bring them all together again.

Soon the boys will join their sisters in public.

In solitude at Bolton, we grow close as the days shorten, and the evenings are filled with family games and the music we play together. When sweet Cecily confides in me that she has fallen in love with Jack's cousin Ralph, I can only be happy that our family may grow again. I assure her that Richard will be happy to grant them permission to marry, especially if Jack requests it.

At Christmas, Cecily is commanded to court, but I persuade Jack that we do not need to attend. Together, we celebrate simple festivities with the boys at home. When Cecily returns, she tells us of the celebrations, how Bess danced with the king and exchanged dresses and jewelry with the queen.

"Did the court think that Richard paid too much notice to Bess?" I ask Cecily. Westminster is a viper's pit of rumours, and it takes little to set tongues wagging. "Your sister knows how to command attention."

Cecily shrugs. "The queen is ill, Lady Scrope. I think Bess felt the need to keep the court entertained when the queen could not stay beyond dinner and had to take to her bed instead."

"And did she? Did Bess keep the court entertained?" I have never forgotten the princess's quick action and triumphant smile in reciting the list of conditions for their leaving sanctuary. Bess has grown up to be a shrewd young woman. I can imagine that she may be thinking of other stipulations if the queen dies.

"To the pleasure of all. Especially the king. He decreed Westminster to be called Camelot until Twelfth Night."

Cecily is sweet but sometimes too innocent. What game is Bess playing now?

"Besides," continues Cecily, "the king put rumours of his enchantment with Bess aside by swearing an oath before Will and the council that he has no inappropriate intentions towards his niece."

Clever Will, who always knows how to anticipate or quell trouble.

Our valley awakens under a spring thaw, and Cecily and I climb to the battlements to enjoy the clear March day. There is a fresh wind on our cheeks, carrying a promise of warming earth and rebirth. As we rejoice in a sky as blue as the Virgin's robe, there is a sudden hesitation in the brightness of the morning, and I look up, expecting to see a hawk or perhaps a flock of crows cross the sun's path. But there are no birds in the sky, and a silence settles upon the land such as I have never heard before.

Around us, the world grows dim. Squinting into the heavens, we cross ourselves. The sun is disappearing, yet the sky is cloudless.

"A sign," breathes Cecily. "Just as there were three suns in the sky when my father claimed the throne, now there are none. This foretells a death."

"What do you mean?" I anxiously search the tracks leading to the castle for a messenger, but the paths are empty.

"When the sun is darkened, there is a death to follow." Cecily reaches for her rosary. I wonder if she too has inherited her mother's witchcraft. The world grows twilight dim and murky. No birds call; no horses whinny. Below us, my servants gather to squint at the dying sun. Some weep, others pray, still more stand in silence.

"There is a death upon the House of Plantagenet," cries Cecily.

"God save us," I reply. I do not know who this could be, and I thank God that the boys are safe with me.

But when the disc has moved across the sun and the light reclaimed the dark, messengers come to Bolton Castle. Richard's queen, little Anne Neville, has died. From sorrow over her dead son, some say. From poison by her husband so he could marry Bess, blabber others.

I wonder if Margaret watched the treacherous sky from her perch at Lathom Park. I know what she is thinking. Richard will have to start his dynasty again with a fertile new wife and pray to God for children if he wants to keep the throne. His is a long road, and a hazardous one that men may not wait for. Time is deserting Richard and running to Henry's side.

Ralph and Cecily's wedding has brought many friends from across Yorkshire to celebrate with us, and I am so grateful for the opportunity to host the people that matter most in the world to the Scrope family. The delicious aromas of roasting meats mingle in the evening air, curling around the smoke from the cooking fires in the meadows surrounding the castle. I leave Bolton's village church across the way from the castle and pause to enjoy the sight of pastures full of our tenants camping around cheerful fires, preparing their evening meals.

To the west of the castle, a cream-coloured canvas tent has been erected, and as the summer twilight turns to purple night, so does the tent glow golden as its own candles are lit. Long trestle tables encourage our guests to bring their food from their fires and eat with neighbours and new friends, and a musician's circle forms, drummers within, lutes and lyres next to pipes and flutes.

The castle windows are equally aglow, for Bolton hosts the king this night. Peasant and squire, lord and lady—all are here to celebrate the wedding of the king's niece to one of their own. Jack's cousin Ralph, a loyal York follower and defender of the king's lands and family since he first served as a young squire, is honoured with the reward of a marriage that some whisper is well above his station. After all, Cecily was once a princess.

I climb the twisting staircase to my chamber high in the south tower and, with the help of my ladies, change into a gown of azure and white with tissue of silver draped as an overskirt. My headdress is a turret with more silvery tissue floating from the cone, my shoes pointed in the latest fashion. I pause and smile to myself as I look in my burnished mirror, remembering how often I deferred to Margaret's proud poise. I think I have finally grown into my own role, and I am pleased with my place in life.

"You are beautiful tonight, my love." Jack comes to my side, stands next to me before the mirror. I lift my hand, caress his cheek.

"And you are handsome, my love," I reply. We stand together, the same passion that has always fuelled us rising as we admire each other's reflections. Jack raises his eyebrow.

"No," I laugh. "Not now."

"Later, then, my lady," he whispers, adding how he would like to dismiss my maids, undress me himself.

"Later," I reply. I tilt my head, let him see the promise in my eyes. And then step to one side before he can grab me and wrinkle my gown. "Time for us to greet our guests, receive the king."

Jack groans. "Come, then, before I forget my manners and any thought of the king's welcome." He holds out his arm to assist me. "Can you get down the stairs in those shoes? And mind your head on the door frame . . ."

The great chamber is dressed for the wedding in its finest decorations. May garlands swathe the walls and fireplace. The tapestries were taken down, beaten within an inch of their lives, and rehung after lavender was rubbed on their backs to scent the room. Jack and I arrive just before the king, and soon the head table is filled with family and friends: Meg and Will, Oliver and Isabel—and, of course, Ralph and Cecily.

I glance to my left, and there, at the young people's table, are sitting Ned and Dickon, still living under my watch as my Pole nephews. I see the secret smile exchanged between Cecily and her brothers. Perhaps by the summer, Henry Tudor will finally realise his ambition is futile, and they will all be safely and happily reunited as one family. When Richard marries again, there will surely be babies quickly in the royal nursery. And with each new child birthed by Richard, my boys will be further and further from danger.

After the feasting, the tables are moved to the sides of the room for dancing, and soon the hurdy-gurdy and hammer dulcimer tune together. The piper tucks his bag under his arm and blows into the mouthpiece, filling it with air and droning the opening chords. A merry tune strikes up, and Cecily and Ralph lead the younger people in a dance combining solemn moves and flirtatious glances that is one of my favourites.

"They look well together," Oliver observes. He sits next to me on a bench, his feet sticking out before him, clothed in his favourite slippers. My brother is not a dancer and has no intention of starting now. "It is certainly an honour to our Scrope family."

I look at Oliver sharply. There is something in his tone that makes me question his words.

"An honour that seems both fast in coming and convenient in arranging," he continues. He shifts over as Will joins us, slightly out of breath after a particularly vigorous saltarello with Meg.

"Ralph's marriage?" Will's sharp mind picks up immediately on Oliver's words. "You speak in truth, Oliver."

My brother crosses his arms, leans forward to speak to Will across me. "You think the same, Will?"

My son-in-law nods. "The king is eager to remove any opportunity for Henry Tudor to tie his claim to the princesses. Now Richard has arranged Bess's marriage to the Prince of Portugal, Cecily is left next in line. He took care of Henry's ambition by marrying her to Ralph."

I sighed. "Really, you are both being annoying. Can you not for once enjoy a love match?" I am enjoying watching the king, who has been persuaded to step into the dance, and the boys, who have been pulled from the table with the other youth. Together with Cecily and Ralph, they join hands to the sound of a lilting country jig, and faster and faster they spin in a circle until the music clamours to a sudden stop and they all collapse together, laughing and breathless.

Jack stands behind me, resting his strong hands on my shoulders. I have removed my uncomfortable headdress, and he leans over and kisses the top of my head.

"This moment," I say to my family, "this moment I would like to keep forever."

Richard holds an informal council meeting the next morning, and I send refreshments to Jack's chamber to sustain them all. A few raw eggs mixed with my special almond tonic is on the tray too, along with oats and spring water, for I fancy there are some sore heads among the men.

As I walk back down to the apothecary, I press to one side of the corridor as another messenger strides by, following my steward to the main chamber. He is the third rider to arrive at Bolton Castle this morning, and the sight of his intent face and travel-stained clothes raises a sudden worry in me.

After checking the stores in the stillroom, I walk through the granary and over to the armaments. Loud hammering echoes from the forge—unusual, for we have no extra horses to shoe that I am aware of. As I draw closer to the ringing, my heart skips a beat to the rhythm of the blows. Stacked up against the half wall must be fifty swords, as well numerous pikes and shields. The armourer looks up briefly as my shadow falls across his anvil and then continues his beating.

I hurry across the courtyard and meet Jack halfway. The wind that always scurries in little eddies around the walls whips my hair across my face, and he tenderly draws a strand from my eyes.

"When were you going to tell me?" I ask.

"When we knew for sure," he replies.

"Is he coming?"

"Yes." Jack brushes my lips with his fingertip. "Shh. It will be all right."

The moment has finally arrived. It is almost a relief. So many months anticipating Henry's invasion, so much thinking about what it might be like. This time he has no false friend in Harry, no hundred-year storm to wreck both ship and shoremen. He arrives unencumbered, prepared to take the throne. And God only knows what Margaret has coordinated to support his quest.

My nephew on one side. My husband on the other. Now I remember how war feels. Encouraging words conceal the fear in my heart. "Then you must go, my love, and God go with you."

A soldier's wife does not get to show her feelings. For who would send their lover to war clothed in worry rather than armoured in love?

I lean into Jack's touch, giving and sharing strength with each other. Horses are led across the courtyard. Armour is stacked onto a cart, breast plates and leg shields eerily resembling bodies as they lie across the wooden planks. Around us, footsteps become more urgent; shouting grows louder; the hammering takes on a life of its own. All mingle as the clarion call of war.

"And Oliver? Does he go too?" If I am to say good-bye to all the men I love, let me be prepared.

"Not yet," replies Jack. "We need him here, to stay with the boys. Just until I return."

A small mercy that I will hang on to. "Where do you travel to?"

"Back to Devon to join Lovell. We expect Henry will land on the south coast."

"When?"

"Now."

I stand on tiptoe, pull his face to mine, look deep into his eyes. I kiss his beautiful mouth, drink his breath until his being fills my lungs. "Remember," I say. "Remember, I will always wait for you."

43

Summer 1485 | Bolton Castle

Barely has Jack left, and certainly before the tears have dried to salt on my cheeks, when I am called to the king before he too rides south. He looks up as I enter Jack's chamber, my heart aching that it is not my husband who sits in the lord's chair by the hearth, disturbed that these men have commandeered my home, my life. A soldier's wife is always last in their thoughts. At Richard's tilted shoulder, as always, stands Will.

"Elysabeth." This time the king approaches me, takes my hands between his strong and slender fingers. "What a curious and winding journey we have had together. And one that I did not expect to find myself on."

"Neither did I, Your Grace," I reply. "A strange road travelled indeed."

"You have been extraordinarily loyal, Elysabeth. Loyal to my purpose, my nephews, and me personally." The weariness has fled his face, the pensiveness shadowing his eyes replaced by a vigour I have not seen for a year. "And now Jack has set out for war again, leaving you behind."

Such is our history I have no need to hide my true honesty. "There have been times it has been difficult. Times when my feelings were torn, my priorities in doubt."

"Your priorities are always the boys," Richard replies. "And that has never been in doubt." He bows his head, kisses and then gently releases my hands.

A small gesture from a man. A world of gratitude from the lips of a king.

He turns to Will. "I would walk with my nephews and Lady Scrope before we leave. Saddle my horse, gather our men, and wait in the courtyard for me."

Will hesitates. He looks tired; his long blond hair is rumpled and finger-combed. "There is unfinished business here, Your Grace." He gestures at a pile of documents on Jack's table.

"You are right," Richard replies. "I have decided that Sheriff Hutton is still the best refuge. Bess is there for safety's sake. I will let the boys know to wait for our message." He claps Will on the shoulder, a man's gruff affection. "Thank you for your counsel, my friend. You can send instructions to the castle steward to prepare for their arrival. And ensure a guard remains here to escort them."

My son-in-law pulls papers and reaches for his quill. His rapid strokes on the parchment prophesy an urgency that stirs a fluttering in my stomach.

Richard turns to me, holds out his arm. "Shall we find the boys, enjoy your beautiful gardens?"

I try to see what Will is writing, but it is impossible. I will have to ask Meg later what he means to do, why Sheriff Hutton now. "They are down by the hawks, Your Grace." I guide the king through the castle corridors to the southern door.

By the mews, the princes are helping feed the gyrfalcons they love so much. As Richard and I approach, they run towards us. Behind them, the wide valley unfolds peacefully to the distant hills. Behind me, the castle stands rooted in the ground, the medicinal garden filled with a myriad of herbs and the hum of bees.

Henry is coming.

But not here. Here we are well hidden. Here we are safe.

I take a deep breath of lavender-scented air.

But Jack is not. My husband rides to war for his beloved king. I clench my teeth to stop a cry escaping, turn, and manage a smile as Richard hugs his nephews.

A soldier's wife. I am a soldier's wife.

It is not the time for me to ask what he meant by his command to Will. Surely Ned and Dickon are just as safe here. Why should we change everything now? As soon as Henry is vanquished, we can travel to Sheriff Hutton, reunite Bess and Cecily with their brothers, and honour them all as children of the royal blood.

We walk as a family to the cages where the birds live.

"Do you enjoy hunting, Ned?" Richard strokes the neck of a hooded falcon, and I see he has a way with these wild creatures that draws them under his power. "We have a fine chase at Sheriff Hutton."

"We love to hunt." Ned is almost as tall as Richard now; he has grown strong during his time at Bolton Castle. "Deer, especially."

Richard nods. "Me too. You have to be exceptionally clever to catch a buck," he continues. "For they can be most wily."

"Sir Oliver has taught us well," says Dickon. He examines a chunk of fur-covered rabbit flesh in his hands, pulls it apart to expose bone and sinew. Always curious, this one. "He has shown us the secret paths to take to surprise them and the places to hide where they least expect."

"I am glad to hear. Lady Scrope's brother is a fine man and someone I would trust to always guide you well." Richard continues stroking the hawk, who is mesmerised by his touch. "And have you ever used a stalking horse?"

Both boys solemnly shake their heads. These brothers have grown close. Even their motions are identical now.

"It is a new term I heard recently from my own master of the hunt," Richard continues. "And one that you should take great care to remember." He gestures for me to come closer, drawing me into the circle of trust he has woven around his nephews. I sense there is another lesson being taught here, one that Richard intends to impress upon the boys—and me.

"If you ever plan on hunting or invading a stag's territory," he pauses, adding weight to his words, "if you are told by your friends to advance without caution . . . then be sure to use a stalking horse."

The boys quirk their heads. "What's a stalking horse?" they ask in unison.

"It is a creature that protects you. It can mislead people into believing it is something it isn't. It can be led between you and your quarry so they don't know you're there."

"Like Lady Scrope did when we left gaol?" Dickon asks excitedly.

I laugh. Dickon still likes to tell of his adventure of escaping from the Tower of London. He was most taken with our guard's disguises and the humble cart in which two princes left like commonplace apprentices through the Byward Gate.

Richard smiles approvingly at me. "I am not surprised. Lady Scrope is a most enterprising woman." He lets the falconer take back the creature and turns to put his arms around both the boys. "And a stalking horse can also be a decoy," he continues. "Something that is sent ahead to test to see if it is safe to advance or if your quarry is going to try and harm you first. It could even be a decoy in the shape of another young man who pretends to be you."

His pleasant tone has a sudden edge to it. I meet his eyes, narrowed and intense. He is telling us this for a reason, I think. It's not just a story.

"You mean if we are to ride on an expedition, let someone else go first?" Ned's bright face is serious. Perhaps he realises there are more to his uncle's words than a simple hunting tale.

"Yes." Richard ruffles his hair, kisses their cheeks. "There are many who will want you to lead, boys. Many who will remind you that your father was a king and that you were once princes. That you have royal blood in you, albeit bastard slips. Do not let yourselves be put at risk. Use a stalking horse to flush out the enemy. Remember that, and trust only those you know."

I swallow a sudden lump in my throat. This is the speech of a man leaving for war, bidding good-bye to his loved ones. His precious son is dead, beyond his teaching. His beloved wife resides in heaven and will not be waiting at the door for his return. But Richard can still impart his wisdom to his nephews. And entrust me to see they are kept safe.

"Promise your uncle you will heed his words," I say urgently, my voice louder than I intended. Richard deserves to know his lesson is heard.

The boys nod. "We promise," they say.

"I pledge to use a stalking horse," continues Ned seriously. "And only listen to those I trust. Like Lady Scrope and her brother."

My boy. My boy king.

Richard nods abruptly, his mouth tightly clenched.

A sudden flapping as a hawk bates next to us and breaks the moment. The boys are distracted by the falconer holding the bird on his gauntlet.

"Are we going to fly her?" Dickon asks.

Richard waves the falconer forward. "I should be going. I will leave you here. Remember, Oliver is a good man. If he tells you he has message from me or asks you to do something, trust and obey him." He hugs the boys once more and kisses my hand. "Elysabeth, walk with me back to the castle, please."

304

"Of course." As we leave the boys behind, I have to walk fast to keep level with his urgent pace. He strikes me as singularly alone, no child to bid good-bye to, no wife to whisper farewell. It is not my place to comfort him, but I knew him as a man before he was king. "Is there anything I can do to set your mind at rest, Your Grace? I feel you are concerned about the boys."

"Will knows what to do," he says. "He will send you instructions. I will be asking everything of Oliver and Lovell. And loyalty and bravery from you."

"In what way?" I do not understand his riddles.

"Henry comes. And this time my army will decimate him. He and his French mercenaries have no hope against true and trustworthy Englishmen."

"And where is my courage needed? I am not fighting. How can I make a difference?"

"You are the one left behind, Elysabeth. Remember the inn, when you told us what women want?"

"*Sovereynté*," I say.

"Yes," he replies. "The power to make their own decisions." The king pauses as we approach the castle walls, flexes his shoulders as if they ache. "You are left behind to be in charge. This is your *sovereynté*. You are tasked with the most important power of all. Keeping the boys alive and sending them safely to their next destination. Wait for Catesby's instructions. Enlist Oliver's help. And, most of all, remember my words. Remember the stalking horse."

The wheel has turned full circle. I cannot help glancing up at my chamber window, the shutters that I threw open in a moment of ennui that seems so recent yet so long ago. "You have entrusted me with the princes for the past two years," I say. "Are you asking anything different of me now?"

"You do not know yet what may be asked of you, Elysabeth. The boys are always your priority," he says softly, pauses, and kisses my forehead in a blessing. "Walk with me to my horse, talk with me more before I go, for I must leave now."

A week after Jack's departure, it is Oliver's birthday, the fifteenth of August. I have planned a small celebration with the boys. The castle is

305

quiet with most of the men gone. But even as we sit to dine, a messenger thunders into the hall, runs to me, and thrusts a paper into my hands. Will's seal is on the parchment, his badge on the man's tunic.

I rip open the letter, read it quickly, and turn to Oliver. "Henry has landed. He advances across country from Milford Haven in Wales." Nowhere near the south coast. Jack is safe—for now. Yet I know he will ride to fight as soon as he hears of Henry's invasion.

Oliver stares at me for a heartbeat and then nods. "War is upon us."

I close my eyes, pray for Jack, Will, the men I love. Pray for their safety and victory for Richard.

I read the rest of Will's letter. He outlines instructions to send the boys to Sheriff Hutton, the royal residence where they will await the king, ride with him in triumph to Westminster. Lovell should be with us any hour, for he has also been told to prepare for this moment. He and Oliver will accompany the boys.

Sovereynté. The decision the king alerted me about has come. And it is in my power to secure the princes, ensure that they are safe from Henry Tudor's attack. I read Will's directions again. Remember Richard's words. Think of the stalking horse.

"Is the order from Will as we expected?" Oliver asks.

"Yes. Lovell will be here tonight. I will send you both on your way with the boys. Though why they should be out on the roads right now, why they can't continue to stay here—"

"It's as the king commands," my brother says firmly. "You were the last he spoke to. Put the question from your mind. Concentrate on preparing them to leave."

"He did grant me the responsibility to carry out his decision."

Does that mean I also have the power to refuse if I think it's the wrong one?

"And that is what you are doing," Oliver assures me. "Just as we removed the boys from the Tower under his command, so we will obey him now."

"Are you prepared to do what the king asks of us?" I clasp my brother's strong hand, a familiar grip that has comforted me all my life.

"Richard knows what is best. He always has." Oliver glances at the boys. "Yes, I am prepared. And so are you."

Sovereynté. I push the uneasiness to the back of my mind so I can think clearly about the urgency of the immediate.

There is a second letter with the messenger, this one from Meg. I crack the Catesby black wax seal, breaking the crowned lion in half and revealing my girl's looping hand.

> *Belle-maman,* she writes. *Will has suggested you stay with me at Ashby Manor now that your nephews are leaving Bolton. Come and keep me and my sons company. It may be a long summer while our men are on campaign, and I don't like to think of you all by yourself.*

Her words are tempting, and suddenly I long for her presence, for she has always been my comfort. Ashby Manor is a mellow-bricked family home, luxurious compared to our northern castle. It is just south of Leicester, and not far from our family's properties at Maxey Castle and Bletsoe. Meg continues in her letter.

> *I have sent a guard with the messenger in the hope that you will return with them.*

She is right. Ned and Dickon will be gone. Our men will be moving around the country, playing cat-and-mouse with Henry. I would rather wait with Meg than by myself.

I will leave when the boys do. And yet in the opposite direction.

They need me.

A sudden anxiety races my heart.

I could still accompany them. They can't go on their own

"You cannot come this time, Elysabeth." My brother catches my thoughts as he so often does. "But you know I will guard them with my life. Lovell too."

I nod fiercely, glare with bowed head at Catesby's letter I have crumpled in my lap. "I know. It doesn't make it any easier."

"Trust us to do what you have instructed, Elysabeth. We will not fail you."

Don't falter, don't fail.

Ned sits on a bench by the fireplace, tossing knucklebones with Dickon, both young men intent on their game. I think of our time in the Tower, our bid for freedom. How I, a mere woman, was able to take them out of the fortress, bring them north to safety. Perhaps their entire future is destined to be always on the roll of a die, a game of chance they cannot escape.

I drag my eyes away from the boys, reluctant to miss them for even one minute. "Let us prepare them to travel," I say to Oliver. "We knew we could not keep them hidden here forever. Let us send them out into the world with all the skills we have taught them."

Oliver and I stay up late as my brother selects the swiftest horses and most durable tack, handpicks a sword for each boy, and chooses four of our most experienced guards, two to accompany each prince. They will travel lightly and swiftly, avoiding the main track and Henry's spies. I organise provisions, supervise packing their saddlebags, snatch just a couple of hours of broken sleep before it is time to say good-bye.

When the great portcullis lifts in the darkest hour, Francis Lovell arrives in black armour on his black warhorse. I know now that there is no turning back from my decision.

The boys stand holding their horses' bridles, their faces alight with excitement at the prospect of an adventure. I know they wish to fight, but I am so relieved they are too young. It is enough that they leave my care and join this world of men. They will never return to Bolton Castle as my Pole nephews, and in my heart I know I am saying good-bye to this part of their lives.

Let me send them away with a soldier's mother's blessing, for that is the best farewell I can give them.

I walk to Dickon first. "Be strong, be brave, my darling." I touch him lightly on his sturdy shoulder. "Your courage will take you far, and you will always bring joy to those around you." I reach in my pocket, give him a piece of oak I picked up from beneath the tree by the mews. "Carve me a falcon and send it when you are ready," I whisper. "Fly free, my darling, fly free."

He grins. "I'll always fly home to you, Lady Scrope. You are like a mother to me."

Swallowing my tears, I approach Ned. "My lord." I curtsey, for I wish to pay homage to my godson, who for just eight brief weeks was once King of England. "You have far to travel in this world, let not your heart falter nor your spirit be in fear." For Ned, I embroidered a small emblem, crimson words stitched in a golden banner resting under a unicorn. "Remember, the unicorn will always bring you home safely. And keep these words always with you, for they are yours to live in the truth."

Ned takes the little badge, reads the words aloud. *"Dieu et mon droit. God and my right."* He kisses my cheek, holds me close before clasping my hands, searching my eyes. He has grown level with me now, a boy no more. "The motto of the Kings of England."

"Yes," I reply simply. "The King of England."

The torches flare alive in the sudden whisper of a predawn breeze. My boys have miles to go. I cannot hold them any longer.

Oliver hugs me. "Don't worry, Elysabeth," my brother says. "Promise you won't worry. Put any anxious thoughts of us from your mind, for we will ride swiftly and in secret." He lifts my chin, winks at me. "What did we used to do when we were hiding from Margaret?"

"Pretend she didn't exist," I smile at our childhood memory, "so that the devil couldn't steal our thoughts and lead her to us."

"Exactly. So do the same, Sister. Put us out of your mind."

My brother and Lovell mount up and lead the way under the portcullis. The princes do not turn back and wave. They are already in their future, leaving the past behind.

"Be safe, my darlings," I whisper as their small party departs. "Guide them well, Oliver. Be safe as you leave Bolton Castle. I will see you again soon."

Sovereynté. I have sent them on their way.

44

Summer 1485 | Ashby Manor

"Have you had word from Margaret?" I ask Meg as soon as I walk through the carved double doors of Ashby, shaking the journey dust from my skirts. It is just three days since I sent the princes on their way, and we slip into our old pattern of *Have you had word?* as we catch up on our news. "I am sure she is ready to don armour and ride at Henry's side the moment he returns to England."

"Aunt Margaret as Joan of Arc?" Meg says mischievously. We both giggle and then quickly sober. "No word. No word from Will nor Jack or Margaret."

"Nothing from Will?" I am surprised. He is usually prolific with his letters.

"No," Meg replies. "But soon, I am sure." She pauses. "And the boys?"

"With Oliver and Lovell," I say, suppressing the quiver of anxiety that sways every thought of them. "My brother has no cause to write. Yet."

Meg nods. "Nor Ned. Tell me of any boy of fourteen who would willingly put quill to parchment. No doubt he is already enjoying the hunt at Sheriff Hutton."

"No doubt."

Don't. Don't think. They are safe without me.

Meg takes my hood, walks me to her solar. "I am glad you are here. We may not have heard from Margaret, but I am sure her spies are everywhere. No doubt she knows you are with me and that Will is with the king. This is, after all, the definitive battle."

"She believes God is on her side. And Henry's." I remember the endless months I was her gaoler, witnessing her anguish at his exile, discovering the conspiracies she created to bring him home. "Her love for her son has never faded. I cannot think how devastated she will be when he is finally defeated."

"How lenient can Richard afford to be when Henry is captured? He is reluctant to kill outside of battle." Meg folds her arms, paces to the window.

"Henry is even more traitorous than Harry ever was. And Richard did not hesitate to execute the man who was once his second-in-command." I join her, longing for a messenger to break from the woods, bang on our gates with word from Jack. The whole world stills under the fierce August sun. Time is suspended, anticipating, watching.

I have to do something. I cannot just wait.

Stark shadows and bright stripes divide the garden, striking the roses until they glow blood-red. I abide in beauty, while in this same land men are slaughtering each other.

"This is a battle to the death, Belle-maman?" Meg echoes my thoughts.

"Richard cannot keep Henry alive, even imprisoned in the Tower for the rest of his years."

"It will kill Margaret. I cannot imagine losing a son," Meg whispers. "Mine are my life. As is Will."

I pull her into my arms. "No talk of dying. You are a soldier's wife. We do not speak of death, we speak of life and victory."

"It is not easy," Meg says.

"I did not say it was," I reply.

Today is the fourth day since I have arrived at Ashby. Still no word, and now, unreasonably, I expect Oliver to write and tell me of the princes, even when he said he wouldn't for their safety's sake, couldn't for fear of the devil catching my thoughts. Last night the moon rose in a shroud, stifling time with no radiance to light our restlessness. Lightning glows inside the clouds, thunder rumbles in the east foretelling death, but no storm flies through the skies to break the heat.

I question the old one-legged steward constantly, for he operates a relay of scouts across the county, relics from his veteran days fighting for the Catesbys.

"Henry's army is marching from Shrewsbury," he tells me this morning. "King Richard's army is moving from Nottingham to Leicester."

"That is just a day's ride from Ashby Manor," I reply, and he concurs. The armies are far too close for my liking. They could collide anywhere in this fair countryside; any fragrant hay meadow could be reaped into a blood-soaked battlefield. When I agreed to be with Meg, I did not think that I was heading into danger, and I wish now I had insisted that she come to Bolton instead.

We are lightly defended, a minimal Catesby guard of old men, a cripple, and ploughboys. Any able-handed man has long left with Will. I walk restlessly through empty rooms, assessing where we may best hide if Tudor's defeated army comes our way to plunder, thinking also of where we could hold our victory celebration when our husbands return. Truly, my mind is all over the place, spinning through our fates as rapidly as a runaway wheel. Their names repeat in my thoughts like the clicking of spokes, over and over.

Ned. Dickon. Oliver. Jack. Will.

Don't think of them . . . don't. I am far away. Fear the devil and trust in God.

"What risk could there be to us?" Meg asks when I tell her I am satisfied that the attics could conceal us, and I carry up water flasks and dried meats to sustain us. She lugs provisions from the kitchens with me, her sons helping before they scurry outside, eager to get back to their games of mock battles and spying. "The king's army has been training for years for this event. Victory is a certainty. No one will attack and plunder Ashby."

I wish I had the confidence of youth. "War is never certain," I reply. "But yes, you are right. The king will dispatch Henry easily. And the armies do not fight to harm the innocent people of this land, but to battle political allegiances."

We stare at each other then, for she is the cousin of Henry Tudor, and I am his aunt. Have we done enough over time to prove where our loyalties lie when York prevails? The king knows we have. The council knows we have. But would a victorious drunk commander of a troop riding under the York banner assume our allegiance is blood over marriage?

"We are taking all precautions," I say firmly. Over Meg's shoulder, through the tall and narrow diamond-paned window of her solar, a cloud of dust rolls towards us from the easterly track.

At last, a messenger.

But the dust grows and spreads and foretells of many more than one rider, one horse.

The cloud sprawls across the hedgerows and fields until it appears as if a storm has descended from the heavens and is bowling along to envelop our manor. Within the dust is the glint of weaponry. There must be a retinue of a hundred horses shimmering under the August sun.

"Dear God," Meg cries. "Who is coming upon us?"

"Quickly," I reply. "Call your sons inside."

"What shall we do?"

"We shall hide as I planned. Until we know who comes this way with such urgency."

Meg takes flight from the solar, and through the window I see her dash to the stables, gather her sons from their play, and run back to the house. I meet her on the stairs, and together we scurry to the attics, where we kneel by a dormer window and peer out at the cloud growing closer and closer.

Below us stretches the path east, and I take Meg's hand as the retinue gallops towards us. Dust billows from the horses' hooves, and with the morning sun at their backs it is impossible to distinguish the flying banners other than dark shapes flapping against the brilliant sky until they come within fifty yards of us.

"It can't be . . ." I say aloud.

Meg squints into the approaching dust storm. "Surely not? Is that orange, tawny . . . ?

". . . and green," I finish. "That's green. These are Lord Stanley's colours."

"Margaret," we say together. "It's Margaret."

As we speak her name, the entourage pulls up in front of the house in a thunder of hooves that we hear even in our high attic, and the guards peel off to the sides, revealing the figure of a woman on a high-prancing mare. She is wearing a leather surcoat, and her full black skirts drape all the way over her horse from withers to tail. She reins to a halt and stares up at the house.

I jump to my feet. "I have to go to her."

"Not alone," replies Meg. "We are family. We are all going to receive her to Ashby Manor."

"I think it better I—"

"Together," she insists.

Feeling slightly foolish for hiding, for Margaret is, after all, my sister, I lead Meg and her sons down the winding attic stairs and through the main house.

We step into the courtyard, our small guard of half a dozen Catesby men flanking us. They are armed but keep their swords sheathed. We are so outnumbered it is laughable, but then, we are not in a battle.

"Margaret," I call. "What are you doing here?"

She lifts the veil that protects her complexion. A guard assists her to dismount. She peels off her riding gloves, stands, and surveys our small party, the manor. "No invitation to step inside, Elysabeth? We will not talk on the step like washerwomen."

Her horsemen line up before us and rein in their mounts. I was right. There are easily a hundred armed guards.

"Of course." I walk to kiss her cheek, take her arm. "Come, refresh yourself." I glance over her shoulder. The men are heated, but not exhausted. "Have you come far?"

"From Maxey Castle," she replies. "I was waiting there."

"Waiting? For what, Aunt Margaret?" Meg interjects. "Have you news?"

My sister's face is impassive. "Yes. I cannot tarry long. Lord Stanley is expecting me." Her face may be expressionless, but her eyes are alight with excitement. She calls a command to the captain. "Water the horses and prepare to leave again within the hour."

We move into the shade of the porch. I stop, for I cannot let her take another step without knowing what is happening. "Your husband expects you? What news, Margaret?"

She looks at me then with triumph in her gaze. "You are to come with me, Elysabeth," she says shortly. "Gather your belongings and change into your riding habit. We must be at Leicester before nightfall."

I drop Margaret's arm like a hot coal. "Come with you? I shall not."

"You must."

"You have no authority to command me to leave with you," I retort.

The dark shadows of the porch emphasise the brightness of the gardens outside, the distortive heat of the August sun. Where have I had this feeling of contrasts before? Suddenly, I recall our rushed conversation in the alley in Burford, when I repeated Richard's warning to her.

Hold your enemies close. And your friends and family closer.

"You have no reason," I repeat. "You do not command me."

"I have every reason," she replies. "Do not think you can delay. Lord Stanley and the king await."

"Why invoke Lord Stanley now, Margaret?" I ask. "And what do your husband and King Richard want of me?"

"Information," she says brusquely. "And it is not King Richard. Richard is dead. You are to meet with my son. Henry Tudor is now King of England."

My head spins with a blood-rush shock, and Meg gasps beside me. I believe we both clutch blindly for each other, but I cannot be sure, for the world darkens and then dazzles. I think Margaret has finally gone insane and that I am plunged into her world of illusion.

"This cannot be." I am flushed and cold at the same time; my heart is racing. I see Richard's quizzical look, his gentle smile, his lifted shoulder and hear his laughter. "You are mad, Margaret, mad."

Richard is dead. This cannot be.

"Will," whispers Meg. "Wherever Richard is, Will is at his side." She trembles in my arms, cries to Margaret, "Where is Will?"

"There was a battle. Near Bosworth." Margaret has the grace to bow her head, her hand creeping for her ever-present rosary. "I do not know, Meg," she continues. "I do not know of anyone's fate except Richard's."

Richard is dead. Loyaulté me lie.

Loyalty let me die.

"How could he die?" I demand. I enfold Meg tighter in my arms, speak to my sister across my girl's quivering shoulders. "How has this happened? What news of Jack? Where's Jack?"

Please God, he did not make it to the battle in time. Please God. Please.

Margaret simply stares at me, reaches a hand to stroke Meg's arm, and drops it as I turn my girl from her touch.

More things fall into place as my head clears. "Your husband? Lord Stanley? He is with Henry? But he is Richard's man—"

"Go and gather your things, Elysabeth." Margaret ignores my questions and turns on her heel, back towards her army of Stanley troops. "Henry demands to see you. He is dispatching a guard immediately to Sheriff Hutton to retrieve Bess. Curious rumours have started to circulate about her brothers, the princes."

Oh God.

Oliver. Ned. Dickon.

No. Don't think of them. The devil will steal your thoughts.

Margaret pierces me with a look. "Henry thinks you may be able to answer some of his questions. He and I were told they are dead. But now . . . now he does not know what to believe." She strides towards her horse. "We leave immediately."

"You don't have to go, Belle-maman." Meg says.

"I do have to go."

"You can't leave . . . Tell him no . . . He's your nephew . . . You don't—"

"You don't understand, Meg."

I have to stop her from pressing me more. I cannot be questioned about the princes in front of Margaret. I cannot stay to comfort Meg, pray with her for Jack and Will. I am commanded by the king. King Henry VII of England. Henry. My nephew.

I am commanded by the king. King Richard III of England.

Richard. Blood relative by my godmother's legacy.

Ned. Dickon.

I cross my fingers against the devil.

Within the quarter hour, I am dressed to ride with my sister.

"Let us go now, Margaret," I tell her. "For this is a wasted journey, and I have nothing to say to Henry."

"That is not what I have heard," she responds. "Take your leave of Meg. We must hurry."

"Be strong, Meg, be brave," I whisper to my darling girl as I kiss her good-bye. My pack has been taken by a servant, a horse provided for me to ride. "We are soldiers' wives. We are strong."

"Good-bye, and Godspeed, Belle-maman," she replies in her sweet, familiar voice, steady and calm. "Be safe, and take *sovereynté*, as Richard empowered you. Do not falter."

Do not fail.

My last sight is of Meg standing with her three sons, her arms protectively around them, framed by the black iron gates of Ashby Manor. Her face gleams white in the unforgiving noon shadows, a prisoner peering from the darkness. She does not smile or lift her hand to wave, but each time I turn around to look back, she is gazing at me with courage in her stance and fear in her eyes, and my heart breaks into a thousand fragments.

45

Autumn 1485 | The Road North

I am surrounded by Lord Stanley's guard, unable to see more than the horses in the row ahead and Margaret to my right. The choking dust enshrouds us, and so even if I could find words, I am reluctant to open my mouth. But no words come except the insistent drumming in my head of *Richard is dead. Richard is dead.*

And all the anxiety that stems from those words now slams down upon me, and although my sister is by my side, we are as far apart as ever two souls could be. She does not look at me, she stares straight ahead as she rides to her son, the King of England.

I am riding pillion with the thoughts of all my loved ones. Jack. Ned. Dickon. Oliver. Will.

Where are you, Jack? Are you still on this earthly realm?

I'd know if you were dead, wouldn't I? I'd feel it in my soul.

With each mile north, my shock is gradually blanketed by a deathly calm, for if there is ever a time I must keep my wits about me, it is now. I am the person who stands between Margaret, Henry, and the truth.

The sun has crossed over our heads as we ride, and now it is on my left, shafts of ruddy August rays piercing the dust and telling me that soon we will be at Leicester.

Henry thinks you may be able to answer some of his questions. Margaret's words are burning in my brain. *Strange rumours have started to circulate about the princes.*

We have been so careful, so vigilant these past months. What rumours, what questions might Henry have? And how does he plan to extract answers from me?

He was told they are dead . . . but now he does not know.

Oliver. Lovell. Did they get the boys to safety?

Oh, Richard, you have bequeathed me sovereynté. I must not let you down.

317

A shout ahead is passed back down the ranks, and the guard slows from a fast trot to a walk. I rein back my mare, and she steps quietly along. We are slowing, slowing, and my heart is beating faster, faster, for this means that we have arrived, wherever arrived is. In a few minutes, I will be in front of Henry, and he will be asking me the questions, demanding answers.

"This way." The captain leads Margaret and me through the entourage, where now men are talking and laughing, clapping each other on the shoulder, quaffing stone jars of ale. We are in a field that hosts an army, and tents are pitched and campfires burning, smoke rising in plumes and meat sizzling on sticks. As far as I can see are banners and men; there is Hungerford and Essex, and we have dismounted in the middle of Stanley. Stanley. Richard's turncoat commander.

"Margaret, I have nothing to say to Henry," I insist as we walk in step towards a pavilion. The standards outside ripple in the warm evening breeze, Welsh dragons flying in the twilight. *Tudor.* "I just wish to go home to Bolton Castle."

"And we want the same for you," Margaret says. "With an escort from my son."

From the pavilion come men's voices and a sudden shout of laughter.

"My son," repeats Margaret, and tears are streaming down her cheeks. "My son."

The guards move to one side, and she runs into the tent, where Henry stands in a group of soldiers. He has not changed much; he is still tall and pale complected, although his face has deep creases, and his hair has thinned. His bright blue eyes catch the light from the tent opening, and he holds out his arms as Margaret almost falls in her eagerness to reach her son. Her hands flutter like doves across his tunic, for she comes only to his breast, and they fly to his face, pattering and touching, finding his cheeks, his hair, return to his shoulders. He catches her and stoops over her protectively. The men around him have fallen quiet, and her sobbing fills the tent until it subsides under his embrace.

"My lady mother," he says, his voice singsong. I hear Welsh and French colour his words, English last.

"The king's mother," Margaret replies.

The men around them raise a spontaneous cheer, and the solemn moment is dispelled by rejoicing.

Henry leads her to a chair, settles her, and approaches me. Tossed on a stool is his battle tabard. I wonder if it is Richard's blood staining the silk.

"Aunt Elysabeth," he says. His face is pleasant, his eyes hard. "Well met. After a long while."

It takes everything I have to curtsey. "Your Grace." I say the words aloud for the first time and then can say no more.

"You have been with my cousin Meg?" He asks. "Will Catesby is under guard here."

I sag with relief. "Thank you," I say. "Thank you for letting me know he is alive."

Henry opens his mouth as if to say more and then shuts it like a trap. "I did not bring you here to talk about Catesby," he says. "I am sending Robert Willing to Sheriff Hutton to collect my betrothed, the Princess Elizabeth."

Oh God, save us.

I jerk down my head to conceal my face. I hope he mistakes my self-defence as humility. "Yes, Your Grace."

"You will ride with him."

"Why?" The word bursts from my lips before I can stop.

Henry looks at me sharply. "You have a problem going to Sheriff Hutton?"

I recover quickly. "No, Nephew, I do not."

Margaret has stopped sobbing and now comes to Henry's side. Together, although they are very different in height, their likeness is so similar. Together, they appear invincible, and I see the core within that has brought them both to this moment.

"Elysabeth, you must assist us," my sister says calmly. "Bess is at Sheriff Hutton, under Richard's guard." She stares at me, reaches for and grabs my hand, squeezes it tightly. "Is there anyone else under Richard's guard at Sheriff Hutton we should know about?"

I stare back at her and say with absolute truth in my voice and conviction in my heart, "That you should know about? No."

Do not let the devil steal your thoughts.

"We heard you left Bolton Castle with a troop of guards. There were young boys in the retinue."

"You spied on me? Your own sister?"

319

Margaret's eyes slide away from me.

"Is this true, Aunt Elysabeth?" Henry's voice whispers like silk on steel.

"There are many pages in my household—"

"—two in particular, fair-haired and well guarded." Henry folds his arms. "I say these young boys sound curiously familiar. And heading for Sheriff Hutton? What say you?"

"You doubt your own cousin Harry's word?" I shoot back. "Buckingham had proof that the boys are dead and buried in the Tower of London. He sent messengers to Margaret confirming this. How could they be at Bolton Castle?"

Margaret steps before me, searches my face, gazes for an eternity, and I stare back at her. I will not drop my eyes. It is like outstaring a dog. I cannot think of anything other than my truth.

Dead. Buried. Gone.

"Elysabeth should go to Sheriff Hutton," Margaret speaks to Henry, does not remove her eyes from me. "And then I suggest you escort her on to Bolton Castle. If there is any evidence, living or dead, that is to be found, she will lead us to it."

"There is nothing to find," I say to them both. "They are long dead. Buried. Gone."

"I want the proof," says Henry.

"Proof," adds Margaret.

"There is no proof," I reply simply. "And therein lies your future. For without proof, there can be no certainty. And without certainty, there can be no peace."

Is it a prison guard of a dozen of Henry's soldiers or a royal escort that accompanies me to Sheriff Hutton? Either, I suppose, based on what we find there when we arrive. Sir Robert Willing is driving an exhausting pace, and we sleep just a few hours to rest the horses. What should take three to four days we achieve in two, and I am so tired I can barely keep on my mare. My eyes are blurred with exhaustion and tears, for as the castle comes into view sitting high on the hill, I can only think of Richard and Jack, Will and Lovell, the times they spent here together.

And, of course, my boys.

We surprise Bess in the great hall, for Sir Robert pushes by the guards and claims the castle in the name of King Henry. The shock on her face is quickly replaced by a carefully arranged expression of welcome.

"You bring timely news, Sir Robert," she says, throwing a hasty sidelong glance at me. "And surprising. I had thought my Uncle Richard would be the victor."

"It was not God's will," replied Sir Robert. "I am to take you south, immediately, to be under the care of the Lady Stanley, the king's mother."

Bess nods slowly. "And not my own mother?"

I can see her mind working, the wheels turning as she assesses her return as Henry's betrothed, not Richard's favourite niece. She ranks above us all now, a future queen, not a bastard girl.

"King Henry is most concerned about your whole family's well-being," I say to her. She's a sharp girl; she will understand my meaning. "There is a need to make sure you are all safe. Best to be under Lady Stanley's care. These times are uncertain. Loyalties are in question."

Sir Robert is in no mood for chatter. "Where is Edward?" he asks brusquely.

Edward?

I speak before Bess can. "Sir Robert, there are no boys here—"

"—and your sisters?" he continues.

"My cousin Warwick is in his chamber," Bess says quickly. "And Cecily is in hers."

Clarence's son, Edward of Warwick. Not Ned.

"Cecily is also here?" I say aloud, clearing my throat to prevent the words from sticking; my mouth is so parched. "I thought she would be at Bolton Castle with her husband."

"Our Uncle Richard commanded her here," replies Bess. "For safekeeping."

Sir Robert laughs dryly. "How convenient," he says. "Saves me the trouble of going to Bolton. Now, if you will excuse me, I have orders to search the castle."

"Princess Elizabeth can guide you," I say, giving her full name and rank. Let Sir Robert be reminded of who he is dealing with. "And then she will want to prepare to travel."

"Of course," says Bess calmly. "You will find little here." She looks at me again, and although I know she dare not make a sign, I fancy I see caution in her eyes. "Take my steward, Sir Robert, for he has keys to every room. Sit with me, Lady Scrope, while Sir Robert follows the king's command."

We are left, two women alone, while the soldiers swarm over the towers and courtyards of the castle. I hear the clanging of footsteps, the shouts of "clear" as each storeroom, chamber, cellar, and larder is searched and found empty. Bess keeps her hand in mine, and there is such a calmness flowing from her fingers that I find strength in her silence. Only once does she speak, when Sir Robert summons his men all to meet in the hall before us and demands if they have found any evidence of the princes. The guards shake their heads.

"Thanks be to God," murmurs Elizabeth of York, my nephew's wife, the future Queen of England. "Thanks be to God."

Thanks be to God indeed. And to Oliver. Who followed my instructions.

After forcing some food into my reluctant stomach and snatching a broken night's sleep, I am told by Sir Robert that he is leaving immediately for Westminster with Bess and Cecily.

"And I am free to go?" I ask. "What exactly did you expect me to tell you here at Sheriff Hutton?"

"Not what you would tell me," he replies, "but what I would find."

"And?" I prompt.

"No evidence that anyone has been here other than the princesses and Edward of Warwick." He stares down at me, a tall man with quiet eyes. I am not fearful of him, but I do not trust him.

"Who else were you expecting?"

"You are so innocent that you have not heard the rumours?" He is gathering his cloak, ready to race south with King Henry's betrothed in his grasp. "I think not."

"What rumours?" I ask.

"Of Bess's brothers. The princes. That they live." Sir Robert pauses. "Do I need to send a guard with you to search Bolton Castle too? Would I find evidence there?"

"Sir Robert," I say. "My husband is missing. My son-in-law is imprisoned, my daughter alone. My nephew has just ascended the throne. I have greater things to occupy my thoughts than rumours about two bastard slips that are long dead."

And the devil take all of you.

"And yet . . ." His eyes search mine. "And yet it seems over the past years whenever there has been gossip about the princes, you have not been far away."

"And neither has my sister, the king's mother," I reply. "Bolton Castle will add several days to your journey. I don't think the king will want to wait for his bride, do you?"

"No . . . but the princes . . ." he wavers, weighing my words.

"The princes are long gone." I piously lower my eyes. "As godmother, I would know more than anyone."

Sir Robert shuffles from one foot to the other. I stare at his boots, let him edge closer to his decision.

"Besides," I continue, "it is a great honour for you to escort the future queen to Westminster. It would be unfortunate if your second-in-command has the accolade of that important duty." Time to finish this. "Now, if you will excuse me, I wish to say good-bye to Bess and Cecily." I sweep from the room with as much dignity as I can on trembling knees, dreading to hear his footsteps following me, announcing he is travelling to Bolton, after all.

Don't falter, don't fail.

Bess and Cecily are already mounted and surrounded by Sir Robert's guard.

"So you travel to your husband," I say to Bess. I turn to Cecily. "And you leave yours. What words would you like me to give to Ralph?"

Cecily looks at me with tears in her eyes. "That I love him. That this choice to leave was not mine."

I nod. "I understand, my darling. And so will he."

"Lady Scrope," Bess's voice is low, urgent. "You know where they are, don't you?"

"Not this moment, not now," I reply in truthfulness, for I do not want to tell her something that she may be forced to admit to. "As far as I know, they are long gone."

But, pray to God, not dead. Not buried. That I have not heard.

"As far as you know?" she asks. "But no proof?"

"No proof," I reply. "No proof."

Her beautiful face quietens, and although her eyes are full of tears, hope is clear on her brow.

"I shall remember that," she says. "No proof. When Henry asks me."

"You can say the same to Margaret," I reply. "Tell her from me that the wheel of fate continues to turn." I pause as Sir Robert joins us, hold my breath until he mounts his own horse, reins it to head the royal party. "My sister may think she is ascending as the king's mother. That now her son is on the throne, the Tudor dynasty has arrived and the Plantagenets are no more. But without proof, Margaret will never be certain of fate's journey. Without proof, she and Henry will never rest easy."

46

Autumn 1485 | Bolton Castle

Five sleepless nights have slunk by like a leper crawling to the church door. I have arrived from Sheriff Hutton to a castle empty of men, watched over only by the women left behind and two brace of guards who would rather be fighting. No word from Jack, which terrifies me. No word from Oliver, which consoles me. Now I am away from Margaret's thought-stealing, perhaps I dare pray for the boys again.

Each endless day I walk—walk to the mews, to the church, through the fields and empty rooms, encountering only memories and ghosts.

Each wakeful night I climb the battlements and gaze upon the valley, willing the waxing moon to illuminate the road home for Jack. And each night only the yipping of a fox or the hooting of owls keep me company.

As I turn to descend back to my lonely chamber, my eyes catch movement on the road below. Too large for a fox, too swift for cattle, the shadow breaks from the trees, and moonlight gleams on a man's armour. A single rider, an exhausted horse—is this the messenger I have been yearning for? Driven by the blood thumping through my heart, I dash to the stairs, and with both hands steadying me on either side of the rough stone wall, I run down from the roof as fast as I safely can.

Down, down past Jack's chamber, past my own rooms, down past the solar, past the chapel, all those familiar places that have held me prisoner these agonising days. Down into the courtyard and past the startled sentries.

"Open the gate," I shout as I stumble across the cobbles, cursing the sheep pens and fences that slow me for one second from knowing the news. "A messenger arrives. Open the gate!"

The mighty portcullis grinds and grates and disappears up into the stone arch. The guards draw their swords, heave open the gates, and steady themselves in case this is an attack and the desperate Lady Scrope is mistaken in her vision.

The horseman rides under, bowed in exhaustion, the horse's head drooping in concert. As they enter the courtyard, both look around as if surprised that they have arrived within.

I run and cling to the stirrup, my fingers clenched around the leather strap, grazing against the rider's foot.

"Tell me!" I cry. "Tell me what news!" My hand clutches the man's calf, and as the warmth of his body runs through my hand, my arm, and straight to my heart, a dizziness hums in my temples. "My God," I whisper. "My God, Jack?"

The man pushes back the visor on his helmet and swings down from the saddle. Wordlessly, he pulls me into his arms, and as I press my cheek against the unyielding breast plate, the armour bruises my flesh, and I welcome the reality of the pain. I wrap my arms around him as far as they can stretch, searching for the man beneath the metal.

"Elysabeth." Jack buries his face in my hair, seeking my mouth with his. Our mingled tears burn on my cheeks, and as we finally draw apart, there is absolute exhaustion and a new sorrow etched in his face.

The guards, who have been standing back, now approach us, one taking Jack's horse, the other unstrapping his breast plate and placing it with a clank on the cobblestones.

"Come." I take his hand and lead him across to our tower's entry. Around us, rubbing sleep from their eyes, women run out to witness the return of their lord, bringing the castle back to life. "Come, my love. You are home."

In Jack's chamber, someone has already stoked up a great fire and pails of water are heating. I help Jack ease off his clothes, and, wrapping him as a child in a thick robe, I sit him in his chair and pull a stool next to him. He is silent, and I do not rush to fill the void, for I remember from my time in sanctuary the overwhelming confusion entering the world again after an age of deprivation. God knows how long Jack has been travelling or on his own, making his way home again, alone on the roads leading north, always north. And entering the light of home from the darkness of whatever horror he has witnessed will take time to adjust.

When the water is hot, I dismiss the servant and help Jack into the tub. Taking the cloth, I squeeze the water gently over his back, his shoulders, where the skin is raw and chafed from the armour, his arms, where the skin is bruised and reddened from the leather grips. I bathe him as I would a child, softly, silently, letting the musical dripping of water and the crackling of the fire bring him back to life.

He finally closes his eyes and lies back, and I carefully trim his tangled beard and stroke peppermint oil into his warm skin.

"Elysabeth." Jack opens his eyes and inhales deeply. "I did not know if you would be here."

"Why would I not be? I will always wait for you," I say simply.

"And I will always find you," he responds, and then his voice cracks. "Wherever you choose to be."

"I choose you." I wonder what deep fear has shaped his doubt. But he is not ready to speak more.

Later, after he has eaten, I am desperate to hear his story, but still he is silent. After his countless days outside, the confines of the stone walls must stifle his voice.

"Come with me," I say, leading him again. He has no more directives left in him, no heart left to command.

We climb the stairs to the battlements, and now the moon lights the entire valley, a glowing orb in the depth of the sky. It is a rare cloudless night, and the constellations sprinkle like raindrops across a black pool.

Jack stands behind me, wraps his arms around me as I rest my hands on the stone. This is my lookout; do I imagine that here the wall has rubbed smooth from my worrying? Perhaps.

Faintly, from way below, a woman sings a familiar love song that drifts from an open window, encircling and drawing us close.

Jack begins to speak, his deep voice reverberating through my spine, into my heart. Weaving through his words and beneath the story, I absorb the pain and shock through my skin.

"I heard of an invasion in Wales. I left the West Country, for they did not come on my watch. And then there was a battle," Jack begins, as any soldier would. "Ten or eleven days past. At Bosworth, near Leicester."

I stiffen. He was there? "I do not see you injured?"

He pauses. "I arrived upon its end, not its beginning."

I do not rush his words, but look out upon the valley where our farms lie carefully tended, our people sleep peacefully in their beds.

"Margaret's husband watched from a distance. Watched as men were slaughtered, as Richard began to lose ground. Stanley joined the field at the last hour. Against Richard. On the side of the invader."

"The traitor. The wretched traitor." I loathe Stanley, despise him with a terrible and lasting hatred.

How long had that been planned? All that Margaret had plotted, her letters, her secret messages. All those instructions galloped by messengers to a patient Henry, waiting with his army in France. And anticipating his arrival, Margaret's husband, Lord Stanley. Richard's top commander. Henry's stepfather. Turncoat.

"Henry prevailed. Richard died."

Margaret Beaufort. Thomas Stanley. Traitors.

Jack pauses again, and I am heartbroken at the suffering those words cost him. His beloved king. My beloved king. Gone.

And then he takes breath.

Oh God, there is more.

"Ratcliffe is dead. Brackenbury is dead. Catesby is dead—executed."

My knees buckle then, and if not for Jack's arms about me, I would have crumpled to the floor. *Oh, Meg. Oh, Meg, that you should know such sorrow.*

"Henry," I whisper through my tears, "murdered Meg's husband."

Jack continues, his voice rough. "I don't know where Lovell is. I searched the field of dead for him. Stayed to look for him in the wounded at Leicester. He was not there, nor was he seen in the battle."

"My love, my love, there is a reason he was not at the battle." My heart is breaking at his anguish. "Lovell—"

"They are gone. All gone." Jack's body feels frail to me suddenly, his mortality under siege. He is deaf to me in his misery. "All is lost."

"Lovell and the boys—"

"Oh dear God. The boys. Catesby sent them to Sheriff Hutton," Jack cries aloud, despair breaking his voice. "I . . . I am just one man. I am all that is left. I must protect them—if they are not already slain."

When he struggles to break free from me, I grip him tightly. Now I must be the strength forging us together.

An owl flies on silent wings below us across the castle lands, flying west towards the sinking moon. West towards the rugged coast, the wild Irish Sea, the sleeping lands of Eire.

I turn within Jack's arms, hold his face between my hands, and look deep into his eyes. "I have something to tell you."

I point over the roofs of the village below us, where the night's last candle flickers in a cottage window. "There, across the sea, far away in Ireland, Dickon is safely concealed with the Earl of Kildare."

I gently turn Jack's gaze to the western sky, where the moon is now a tor upon the highest hill, a beacon lighting the horizon.

"There," I say. "In England's West Country, Ned hides in Devon. Waits for the signal to return. Waits for you."

Jack stares to the distant hills, and I know his mind is journeying to the wild lands afar, to the hope that lies beyond our borders.

"They survived?" his words are whispered so softly that the night breeze steals them from his mouth, and they are meant for my ears alone. "You know for sure?"

"They survived," I tell him. "Catesby had instructions to send them to Sheriff Hutton."

"He did—"

"Richard told me to send them farther." I look down upon the path from the mews to the castle, the path Richard and I walked after he said good-bye to the boys. Where in just a few words he gave me his final command. "He entrusted their future with me. With Oliver and Lovell."

"How? What do you mean?"

I speak slowly, share my secret.

"Richard advised me to employ a stalking horse."

"A what?"

"A stalking horse. A decoy."

"What did you do?" I feel Jack's muscles tense.

"I rode out with a Scrope guard and two boy pages and sent them to Sheriff Hutton. They much resembled Ned and Dickon. And they rode in broad daylight to be noticed by all. Friend and foe."

"Go on."

"Earlier, during the night, Oliver took Dickon to Ireland, to the Earl of Kildare. Lovell took Ned to Devon, to his brother Thomas Grey." There. The secret of my *sovereynté* is revealed.

"I have been taming Devon these past six months—"

"The king trusted no other to secure the county for Ned."

As the sun rises like a phoenix in fire of gold, I share Jack's gaze over the purple valleys and rolling hills, the high dales surrounding Middleham, Richmond, Sheriff Hutton; Richard's castles of Yorkshire defending the Northland against all invaders. Hiding their lords from all usurpers.

Henry Tudor will never reign in peace. Will never stop wondering if the throne is his to keep. Or if another will return and claim it from him, as he has stolen it himself.

Let Margaret summon me to Westminster. I will not go.

Let Henry Tudor search all of England. He will not find them.

Let both son and mother sleep uneasy in their beds, suspecting but never finding proof of my secret.

My life is here.

My *sovereynté* is York.

Author's Notes

Author's notes on this complicated and emotional story could be as long as the novel itself. Ultimately, this is a work of fiction, and so the notes I am adding support the story I've created. I'd encourage you to explore a variety of fictional and non-fictional materials that have circulated since the princes went missing in 1483, for there are almost as many opinions as there are decades that have passed, and each one carries a different perspective on the mystery of their disappearance.

How did I start this novel?

Two converging threads.

Firstly, when I was working on my 17th Century novels, The Lydiard Chronicles, I came across a fascinating research paper about the supposed discovery of the princes' bones in the Tower of London in 1674. I filed it away, but never forgot it. Later, when I was at the Tower, I enjoyed in-depth discussions about the likelihood of these being the bones of Edward V and Richard, Duke of York; and subsequently, I was fortunate to have similar discussions at Westminster Abbey. Although they were examined early in the 20th century, the report was scientifically inconclusive. The bones have never been DNA tested, nor are they likely to be in the near future. So they remain as much of a mystery as the disappearance itself.

Secondly, I was asked to contribute to an anthology of historical fiction short stories around the theme of "Betrayal". I had no idea what to write, but one afternoon I was searching through our digitized St.John family tree, and decided to enter my own name. A dozen or so "Elizabeth St.John" listings appeared. I knew of the 17th Century women, but my eye was caught by an Elysabeth who was born in the 15th century. When I researched a little deeper, I found that she had been the godmother to Edward V, the oldest "Prince in the Tower."

In the 15th century, a godmother was regarded as a blood relative – so much so that dispensation had to be obtained to marry within the godchild's family. So she had a close relationship with Edward IV, and Elizabeth Woodville, the queen. In fact, she was appointed to accompany the queen into Sanctuary to witness Edward's birth. When I realised which generation she belonged to I became really excited. For not only was Elizabeth godmother to the York heir, Edward V, she was the half-sister of Lancastrian Margaret Beaufort, and therefore the aunt of the future king, Henry VII.

I had my story. If anyone would know what happened to the princes, I thought, Elysabeth would.

Now I wanted to think of a theme for my novel, and decided upon *sovereynté*. A woman's right to make her own decisions. This was a pretty radical concept in the 15th century, and one that is reflected in the Tales of King Arthur. Writing about a woman who left little evidence of her existence, but lived very much in the centre of one of the most turbulent times in English history was a challenge. In order to avoid anachronistic behaviour, I wanted her driven by an inner strength, and a quiet power. The concept of *sovereynté* fitted Elysabeth perfectly.

In my world of historical and biographical fiction, I had a few incontrovertible facts that supported my writing. The princes went missing. No proof has ever been found of their death, their murder, their bodies, their murderers. But as I cast my net wider, I was intrigued by the web of my own family connections and coincidences as I started my research.

To recap, the known facts of the family relationships and people in my novel:

- Elysabeth was born c.1430, and married to John "Jack" Scrope, 5th Baron Scrope of Bolton Castle. She was in sanctuary with Elizabeth Woodville for the birth of the prince, appointed godmother of Edward V, pardoned by Edward IV, and lived until c.1494;

- All of the St.John / Beaufort / Welles / Scrope relations and family tree at the front of this novel are based on validated family research. Elysabeth's half sister was Margaret Beaufort. Her nephew was Henry VII. Elysabeth's stepdaughter Margaret "Meg" Zouche married Will Catesby;

- John "Jack" Scrope's family tree is also validated. His sister Elizabeth/Isabel married Oliver St.John, Elysabeth's brother. Jack's sister Agnes married Richard Ratclyffe. Jack's cousin Ralph married Cecily Plantagenet, Elizabeth of York's sister;

- The famous doggerel written by William Colyngbourne: *The Cat, the Rat and Lovel our Dog Doe rule all England under a Hog,* refers to the power William Catesby (The Cat) Richard Ratclyffe (The Rat) and Francis Lovell wielded as King Richard's (The Hog) trusted advisors. Two out of three of them were close relatives of Elysabeth;

- Elysabeth's brother, Oliver St.John, lived a few miles from Bolton Castle, as well as at Lydiard Tregoze in Wiltshire. He was close to both Elysabeth and Margaret Beaufort; with his wife Isabel Scrope he had two daughters, Elizabeth and Eleanor. After Bosworth, Elizabeth married Gerald Fitzgerald, 8th Earl of Kildare, sponsor of "The Dublin King", royal pretender Lambert Simnel. Eleanor married Thomas Grey, 2nd Marquess of Dorset, whose father Thomas Grey, 1st Marquess of Dorset, was half brother to Edward V. Both of these men are associated with the missing princes. Edward V, Thomas Grey and their connection with Coldridge in Devon is currently under investigation by Philippa Langley and the Richard III Society;

- Elysabeth's half sister, Margaret Beaufort, was a woman of immense piety and character. She was also very fond of all of her St.John half brothers and sisters, and throughout her long life she consistently ensured they were well looked after, rewarded with positions and land, and received the due respect of being King Henry VII's aunts and uncles;

- When Lambert Simnel, the "pretender" supported by Kildare, landed in England in 1487, Jack Scrope and his cousin Thomas Scrope held York in his name and fought against Henry VII's troops to overturn him. Simnel (who was purported to be Dickon) was pardoned by Henry and was taken into his household. Instead of being executed for treason, Jack was put on house arrest and subsequently released;

- After taking the throne, King Henry VII never officially "searched" for the princes. nor declared them dead nor discovered their bodies or burial place. I have found no record that his mother, Margaret Beaufort, did so either.

As far as historical events within my novel, I have tried to peel away the centuries of speculation, gossip and rewrites that have occurred. There are a couple of incidences that took place that have little or no written evidence, but enough mentions to think they did happen.

The first attempt to remove the princes from the Tower did occur, fires were lit and extinguished; John Welles (Elysabeth and Margaret's half brother) was definitely mixed up in it, and Jack Scrope was appointed to question his brother-in-law when he was arrested. I saw the hand of Margaret behind both the attempt and Welles's subsequent lenient treatment.

The encounter between Margaret Beaufort and the Duke of Buckingham just before Buckingham arrives in Gloucester is not documented that I could find; plenty of speculation that it did occur, with various places suggested as the rendezvous. It worked in my novel for me to include this, and so I set it at Burford.

Finally, my fictional telling of The Godmother's Secret results in an ending that still leaves room for question, but hopefully satisfies the mystery. I wanted, more than anything, to tell a story of family love and tolerance, and a woman's loyalty and courage: Elysabeth's *sovereynté*. I didn't want to spend three years writing about the darkness of infanticide and war. I thought, more than anything, that if I could write a decent historical fiction novel, based on the known facts, my work would entertain and encourage readers to search for their own interpretation of the disappearance of the princes.

I hope you enjoyed The Godmother's Secret. Thank you for reading this far, and do visit my website or email me if you'd like to join the conversation. I'd love to hear from you.

www.ElizabethJStJohn.com
ElizabethJStJohn@gmail.com

For further reading, please enjoy this extract from my most recent novel, The King's Intelligencer, companion book to The Godmother's Secret:

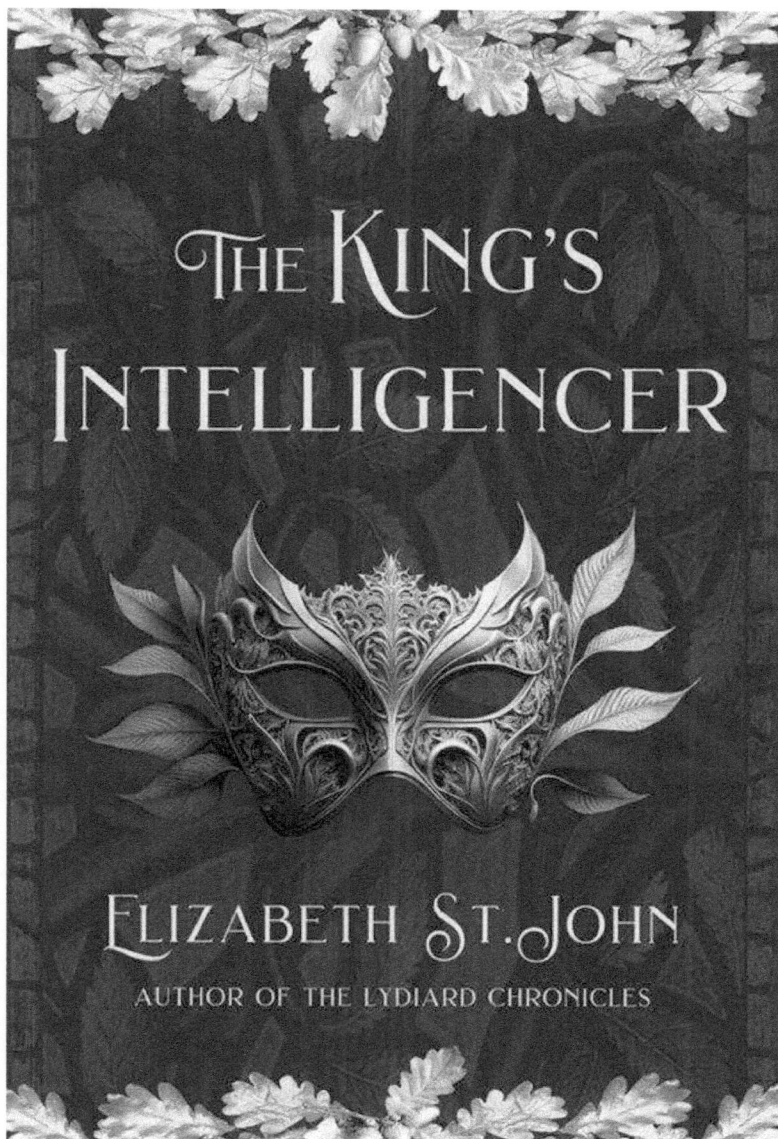

THE KING'S
INTELLIGENCER

ELIZABETH ST.JOHN

AUTHOR OF THE LYDIARD CHRONICLES

The King's Intelligencer

The Discovery of the Missing Princes in the Tower

London, 1674: When children's bones are unexpectedly unearthed in the Tower of London, England's most haunting mystery—the fate of the missing princes—is reignited.

Franny Apsley, confidante to Lady Mary Stuart, heir to King Charles's throne, becomes embroiled in the royal court's excitement over the discovery of children's bones. Could they be the missing princes? As a devastating family secret emerges, Franny is recruited by her cousin Nan Wilmot to unearth the truth behind the bones. Her investigation, complicated by an attraction to the secretive court artist Nicholas Jameson and the influence of an enigmatic royal spy, reveals a startling plot threatening the throne and England's stability.

In a glittering and debauched society where love is treacherous and loyalty masked, Franny must navigate a world where a woman's voice is often silenced and confront the ultimate question: What is she willing to risk for the sake of her country, her happiness, and her family's safety?

A captivating historical novel of conspiracy, passion, and courage, The King's Intelligencer is one woman's quest for a truth that could change the fate of a nation. A companion to the critically acclaimed best-selling novels The Godmother's Secret and The Lydiard Chronicles, The King's Intelligencer weaves together beloved characters and actual events to bring a suspenseful mystery to life.

Fore Word

I destroyed all the evidence, of course. Any intelligencer worth their salt always covers their tracks. As I have mine. There may still be a whisper in a thrice-notched and folded letter, or a payment in the king's accounts that pens a trace of our network. Perhaps even a cuckoo's egg in a will and testament which begs a question.

But all in all, I think I have succeeded.

One day, a descendant may find the same clues I did. Might stitch together scraps to quilt a full design. We'll be long dead and buried by then. Perchance the monarchy will be gone—just as my Aunt Luce once sought. Our time of revolution and restoration will be no more than a notch in the arc of history.

But it's my arc. And I know if it wasn't for our work, my family and England would have turned out very differently. If they had survived at all.

Franny Apsley
Intelligencer
1678

1

London, 1674

Footsteps rattled across Westminster Abbey's chessboard floor, tip-tapping a reveille rude enough to wake the dead. Franny Apsley frowned. She welcomed an entertaining disruption from escorting her royal mistress around the dismal graves, but they had yet to visit the tomb that really mattered. The one that served Franny's purpose, if not her desire.

The excursion was the girl's idea, of course, because Lady Mary Stuart, King Charles's precious twelve-year-old niece, relished visiting macabre monuments of her ancestors. Later, Mary would no doubt scream for her favourite lady as the dead rode night mares across her swagged four poster, keeping Franny awake and yawning at her side, and proving once again her opinion that a place in the royal household was more duty than honour. The least she could salvage from today's expedition was another rung up the ladder of ambition.

Gibstone, the court's drawing master, scuttled towards them, his anvil-jawed face mulberry-flushed, stubby legs pumping. He flashed a satisfied glance at Franny; he was her co-conspirator in entertaining Mary.

"Do you carry news, Mr. Gibstone?" The interruption was timely, but not at the expense of Franny's story. In its telling, she required the presence of a significant tomb to capture Mary's vivid imagination. "Can it wait? We must go to the Lady Chapel."

"What is it?" cried Lady Mary, eager, apparently, for a diversion. "Oh, what has happened, Mr. Gibstone?"

"Bones! Bones! The Tower—" panted the dwarf, wedging a thumb under his elaborate cravat "—I've been at the demolition at the Tower of London. Kit Wren is examining ancient bones found by the stairs at the White Keep. Children's bones. Two sets. Two children. In the Tower."

A distant story nagged just beyond Franny's recollection. "Bones? Whose bones?"

"Could it be the murdered princes?" Mr. Gibstone rolled his eyes in excitement. "Come now! Come and see for yourself."

Courtiers circled, enticed by the whiff of distraction from Lady Mary's obsession. She may enjoy predicting her own future by communing with her royal ancestors in the abbey. But the Tower of London? Children's bones? Evidence of a royal murder?

Infinitely more interesting.

Beyond Mr. Gibstone's bobbing head, behind the familiar clutch of cousins, friends, and foes, a stranger stood tall, his green-eyed gaze piercing the abbey's gloom. He watched Franny, not the news-bearing dwarf. She had not seen this man before.

Franny blinked, looked away, met the unforgiving stares of the painted plaster saints in their niches. "Jesu," she breathed and crossed herself. "The murdered princes? Jesu save their souls."

Mary clapped with delight. "Bones! Another adventure." Her voice squeaked excitement. "Franny, we must go, this very minute!"

Not until she had finished her business in the Abbey. "We have one more tomb to visit." Franny bent to Mr. Gibstone, gathered her thoughts. "Arrange for the coach to meet us in the sanctuary courtyard. We will be there shortly."

Mr. Gibstone wavered, torn between Franny's instructions, Mary's excitement, and his opportunity to win favour. "They think it might be the missing princes," he offered again hopefully, "in the Tower."

The Tower. The princes. Franny inhaled deeply. She hadn't been to the Tower since she was nine years old. And never thought she'd have reason to return.

"Thank you, Mr. Gibstone."

The Lydiard Chronicles

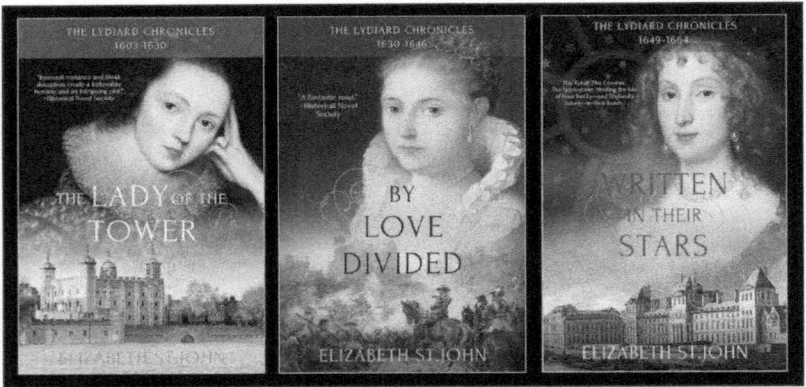

If you enjoyed The Godmother's Secret, please consider reading more St.John family history in The Lydiard Chroniclers

For further reading, please enjoy this brief extract from The Lady of the Tower, the first book of The Lydiard Chronicles:

London, 1609. When Lucy St.John, a beautiful highborn orphan at the court of King James, is seduced by the Earl of Suffolk, she never imagines the powerful enemy she creates in his beloved sister, the Countess of Rochester. Or that her own sister Barbara would betray her and force Lucy to leave the court in disgrace. Spirited, educated, and skilled in medicine and precious remedies, Lucy fights her way back into society, and through an unexpected love match, becomes mistress of the Tower of London. Living inside the walls of the infamous prison, she defies plague, political intrigues and tragic executions to tend to aristocratic prisoners and criminals alike.

Now married into the immensely powerful Villiers family, Barbara unites with the king's favorite, the Duke of Buckingham, to raise the fortunes of Lucy and her family to dizzying heights. But with great wealth comes treachery, leaving Lucy to fight for her survival—and her honor—in a world of deceit and debauchery.

Elizabeth St.John's critically acclaimed debut novel tells the true story of her ancestress Lucy through her family's surviving diaries, letters, and court papers. Lucy's personal friendships with historical figures such as Sir Walter Raleigh and the Stuart kings brings a unique perspective to the history of seventeenth century England.

Available on Amazon and Kindle Unlimited
https://geni.us/MyBookLOTT

PROLOGUE

God, who holds my fate in Thy hands, give me strength, I implore, for today I enter a prison like no other on this earth, and perhaps one that even Hell does not equal in its fiery despair. Give me fortitude to walk through those gates where so many traitors have gone before and never left. Give me compassion to hear the cries of forgotten men and not turn my head away. Give me, above all, Heavenly Father, courage to bear myself with dignity and Your grace when I am inwardly trembling with fear at the horrors that lie behind those walls.

Lucy
23 March 1617

Silver drizzle veiled the stone walls rising from the moat's stagnant water. To the north, the White Tower glistened but bade no welcome for all its shining. Gabled roofs with ornate chimneys pierced the mist and hid again, hinting at a house within the fortress. I was not comforted, for it reminded me that the kept must have their keepers.

Thunder resounded through the fog from water swirling around the center arches of the bridge, just upriver from our tethered barge. The first time I was rowed in a shuddering boat through the narrow span of columns was terrifying. "Shooting the bridge" the locals called it, the currents created by the arches manifesting river water into whirlpools. Recollections of impaled traitors' heads grinning from the pikes appeared before my closed eyes. What hell's gate was I approaching?

"Ho! Tie here!"

A clash of metal resounded as the pikemen stood to attention on the wharf. I pulled my mind back to the present.

"Aye, make way for the lady."

Roughened hands guided me from the rocking boat, and I carefully picked my way up the water steps. My heart beat faster as I gazed up at the sheer ramparts. They loomed over my head, broken only by a low arch with an iron portcullis. Blackened bars jutted forth, a reminder I entered a prison.

I shivered from the damp air, and not a little from apprehension, and stood still on the wharf. Behind me, the Thames ebbed now, and the ferrymen urgently called patrons to catch the running tide. In front, the moat lay impenetrably black and still. The cold seeped through the soles of my shoes, for in my anxiety I had forgotten my pattens. Out of the gloom, a man appeared beside me.

"Princess Elizabeth paused here," the Keeper spoke quietly, his words brushed by the lilt of an Irish accent. "She declared she was no traitor and refused to enter through that arch, for those who arrive through Traitors' Gate do not leave again."

The dark water gate, its walls defining the width of the ramparts above, did not welcome guests. I thought of the young princess defying her guards, perching on a wet stone on a rainy day similar to this, her own future cloudy with doubt and dread. I recalled the moment I heard I was to enter the Tower and how my stomach twisted with fear at the news.

"When I served her, none could see the frightened girl behind the majesty," he continued, "for we were all in love with her, each one of us outdoing the other in deeds and poetry to gain her favor."

The Keeper waved the bargeman away, and the boat was quickly untied and pushed from the wharf, the crew not looking back as they rowed rapidly upriver.

"Her 'adventurers,' she called us, and all through her life she played us one against many, declaring her affection and encouraging our competition—who could sail the farthest, dance the longest, fight the strongest." He pulled his black leather cloak closer against the cold. "She challenged us, and she baited us like dogs to a bear."

I looked at the Keeper, his faded blue seafarer's eyes gazing toward invisible horizons as he sailed into memories. Briefly, I glimpsed the queen's man in his prime, standing tall and strong, bronzed by foreign suns, his white beard a rich chestnut brown, his shoulders broad.

"Another woman whose own sister betrayed her, who knew not whom she could trust." My voice competed with the rushing water; there was no telling if he heard.

"All the princess recalled that sorry afternoon was her mother, who entered the gate at the king's command and never left." He turned away abruptly and hailed a guard standing by.

Just as I am commanded.

"Escort my lady to her lodging. Ensure my steward is there to greet her and introduces her to her household. I shall be at the armory."

He strode off, leaving me lonely on the wharf, my skirts heavy with the weight of the rainwater, thoughts swirling. I followed the guard along a narrow path to a bridge across the moat and toward the gabled house I'd glimpsed earlier.

Married to a man I trusted not, parted from family and friends, I entered the Tower of London. A bleak March morn in the year of our Lord 1617, and I was the new mistress of the prison.

For further reading, please enjoy this brief extract from By Love Divided, the second book of The Lydiard Chronicles:

London, 1630. Widowed and penniless, Lucy St.John is fighting for her family's survival and makes a terrible choice to secure a future for her children. Worse still, her daughter Luce rejects the royal court and wealthy marriage arranged by her aristocratic family and falls in love with a charismatic Parliamentarian. As England tumbles toward bloody civil war, Luce's beloved brother Allen embraces the Royalist cause and chooses to fight for the king as a cavalier. Lucy is helpless to prevent her family being torn apart, and as war flares across England, Allen and Luce are swept up in bloody battles and brutal sieges as they fight for their opposing causes.

Along with thousands of others uprooted by the turmoil, Lucy, Allen, and Luce face a devastating challenge. Will war unite or divide them? And will they find love and a home to return to—if they survive the horror of civil war. In the dawn of England's great rebellion, love is the final battleground.

A true story based on surviving memoirs, court papers, and letters of Elizabeth St.John's family, By Love Divided continues the story of Lucy St.John, the Lady of the Tower and her influential relationships with historical characters such as Oliver Cromwell and King Charles I. This powerfully emotional novel tells of England's great divide and the heart-wrenching choices one family faces.

Available on Amazon and Kindle Unlimited:
https://geni.us/MyBookBLD

Prologue

The fire is most fervent in a frosty season.

Luce
21st August, 1642

These were the times in which Lucy Apsley questioned if God had deserted her.

Around the table, her children gathered. When had they grown into men and women? Where went the innocent Allen, the child in Luce? These young people talked recklessly tonight.

Lucy shook the ghosts of yesteryear from her thoughts.

Be grateful for the hour at hand, the joy shared in this pleasing home.

Still, the doubts chattered in her mind. The past crept close tonight, the door ajar between dead and living.

This dinner was a happy occasion, a celebration of Allen's knighthood. A fresh carp caught in their own fishponds graced the table. Elegant clothes were unpacked from trunks, dried lavender shaken from the skirts. Even Luce, always careless with her dress, wore a fine gown of blue watered silk, dotted with moonstones.

And then, as unpredictable as a summer storm, a lightning exchange heralded dispute.

For the king. Against the king. Favored by Villiers. Betrayed by Parliament.

Those old arguments restored her husband's memory, twelve years departed from this life. And now, their past disputes echoed in her children.

"Where lies your loyalty, Allen?" demanded Luce. "Your family deserves the truth."

He shrugged, his broad shoulders strong under the fine holland shirt, the beautifully cut doublet. Court was good to her son.

"Why, Luce," he replied, "As God is my witness, I am loyal to His Majesty and faithful to the Parliament. My heart lies with the men of this country, and their wish for peace."

"By forming armed bands of Cavaliers?" cried Luce, her voice rising. "My heart is loyal and faithful too—loyal to the Parliament who represent the rights of men, faithful to the tradition of monarchy. Consider your own world order, not mine."

Allen stood too, his soldier's physique suddenly charging the atmosphere. His color rose. "The king is as a father to the people of this nation. He knows what is best for them."

"Is that why he commandeers our ammunition, leaves our towns defenseless, our woman and children vulnerable to any band of armed men?"

"Keep to your writing and notebooks, Sister, and leave the business of government to men."

Lucy prayed for the storm to subside. Thus always ranged their arguments, until one caught the other's eye, and a shared smile would appear, contagious and healing.

Please, God, let this night be no different.

"Tomorrow, we ride to Nottingham to attend King Charles," she said. "He speaks to unite our country, to stand down the armies. Tonight, let not differences divide us."

A mother knows what is best for her children. And still, they seek out their own destinies. Perhaps, once more, she could protect her children with a lie.

God save us. For again, the fate of my family and of England lies within this deceitful king's hands. And if he cannot have his way, he will destroy us all.

1

Our uncle Lord Grandison was married to a lady so jealous of him, and so ill-natured in her jealous fits to anything that was related to him, that her cruelties to my mother exceeded the stories of stepmothers.

Luce Apsley
16th January, 1631

Leaving sweet Chelsea for the Battersey shore, Lucy was ferried to the underworld, where Cerberus guarded the gates to Hades. Only this hell was her childhood home, and the sentinel, Aunt Joan.

"Hold tight to the side, my Lady Apsley." The Thames boatman, etched black against the lowering January sky, stood and plied his oar. "The current runs strong upon the shallows."

Lucy already gripped the weathered wood, for she knew this treacherous river of old. On the southern bank appeared St. Mary's spire, an obelisk marking the family crypt. There, her uncle would reside, laid beneath the chancel, where the flesh would fall from his bones and his spirit be exalted to the heavens.

Lord Oliver St.John, Viscount Grandison, no longer of this world. Another funeral, when her husband's death still shrouded her heart.

Would she ever be free of the melancholy? A tear stung her eye—surely from the hostile wind, unfurling silvery banners all the way from the Tower and the cold northern sea beyond.

"Do not despair, Mother. You have me to care for you," murmured her son, Allen's namesake, fourteen and caught between youth and manhood. Her eldest boy, a witness to more in the Tower than any child ought.

He huddled close to her on the rough plank bench, his threadbare cloak pulled tight across his chest. Those final years in the Tower afforded no new clothes, for the departing prisoners left but shabby pickings. At least she'd salvaged mourning silks, payment obligatory for their keeper duties.

Lucy sighed. Her husband had been so proud of his appointment. Sir Allen Apsley. Keeper and Lieutenant of the Tower of London, with all the fees and privileges that accompanied the position. Three thousand pounds he'd paid for that perquisite, moving them into the

Tower to administer the prison. And so little income, after the Duke of Buckingham's death ended his favors. All had turned to dust in their last years of residence.

Her son nudged her, breaking her thoughts. Those clear glass-gray eyes. Lucy's heart clenched at the youthful reflection of her husband, before the ruinous debts and the devastating consumption had drained the life from him. Death came as a relief, his Calvinist soul content with its destiny. Who was she to challenge the doctrine that sustained her through her darkest hours? Sir Allen Apsley's time was done.

Lucy smiled and took his cold-reddened hand. "Boon—"

"Allen," he corrected her.

"Allen," she continued. So, his childhood nickname departed also. "No mother could ask more of her son, and the example you set for your brother and sisters. In these difficult times, you are still our boon."

He flushed, his young skin translucent, the down on his chin almost stubble. "Father would have wished this so. He instructed me to protect our family upon his death. My training with the Yeoman Warders will serve me well."

The wind gusted bitter at the river's center, pushing their craft upstream as the boatman struggled to steer a straight course. A fragment of muddy ice floated by, and as they approached the bulrushes, more appeared. How deep the winter gnawed.

"Eleanor is waiting for us." Lucy's heart quickened. Her beloved sister stood on the snow-covered landing, bundled in black furs and a deep hood. As the boat edged closer, Eleanor's delicate face reflected the brittle light, framed by the glossy beaver skins.

"My darlings," she called. "Praise God, you arrive safely."

Lucy stepped from the rocking boat and stumbled into Eleanor's arms.

"I have missed you sorely," she whispered.

"Sweet Lucy, your life has transformed since leaving the protection of the Tower. I am heartbroken at your suffering," responded her sister softly. Her tone lightened, "Ah, Allen, look at you—how much you have grown!"

She held her hands out to Allen as he clambered to the landing. The boatman handed up their packs and tipped his hat in thanks as Eleanor paid him.

Lucy stood silently on the dock, memories surfacing. This riverbank once was her haven, until she'd discovered the plague man, dead in the reeds. Then came the summer of change, when Uncle Oliver returned from the Irish wars, bringing with him her cousin William.

"How is Will?" she asked. "You wrote he is at sea?"

Eleanor nodded, her eyes softening. "My husband is happiest when on his ship, Lucy; you know that." She shrugged under the heavy furs, making light of her feelings as only Eleanor could. "He sails regularly to the Americas. And yet, the commerce is still not forthcoming."

Lucy glanced through the black lacework of twisted apple trees to the manor. Unrecognizable since her time here, what with Aunt Joan's vulgar adornments of turrets and a false front. Beneath, the old house she knew still rested, ancient bones settling into the ground, decay concealed behind its rendered face. Best get this over soonest.

Lucy reached for the comfort of Allen's hand. "Should we go? This cold bites to the bone."

"And even more so inside. Joan has not changed her frugal ways, despite her title." Eleanor led the way along the frosty path, her boots squeaking on the gravel. "She will expect to see you tonight at the funeral, not before. She has kept to her rooms since Oliver's death."

"And Barbara?" Lucy's voice hung with the mist of her breath in the frigid air.

"She arrives later this evening."

So, Barbara attends. Of course. She was Joan's favorite. My sister. My enemy.

For further reading, please enjoy this brief extract from Written in their Stars, *the third book of* The Lydiard Chronicles:

London, 1649. Horrified eyewitnesses to King Charles's bloody execution, Royalists Nan Wilmot and Frances Apsley plot to return the king's exiled son to England's throne, while their radical cousin Luce, the wife of king-killer John Hutchinson, rejoices in the new republic's triumph. Nan exploits her high-ranking position as Countess of Rochester to manipulate England's great divide, flouting Cromwell and establishing a Royalist spy network; while Frances and her husband Allen join the destitute prince in Paris's Louvre Palace to support his restoration. As the women work from the shadows to topple Cromwell's regime, their husbands fight openly for the throne on England's bloody battlefields. But will the return of the king be a victory, or destroy them all? Separated by loyalty and bound by love, Luce, Nan and Frances hold the fate of England—and their family— in their hands.

Winner of The Coffee Pot Book Club's 2019 Book of the Year, Written in Their Stars is a true story based on surviving memoirs of Elizabeth St.John's family.

Available on Amazon and Kindle Unlimited:
https://geni.us/MyBookWITS

FRANCES

Frances shifted under the fine Rennes linen sheets, thoughts skittering in all directions, sleep running from her. A door closing, whispered voices and then a muffled cry murmured beyond the partition wall told of John and Luce's triumph. She unclenched her fists and slowly opened her fingers, flexing her stiff hands.

"Frances?" Allen drowsily reached for her.

"Hush. Go back to sleep, my love."

It is done.

John had signed the warrant this night. Death would be immediate. Parliament would not permit time for the exiled prince to return at the head of a Catholic army, rallying the Royalists.

She touched her neck. Crossed herself.

Mother of God.

Allen's breathing deepened, the brandy pulling him back into its warm embrace.

She fidgeted again. After John's decree, would her sister-in-law make love so passionately, so that moans and exclamations kept Frances awake?

Yes.

For had not Allen fallen in love with Frances herself in the shadow of war's surrender? Ardor healed where words failed.

Will tomorrow's execution toss Allen back into his mind's abyss?

A small hiccup next to her, the sound the baby made just before she cried. Frances held her breath, willing Isabella not to wake. Surprising she slept at all, given her parents' anguish. A few minutes, and she quietened.

Frances slid her arm from between Allen's head and the bolster. He mumbled and reached for her, but she inched from his grip. Let this troubled husband of hers rest, for he bore the burden of a hundred deaths, of those he knew and loved and those by the numbers only.

Mother Mary, grant these men eternal rest.

Allen's beloved cousins. Luce's too. And yet her sister-in-law's religion forbade prayers for the dead. What hope for salvation if God did not guide them from purgatory?

Frances rolled over to face Allen. Exhaustion and brandy had loosened his expression, a sweetness playing around his full lips and long lashes. She tucked a lock of curling dark hair from his forehead. A frown flitted across his face and disappeared as quickly as it had arrived.

How she loved this man and his mercurial passion. Tonight, as he drank steadily, Allen had recounted a boyhood story of his cousins at this manor house. They'd stolen their uncle's wine, raided the kitchens of a fine feast, and drank themselves silly as they teased and talked about the university years ahead. He'd laughed heartily at the memory. And then wept bitterly for his loss.

Only he remained.

And tomorrow, because of John's signature, the divinely appointed king whose life they had defended with their own, whose beliefs were the very essence of England's soul, would join Allen's soldier-cousins in death.

"Is it done?"

While she reflected, Allen's smoke-grey eyes had opened.

"Yes."

"John has signed the death warrant?" The familiar blankness shuttered his face.

"I believe so." John would not have come home with the business unfinished.

"My best friend. My sister. Traitors to the king." Allen's bitter whisper travelled to her ears alone.

Frances remained silent.

"These past two years John and I negotiated England's solution. We carried the messages back and forth from king to Parliament. We talked, we found common ground." He sat up abruptly, as if to march to John now, continue their parley. "A way to govern England, give voice again to Parliament. And yet, tomorrow, the axe severing the king's life finishes ours as we know it too." Allen rubbed his eyes wearily. "John betrayed our agreements. Luce encouraged the king's death. And now you and I are doomed by their decisions."

"You never gave up, neither of you. Perhaps in the end the king could not accept the advice of anyone but God," replied Frances. Scant comfort, but anything to shift the blame from Allen's conscience. "Perhaps you and John can still find your brotherhood."

Allen ran his fingers through his hair. Such fine hands, the sword scar on his forearm glinting white in the dim light. Frances studied him, cheek pillowed in her hand.

"Not at the price of the king's death," he said. "I go tomorrow. Nan too."

"Your cousin told me this evening she must attend."

"Naturally. To honour my cousins, her brothers who died in the king's service. Don't come if you do not wish to."

"Of course I will." Frances sat up, the velvet covers falling from her, the night cold descending upon her shoulders. "Why would you think otherwise?"

Allen shrugged. "It is not a scene for a woman to observe."

"Nan attends."

And had made a point of telling Frances within minutes of their meeting this evening.

"She has her reasons."

Frances's temper flashed. "And I don't? I cared for the king's infant daughter, Queen Henrietta, her ladies. I held the prince by the hand and comforted him when he lost all hope of seeing his father again. When the court sought refuge with us, I risked everything to aid them."

Isabella stirred, disturbed by Frances's anger. She whimpered.

Allen rolled from the bed, leaned over the crib and picked her up. The little girl immediately settled, snuggling into his arms.

"You're right. I'm sorry. You were as a sister to Prince Charles. Of course. We will go together with Nan."

"Are you sure you should be there?" Allen's condition lay between them, unspoken but present.

"He is my king. He is dying for me."

Floorboards creaked from the next chamber. Someone had arisen. Allen climbed back into bed, tucked Isabella between them. The fire died and darkness flowed over them, except for a bead of light trickling from the adjoining room.

"And Luce? What words for her? She will attend too."

"Luce is lost to me." Allen's words were muffled in the softness of Isabella's hair.

Frances curled under the covers and turned to face the window. Candlelight flickered through the partition. Today's judgment gave John and Luce victory. But tonight one of them could not find peace.

Allen's words lingered. The world they knew ended tomorrow. She must think past the moment of death to life beyond. Mary, Mother of God, guide her well, for survival lay in her hands, not her husband's.

9 798227 159458